STONEBRIDGE SECRET

~A Novel~

DAVID MOORE

Cover design by Mahlon Dennis
Author photograph by Michelle Halverson

ISBN-13: 978-1475159899
ISBN-10: 1475159897

For Michele

Your love and support make everything possible.

Acknowledgements

My heartfelt thanks to my wife, Michele, for her patience in reading and re-reading the manuscript, and for assisting me with her creative input.

Special thanks, also, to the following manuscript readers: David Barnes, Katie Barnes, Brett and Sarah Carpenter, Chad and Michelle Halverson, Don and Georgia Lamirande, Tammi Lamirande, Fred and Ruth Moore, and Tommy Wilhite.

PART 1

Prologue

The old church was empty and quiet, just the way the altar boy liked it. Soft rays from the afternoon sun filtered through the stained glass windows, bringing the iconic scenes to life on the leaded glass and creating a subdued, almost mystic glow around the altar. The boy sat transfixed on the front pew, on the end near the center aisle, gazing at the crucifix suspended over the altar. As he meditated on the image of Christ—arms outstretched, hands and feet pierced, crown of thorns pressed into His bleeding head—a familiar peace settled upon him. A peace that had become like a friend. A peace that at times could be so tangible he felt transfigured, as though he was an angelic being floating above the coarseness and pain of life, floating upward, higher and higher toward the heavenlies until all his thoughts yielded to the whispers of God.

He needed that peace today.

It was exactly one year ago that his father died—October 25, 1961, at 4:37 a.m. He would never forget that date and time. He saw it on the death notice that his mother had left on the kitchen table when she returned from the hospital that day. That was how he found out. The pain of his loss was more acute than ever, and he needed something to fill that emptiness. Spending time in church like this helped. Somehow, it made him feel closer to his father's memory.

His father was not a religious man, but he was spiritual. His son was both. The two often spoke of heaven and hell and eternity. Now the father alone knew if the things they discussed were true. And the boy wished he could cross that divide, if just for a moment, to experience that reality with him.

The rear sanctuary door slowly creaked open, jarring the boy from his thoughts. Mr. Knapp, the janitor, limped in to replenish the holy water fonts on the back wall. Within minutes he was finished, and he quietly left. By now the boy was aware of the chill in the room. It had been an unusually cold day, and the old

1

stone building was beginning to feel as dank as a crypt. The boy
moved to the kneeler at the right of the altar to get close to a
ventilation register, where a weak flow of warm air had just
started trickling out. Dropping to his knees onto the soft upholstered padding of the kneeler and leaning forward against the
polished oak altar rail, the boy began to murmur the prayer he
had repeated since he was a child: "Our Father who art in heav-
en, hallowed be Thy name . . ."

The altar boy paused. He heard a still, small voice coming
from his right. He opened his eyes but saw no one. The voice
persisted. It sounded like it was coming from the heat register.
He put his ear to the vent and realized it was the voice of Father
Francis, his pastor. His office was in a wing of the rectory attached to the church behind the altar backdrop, but the metal
heat duct was transmitting his voice as if he was standing just
feet away. Once the boy realized this, he pulled away from the
vent, embarrassed that he was eavesdropping on a private conversation. It reminded him of an awkward moment two years
earlier when he was kneeling in the confessional for the first
time and heard a man in the adjacent booth confessing his trans-
gressions in a feverish pitch to the priest. That time he plugged
his ears until it was over; this time was different.

Something about the tone of the priest's voice intrigued the
boy. He looked around the sanctuary to assure himself he was
alone, and lowered his ear to the vent.

"Jean, I can't resist you anymore," the priest said.

"Father, we can't . . . we shouldn't." The woman's voice
sounded familiar to the boy.

"I told you, call me Michael," the priest said.

"Michael . . . I . . . I . . ." The woman's voice faded into low,
sensuous groans.

The boy tensed when he realized what was happening.

Who is that woman? Jean . . . Jean . . . she sounded like . . .
His stomach felt sick when he made the connection. He plugged
his ears with his fingers, pressing as hard as he could, while

shaking his head violently. *No! No! How could they do this?*

The boy grabbed the altar rail with both hands, staggered to his feet, and backed away from the vent. He could still hear the voices. Plugging his ears again, he turned and stumbled down the aisle of the sanctuary, toward the rear door. Stepping outside, he bent over and grabbed his knees, gasping for air. Though it was a clear, crisp fall day, everything looked gray to him. It was as if a veil had dropped over his eyes, and he knew he would never be able to picture his pastor and his mother any other way again.

Chapter 1

The raw autumn air stung Alex's face as he raced his bicycle down the hill leading into the waking village of Stonebridge. He overslept after spending a long, torturous night with his troubled thoughts, and now had only seven minutes to get to church, slip into his cassock and surplice, and light the altar candles in time for the early morning Mass.

Alex wondered if Father Francis would realize that he knew his secret. He wondered if the priest would even care. Alex Michael Spencer was just a bare-faced, wavy-haired, thirteen-year-old altar boy. Father Francis was the pillar of St. Andrew's parish, a priest for nearly twenty years, a priest who carried himself with a dignified air in his black Roman cassock, white clerical collar, and soft leather shoes, a priest whose slightly graying hair presented him as a sage and prophet to those who didn't know better, a priest the boy once revered but now loathed.

Alex leaned his bike against the cold fieldstone wall at the side entrance to the church and rubbed his chilled hands before pulling open the weathered oak door that creaked like the closing lid of a wooden coffin. Towering above the boy in the entryway was the priest, arms folded, wristwatch exposed, his gray eyes shifting from the watch to the boy.

"Running a little late this morning, Alex?"

"Yes, Father Francis, I'm sorry." His stomach tightened as he resisted spewing his true feelings toward the man.

"Well, hurry up. You know I like to start at six-thirty sharp."

"Yes, Father. I'll make sure everything is ready."

Alex hurried down the stairs to the church basement to put on his vestments, all the while clenching his fists. Should he confront the priest and demand that he tell him what he was doing with his mother yesterday? Should he threaten to expose the priest's hypocrisy and sin to the members of St. Andrew's? Or should he just leave it in God's hands?

"Hey, Spencer, I already lit the candles for you. You can snuff them out after Mass," a voice called down from the top of the stairs. It was Dan Wallace, the other altar boy serving this morning. He and Alex both attended St. Andrew's Parochial School and had been friends since first grade.

"Thanks, Wally. I owe you," Alex replied, while slipping the surplice over his head.

"Two minutes till show time," Dan said.

"I'm comin', I'm comin'."

Alex performed his duties flawlessly throughout the Mass. He never took his eyes off the priest—watching him lift the Eucharist, kiss the altar, and bend the knee with the precision of the finest classically trained actor.

After the pronouncement of the benediction, Father Francis made his way to the rear of the church to greet the faithful. Alex quickly found the candle snuffer and began extinguishing the candles around the altar. He was finishing just as the priest was making his way back to the altar.

"Alex, can I see you in the vestry before you leave?"

"Yes, Father, I'll be right in." *Okay, so he probably knows that I know about him and my mother. Now what?* Alex followed the priest into the vestry, placed the brass snuffer on its stand, and turned to see Father Francis holding out a book.

"I would like you to give this to your mother for me, Alex. I know the anniversary of your father's death has been hard on her, and I think this book could help."

Alex looked at the hardcover book placed into his hands— *A Grief Observed*—written by some author he had never heard of before.

"Uh . . . okay, I didn't know she even thought about him still." Alex felt a faint pleasure in knowing this came out with a trace of an attitude.

The priest gave him a reprimanding look. "Of course she does. His death has not been easy for her to get over."

"Well, she just doesn't talk about him anymore, that's all."

"I am sure she is trying to be strong. She knows that this has not been easy for you either."

"Yeah, sure. Well, thanks for the book, Father. I'll make sure she gets it."

"Thank you, Alex. Please be sure to turn the lights out as you leave." With that, Father Francis strode out of the vestry toward the hallway leading to his office, with the gait of a lesser kind of deity—a man assured of his position and used to living life on his own terms.

§

Riding back to his house, Alex's head was spinning. He felt the book tucked underneath his jacket and rehearsed what he would say when he presented it to his mother. "Oh, here Mother, your lover boy thought you might like to read this. He thinks you're still sad about Dad. But we know better, don't we?" It was what he wanted to say, but knew he wouldn't. He thought about his father and how disappointed he would be to hear him talk to his mother with a disrespectful tone. "Respect your elders," he always told his son, leaving the assumption that elders were always worthy of such respect.

Alex walked into a quiet house. His mother was still sleeping, so he set the book on the kitchen table, grabbed a napkin and pencil, and scribbled *from Father Francis*. He left the napkin on the book and went to his room to dress for school.

St. Andrew's Parochial School was a one-story brick structure placed on the edge of ten acres at the northeast corner of Stonebridge. It was built nine years earlier, the first of three new buildings raised by Father Francis during a seven-year building program that also yielded a new convent and rectory. This was Alex's last year at St. Andrew's school, which only went up to eighth grade. Most of his friends were going to attend public high school the following year. Others, whose parents could afford it, would attend St. Bartholomew's Academy in a neighboring town. Alex was certain his only option was to attend the public school, and he had accepted that as his fate. In fact, he had come to accept that life was seldom what he wanted it to be.

§

Alex filed into his classroom a few seconds before the morning bell rang, walked to his desk next to Dan Wallace, and turned toward the flag to join in the Pledge of Allegiance. Following the morning prayer, he sat down with the rest of his class to await Sister Angelica's announcements.

"Class, we will be doing something special this morning," she said. "Father Francis will be coming to our classroom to talk to the boys only. All of you girls will be joining me down in the cafeteria."

The boys rolled their eyes, and the girls snickered, each knowing that this was the annual "talk" given to eighth graders to educate them on how to behave properly with members of the opposite sex. The ritual had become a joke to many of the boys, who wondered what expertise the priest brought to the topic at hand. Alex now saw the irony in their assumption and became flushed with the thought that some of the carnal knowledge the priest had acquired came through his relations with his mother.

"Good morning class," Father Francis said, entering the room.

All of the students stood and replied in unison: "Good morning, Father Francis." Sister Angelica motioned to the girls to begin filing out of the room.

"You young men can be seated," the priest said, smiling at the girls walking out the door. "What a fine group of young ladies in our eighth-grade class this year."

After the last girl exited, Father Francis closed the door, turned toward the boys, with his hands clasped in front of him, and said, "I am sure that most of you are aware of what we will be discussing this morning. I have made it a practice over the years to talk to the eighth-grade boys about their relationships with young women. You have reached the age when your interest in girls has begun to stir . . ." His eyes slowly and methodically probed the reactions on the faces throughout the room. Each boy struggled to keep a blank expression, while focusing toward the front.

"And as Christian young men," the priest continued, "it is important that you remember to keep those stirrings in check at all times. Many of you will be entering the public school system next year and will have to struggle even harder to mind the voice of your conscience in these things. Remember, women are the weaker vessels. You will need to take the lead in protecting your virtue and theirs. And two good rules to follow are to treat a young lady with the same respect you give your mother, and do not do anything with a young lady that your mother would not approve of."

Alex's jaw dropped. His heart was pounding, his body tensing in reaction to the priest's canned speech. Before he could stop himself, he shot his hand in the air and heard himself blurt, "Father Francis, do those rules apply to priests too?" All heads turned in unison toward Alex, their eyes wide with shock at the boy's brazen questioning.

"Why no, Alex," the priest replied, turning slowly, his raised left eyebrow being his only sign of irritation. "As servants of Almighty God, priests live by a much higher standard, a standard that prohibits us from doing many things that others can freely do." After fixing his gaze on Alex a few seconds longer, he turned back toward the class and said, "All right gentlemen, let us continue."

Alex felt himself recoil on the inside, his adrenalin rush having subsided under the cool retort of the cleric. He realized he was no match for the priest's confident superiority. Not now anyway. He kept to himself the rest of the school day, like an injured animal licking its wounds. But in his mind he began imagining the day when he would get his revenge. He didn't know how, and he didn't know when. But he was determined that one day he would balance the scales.

§

The school bell rang, signaling the end of the school day. As Dan and Alex gathered their books, Dan asked, "So, you going over to church today, Alex?"

"No . . . not today."

"Wanna ride over to Beaman's and get a bottle of pop?"

"Okay, I guess." Alex fingered his pocket to see if he had enough change.

"I'll buy today, Spencer. Still got some of last week's paper route money left over."

The two boys mounted their bikes and rode the half-mile trek through the village in silence, but for the sound of dried leaves crunching under their tires. The maple trees lining Main Street had dropped most of their brilliant red and yellow leaves, leaving only tawny remnants clinging desperately to the limbs, reluctant to make their descent to the street below where they would be crushed by passing motorists or boys on bicycles. Coasting their bikes under the railroad bridge, the boys made a quick left turn up East Prospect Street and pedaled into Beaman's parking lot.

Beaman's was a small grocery store situated on the outskirts of the village business district. With its brown brick façade, mullion windows, and recessed entry trimmed with richly carved molding, the store looked like it had been transplanted from a Dickens' novel, better suited to being a law office than a general store.

The boys pushed open the front door and were greeted by the familiar jingle of the bell that alerted old man Beaman and his wife that they had a customer.

"What'll it be today, boys?" the merchant fairly shouted to the young patrons. Alex never knew if old man Beaman was hard of hearing or talked loudly for effect.

"Just a few pretzel sticks and a couple of Dr. Peppers," Dan said, reaching into the pretzel jar.

"That'll be thirty cents!" Beaman bellowed, looking down from his six-foot two-inch frame, his hands resting on his protruding belly, both thumbs hooked behind the front of his spotless white apron.

Dan spread his coins on the counter and sorted out the correct change. Old man Beaman slid the coins into the palm of his hand and cried, "Bingo! You got it!"

The boys walked over to the soda bar and hopped onto a couple of vinyl covered stools as old man Beaman popped the tops on their soda bottles. He plopped them in front of the boys, and strolled back to the check-out counter. Dan, crunching on his pretzel, finally glanced at Alex and asked, "So what was that all about with you and Father Francis this morning?"

"What do you mean?" Alex responded, feigning ignorance.

"What do I mean? For cryin' out loud, Alex, you might as well have asked Father Francis if he's ever done it with a girl."

"Well, what if I was, what's wrong with asking?"

"What's wrong? You could probably go to hell for asking a question like that."

"A person doesn't go to hell for asking a simple question."

"Well purgatory then. Anyway, I thought you liked Father Francis."

"I used to. I don't anymore."

"Why not?"

9

"I don't wanna talk about it."

"Something happen?"

"Wally, can we just drop it for now?"

"What? A friend can't ask a question?"

"C'mon Wally . . ."

"Fine. Whatever you want." Dan spun his stool toward the counter and sipped on his soda pop. He reached into his jacket pocket, pulled out a coin, and started flipping it.

"Listen, Wally. I'm sorry . . . it's just . . . I just don't want to talk about it."

"I get it, Spencer. You don't want to talk about it, so we won't."

Mrs. Beaman waddled over to the soda bar and began wiping the counter. Short and round, she always reminded Alex of a penguin whenever she walked. "How's your mother, Alex?" she asked. "I haven't seen her around town lately."

"She's fine, Mrs. Beaman. Been keeping to herself pretty much."

"Trudy Hogan said she saw her coming out of the church office yesterday. Said she was looking like a new woman, color in her cheeks, smile on her face. I'm glad she seems to be getting along. Father Francis seems to have a way of comforting people in their distress."

"Yes, ma'am," Alex replied, flushed and fidgeting.

"You tell her I said hi, now," Mrs. Beaman said as she waddled away to straighten the grocery aisle nearby.

§

Dan noticed the sudden change in his friend's composure and attributed it to the discussion about his mother. He knew the relationship between Alex and his mother was distant at best, a distance that had only increased after Alex's father died. In an unguarded moment, Alex had confided to Dan that he always felt like he was an intrusion in his mother's life. Dan understood why after overhearing his own parents talking one night about

Alex's mother and her past. Dan's mother told his father that she thought the combination of marriage and family were like a railroad switch that redirected Jean's life down a lackluster track far removed from the fairy-tale life of her dreams.

His mother recalled how Jean had told her she was raised the only child of a prominent New England family—the Davidsons—and grew up surrounded by all the material trappings that accompany wealth. Her parents provided her the finest of educations in the most prestigious private schools in Massachusetts, but they found little time to cultivate a meaningful relationship that established healthy and loving boundaries. Consequently, Jean's was a wild refinement, which, as she put it to Dan's mother, instructed her how to dress for a formal dinner but enticed her to do so without wearing a stitch of underwear.

At twenty years old, Jean returned home for summer break from her studies at Harvard and became infatuated with Bill Spencer, the new master carpenter for her family's sprawling estate, Woodland Hills. The carpenter's chiseled features and muscular frame caught the young girl's eye, and his easy-going, adventurous manner won her heart. Although fully aware that the tradesman was well beneath the social standing of her family, Jean eloped before summer's end to become Mrs. Spencer, and her parents wrote her off like a bad investment.

The newlyweds moved to Western New York to begin their married life out from under the Davidson shadow. It wasn't long before Jean's infatuation for Bill was replaced by a respectful tolerance. The responsibility of marriage tempered Bill's adventurous spirit. He was less willing to take risks now that he had a wife to support, especially one who was used to having everything she wanted. He settled into a job as a high school building superintendent, working long hours for mediocre, but regular, pay. Jean thought about having the marriage annulled. But where would she go? And who would support her? And when Alex was born two years after she and Bill eloped, Jean accepted her marriage and family as an irreversible reality and her cross to bear.

"You all right, Alex?" Dan asked after Mrs. Beaman left.

"Yeah, yeah I'm fine."

"Hey you going to Kitty McAlister's Halloween party to-morrow night?"

"Planning on it."

"What're you gonna dress up as?"

After a slight pause, Alex responded, "I think I'll go as a priest."

§

Autumn dusk was settling on the neighborhood when Alex turned his bike into the McAlister's driveway. He could hear the sounds of laughter and chatter wafting from the open rec-room window through the crisp night air and recognized the sound of Bucky Enman belching the alphabet, to the girls' disgust and the boys' delight.

Mr. and Mrs. McAlister knew how to put on a Halloween party for their daughter and her friends. In fact, anything less than the best was unthinkable to the couple. Bob McAlister was a manager on the rise at a General Motors factory about ten miles from Stonebridge. And Betty, his dutiful wife, had the job of keeping up appearances. They lived in the newest subdivision in town, in a split-level with young crimson maple trees in the yard, an inviting sidewalk winding to the entrance on the lower level, and a sloping, manicured front lawn, dotted with carved pumpkins, and skeletons, ghosts, and goblins.

Alex dismounted his bike and pulled the bottom of his cassock down to cover his slacks. Suddenly he felt awkward in the priestly garb. It was a gift from his father about two years ago, found in a pile of costumes Bill was trashing for the high school drama department. Alex had told his father that he dreamed of becoming a priest one day. After giving his son the cassock, Bill occasionally watched him pretend to say Mass in the basement, with an old door stretched across a pair of sawhorses serving as the altar and an old trophy filled with grape juice, the chalice. The cassock hung loosely on Alex then, but now it fit like it was made for him. He was just not sure anymore if he was made for it.

After adjusting his white collar and zipping his jacket, he strolled up to the door and pushed the doorbell. The door swung open to reveal a smiling Kitty McAlister dressed as a Barbie doll.

"Hi, Alex . . . or should I say, Father Alex," Kitty quipped.

"Hi, Kitty. Alex is just fine."

"Well hel-lo there, Alex," Mrs. McAlister said as she came down from upstairs— her arms laden with bowls of potato chips and pretzels—slowing as she noticed Alex's attire. "Don't you look . . . dignified . . . tonight. Kitty, why don't you show Alex where he can hang his jacket."

"Follow me," Kitty said, motioning Alex into the rec room where the shellacked knotty pine walls and cream linoleum floor glistened from a fresh coat of Johnson's paste wax. Its distinct odor provided a strange olfactory backdrop to the scents of Chanel No. 5 and Old Spice filling the room.

"Hey, if it isn't Father Spencer!" Dan Wallace shouted from the opposite side of the room over the din of a Four Seasons' song, which had just started playing on the stereo console. Alex acknowledged Dan and the other guests with an inconspicuous wave as he removed his jacket and handed it to Kitty.

"Soda pop is over there," Kitty said, pointing to a round table covered with an orange cloth. "Help yourself, Alex."

"Thanks, Kitty."

Dan, flipping a coin as he walked, intercepted Alex on his way to the table. "Geesh, I thought you were just joking about dressing up as a priest. Did Mrs. McAlister have a conniption?"

"No, she just gave me that look."

"You oughta come over and listen to Bucky. He's belting out some good ones tonight."

"Yeah, I heard him from outside. I'll be there in a minute."

Alex popped the cap off his bottle of Coke.

"Don't take too long. I'm not sure how much more Bucky's got in him." Dan turned and walked away.

Alex slowly looked around the room as he lifted the Coke bottle to his lips and took a swig. The fizz from the drink caused him to sputter and spit uncontrollably. Kitty came up, grabbed a napkin, patted the sides of his mouth, and said, "Easy does it there, Father Spencer. Maybe this stuff is a little too strong for you."

"Man, I feel stupid," Alex said.

"You know, you look cute when you blush like that, Alex."

"Cut it out, Kitty."

"Aw, lighten up. You don't always have to be perfect you know."

Alex looked at her sheepishly.

"So, how you doing?" Kitty asked. "You haven't seemed yourself the past few days."

"It's complicated, Kitty."

"Too complicated to explain, or too complicated for me to understand?"

"It's too complicated for me to understand."

"The usual problems with you and your mom?"

"I wouldn't exactly say these were usual."

"Oh Kit-ty!" Mrs. McAlister's singsong voice pierced through the party racket. "You have guests at the door."

"Coming, Mother. Well if you need a good listener, Alex," Kitty said, touching his shoulder lightly, "you know where to find me."

"Thanks."

Alex made his way over to Dan to enjoy the last few expulsions from Bucky Enman. He had burped himself hoarse getting to the letter Z.

§

Sunday morning, Alex and his mother rode to church to-

14

gether. They seldom saw each other throughout the week because Jean worked the evening shift at the General Motors factory. She was an assembly worker—a job she acquired, with the help of Mr. McAlister, after her husband died. Alex had been able to avoid his mother since hearing her with Father Francis two days earlier. Now, riding in the car together, the tension was palpable.

"I haven't seen you to thank you for bringing that book home from Father Francis, Alex."

"Yeah."

"How's school?"

"Okay."

"How was Kitty's party last night?"

"Okay."

"I'm sure Mrs. McAlister outdid herself."

"I guess."

After an awkward pause, Jean said, "Father Francis invited us to have lunch with him in the rectory, following Mass today."

Alex bristled at his mother's comment. "Why?"

"He's hosting a luncheon for some of the single mothers from the church and their children and was kind enough to include us."

"When did you find that out?"

"When I met with him on Thursday for grief counseling."

"And how was your grief counseling, Mother?"

"I don't appreciate the tone you're taking with me right now, Alex. What's your problem?"

"No problem. Thought I was just asking a simple question."

"Well it didn't sound like that to me."

Alex grunted, turned away from his mother, and stared aimlessly out the side window.

"Well if you really want to know," Jean said, "it was very helpful, as always. Father Francis is a good listener. I'm glad for our sessions."

Alex continued glaring out the window in silence. Jean

huffed, pushed in the dashboard lighter, and reached into her purse for a Winston.

§

The rectory dining room bustled with the chatter of women and the squeals and whines of restless children who had suffered quietly through the forty-minute Mass but now freely vented their pent-up energy and demands for food. Alex was the oldest of the children present, and he tried to pacify a four-year-old boy sitting next to him who was whining about being hungry. The boy's mother, Shirley Foster, was busy talking with Barbara Mason and seemed oblivious to his pleas.

Miss Windom—a spinster in her mid-sixties who had the energy of a woman half her age and served as the rectory house-keeper, cook, and occasional secretary—was busy bringing bread and butter to the table and filling glasses with water when Father Francis entered the room, beaming.

"Good afternoon, ladies. Hello, children. I am so glad you could join me for lunch today." His gray eyes twinkled as they gazed upon each of the five women, all younger than him, all attractive. Five sets of eyes returned his gaze with a collective look of awe-struck wonder. It was then that a thought entered Alex's mind, a thought he pondered for a moment, a thought that, if found to be true, was ripe with scandal.

Miss Windom returned, pushing a squeaky stainless steel kitchen cart containing a pot of soup and a plate of assorted sandwiches, and she began serving the guests. Mrs. Foster turned to Alex and smiled.

"Thank you for keeping my son occupied while I was talk-ing with Mrs. Mason," she said. "He is forever whining. I some-times tune him out just to keep my sanity. Outside of my counseling sessions with Father Francis, I don't get many oppor-tunities to speak with other adults."

"No problem, ma'am," Alex said. "I understand Father Francis is a good listener, has a way of comforting people in their distress."

"He's wonderful. We meet every Tuesday afternoon at three o'clock. It gets me through the week."

Alex nodded and smiled, making a mental note of the day and time of Mrs. Foster's counseling sessions. *I just might feel like praying in the sanctuary this Tuesday afternoon*, he thought. Father Francis closed his eyes and lifted his voice to say grace: "In the Name of the Father, and of the Son, and of the Holy Ghost, bless us oh Lord and these Thy gifts . . ."

§

On Tuesday afternoon at 2:30, the school bell rang right on schedule. Alex slipped on his jacket, gathered his books, and headed for the door.

"Going over to church today, Alex?" Dan asked.

"Yeah."

"Mind if I join you?"

"Since when did you want to spend extra time in church?"

"With that history exam coming up on Friday, I figure I need all the help I can get."

"Wally, I've got some advice for you: try studying. Anyway, I'd sorta like to go alone today, okay?"

"As long as you say a prayer that I pass the exam."

"I'll say a prayer for you, Wally."

"Thanks, pal. It'd probably be better if it came from you anyway."

Alex shook his head and walked out into the stream of students flowing down the school hallway toward the exit.

§

After parking his bike on the side of the church away from the road, Alex entered the building through the back door. From the foyer, he pushed open the sanctuary doors to hear the familiar lonely creaking. He instinctively turned right, dipped his fingers into the holy water font on the back wall, and made the sign of the cross. As he turned forward to face the front of the church, the smell of melting beeswax reached his nostrils.

He was not alone.

A tall man with white hair had just finished lighting a candle and was walking, head bowed, toward the kneeler near the heat register. From the back of the church through the dim light, it was difficult to make out who the man was. Alex looked at his wristwatch: 2:45. He decided to slip into the back pew and wait for the man to leave.

Minutes ticked by, and Alex prayed for everyone he could think of, including Dan Wallace, but the man hardly moved while he knelt with his elbows leaning on the altar rail. At 3:00 Alex decided to move to another pew closer to the front, a respectable distance from the man but within earshot of the heat vent. He could see, now, that the man held a set of beads between the fingers of both hands and was silently praying the rosary, which meant he probably wasn't leaving any time soon. Alex checked his watch again: 3:05. The tranquility of the sanctuary was only occasionally interrupted by the sound of the prayer beads sliding against the wooden rail.

Another five minutes passed. Then a faint sound. At first Alex thought it might be murmurs from the praying man, but then he recognized it as the muffled playful giggles of a woman. He strained his ears and heard the familiar authoritative voice of the priest. Alex wasn't sure, but it sounded like he said, "There's no need to be nervous, now." He glanced at the man praying. *Can he not hear that?* More giggling followed by an approving comment from the priest. The giggles subsided into sounds more provocative and less restrained, sounds that climaxed with low, sensuous groans of pleasure.

Several minutes later, the man at the altar slowly pulled himself up from one knee and then the other, made the sign of the cross, and turned to leave. Alex quickly bowed his head as though he was busy with his devotions, looking out the corner of his eye long enough to see that it was old man Beaman, walking away as though a weight had lifted from his shoulders. *He didn't hear a thing. He really is half deaf.*

Once the grocer left, Alex shuffled out of his pew, knelt next to the heat vent, and listened. All was silent. He got up, hurried out of the sanctuary, and hopped onto his bike, making a wide sweep down one side street and up another, bringing himself in position to view the church office from a safe distance, seemingly unnoticed. Then he waited. Fifteen minutes later, a flushed Mrs. Foster exited the doorway, smoothing her skirt as she stepped down onto the sidewalk and strolled to her car. His suspicions confirmed, Alex shook his head and said to himself, "I've got to talk to Kitty."

As he started to turn his bike around, he felt like he was being watched. He looked again at the church office and noticed that two slats of the Venetian blinds covering the window were slightly parted, and then suddenly snapped closed.

Chapter 2

The two priests toasted their friendship, lightly clinking their long stemmed Waterford goblets and sipping the rich red Chianti. "Pretty fancy crystal for a common table wine, Father Francis."

"The Waterford I inherited from my mother, Father Vincenzo. It was one of the few extravagances in her life. As for the Chianti, well I spared no expense, knowing the bishop's right-hand man was coming. And it goes well with Miss Windom's remarkable chicken cannelloni."

Father Vincenzo nodded and smiled.

"So how do you like working so close to the seat of diocesan power?" Father Francis asked, tearing a warm slice of garlic bread.

"Do I sense a hint of jealousy, Father, or was that sarcasm?"

"Perhaps a bit of both, Father."

"Still roiled because I got the position of vicar general instead of you? When will you let it go Michael? It has been over
a year. Must we always compete?"

"I have accepted your promotion, Thomas, and I am happy
for you. Truly, I am." Father Francis lifted the basket of bread
and gestured to his friend to partake. "However, I do not deny
that I think I was the better choice for the job."

"You have always thought you were the better man," Father
Vincenzo said, chuckling, while lifting a slice of bread from the
basket. "As far back as high school I can remember you having
to win at everything—sports, academics, debates, girls. And that
did not change when we attended seminary . . . well, accept for
the girls."

Father Francis swallowed a sip of wine. "It is in my blood. I
am a competitor, and competitors compete to win. When I completed the seven-year building program at St. Andrew's—one, I
will remind you, the bishop fully endorsed—I had my eye on
winning a position within the diocesan curia."

"The fact of the matter is the bishop chose me over you, Michael. Now are we going to spend the first luncheon we have
had in ages quibbling over irreversible facts, or shall we discuss
your chances of becoming the next episcopal vicar?" Father
Vincenzo poked his fork into his last portion of garden salad.

"Episcopal vicar?"

The dining room door opened, and Miss Windom entered,
carrying a tray with two plates loaded with cannelloni stuffed
with chicken and ricotta and covered in a rich homemade tomato
sauce tinged with garlic.

"Ah, Miss Windom, that aroma takes me back to my visits
to Italy." Father Vincenzo said. "You have captured the fragrance of a Tuscan kitchen."

"Thank you, Father. You are too kind," Miss Windom replied, blushing.

"And I assure you, it tastes as good as it smells," Father
Francis said.

"Thank you, Father. May I take your salad plates?" The housekeeper looked uncomfortable with the attention.

"Yes, please, Miss Windom," Father Francis replied. "And I will ring when we are ready for dessert. Father Vincenzo and I have some important matters to discuss over lunch."

"Certainly, Father. I understand." Miss Windom removed the salad plates from the table. "Is there anything else I can get for either of you before I leave?" Both priests shook their heads. Miss Windom nodded politely and left the room, closing the door behind her.

"This cannelloni looks delicious," Father Vincenzo said as he began slicing the stuffed pasta.

"While you are eating your delicious dinner, Thomas, I would like to finish the appetizer you served me before Miss Windom interrupted. What is this talk about me being appointed episcopal vicar?"

"I said nothing about you being appointed to that position. You act as though the bishop has already made up his mind."

"Has he?"

"No, he has not. But your name has surfaced whenever we have discussed it."

"Clearly, the diocese has grown enough to substantiate the added position . . ."

Father Vincenzo swallowed a bite of cannelloni. "Your assessment is correct, Michael. And with that growth is a need for more buildings. The bishop wants someone who is experienced with building programs, someone who knows the local building codes and can show parish priests how to navigate through the government bureaucracy. We have two parishes that are clamoring for parochial schools and three others that need additional space for their sanctuaries. So, you see, your seven-year building spree at St. Andrew's may have served your purposes after all."

"And what is the timeline the bishop has in mind for completing all of these building projects?"

"Five years."

"So at the pleasure of the bishop I work myself at a break-neck pace for five years, help him establish his place in the diocesan annals as the Great Architect, and then what?"

Father Vincenzo lifted his glass of wine to his lips, sipped, and slowly lowered the goblet to the table. Looking at his friend, he said, "A college."

"A college?"

"Bishop O'Keane believes it is the Lord's will that this city should have a Catholic college. He believes that post-war materialism has produced a new generation of young Catholics void of any depth of understanding of philosophy, theology, and church history. And I think he is correct. As we have seen in these last few weeks with this Cuban missile crisis, these are perilous times in which we live. Thank God we have a strong Catholic leader in our young president who is not afraid to confront evil when he sees it. Bishop O'Keane thinks the Church needs to capitalize on this country's new openness to Catholics in politics. We need to raise up young men and women who are ready to be the vanguard of this movement."

"Do you think this city is ready for a Catholic college?"

"Bishop O'Keane is a visionary, Michael. And one of his greatest frustrations, indeed, the greatest frustration of any true visionary, is waiting for the rest of the world to see what is already too evident to him. No, this community would not see the need for another college if the bishop were to present his vision today. But five years from now . . ."

"Just about the time the diocesan building program is finished."

Father Vincenzo nodded. "With the addition of two new parochial schools within the diocese, our families will begin to see the value of investing in a post-secondary Catholic education for their children. And we will be ready to provide that when the time comes."

"So am I to presume that my sole ministry within the curia is to be a general contractor?"

"I thought you had more foresight than that, Michael. The bishop will hire a general contractor for a project the magnitude of the college. But where will he find its first chancellor, its first dean? I dare say it will be from among those who have proved themselves in the little things, as our Lord has stated."

"And serving as episcopal vicar constitutes a 'little thing,' Thomas?"

"Not just serving as episcopal vicar, but proving yourself in that role. That is what will make the difference to Bishop O'Keane."

"And what do I need to do to let Bishop O'Keane know that I am interested in this position?"

"I will tell him myself that you desire the position. And as we both know, desire is the force that directs the course of every man."

Father Francis smiled at his friend while reaching for the dinner bell. "Shall we have dessert, Father Vincenzo?"

"Why of course, Father Francis."

Chapter 3

A collective clamor ascended from St. Andrew's school cafeteria, where the boys sat on one side of the lunchroom and the girls on the other. Their voices merged into a cacophony of cracking baritones and shrieking sopranos during the one time of day students were allowed to be kids. Alex's voice cut through the chatter as he slipped past Kitty's table on his way to throw his lunch bag into a garbage can.

"Kitty, can you wait for me after school today? I need to talk to you about something," he said while he continued walking.

"Okay . . ." Kitty's gaze followed Alex as he passed, tossed his garbage into the can, and came past her again.

"Wait for me in the parking lot," he said quickly, hoping Sister Angelica hadn't seen them talking. He was in luck because just at that time the nun was grabbing one of the fifth-grade boys by the ear and marching him toward the principal's office.

§

When the last bell of the day rang, Alex grabbed his jacket and raced toward the parking lot to find Kitty. It was a gorgeous fall afternoon, warm and sunny with a soft breeze that was blowing Kitty's auburn bangs over her eyes while she stood waiting near her bus. Alex approached, slightly winded, and said, "Kitty, you remember at your party you said if I needed a good listener I could talk to you?"

"Yeah, I remember."

"Do you think I could meet you at your house this afternoon, and we could ride our bikes over to Simms Park to talk?"

"Why can't we just talk at my house?"

"Like I said before, it's complicated. I'm not sure I want your mother to overhear us."

"You're making me a little nervous about this, Alex. Can you give me a hint what it's all about?"

"Not here. Will you ride to Simms Park with me?"

"I think I can, as long as I'm back before dark. That only gives us a few hours. I've gotta go; my bus is getting ready to leave. Be at my house by three-thirty."

Kitty brushed a strand of hair out of her eyes and gave Alex an assuring smile when she turned to climb the steps of her bus. While Alex watched, a warm sense of security enveloped him, and a sudden pang of desire for Kitty's presence took him by surprise. He had never noticed how soft and inviting her hair looked. How her eyes seemed to look right into his heart. And the sweet floral scent she left behind, though familiar, seemed to awaken new feelings in him . . . feelings quickly quenched by the pungent odor of diesel exhaust from the departing school bus. He then remembered he better get moving if he was going to take his books home and ride over to Kitty's by three-thirty.

§

Alex turned his bike into the McAlister driveway and found Kitty sitting on the front steps, her elbows on her knees, resting her head on her hands. She had changed out of her school uniform and into a pair of blue jeans, rolled up to her calves, and a green hooded sweatshirt with the St. Andrew's insignia across the front. As soon as she saw Alex, she smiled, stood up, and brushed the back of her jeans with her hands. "We need to go in and tell Mother we're leaving," she said when Alex glided his bike to a stop near the sidewalk. The two bade Mrs. McAlister goodbye, hopped onto their bicycles, and turned left out of the driveway toward the village.

Simms Park was nestled alongside a canal that snaked purposefully through Stonebridge. The canal's crushed stone towpath commemorated an earlier time when the waterway served as a main artery for commerce. Now the path was reserved for young lovers frolicking and flirting and for old sweethearts rambling and remembering.

During one week in June every year, the park came alive with carnival rides, beer tents, and marching bands as the village ushered in a new summer season. On this late October day, though, all was quiet, but for the sound of the breeze gently whistling through the gazebo where Alex and Kitty parked their bikes. They sat down on the rustic picnic bench overlooking the murky canal, quietly watching a pleasure boat making a late season excursion up the waterway. The familiar bell from the lift bridge signaled to village traffic that the bridge was about to go up to let the boat pass under.

"When I was little, my dad used to tell me that pirates would sail up the canal and hide their treasure underneath that bridge," Alex said.

"Did you believe him?"

"I believed everything he told me back then."

"You miss him, don't you?"

"Every day. I thought it'd be easier as time passed. But

things seem to be getting more complicated, and I sure could use his advice."

"Tell me what's going on."

Alex paused and took a deep breath. "Well, it all started last week when I was praying in the church after school. In fact, it was on the one-year anniversary of my dad's death. I know some people think I'm weird because I like to spend time in church even when I don't have to . . ."

"I don't think you're weird, Alex." Kitty's brown eyes confirmed the sincerity in her voice, assuring Alex it was safe to be himself with her.

"Well, it gives me a peace I can't find at home anymore. Anyway, while I was kneeling at the altar, I heard voices—a man and a woman. At first I thought I was losing it. Then I realized the sounds were coming from the heat vent, from Father Francis's office. I put my ear to the vent, and I realized it was Father Francis and my mother. And they were making out."

Kitty gasped. "What do you mean, 'making out'?"

"Making out, y'know, doing it," Alex replied, blushing.

Kitty looked around and said quietly, "You mean having sex?"

"Yeah, that's what I mean. At least I think so."

"My gosh, no wonder you haven't been yourself all week."

"There's more."

"More?"

"Last Sunday I had to go with my mother to a lunch that Father Francis was hosting for some of the single mothers in the church and their kids. It was weird, but it seemed like he had some kind of spell over these women. They all looked at him like he was, I don't know, a movie star or something, not a priest." Alex paused and looked at Kitty.

"Go on," Kitty said, prodding.

"You know Mrs. Foster at church?"

Kitty nodded.

"She was sitting next to me and was going on about how Father Francis has been such a help to her and how he counsels her every Tuesday afternoon at three o'clock. And it made me wonder. So I decided to go to the church after school Tuesday to listen for any strange sounds coming from the heat vent."

"What did you hear?"

"The same sounds I heard when my mother was with him. I think he's doing it with other women too."

"You think anyone else knows about this?"

"When I was at the church Tuesday, old man Beaman was praying the rosary at the altar, near the vent. He must be half deaf, though, because he acted like he didn't hear a thing."

"You sure of that?"

"No . . . I'm not sure . . . but he didn't even flinch when the noises started."

"Where were you sitting?"

"Second row, straight out from the vent."

"And you could hear from there?"

"Yeah."

Kitty paused. "We need to think this through, Alex. This is the kind of thing that could ruin a lot of people's reputations, including your mother's. I mean, think about it . . . accusing a priest, well a scandal this big could turn this whole village upside down."

"We can't just pretend it's not happening."

"I agree. But right now, we just have your side of the story. We need more evidence, more witnesses."

"What do you suggest?"

"Think about it. Who is closest to Father Francis and would be most likely to know if something like this was going on?"

Alex thought for a moment. "What about Miss Windom?"

"Exactly. She's in the rectory more than anyone else and knows who's visiting and why."

"And she's going to be hush-hush about it, Kitty, which could be why she's kept her job as long as she has."

"I think you underestimate Miss Windom, Alex. She seems

like a very devout woman. I don't think she'd put up with the kind of behavior you described, Father Francis or not."

"So what do we do, go up to Miss Windom and ask, 'Hey Miss Windom, you think Father Francis is having sex with women from the church?' I'm sure that'd go over real big."

Kitty squinched her face and shook her head. "What if we could find out from Miss Windom if Father Francis counsels any of the other women who were at the lunch last Sunday? And what if we could find out the times and days they meet with him? Then, you and I could go to church and listen."

"That'd give us more proof, I suppose. But how would you get that information from Miss Windom?"

"First things first. Can you remember who else was there?"

"Sure. Besides my mother and Mrs. Foster there was Mrs. Mason, Mrs. Thornton, and Mrs. Bartell."

"Good. Now it just so happens I volunteered to help Miss Windom two weeks from this Saturday. We're getting the church Christmas decorations out of storage for the holidays. I'll see what I can find out from her that weekend. Leave it to me."

"You realize this'll make you a co-conspirator, Kitty."

"Yeah sort of like Nancy Drew and the Hardy Boys. I'm okay with that."

A loud honking sound in the sky broke the late afternoon calm. Alex and Kitty looked up to see a flock of Canada geese flying south in a tight V formation.

"Don't you wish our lives could be that organized?" Alex said. "Think of the confidence that flock has in their leader. After all I've seen and heard lately, I'll never trust another leader again."

"Really, Alex? You can't believe every priest is as bad as Father Francis."

"Two weeks ago I wouldn't have believed Father Francis was as bad as he is. I've watched him all my life. He was my role model, Kitty. I wanted to be just like him. But he's a fake, and I didn't see that until last week. No, I won't be fooled like that again."

"You know, the thing I always liked most about you is your kind heart. You're not like other boys, Alex. You're compassionate . . . tender. I hope you don't let Father Francis change that."

Alex looked at Kitty for a moment, dropped his head, and then looked aimlessly toward the canal. "Maybe we should start heading back home."

Kitty pursed her lips. "Okay, if you want to."

The two rode home in an awkward silence. When they reached the McAlister's driveway, Kitty turned to Alex and asked, "So . . . you still want me to talk with Miss Windom?"

"Yeah, why wouldn't I?"

"Just wanted to be sure, that's all. See you later, Alex."

Alex nodded and then rode away, replaying Kitty's words in his head and wondering if his heart had already been changed.

§

"Looks like it's just you and me today, Miss Windom," Kitty said after looking at the clock in the rectory reception area.

"I think the two of us can handle this. Let's head to the attic." Miss Windom motioned Kitty with her hand, and the two of them walked down the corridor leading to the attic stairway.

"Will Father Francis be around if we need some help?"

Miss Windom laughed while she began climbing the stairs. "Goodness no. Father Francis is better at preaching and teaching than lifting and sweating. When he knows I've got work like this scheduled, he skedaddles. He left just before you got here. Meeting someone for brunch I think."

"I bet he has a pretty busy schedule."

"Oh yes, he's a busy man. I sometimes don't know how he keeps everything straight."

"That's why he has you, Miss Windom."

"I suppose . . . here we are. Move down a step, so I can open this door."

Kitty responded and watched Miss Windom pull open the door to the expansive attic. The high pitched gable roof provided enough headroom for the housekeeper to stand upright with room to spare. She switched on the overhead lights and motioned for Kitty to come in. Kitty's eyes scanned the rows of wooden shelving filled with familiar odds and ends used during different seasons of the church calendar and unfamiliar surplus supplies that had been gathering dust and tarnish from years of disuse.

"There sure is a lot of stuff in here," Kitty said.

"Well, Father Francis is a bit of a pack rat. He thinks we might find a use for something like this someday." Miss Windom wrinkled her nose as she held up a garish sterling candle holder, dulled dark gray with age.

Kitty chuckled. "My dad is the same way. He doesn't like throwing anything out."

"Let's get started on the Christmas decorations; they should be right over here. Let's pull them out to the middle of the attic, so we can see what we have. Now where is that list Father Francis wrote?"

"What list is that, Miss Windom?"

"Oh, Father Francis told me before he left this morning that he had made a list of the specific Christmas decorations he wanted on display this year. I bet it's still sitting on his desk. Kitty, would you mind going down to his office and getting it for me? Your young legs can take you up and down those stairs quicker than mine will."

"Sure. You said it's on his desk?"

"I'm almost certain that's where he said he left it. Remember to close the door to his office when you're finished."

"Okay." Kitty turned and walked out of the attic, down the flight of stairs, and into the hallway that led to the pastor's office. She cautiously knocked on the office door, to be sure no one was inside, and then stepped into the priest's inner sanctum. She turned on the light and gently pushed the door closed behind her. In front of her sat a polished mahogany desk with a rich cordovan leather executive chair. She felt intimidated.

On the wall behind the desk hung multiple plaques and certificates, attesting to the priest's achievements throughout his years of ministry at St. Andrew's. A series of three mahogany bookcases filled with hardcover volumes of philosophers, religious thinkers, and biblical studies lined the wall to the left of the desk. Along the wall to the right was a plush sofa—its leather creased from use—centered between two heat vents at the base of the wall.

"No wonder those women have been putty in his hands," Kitty said to herself as she looked around.

She walked over to the desk and saw a piece of yellow legal note paper with handwriting on it lying on the desktop. Scrawled at the top of the paper were the words *Christmas Decorations*.

"This must be it." Kitty reached to grab the list and noticed a black leather booklet next to it. A brass plate attached to the cover of the booklet was engraved with the initials *Fr. M.D.F.*

"What's this?" she whispered, clutching the cover and slowly pulling it open. Inside was the priest's appointment booklet, showing all of his scheduled meetings for the month of November. Kitty, glancing up to check the closed door, quickly thumbed to the first Tuesday in the booklet, November 6, and scanned the page to find 3:00 p.m. There in black ink, blocking out the 3–3:30 time slot, was written *Counseling – Mrs. Foster*. She turned to the same time on Thursday and saw the words *Counseling – Mrs. Spencer*.

Kitty frantically searched for a pen and paper. She pulled open the center drawer of the desk and found a pencil and a small notepad. Grabbing both, she began to search for the names of the other women who attended the church luncheon with Alex. She quickly saw a pattern: Monday 3–3:30, *Counseling – Mrs. Mason*; Wednesday 3–3:30, *Counseling – Mrs. Thornton*; Friday 3–3:30, *Counseling – Mrs. Bartell*. She jotted this information on the notepad. Then she turned to the next week on the calendar and saw that the appointments repeated on the same days at the same times. However, when she got to Friday, November 16, the 3–3:30 time slot for Mrs. Bartell had been crossed out. Thinking the woman may have re-scheduled, Kitty began to flip through each page of the calendar. But there were no other entries for Mrs. Bartell.

Suddenly, Kitty froze. She heard the sounds of heavy footsteps coming down the corridor in an even, determined stride. They slowed as they approached the pastor's office door and then stopped. Kitty heard the doorknob turn and panicked. Fumbling to tear the sheet off the notepad, she knocked the calendar on the floor, just as she heard Father Francis say, "Good morning, Miss McAlister."

"H-Hello Father Francis. You startled me."

"May I ask what you are doing in my office?"

"I'm helping Miss Windom with the decorations. She sent me to your office to get the list you wrote." Kitty noticed the priest look down at his calendar on the floor next to her feet. "I'm afraid I knocked your calendar over accidentally when I was getting the list."

"If you would please hand it to me, Miss McAlister, I need it for an appointment for which I am running late. And since you have your list, you can run along."

"Yes Father." She quickly bent down, grabbed the calendar booklet, and gave it to the priest on her way out of the room.

§

After Kitty closed the door, the priest thumbed through the booklet as though sensing something was amiss. Out of the corner of his eye he saw lying on the desk the pencil and notepad he always kept put away in the center drawer. Clearly, Kitty McAlister was looking for something more than the decoration list. But what? He would have to look into this later, for now he had an appointment to keep. He opened the calendar to Saturday, November 17, and found the entry for 10:30: *Brunch with Fr.*

Vincenzo at the Crescent Inn (Phone: EL 24182). Picking up the phone on his desk, he called the restaurant and asked them to tell Father Vincenzo when he arrived that Father Francis would be a few minutes late.

Chapter 4

"Well it's about time you showed up," Father Vincenzo said, chiding Father Francis who was pulling out his chair to sit down.

"My humble apologies. I trust you got my message."

Father Vincenzo nodded and grinned.

"I had forgotten where we were meeting and realized that I left my calendar in my office. I had to turn back to get it."

"One of the hazards of growing old, I am afraid, Michael."

"One of the hazards of being too busy, Thomas."

"You are about to become much busier, my friend."

"Oh?"

"Bishop O'Keane has asked me to offer you the job of episcopal vicar."

Father Francis smiled and said, "He is a wise man."

"Of course, the bishop will present a formal offer to you personally once he knows you will accept the job."

"Of course."

"So, I assume you accept?"

"Unequivocally."

"Good. He will be pleased to hear that. He was quite impressed with the ideas you shared in your meeting with him last week."

"I sensed that he was, but I did not expect an offer so soon."

"You will find that Bishop O'Keane usually has his mind made up on something long before he brings the issue to your attention. And, surprisingly, he is almost always correct in his assessments." The priest paused, then added, "I trust you will not be the exception to that, Michael."

Father Francis gave his friend a perplexed look.

"Two days ago, I received a troubling letter in the mail," Father Vincenzo continued, "a letter about you. The writer did not have the courage to sign her name, but I suppose she has her reasons."

"A letter from a woman? And what did she have to say about me that troubled you?"

"She alleges you made inappropriate advances toward her during a counseling session."

Father Francis shook his head and sighed. "Mrs. Bartell, no doubt."

"Is there any substance to her allegations?"

Father Francis looked up to respond and saw a waiter approaching the table, smiling at Father Vincenzo.

"Well I see your guest has arrived, Father. Are you ready to order?" the waiter asked.

"I will have the buffet today, Jonathan," Father Vincenzo said.

"Very good, sir. And for you, Father?"

"The same," Father Francis replied, mildly annoyed by the interruption.

"Thank you, gentlemen. Please help yourselves whenever you're ready." The priests nodded, and the waiter gave a slight bow and left the table. Father Francis looked around the dining room to assure no one could hear him and resumed his narrative.

"You asked, Thomas, if there is any substance to Mrs. Bartell's allegations. The short answer is no. Mrs. Bartell is a single mother who attends St. Andrew's. About two months ago her husband abandoned her and their two-year old daughter. He ran off with some young woman he met at his office. Mrs. Bartell came to me for counseling shortly after this happened. She holds much bitterness toward her husband for leaving her, and I could see that the incident clearly affected her self-esteem. A week ago we were having our third, or maybe it was our fourth, session together, I cannot recall. She was being extremely hard on herself, saying she must be unattractive and unappealing or why else would her husband have left her. I walked over, put my arm around her, and tried to assure her that she was very attractive."

Father Vincenzo grimaced.

"I realized right away that she misunderstood my intentions. She stiffened her back and said, 'I'm not comfortable with you being so close to me, Father.' I immediately moved back to my desk, and our session ended shortly thereafter."

"And that was your last session with her?"

"We had another session scheduled for yesterday, but she called Monday and canceled. I assumed it was because of what transpired last week."

"I think that is a safe assumption. What were you thinking, Michael, putting your arm around her? With all of your training, you should have known better."

"I am a pastor, Thomas, not just a trained counselor. And sometimes my compassion for my sheep overrides my better judgment as a counselor."

"Well, it certainly did in this case. The last thing Bishop O'Keane needs is to have this get blown all out of proportion and come to the forefront just as he is about to bring you on staff. If I did not think you were the right man for the job, I would recommend he look elsewhere."

"But we both know I am the only man for the job. And I hardly think this woman can accuse me of anything more than poor judgment."

Father Vincenzo glared at his friend. Pointing his finger at him, he said, "Let me tell you what you are going to do Father Michael Francis. You are going to cancel any further counseling sessions you have with any women, and you are going to keep a very low profile until I find your replacement. Your accuser does not want her name known, which is a good thing for you. Hopefully she will see your transfer as the end of this matter. Now please tell me there are no other surprises I or the bishop will face as the result of your poor judgment."

"You are being unduly harsh, Father Vincenzo."

"Welcome to the big leagues, Father Francis."

Chapter 5

Alex was sitting on the edge of his bed, strumming his father's old acoustic guitar, when he heard the phone ringing in the kitchen. His mother had just left for the factory to work the Saturday afternoon overtime shift, so Alex was alone in the house. He rested the guitar against the bed, walked to the kitchen, and lifted the receiver.

"Alex, this is Kitty," the voice said breathlessly.

"Kitty, are you all right?"

"I need to talk to you. Can you come over?"

"Yeah, I'll be over in a few minutes."

"Good. Hurry."

Alex slipped into his winter jacket, pulled his wool cap over his head and his knit gloves onto his hands. He grabbed his bike out of the garage and headed to Kitty's. A slate gray November sky hung over the neighborhood houses, their chimneys puffing colorless smoke that floated over a landscape of brown grass and barren trees. A frosty breeze nudged Alex's back as he sped past the houses toward the McAlister's. He reached behind him and pulled up the collar of his jacket, and thought about the urgency in Kitty's voice.

They had not spoken much to each other since their conversation at Simms Park. The awkwardness he felt after Kitty expressed her concerns about him losing his tenderness had not abated and left him feeling vulnerable. He desperately wanted to make sense out of his life, and this sordid revelation about Father Francis had left him struggling to find his equilibrium. No one seemed to understand this about him better than Kitty, and for some reason that scared him.

Alex pulled into the McAlister driveway and saw Kitty

watching out the living room window, looking worried. While Alex was walking up the sidewalk, she opened the front door and stepped out, bundled in her coat and hat.

"I told my mother we were going to take a walk around the neighborhood."

"What's going on?" Alex asked. Kitty tugged on the arm of his jacket and said she would tell him once they got away from the house. When they reached the street, they slowed their pace, and Kitty began telling Alex all about her encounter with Father Francis in his office that morning.

"It sounds like you did okay. I doubt if he suspects anything," Alex said when she was finished.

"Alex, I didn't have time to put the pencil and notepad away. I'm sure he noticed that, and he might think I was snooping. I'm terrified he might say something to Miss Windom or my parents."

"Well . . . all the more reason for us to finish what we started. If you're going to be accused of snooping, you might as well have evidence that explains your actions. You said you wrote down the times for his counseling sessions with Mrs. Mason and Mrs. Thornton, right?"

"Yeah."

"So we go to church together this week and listen. You're the one who said we need more evidence. If you hear the same thing I heard, then we'll tell some adults we can trust and let them take it from there. It's that simple."

"If it's that simple, how come I'm so scared?"

"Kitty, if you don't want to do this, say so."

"I'm already involved."

"Then there's no turning back. So we'll meet in church Monday after school, okay?"

"What'll I tell my mother? I'm not going to lie to her."

"Can you tell her you need to stay after school to work on a special project? That's the truth."

"I suppose, but you know my mother, she'll ask questions:

'What kind of special project?' and 'What time will you be done?'"

"Geesh, Kitty, I don't know," Alex said, lifting his gloved hands in exasperation as he continued walking. He despised Mrs. McAlister's interrogations, having experienced them himself on occasion. She had a way of putting people on the defensive unnecessarily with her pointed questioning. "Tell her you're going to church to pray for world peace. You can certainly do that while we're waiting."

Kitty stopped abruptly. "Please don't get sarcastic with me, Alex. I'm trying to help you, remember?"

Alex turned, mid stride, and faced Kitty. "You're right. I'm sorry. I think maybe we're both a little on edge about all this stuff."

"A *little* on edge?" Kitty raised her voice and glared into Alex's eyes. She then paused for a moment and composed herself. "I'll try to think of something to tell my mother. Let's plan on meeting in the church after school on Monday. We should probably walk over separately, so it doesn't look suspicious."

"Good idea."

Kitty began shivering. "Can we walk back to my house now? This wind is going right through me."

Alex suddenly felt miserable. He wanted to put his arm around her to warm her, wanted to tell her how much he appreciated her, tell her how much he had been thinking about what she said to him at Simms Park. He wanted to, but he didn't. He walked Kitty to her door, got on his bike, and rode home.

§

Jean Spencer entered the empty break room, pulled out a folding chair, and sat down, letting out a long sigh. She poured herself a cup of coffee from her thermos and watched the steam rise and swirl as she sniffed its comforting aroma. "Aahh," she said softly, then reached into her purse and pulled out her Winstons.

"Can I bum a cig, Jean?" Kathy Bartell walked in and sat down across from her friend. "Where's Don Loamke? I thought you guys took breaks together."

Jean smacked the end of the red and white cigarette pack and offered it to her friend. "His line is down, so he's working through break."

"Y'know, people are talkin', sayin' you got something going with the foreman . . ."

"People can talk all they want. Don's not foreman of my line, so it's not like there's favoritism or anything." Jean leaned forward to light Kathy's smoke. "Besides, we're just friends. He's from Boston, so we've got some things in common. That's all."

"Hey, I say go for it. The guy's divorced; you're widowed. Might be a good thing for both of you."

"We're just friends, Kathy, okay?" Jean held the lighter to the end of her own cigarette and lit it.

"You still counseling with Father Francis?" Kathy asked.

"Yeah, pretty regularly. How about you? How are your visits with him going?"

"They're not."

"How come?"

"Listen, Jean, I didn't want to say anything about it, since you recommended him to me and everything."

"Say anything about what?" Jean flicked her cigarette against the side of the ash tray.

"The man gives me the creeps. I mean the first few sessions were fine. Seemed like he was listening, showing compassion. It helped some. My last session, though, I was feeling really down, and he comes over and puts his arm around me. Whispers in my ear how beautiful he thinks I am. I told him he was making me uncomfortable, and he went back to his desk. I mean come on. The man's a priest for Pete's sake. He shouldn't be acting like that. Needless to say, I'm not goin' back."

Jean felt the blood drain from her face as she listened to

Kathy's story. "Do you think you might've misunderstood his intentions? Could he have just been trying to comfort you, maybe?"

"Trust me, Jean. The guy was coming on to me. He had that look."

"What look?"

"The same look all men get when they want sex. The wild look of an animal in heat."

Jean had never seen that look from the priest during her own visits with him. His looks toward her were more of a man who was hungry but not starved. If he had to wait, he could. She began to feel strangely jealous. Jealous that she was not the only woman Father Francis was interested in. Jealous that his interest in Kathy was apparently more intense than his interest in her. "Well, I'm sorry I recommended him to you, Kathy."

"My guess is he'll be sorry too."

"What do you mean?"

"I wrote an anonymous letter to the bishop's office, telling them all about his inappropriate behavior."

"You think that was a wise thing to do? I mean something like that could cause him a lot of trouble."

"Well that's the point, Jean. Somebody needs to come down on him before he takes advantage of some other woman who's too weak to resist."

Jean suddenly felt flushed with embarrassment. Was she one of those weak women who couldn't resist the priest's advances, or was she content to throw herself at him because she enjoyed the thrill of the adventure, the thrill of kicking against societal norms like she did when she married Bill? She had convinced herself it was the latter, but now she wondered. She had lacked the courage and strength to leave her husband when her marriage hadn't lived up to her childish expectations. Maybe fear was influencing her openness to her pastor's advances. While she was contemplating this, a loud horn blew, signaling the end of the ten-minute break, and the churning, thumping rhythms of the assembly line resumed.

"Listen, Jean, I'm sorry if I upset you about this. I'm sure you'd feel the same way if he did something like that to you, wouldn't you?"

"Yeah . . . of course. We'd better get back to work." Jean took one last drag on her Winston and exhaled.

Kathy stubbed out her cigarette in the ashtray. "Talk to you later, Jean."

"Yeah, see you, Kathy." For several seconds after Kathy had gone, Jean stared at the doorway, moving the palm of her left hand in circles on her belly. Where did this leave her with Father Francis? Certainly she knew nothing would come of her relationship with the priest. She realized now that she had duped herself into believing he was involved with only her. The more she thought about it, the more foolish she felt. She was determined she would confront him about it at her next counseling session on Thursday.

§

The line filing out of St. Andrew's on Sunday was moving at its usual snail's pace as some parishioners lagged to chat with each other while others paused to complement Father Francis on his sermon. Jean Spencer was in the latter group and stayed back to be at the end of the line.

"Excellent homily about truthfulness this morning, Father," Jean said as she shook her pastor's hand. "I am looking forward to our Thursday meeting to ask you some questions about it." The priest's eyes widened, and he glanced around, releasing her hand.

"Did Miss Windom not contact you Mrs. Spencer?" he asked with a somber expression.

"Contact me about what?"

"I am afraid I will have to cancel our Thursday meeting."

"Oh? Is there another day this week you're available?"

"I am afraid not."

Jean felt uncomfortably perplexed and said, "Then, I guess I'll have to wait until a week from Thursday."

"Mrs. Spencer, I am afraid I will be unavailable for counseling for the foreseeable future. The bishop's office has me working on some special projects that will keep me quite busy." The priest looked like he was trying to hide his discomfort behind a pharisaical pose.

Jean remembered Kathy Bartell's comment about reporting him to the bishop's office, and she immediately wondered if the bishop's retribution was to suspend the priest's counseling privileges until everything settled down. That would mean there was substance to Kathy's accusations, for Jean presumed Father Francis was not one to bend to pressure unless it was warranted.

Jean glared at the priest and folded her arms. "I'm sure Kathy Bartell will be pleased to hear that," she said. She noticed the priest's jaw clench and knew she had hit a nerve.

"And why would Mrs. Bartell be interested in my projects for the bishop?"

"Oh, I think we both know why she would be interested, Father. And I'm sure there are others who would be interested as well." She threw the last line in for good measure.

The priest looked around as if verifying no one else was listening to their conversation. He leaned forward, glowering at the woman, and began threatening her with the controlled voice of a seasoned trial attorney.

"Have you stopped to think about how your allegations might come back to affect you, Mrs. Spencer? Let me be perfectly clear that I will not only deny any charges that you conjure against me, but I will systematically dismantle them and shred your reputation in the process. And what will all of your son's friends at St. Andrew's think when they find out that you are nothing but a desperate widow who tried to seduce her pastor into satisfying her sexual appetite? I dare say that neither you nor your son will be able to show your faces in this community after that. So, you had better think long and hard about what you say about me, my friend."

Jean felt a surge of indignation rise from within, an attitude she had cultivated as a Davidson and had almost forgotten she still possessed.

"First of all, I am not your friend. Secondly, I stopped worrying about my reputation fifteen years ago, when I married beneath myself. As for my son, he has enough resilience to face ten of you. So you had better think long and hard about how you might make a living once your reputation as a priest has been laid to waste. Good day to you . . . Father."

With that, Jean Spencer turned and walked out of the sanctuary, struggling to project the outward composure of a woman in control. But inside, she felt bruised and sore, like she had gone twelve rounds with a heavyweight and barely escaped with her life.

§

Alex walked in the house and heard the soft sounds of a Frank Sinatra record coming from his mother's bedroom. He had spent the night at the Wallace's, and Dan's mother dropped Alex off after first stuffing him with her famous Sunday dinner of roast beef, mashed potatoes, and homemade gravy. As Alex walked past the kitchen, he noticed a half-empty bottle of Chardonnay on the kitchen counter. It was the bottle his father and mother said they would save for a time when they had something to celebrate. Continuing down the hallway, he approached his mother's bedroom and heard the sounds of crying mixed with the crooner's melancholy strains of "All Alone." Alex stopped in front of the door and knocked lightly.

"Are you all right, Mother?"

After a few seconds, the door opened, and Jean Spencer, in her worn pink housecoat, her cheeks wet with tears, stood clutching the doorknob. She smiled sadly at her son and said, "I'm glad you're home, Alex. Can you come in and talk with me for a minute?"

"Yeah, is something wrong?"

"No . . . yes . . . yes everything is wrong. I am wrong. Our lives are wrong." Alex had only seen his mother under the influence of alcohol once, and he remembered that in that state she had shown an emotional transparency that made him feel uncomfortable. He braced himself for a spontaneous outflow of sentiment. His mother seemed to sense his apprehension and backed away.

"You probably have better things to do than talk to your mixed up ol' mother." Something about the humility in her voice softened Alex. He glanced in the room and saw a shoebox with old photographs on the bed and several pictures of his father and grandparents spread out on the quilt.

"I can come in and talk if you want."

His mother pulled open the door and stumbled over to her rocking chair, tripping on one of the slippers she had kicked off earlier. Alex quickly grabbed her arm and helped her to the chair. He then sat down on the side of the bed, glancing at the pictures of his dad lying next to him.

"He looks a lot like me, doesn't he?" Alex said.

"Yep, very handsome," Jean replied. After a few seconds, she added, "Alex, I've not been the mother for you I should have been all these years. I've been so focused on my own needs I hardly gave a thought about what you might be going through, before or after your father died. You and your dad were always so close. I guess I felt like you really didn't need me. Or maybe I didn't want you to need me because then it would've required something of me."

As Alex listened, his mother reminisced about growing up as an only child with all of the privileges of being a Davidson. She explained how it encouraged her to be proud and self-absorbed, a trait she, regretfully, had carried into her marriage.

When Jean paused, Alex asked, "Why are you telling me all of this now, Mother?"

"Alex, I miss my parents. It's been over fifteen years since they wrote me off for marrying your father. They tried to reconnect with me after you were born, but I was too proud to let them back into my life. I don't even know if they're aware your father died. God knows they can be very superficial people. But they can offer you a future I can't. Not on my income."

"What are you saying, Mother?"

"I'm saying I'd like to try reconciling with your grandparents and see if they'd allow us to move into their guest quarters."

"But all my friends are here."

"Dan and Kitty will both be going to St. Bartholomew's next year, and you know I can't afford that tuition. How much do you think you'll get to see them when you're going to different schools?"

"I can still see them at church. And what about you and your counseling sessions with Father Francis? I thought you said you were getting a lot out of talking to him?" Alex was sorry he said it as soon as he heard the words come out of his mouth. He saw his mother wince.

"Father Francis isn't the priest I thought he was. And I won't be meeting with him anymore. In fact, I won't be attending St. Andrew's for a while. That doesn't mean you can't keep going. I just need a break for now. And I plan on contacting my parents, Alex. What happens after that, I don't know. But please know I love you and want more for your life than I'm able to provide you right now."

Alex had not heard his mother say those three words in a long time. They sounded strange to his ears: "I love you." For some reason, tonight he believed her when she said it. There was a sobriety to her words that belied the slight slur in her speech. He wondered what happened to bring on this sudden change—her desire to move close to her parents, her disdain for her pastor, her concern for him.

"You still want to be a priest when you grow up, Alex?"

"Uh . . . I don't know. Why?"

"Promise me you'll be a good priest. Promise me you'll treat people kindly and not take advantage of their weaknesses. Promise me you'll be a *good* priest, Alex."

"If I ever become a priest, and that's a big *if*, Mother, I promise I'll be a good one." He saw his mother smile, and noticed that her eyes were starting to droop. "You look tired. Maybe you should take a nap."

"I am tired, Alex. So tired. I think I'll just close my eyes right here and rock myself for a little while." Jean began slowly rubbing her belly as she gently rocked the chair.

Alex slid off the bed, grabbed the afghan lying by the pillow, and covered his mother, noticing her hand on her belly.

"Does your stomach hurt, Mother?"

"No . . . no I'm fine. Thanks for talking with me, Alex."

"You're welcome." Alex stood for a moment looking at his mother as she cuddled the coverlet close to her face. He suddenly felt grown up, as though he was someone his mother could lean on now. He felt a warmth on the inside he hadn't experienced in a long time, and he whispered, "I love you, Mother." Had he known then it would be his last chance to tell her, he would have said it loud enough for her to hear.

§

The sanctuary of St. Andrew's Church pulsated with the sounds of a silence so complete that a finely tuned ear could almost hear the voices of the faithful from generations past, breathlessly praising their God. It was three o'clock, and Alex and Kitty were kneeling alone in front of the altar, just to the side of the heat vent.

But the heat vent was quiet.

Alex and Kitty remained motionless while ten, fifteen, twenty minutes passed, and not a sound was heard. Alex leaned his head closer to the vent, only to be disappointed.

"I don't get it," he whispered to Kitty. "You sure Mrs. Mason was supposed to meet with him today between three and three-thirty?"

"I'm sure. It was right there in his calendar booklet."

"Well, maybe she canceled or something. Seems sort of pointless for us to keep waiting here. I know Mrs. Foster meets with him tomorrow. Can you come tomorrow?"

"I'll be here."

The results Tuesday afternoon were the same. Neither Alex nor Kitty heard anything coming from the vent. Alex was starting to feel awkward. He wondered if Kitty thought he had just been hearing things, or, worse, thought he made it all up.

"What do we do now?" Kitty asked.

"Can you come tomorrow?"

"Alex, I can't. My mother doesn't like that I'm getting out late two days in a row. I don't want to push it."

"Is she picking you up soon?"

"In about ten minutes."

"I'm going over to Beaman's. I've got to find out if old man Beaman heard anything the day Mrs. Foster was with Father Francis. I know I'm not nuts. I heard Father Francis making out with women."

Kitty looked at him sympathetically and shrugged her shoulders.

"You think I was just imagining things, Kitty?"

"I never said that. But without evidence . . ." She shrugged her shoulders again.

"I'll find the evidence; don't worry. Somehow, I'll find the evidence."

§

Alex pushed open the door to Beaman's store and found Mrs. Beaman standing behind the counter, smiling.

"How are you, Alex?"

"Fine, Mrs. Beaman." He reached his hand in the pretzel jar and pulled out two sticks.

"No friends with you today?"

"Nope, just me. Where's Mr. Beaman?"

"He's in the back room working on this week's order. Did you need him for something?"

"No, ma'am, just wondered. I saw him at church a couple weeks ago after school. Wondered if he went there every day."

Mrs. Beaman rang up the pretzels for Alex, considering his comment. "Mr. Beaman at church a few weeks ago, you say? On a weekday? Hmm . . . Oh, I remember now. That was the week we were all upset about the missiles in Cuba. Mr. Beaman was worried about his favorite nephew. He's in the marines, y'know. His platoon probably would've been the first to go if there was trouble. My husband went to church to light a candle and pray for him. Said it made him feel much better afterward, like God heard his prayer. And He did, didn't He?" She smiled.

"Yes, ma'am, sure looks like it." Alex took a bite out of a pretzel. "He didn't mention hearing anything unusual while he was at church praying, did he Mrs. Beaman?"

"If he did, he didn't say anything to me." Mrs. Beaman put her hand to the side of her mouth and whispered to Alex, "You know, most people probably don't know it, but Mr. Beaman's hearing is not what it used to be. I try to get him to wear his Beltone, but he can be a stubborn old man."

Alex smiled politely at the woman, but inside his heart sank as he felt his last hope for justifying himself to Kitty disappear.

"Well, thanks for the pretzels, Mrs. Beaman."

"What did you mean about hearing something unusual, Alex?" the shopkeeper pried.

"Oh, nothing. Probably just my imagination getting the best of me. See you later."

The woman gave Alex a side glance that implied she thought the boy was just a bit odd.

Alex hurried out of the store and felt the sting of freezing rain against his face. The drizzle began while he was inside, and in that short time, it coated everything. Alex felt as though he had been instantly transported to a fragile crystalline wonderland, where everything around him could shatter in an instant.

He realized it was probably best that he hadn't ridden his bike to school that morning. Riding would be treacherous now. Even walking was a challenge. The mile-long hike to his house would probably take him a good half-hour. He pulled his collar up and cap down, stuffed his hands into his coat pockets, and forged ahead, shuffling his feet along the glazed sidewalk.

Twenty-five minutes into his walk, Alex had finally reached his street when he heard the lonesome wail of the town fire siren blowing in the distance. It sounded every day at noon and at six in the evening. He checked his watch and saw it was almost four-thirty. *Must be a fire or an accident. I'd hate to be a fireman in weather like this.*

When he arrived home, he quickly removed his wet clothes and dried himself off. After putting on a clean sweatshirt and a pair of jeans, he went to the kitchen. His mother had a pot of chicken soup warming on the stove, and the rich aroma was both comforting and inviting to the boy. He was reaching for a soup bowl from the cupboard when the phone rang.

"Is Jean Spencer there?" a man's voice on the other end inquired.

"My mother's at work. Can I ask who's calling?"

"This is Jean's supervisor. You sure she left for work because she's not here yet, and she's supposed to start at four o'clock sharp." The man sounded agitated.

"Maybe she was held up by the weather, sir."

"Well if she's not coming in, tell her to give me a call. I need to keep this assembly line moving."

"I'll tell her, sir."

The supervisor hung up his phone abruptly, leaving Alex with a dead line next to his ear. He shook his head and laid down the receiver. *That's not like Mother to be late for work.*

§

On the other side of town, Lieutenant Harry Wallace watched as his men worked frantically with a Halligan bar to pry open the ice-coated driver's door of a white 1960 Corvair. The woman driver, colorless and slumped over the steering wheel shoved against her chest, lost control driving north on Canal Street and slammed into a telephone pole. The front of the rear-engine car crumpled like a tin toy upon impact. Witnesses said the woman was driving too fast for the icy conditions. The firemen had already smashed through the side window and were able to detect a faint pulse in the driver, who had blood oozing from her mouth and shards of glass sprinkled over her tangled hair.

Harry Wallace, Dan's father, had seen his share of gruesome accidents. He had been a volunteer with the town's fire department for more than a decade, and it never ceased to amaze him how much damage people could inflict upon themselves and others with one careless action. As he surveyed the accident scene, he thought *There is no way that woman will survive this.*

Moving to the front of the car to get a better look at the driver, Harry stopped cold when he saw her face.

"How soon before you get that door open boys?" he asked, trying to mask his emotion.

"Almost there, sir."

The sound of flexing metal and pounding hammers continued for another few minutes until a sudden loud pop indicated the door latch had released. The firemen forced the door open on its battered hinges, exposing the driver's full injuries. The collapse of the car's front end had snapped her legs at the knees, leaving them contorted with bone visibly protruding through the skin. Harry looked at her and grabbed his radio.

"This is Lieutenant Wallace, over."

"Go ahead, Lieutenant."

"Somebody contact St. Andrew's and have Father Francis get out to the accident scene on Canal Street. Tell him one of his parishioners, Jean Spencer, is going to need last rites. Now."

"10-4, Lieutenant."

§

Within less than a minute, the rectory phone at St. Andrew's began ringing. Miss Windom took the call from the fire dispatcher and twice asked him to confirm that the accident victim was Jean Spencer.

"Oh dear," she said, "She was just here at the church less than a half-hour ago. I'll let Father Francis know right away."

As she hung up the phone, Miss Windom remembered that Mrs. Spencer had left the priest's office in tears. She remembered telling her to drive safely, that the roads were getting pretty slippery. The woman had just nodded to Miss Windom and looked like she couldn't get out of the building fast enough.

Miss Windom knocked on the pastor's office door, and heard him say, "Come in."

"Father, the fire dispatcher just called. Jean Spencer has been in a terrible accident on Canal Street, and they're requesting you to come and administer last rites."

At the news, the blood drained from the priest's face. "Is she conscious?"

"I don't know. The dispatcher just said she barely has a pulse."

"Then . . . I . . . I should probably go."

Probably go? The priest's hesitation puzzled Miss Windom. She had always seen him react to emergencies with calm resolution—he knew what had to be done, and he did it. Now he seemed unsure of himself.

"Did the dispatcher say where on Canal Street, Miss Windom?"

"About two miles north of the church, Father."

"Thank you . . . thank you."

Miss Windom nodded and left the office, closing the door behind her.

§

The priest looked at his watch, then eased open a desk drawer and pulled out a bottle of anointing oil. He slowly pushed himself up from his chair and reached for his black London Fog and wool scarf hanging on the coat rack near his desk. He carefully slipped each arm into the rain coat and meticulously buttoned each button down the front, as if he was testing the fit and function of the garment for the first time. After wrapping the scarf around his neck, he slipped the bottle of oil in his coat pocket and ambled to the rectory garage.

Several minutes later the priest's black Chevy Impala pulled out onto Church Street and slowed to a stop at the intersection of Church and Canal. The priest pushed down on the turn signal lever, indicating he was turning north on Canal Street. Pulling out, he suddenly veered to the right and headed south, determined he could not face Jean Spencer again. Not while there were other people around. And not while there was even a remote chance she could still talk.

§

At 6:30 in the evening, Alex heard the sound of a car pulling into his driveway. He ran to the living room and knelt on the couch in front of the picture window. Pulling the curtains back slightly, he peered out just as the driver and passenger doors slowly opened in unison. A man and a woman stepped out, looking reluctantly toward the house. They walked around to the front of the car, and the woman grabbed the man's arm to steady herself as they plodded side by side across the icy sidewalk toward the front entrance. Alex reached the door just as the bell rang, and he opened it to face Dan Wallace's parents, their faces somber and Mrs. Wallace's eyes moist with tears.

"Alex, Mr. Wallace and I need to come in and talk with you for a few minutes."

"Sure Mrs. Wallace. Is everything okay with Dan?"

"Dan is just fine." She walked into the house and put her hand on Alex's shoulder. Alex sensed she was struggling to keep her composure. "It's your mother, Alex."

Alex gave Mrs. Wallace a puzzled look. Surely his mother

had made it to work by now. Did something happen to her once she got there? Or did the Wallaces know about his mother's liaisons with Father Francis?

"What about my mother Mrs. Wallace?"

"I'm afraid she's been in an accident."

"An accident? What kind of accident?"

"She lost control of her car on Canal Street. She slid on the ice . . . and hit a telephone pole."

Alex immediately tensed as panic began to rise within him. "Is she all right?"

Mrs. Wallace looked at her husband, who nodded his head for her to continue. "Your mother was hurt very badly—"

"But she'll be okay, right?"

"Alex . . . honey . . . your mother . . ." The woman's voice started to crack." Your mother is . . . dead."

Alex felt as though everything around him stopped, as though time stood still. He felt like he was trapped within a photograph. But his insides felt like he had just begun a steep decline on a high speed roller coaster. The same sense of finality that shook him when he read his father's death notice on the kitchen table a year earlier struck him once again. Only now the blow was complete. He suddenly realized he was alone in the world. No father, no mother, no siblings. And only one set of grandparents whom he had never heard from or known. He was an orphan. His mouth became dry. He tried to utter something, anything to vent his despair. But nothing would come. He began to feel like he was suffocating and realized his face was buried in Mrs. Wallace's wool jacket while she was trying to console him. He pushed himself away and gasped for air. Harry Wallace tried to soothe him, taking him by the shoulders and encouraging him to calm down and breathe slowly. Alex gradually responded. Within a few minutes, he was sitting in a kitchen chair, breathing normally again, his eyes fixed in an empty stare.

"Alex, Mr. Wallace and I would like you to come home with us tonight. Why don't you let me help you pack the things you'll need."

"Yes ma'am." His voice was barely audible.

Within minutes, Mrs. Wallace and Alex had packed his duffle bag with his essentials. Alex grabbed his coat, still wet from his walk home from Beaman's, and he remembered the fire siren. He wondered why his mother had been late for work. She should've been on her way about the time he had arrived at Beaman's store, before the sleet had made the driving hazardous. And why was she taking Canal Street when she always took the parallel route west of town? He was too tired to try to figure it all out now. He slid into the backseat of the Wallace's sedan, slumped down, and closed his eyes, hoping he would fall asleep and wake up to realize this was all just a bad dream.

Chapter 6

On Wednesday, Harry Wallace called and notified Jack Davidson of Jean Spencer's death and of the impending funeral. He puzzled over Jack's emotional detachment when hearing the news about his daughter. He was all business: "How did she die?" "Where and when is the funeral?" "Where is her son?" After answering Jack's questions about Jean, Harry told him that Alex was staying with him and Mrs. Wallace. Jack decided to discuss Alex's future when he and his wife, Doris, arrived from Boston on Friday.

§

"The boy will come live with us," Jack said when Harry met with the couple at their hotel on Friday. "It's what our daughter wanted."

"Good," Harry said. "I'm glad you and your daughter had a chance to talk about these things."

Doris Davidson huffed and rolled her eyes.

"Mr. Wallace," Jack said, "I've not spoken with my daughter in fifteen years. Never will again. Only reason I know what she wanted is because my wife and I received a letter from her this week, mailed on Monday, according to the postmark. Asked if she and Alex could move in with us. My daughter made a number of bad choices in her life. Seems one of those finally caught up with her."

Harry slid his hands into his pockets, trying to conceal his agitation over the Davidsons' cold disregard for their daughter. "Well it's not for me to meddle in anyone's family business, Mr. Davidson, but in my opinion your daughter handled the loss of her husband better than most women. And she did a fine job of bringing up your grandson—"

"And now my wife and I will raise the boy, Mr. Wallace. Hopefully he'll have more sense than his mother. Appreciate you keeping him while you did. My law office will settle my daughter's estate and cover all funeral expenses."

"All right then . . . When will you be coming to get Alex?"

"If you and Mrs. Wallace would be kind enough to keep him another night, we'll take him with us after the funeral service tomorrow. My wife's a bit tired from the drive today."

Harry nodded and wondered to himself what kind of life lay ahead for his son's friend.

§

The church bell atop St. Andrew's chimed once every ten seconds as pallbearers carried the casket containing the remains of Jean Spencer down the long aisle to the foot of the altar. More than one-hundred mourners from Stonebridge attended the Saturday morning funeral Mass. Some came to pay their respects. Others came as an act of contrition in hopes that their penance would keep the Grim Reaper at bay in their own lives for a bit longer.

Alex sat with the Wallaces in the front pew near the center aisle, gazing at the crucifix and thinking that Christ's sacrifice meant little to him now. He had always wanted to believe in the promise of an abundant life, but as far as he could tell, it didn't exist. Not for him anyway.

Before him, towering in the pulpit and wearing a sanctimonious expression, stood a scoundrel in priestly garb, eulogizing Jean Spencer. A priest who left a trail of disposable women, whose bodies he used for his own pleasure with no regard for the price they might pay.

Before him sat a casket that held the remains of one of those women, and God alone knew what eternal price she was paying for her indiscretions with the priest. Alex concluded that life was simply about the powerful manipulating the powerless. And the fact that Father Francis stood piously in his pulpit, seemingly unscathed by his actions, left Alex to surmise that God endorsed this life view.

Alex determined then and there that he would not live as one of the manipulated. He determined he would find his voice, and it would carry authority, and it would be louder than the voice that thundered from the pulpit, smoother than the voice that floated from the heat vent, and sharper than the voice that delivered cool retorts to innocent inquiries. And when he found his voice, he would use it to take control of his life.

Father Francis finished his eulogy and brought the Mass to a close. Pallbearers lifted the casket and carried it out to the hearse that would bring it to its final resting place in the church cemetery. There would be no graveside service, so some people approached Alex at his pew to express their condolences before leaving the church. The last to come was Kitty McAlister, her eyes red from crying. She gave Alex a hug and told him how sorry she was.

"It's all right, Kitty. I'll be fine."

"I heard you're moving away to live with your grandparents."

"Yeah, I'm leaving this afternoon."

"I'm gonna miss you, Alex. Can we write to each other?"

"Sure, I'd like that. It'll seem weird not having friends close by."

"You'll always have a friend with me. Don't forget that."
Kitty's eyes started to water, and she gave Alex another hug.
"I'd better go. Take care of yourself, Alex."

"I will, Kitty."

Once Kitty walked away, the Davidsons slipped out of their
pew and walked toward Alex. As Jack approached, he held out
his hand toward the boy.

"Hello, Alex. I'm Jack, your grandfather."

"Hello, sir." Alex tried to match the man's firm handshake.
Doris Davidson followed her husband with the confident stride
of a matriarch. She stopped within two feet of Alex, both hands
in front of her, clutching her purse. She looked him over from
head to toe, as though assessing whether he was worth her time
and effort.

"I see you have your mother's eyes, but the rest of you looks
just like that carpenter she ran off with."

"None of that now, Doris," Jack said. "Alex, this is Doris,
your grandmother."

"You look like my mother," Alex said.

"Your mother looked like me, young man."

"Yes ma'am."

"Let's get your things, Alex," Jack said. "We've got a long
drive ahead of us."

Chapter 7

Jack Davidson slowed the black Lincoln Continental to
make the turn onto the long sloping drive ascending to Woodland Hills Estate. Alex peered out the window, gaping at the imposing yellow and white mansion perched atop the hill. Its ivy
covered chimneys, railed balconies, and fluted ionic columns
provided a look of grandeur beyond anything he had seen. In the
morning light, the terraced gardens with their symmetrically

aligned ornamental evergreens looked as though they could be stairways leading to heaven. Beyond the gardens, lush woods provided a rustic backdrop to the manicured grounds and served as a haven for wildlife. On the edge of the woods, Alex saw rabbits scatter and a doe and her fawn look up from their grazing when the car climbed steadily past.

The Lincoln came to a stop under the portico leading to the front entryway. A tall, slender man wearing a gray suit, white shirt, black vest, and bow tie was waiting near the front door and stepped smartly toward the car once it stopped. He opened the passenger door and greeted Mrs. Davidson, extending his arm to assist her.

"Thank you, Howard," she said.

Alex opened his door and climbed out just as Jack was coming around the car. He saw Jack hand the car keys to Howard then turn to join Doris, who had already started walking toward the front entrance. Alex looked awkwardly at Howard and asked, "So . . . are you the doorman?"

"I am Mr. Davidson's *valet*, sir," Howard replied, tipping his head down toward Alex. "And you are Master Alex, I presume."

Alex was intrigued by the man's British accent. "Just plain Alex will do. What should I call you?"

"You may call me Howard."

"Well . . . uh, Howard, my stuff is in the trunk. Would you mind opening it for me, so I can get it out?"

"I will be happy to bring that to you, sir, after I have parked Mr. Davidson's automobile in the carriage house."

"I don't mind taking my stuff myself—"

"You coming, young man!" Jack shouted from the entryway.

Alex looked toward Jack and then glanced at Howard. "Coming, sir."

Once in the main entry hall, Jack pointed to a padded bench and told Alex to sit there until Howard came in to take him to his room.

"When you're all settled, I want to talk to you," Jack said. "Meet me in the billiard room in fifteen minutes."

Alex glanced around at all the doorways leading out from the hall and gave Jack a puzzled look.

"Howard will show you where to go."

"Thank you, sir."

Jack walked out of the room, his leather heel shoes making a distinctive clicking sound on the cold marble floor. The sound reminded Alex of Father Francis pacing across the floor of St. Andrew's vestry before Mass started. The boy had always associated that sound with authority, and when he heard it, he usually felt tense and intimidated. He was feeling that way now, listening to Jack's footsteps. He determined that one day he would own his own pair of leather heel shoes and project his own authority. And if that intimidated others, all the better.

Alex sat down on the bench and looked around. This was not home. This didn't even seem like the same world. This was the Davidson world, where everything was played out on a larger-than-life scale, a reality that had quickly become apparent to him on the drive over with his grandparents.

They had stopped in Albany for the night because Jack wanted to meet with the lieutenant governor of New York, Frank Bechtold, an old friend of his. The politician joined them for dinner at a posh Albany restaurant where the Davidsons and he talked about politics and law for almost two hours.

Alex listened attentively to the Davidsons, who had hardly spoken in the car. He wanted to find out all he could about his grandparents, now that he was destined to spend his adolescence with them. Not once did he hear them mention burying their only child that day. They simply introduced Alex as their grandson and left it at that. He observed that Doris was as sharp at politics as the men and more than held her own in the conversation.

He recognized the tangible presence of power at the table. He had sensed something similar around Father Francis at times. Only this was more palpable, more vibrant; it made his skin tingle. And he found himself attracted to it, like a bug to a warm light.

§

The front door opened, and Howard stepped in, pulling a luggage cart. Alex jumped up and walked over to grab his bags.

"If you can show me where my room is, Howard, I can take these up."

"Very good, sir. Your room is at the top of the stairway and to the right." Howard tipped his head toward the white paneled staircase with its dark oak rail and white spiraled balusters that seemed to climb to infinity. "If you will follow me, I will take you to it."

Alex grabbed his suitcase and duffle bag and trudged behind the valet. The top of the stairway opened into an expansive square hall with six doors equally spaced along the walls. Howard turned to the right and opened the door to the room adjacent to the stairway.

"This is your bedroom, sir."

"Howard, you really don't need to call me—" Alex's mouth dropped when he looked into his room. Facing him was a white fireplace with an ornate mantel and fluted mantel legs. A soft fire was crackling inside the firebox. Centered on the far wall between two windows facing out to the front grounds was a four-post bed with a cherry headboard and footboard. To the left of the bed was a Queen Anne reading chair and a cherry lamp table. To the right was a small desk with a bow-back Windsor chair. On the wall opposite the fireplace stood an armoire and a door leading into the private bathroom.

"Is the room to your liking, sir?"

"Are you sure this is my room, Howard?"

"I am certain it is, sir. This will be your room when you are not away at school."

"School . . . I had almost forgotten about that. Maybe that's what Jack wants to talk to me about. Howard, can you take me to the billiard room in a few minutes? I need to meet with Mr. Davidson."

"It would be my pleasure, Master Alex."

§

Alex stepped into the room just as Jack finished hitting the last ball into the corner pocket. "My dad told me you were good at pool," Alex said.

"Well your dad was wrong. I'm great at pool. Taught him a thing or two about the game when he worked here. Ever teach you how to play?"

"He took me to the YMCA a few times; they had a table there. Learned the basics, that's about it."

"Grab a cue stick. Let's see what you can do in a game of eight ball."

"Uh . . . I'm not sure if I can—"

"Boy, let's get something straight. When I tell you to do something, I'm not interested in whether you think you can or not. Pick up the stick, and show me what you can do."

With sweaty, shaky hands Alex grabbed a cue stick and chalked the tip, while Jack racked the balls.

"Go ahead and break," Jack said after setting the billiard table.

Alex slowly walked up to the table, took a deep breath, and held it for a moment. As he exhaled, he felt his tension start to subside. Positioning the cue ball about two balls width away from the side rail, he leaned over and eyed his shot. He placed his hand on the table to level his cue stick and slammed the cue ball, scattering the other balls and pocketing two—both striped.

"Just learned the basics, huh?" Jack said, raising his left eyebrow. Alex turned up the palm of his hand and shrugged.

Ten minutes into the game Alex was feeling more relaxed around his grandfather. Sure Jack was a crusty old sod who wasn't afraid to speak his mind, something to which Alex was unaccustomed, but Jack was a man. And Alex had missed having man-to-man interaction since his father died. At one point in the game when Jack was eyeing a shot, he started venting to Alex about Jean.

"Your mother should never have married your father, you know. We provided her every opportunity for success. What did she do? Threw it away. For what?" Jack finished his shot, landing a solid ball in the center pocket. "And out of the blue she writes us last week and asks to move back here."

"She told me she missed you and Doris."

"Missed us? In a pig's eye!" Jack drove the butt end of the cue stick against the floor, his blood rushing to his face. "Got herself pregnant and needed somebody to take care of her. How convenient."

Pregnant! Alex felt like Jack had slammed the cue stick into his gut. He grabbed the side rail of the table to steady himself, trying desperately not to let Jack see his surprise.

"Your shot," Jack said.

Alex struggled to focus on the shot. It felt like a floodgate opened in his mind, and a barrage of thoughts poured in: *Mother pregnant? Did anybody know? Did Father Francis know? I hate that man. Got to make him pay.* Smack! The cue ball slammed into a ball and spun up and off the table, bouncing onto the hardwood floor.

"Level your cue stick next time," Jack said.

"Yes, sir." Before Alex could finish processing Jack's comment about his mother, the man threw him another curve ball.

"Don't get too settled in your new room. Enrolling you in Drexler Academy. One of the best prep schools in the Boston area for a young man who's going to be a lawyer. Any luck, you'll be living on campus in a few weeks. Had to call in a favor from Lieutenant Governor Bechtold last night to get you in. He's a big supporter of the school. Went there when he was your age. Spending a lot of money to send you there, boy. I expect a good return on my investment. Screwing up is not an option, you understand?"

"My mother and I talked about me becoming a priest one day . . ."

"A priest? For crying out loud, boy, there's no money in that. Did your mother want you to stay poor, scraping and struggling like her? And a life without women? You aren't made of stone, are you? If your flesh hasn't started craving a female yet, it will soon enough. No, sir. It'll be the law for you, just like it was for me. Play your cards right, and you'll find yourself at Davidson and Associates Law Office someday. I'm sixty years old. Don't expect to work all my life you know."

Alex stared at his grandfather, not really sure how to respond. A week ago the boy didn't even exist in the mind of Jack Davidson. Now the man had mapped out his life and career for him, regardless of what Alex wanted. But what was it Alex really wanted? He remembered his thoughts during the funeral, thoughts of finding his voice, rising to a place of authority, and exacting revenge. He suddenly realized that Jack could unwittingly be setting him up to accomplish all three of these goals. A lawyer . . . Alex Michael Spencer, Esq. He liked the sound of that. He wondered what Kitty would think. Did it really matter anymore what Kitty thought? She was four-hundred miles away, and the worlds they lived in now were so very different. No, what really mattered is what he thought, and he felt his face brighten as he contemplated the possibilities.

"I think I'd like that, sir."

"Why wouldn't you?" Jack said, hitting the eight ball into the side pocket. "I think we've had enough pool for today. Dinner's promptly at two o'clock in the dining room. Doris will expect you there. Don't be late, or she'll have your hide."

"I wouldn't want that, sir. I noticed Doris seems pretty smart about politics. Where did she learn all that?"

"Where did she learn it? Spent twenty-five years as secretary to our state's most powerful representative in Washington—Congressman John Walters. Didn't my daughter tell you anything about us?"

"I knew you lived in Chestnut Hill . . ."

Jack rolled his eyes and said, "Dinner at two o'clock. Sharp." He then walked out. Alex noted that Jack's gait was similar to that of Father Francis, except Jack walked at twice the pace.

§

Alex stretched out on his new bed, the fluffy down comforter underneath him warming his back. He brought his arms up, and laid his head in his hands resting on the pillow. The room was quiet except for the sound of the crackling fire. He had one of his windows opened slightly, and he could hear the faint sound of a dog barking somewhere off in the distance. This was his first chance to be alone with his thoughts since his mother died, and he began to reflect on all that had happened.

The revelation from Jack about his mother's pregnancy was foremost on his mind. Alex now realized why his mother was acting the way she was last Sunday—the wine, the pictures on the bed, her crying, rubbing her belly. It all made sense now.

He wondered if she had told Father Francis she was pregnant with his child. *It had to be his kid, right? She wouldn't have been sleeping with more than one man, would she?* He couldn't allow his thoughts to go there. That would make Father Francis the victim and his mother the tormenter. No, he wasn't going to let the priest off that easy.

He thought about his mother's death. *Was it really an accident, or had she been so upset that she . . .* No he couldn't allow his thoughts to go there, either. He wanted to think she was stronger than that. It occurred to him that, other than his initial reaction of shock, he never showed any emotion about her death. He never once cried. Not even a tear. He wondered if Kitty was right. Maybe he had lost his ability to be compassionate and tender. *Shouldn't a person cry when his own mother dies?*

He thought about Kitty. She'd be home from church by now, probably eating lunch with her family. Living life as though nothing had changed. *Tomorrow she'll go to school. She'll talk to Dan; Dan will talk to her. Maybe they'll mention my name tomorrow, maybe even the next day. But before the week is over, it'll be like I never even existed.*

A tug on his insides halted his pity party. He remembered that Kitty had asked if they could write to each other. Maybe he was being too harsh. Maybe she would still think about him. Maybe they could still be friends, long distance friends. *She doesn't even know my address.*

Alex sat up, scooted his legs over the side of the bed, and hopped down to get to his desk. He pulled open the desk drawer and smiled. A pile of cream colored postage-paid envelopes were neatly stacked next to a supply of matching stationary emblazoned with a picture of the Davidson mansion, its address centered at the top. Two ballpoint pens were nestled in the pencil tray along the inside of the drawer. Alex sat down, pulled out a piece of stationary and a pen, and began writing.

November 25, 1962

Dear Kitty,

    I'm at my grandparents' now. If you want to write to me, my address is on the top of this note.
Alex

§

Alex had just finished dressing after taking a shower and was still combing his damp hair when he heard a sharp knock on the door. It was Howard.

"Excuse me, Master Alex. Mr. Davidson requested that I escort you to the dining room for the two o'clock meal. It is important we do not keep Mrs. Davidson waiting. She expects all of her dinner guests to be in attendance when she arrives in the room."

"I'm almost ready, Howard," Alex said. "Is Doris always grumpy, or is she just that way with me?"

"Mrs. Davidson is the matron of Woodland Hills. And on this estate she may act as she pleases to whomever she pleases. It will do you good to remember that, sir." Alex felt the heat of embarrassment when he realized he had allowed himself to become too casual with Howard.

"Thank you, Howard. I'll remember."

Alex and Howard walked down the stairs, passed the padded bench in the main hall, and turned left into the dining room. They were the first to arrive. Howard took Alex to his assigned seat and instructed him to remain standing next to his chair until Mrs. Davidson sat down. Alex nodded, and Howard left the room.

The dining room extended out on one side to a three-sided bay fitted with windows that overlooked the gentle terrain of the estate. Raised mahogany paneling covered the dining room walls, providing a rich accent around the Italian marble fireplace. The oblong mahogany table was covered with a crisp white linen cloth, and its two tripod pedestals sunk into a deep blue Oriental rug. Alex noticed that the table was set for three.

Jack strolled in just seconds before the pendulum clock on the wall struck two. He pulled out his chair at one end of the table and sat down. Alex was tempted to do the same and then remembered the instructions Howard had given him. He continued standing next to his chair like a sentinel. The sound of a woman's high heels echoed in the main hall, and seconds later, Doris entered the room. Without looking at Alex, she sauntered to the chair at the end of the table opposite from her husband. Seemingly from out of nowhere, a server appeared behind Doris, pulled out her chair, and assisted her. Seconds later, the server brought in three fresh garden salads, gently placed the salad plates in front of each person at the table, and left the room.

Alex folded his hands and bowed his head in preparation for the blessing over the food. He heard the sound of silverware clinking against chinaware and looked up to see Jack and Doris eating their salads and looking at him.

"Don't you pray before you eat?" Alex asked.

"We pray at church," Jack said. "We eat in the dining room. I suggest you do the same."

Alex looked at Doris, who was ignoring the exchange. After glancing back at Jack, he dropped his head and began eating his salad. For the next three minutes, the only sounds he heard were teeth chomping, silver clinking, and the clock ticking, ticking, ticking. He wondered if every mealtime in the Davidson house was this boring and rigid. It was definitely a contrast to what he witnessed at the dinner in Albany on the trip over. He wondered if asking a question about politics might spark some table conversation.

"Isn't President Kennedy from around here?"

Jack and Doris set their silverware down and turned toward Alex, each giving a look of disdain. This time Doris responded, periodically tapping her stubby right index finger on the table for emphasis.

"I don't ever want to hear that family's name brought up in this house," she said. "They may live in Massachusetts and they may be Catholic, but they are Democrats. The Davidson's are Republicans first, and have been for as far back as people can remember. As long as you are under our care, you will be too. Is that clear?"

"Yes, ma'am." Alex had finally elicited a reaction from Doris. He didn't care that it was an admonishment; it was better than being snubbed, especially if he was going to learn from her. He sensed that Doris, like Jack, knew a lot about power and how to wield it. And he found himself increasingly eager to learn all his grandparents could teach him about the subject.

The server brought in the main course of the meal—roast beef, gravy, mashed potatoes, and corn. The smell reminded Alex of Mrs. Wallace's kitchen and the Sunday meals he occasionally shared with the Wallace family. There was never any want for banter at their dinner table. But he couldn't recall them ever discussing topics related to the more serious aspects of life, and he didn't remember caring about it at the time. He felt differently now.

"Would you teach me how to be a Republican, Doris?" he asked. Doris had been slicing a piece of her roast beef, and her hands, still holding the knife and fork, froze. She slowly raised her head and looked at Alex.

"Teach-you-how-to-be-a-Republican?" she said, emphasizing each word.

"Yes, ma'am."

Doris glanced at Jack, who was smirking, and then looked back at Alex.

"One does not learn how to be a Republican like one learns how to swim or ride a bike. One is a Republican because of the principles he believes in." She continued looking at Alex for a moment longer, to be sure she had made her point, and then resumed cutting her meat. Alex scratched his head and squinched his face. He determined it was probably best not to question her further.

Nothing more was said throughout the remainder of the meal. Jack seemed to be quite content savoring each bite of his apple pie and ice cream dessert, but Doris seemed as though she was laboring over a decision. When she finished eating, she rang a small brass hand bell. The server stood behind her chair and gently pulled it away as the woman stood up. Doris turned toward Alex.

"I believe it would do you some good to attend the next Republican Party meeting on Tuesday. If you can keep from asking a lot of silly questions, Jack and I will take you with us."

"I promise I'll keep my mouth shut, ma'am. Thank you." Alex thought he saw a trace of a smile on Jack's face, but Doris wore her usual stoic countenance. She turned and exited the room, her heels clicking a steady, determined rhythm. Jack slid his chair back, took his linen napkin from his lap, and set it on his plate. He pushed himself up from the table and looked at Alex. "I do believe she likes you, boy. For now anyway."

§

On Tuesday, the committee chairman called the meeting to order at precisely 7:30 p.m. and led the attendees in the Pledge of Allegiance. Alex, standing in the third row, instinctively placed his hand over his heart. To his immediate left, Jack and Doris were standing erect, like soldiers at attention, focusing straight ahead at the flag. They placed their right hands over their hearts and annunciated each word of the pledge as though they were committing their lives to a sacred cause.

Following the pledge, the chairman reviewed old business and discussed the budget and state committee reports. While the man droned on, Alex scanned the audience of mostly older men wearing charcoal gray or navy suits, white shirts, dark ties, and leather shoes. Doris was the only woman present. If that bothered her, she didn't show it.

Alex spotted a man in the front row who, although dressed in similar conservative attire, stood out from the rest of the crowd. His age had something to do with the distinction; he looked to be in his late 30s or early 40s. But it was the appearance of the man that captured Alex's fascination. He had a dark brown mane, slightly thinning at the crown and neatly trimmed around the ears and neck. He sat erect and square-shouldered, his medium-sized frame rocking slightly from left to right as he shifted his weight from one buttock to the other. His left hand seemed to be tapping out a song lightly on his knees.

"And now I have the pleasure of introducing our guest speaker for the evening," the chairman said. "A man who is no stranger to those of us who hold a place in our heart for Drexler Academy. As chairman of the history department at Drexler, our speaker is driven by a vision to not only educate his students about our unique political heritage, but also to energize them to become involved citizens who will make a difference in Massachusetts, the nation, and the world. Please give a warm welcome to fellow Republican James Pearson."

Alex watched the man on the front row stand and bound up

to the podium to the warm applause of the room. From the second James Pearson opened his mouth, Alex was captivated. For the next thirty minutes, the teacher expounded on the history of the Republican Party in a way that made Alex feel like he was living it as it happened. The speaker detailed the path he believed the party needed to follow for the remainder of the 60s, and that path included younger leadership with a fresh vision. He challenged his audience to look for ways to mentor those who would soon take the reins of leadership and to leave a legacy that would inspire, not discourage. He warned them that ignoring that challenge would be handing the decade to the Democrats.

The room was silent for several seconds after Mr. Pearson finished his speech. It was as if a whirlwind had blown through the room, and the audience was trying to catch its breath. A hesitant applause began in one corner and soon gained momentum until all fifty or so in attendance were on their feet, giving a resounding approbation.

Jack leaned over to Doris and said, "Amazing. This guy just dressed these old geezers down, and they're thanking him for it."

"They should be," Doris said. "He's right."

Alex lifted his voice over the din and said to Doris, "I like him. Will he be one of my teachers?"

"As long as I have anything to say about it he will. And I expect you to pay close attention to what he tells you. That man has more sense than most of the so-called leaders in this room."

Once the applause subsided and the men started leaving, the Davidsons and Alex made their way toward the front of the meeting room to greet the speaker.

"Mr. Pearson, I like your ideas," Doris said. "You should consider running for office. The party needs young men like you. If for nothing else, to stop the Kennedys from taking over this country."

"Thank you, Mrs. Davidson. Your candor is always so refreshing. But I think I'll be more useful in my role at Drexler, grooming future leaders."

"I thought you might say that. Well, if that's the case, you can start grooming this young man for Jack and me." Doris turned toward Alex. "This is Alex Spencer. Jack's pulling some strings to get him into Drexler in a few weeks. I'd like very much for you to be his history teacher."

Mr. Pearson turned toward Alex and stuck out his hand.

"Pleasure to meet you, Alex. What grade are you in?"

"Finishing eighth grade, sir." Alex returned the teacher's handshake with the firmest grip he could muster.

Mr. Pearson turned to Jack and Doris and asked, "Is Alex a friend of the family?"

"He's our grandson," Jack responded.

"Grandson? That's splendid. I didn't even know you had children."

"You didn't need to know," Doris said. "But I need to know I have your assurance Alex will receive his history instruction from you."

"I normally teach junior and senior history classes, Mrs. Davidson. We do, however, have one of our eighth-grade teachers going out on medical leave starting next month. I planned on having one of my subordinates take on the extra workload. I need to focus my energies on fundraising for improvements I want to make in the department."

"And just how much will those improvements cost, Mr. Pearson?" Jack asked.

"About $10,000."

"And if you were relieved of your fund-raising activities, you could teach the eight-grade history class?" Doris asked.

"Most certainly."

Doris looked at Jack.

"Consider yourself relieved," Jack said. "I'll have a check for you the week Alex starts school."

Mr. Pearson smiled, turned toward Alex, and placed his hand on his shoulder. "Looking forward to having you in my class, young man."

§

Drexler Academy looked like a winter wonderland the afternoon Alex arrived. A light snow had blanketed the campus that morning and dusted the tops of the Georgian brick buildings. The red bows and holly berries on the snow-covered Christmas wreathes hanging on the doors stood out in stark contrast to the white backdrop, reminding Alex of the blood-covered entryways warding off death in the Passover story. He hoped the similarity was only coincidental.

Jack took Alex to the admissions building to make sure all of Alex's paperwork was in order and then left him with the Dean of Students, who assured Jack that Alex would be well cared for. The dean took Alex to his dorm and introduced him to his roommate, Reed Wentworth, who was sitting on the edge of his bed, tossing a Duncan yo-yo.

"Nice to meet you, Reed," Alex said, reaching out his hand.

Reed gave Alex a disinterested look. He slowly lifted his arm and flapped a limp hand at his new roommate, with the yo-yo still attached to his finger. "Likewise."

"So how long have you been at Drexler?"

"Long enough." Reed resumed tossing his yo-yo.

"Look sorta big to be in eighth grade. How old are you?"

Reed looked up at Alex. "And you look short and scrawny. You writing a book or something?"

Alex lifted the palms of his hands toward Reed. "Hey, just curious."

"Fifteen, Mr. Curious. Started late because of my birthday and got held back in fifth grade."

"That's tough luck. Your family from around here?"

Reed gave Alex a side glance and sneered. "My family *owns* this city. What cave have you been living in?"

"Just moved here."

"Looks like you've got a lot to learn."

Alex noticed several pencil drawings of animal-like creatures in strange environments taped to the wall above Reed's bed. Though the subjects were a bit unconventional for his taste, Alex appreciated the detail of the work.

"You draw those?" he asked.

"What's it to you?"

"I just thought they were nice, that's all. So . . . you always this grouchy or only when you meet your new roommate?"

Reed looked up with a smirk on his face. "Always."

"Good, at least I know it isn't just me, then." Alex turned away and threw his duffle bag onto his bed on the other side of the room. He bent down to grab his suitcase, and out of the corner of his eye he saw Reed reaching for something.

"Hey kid," Reed said.

Alex turned and looked up to see him lobbing a bright red spool in his direction.

"Have a yo-yo."

Alex caught the toy in mid-air and said, "Thanks, don't mind if I do."

"And yeah, I drew the pictures."

§

Mr. Pearson stood before his history class of twenty boys, who were all dressed in white shirts and black ties and were mesmerized by the man's oration.

"Who can tell me what populist movement in the mid-1700s helped alter the course of American history?"

The class paused, stumped.

"Think boys. What did we say populism is? Mr. Unger?"

"Uh, something that's popular?"

The class snickered.

"It's more than that, Mr. Unger. How about you, Mr. Spencer?"

Alex remembered Sister Angelica talking about this very subject at the beginning of the school year, and he didn't hesitate.

"The belief that the common people are the backbone of society, and should be protected from the rich and privileged people."

"Very good, Mr. Spencer. And who are the rich and privileged people from whom they should be protected?"

"Me." A voice spoke up from the back of the room.

"And why do you say that, Mr. Wentworth?"

"Cause I'm rich and privileged."

More snickers.

"Then you should know that our history shows your position is subject to change. Wealth comes, wealth goes. The privileged today can become the disadvantaged tomorrow. The question you should be asking yourself, Mr. Wentworth, is how you will use your wealth and privilege to advance society and help raise others to a higher level. Remember what Thomas Paine said: 'We have it in our power to begin the world all over again.'"

Mr. Pearson stepped back and scanned the class. "And now back to my original question: What populist movement in the mid-1700s helped alter the course of American history? Who can tell me the answer?"

Alex raised his hand.

"Mr. Spencer?"

"I believe it was the Great Awakening."

"That's correct. The Great Awakening. A series of religious revivals from the 1740s to the 1760s that helped unify scattered colonists and caused them to reconsider their assumptions about church and state. It encouraged men and women to take an active role in their spiritual well-being, and caused them to question their attitudes toward traditional authority. In short, it provoked a revolutionary attitude in the colonists, preparing them for the revolution of 1776."

Mr. Pearson lectured like this for the remainder of the class, and when the bell rang, he asked Alex to see him before leaving.

"Mr. Spencer, what school did you attend before coming to

Drexler?"

"St. Andrew's, sir. It's a parochial school in Stonebridge, New York."

"Well it seems they did a good job teaching you history."

"Thank you, sir."

"Alex, I'm looking for a few students to help me with running the political campaign for Steven Roberts. He's a candidate for city council. I think this might be something your grandmother would like you to experience— Mr. Roberts is a Republican, after all. Are you interested?"

"Yes, sir. When do I start?"

"We have our first meeting this Saturday morning in Walker Hall at ten o'clock. I'll see you there. Oh, by the way, have you met Brother Paul yet?"

"I saw him in chapel this morning, and I have his religion class tomorrow."

"Get to know him, Alex. He's a good man. I understand you've gone through a lot over the last year with losing your father and mother. He's a good listener. Don't be afraid to talk to him."

§

"Hey kid, you trying to make us all look dumb in Pearson's class this morning?" Reed Wentworth approached Alex, who was on his way to Walker Hall.

"Reed, stop calling me kid. My name is Alex. And no, I was just answering his question. Is that a problem?"

"Touchy, touchy. What's eating you?"

"It's not *what*, it's *who*? I haven't heard one nice thing come out of your mouth since I met you, man. What gives? Do you think just because your family has money, you can treat other people like they're beneath you?"

"Well, of course."

"You're hopeless, Wentworth."

"It didn't take you long to figure that out. My old man has

told me that ever since I was held back in fifth grade." Alex heard pained undertones in Reed's sarcastic response that grabbed his attention and caused him to back off his attack.

"Listen, just stop calling me kid, all right. I don't like it."

"I'll think about it. So you headed to Walker Hall?"

"Yeah, why?"

"Just thought you'd want to know you have mail in your box. Looked like a girl's handwriting on the envelope."

"For crying out loud, Reed. Did you go through my mailbox?"

"What are roommates for, man?"

Alex shook his head and walked away. His heart raced at the prospects that the letter was from Kitty. Two weeks had passed since he sent her the note with the Davidson's address, and Howard assured him he would forward any mail to him at Drexler. When Alex reached his mailbox, he saw that Howard was true to his word. Inside was a white envelope with Kitty's handwriting, and *Miss Kitty McAlister* written in the return address section.

He walked over to the dining room and sat down at a table where he could be alone. He gazed at Kitty's handwriting, caressing her words with his fingertips before sniffing the envelope for any traces of her familiar floral scent. He carefully peeled the flap of the envelope, removed the note, and gently unfolded it.

December 4, 1962

Dear Alex,

I was so happy to get the letter you sent with your new address. I wish you would have told me more about where you live. The house on your stationary looks beautiful, like a mansion. I didn't know your grandparents were so rich. Do you like living with them? Where do you go to school? It seems weird not having you at St. Andrew's any more. I miss talking to you. I guess you'll have plenty of girls to talk to at your new school.

Dan Wallace says hi. He said to tell you not to expect a letter from him. You know how much he hates writing. So I guess if he has something to say, he'll tell me, and I'll let you know.

Father Francis is leaving St. Andrew's after Christmas. He's going to work for the bishop. I heard my parents say he'll be building new schools and stuff like that. After all you told me, I'm glad he's leaving.

I helped Miss Windom at church the other day, and she told me Father Francis talked to her about me going into his office that day I helped with Christmas decorations. She didn't tell me what he said or anything. She just said she probably should've gotten the list herself.

She said something else, too. She said your mother was at church, meeting with Father Francis, right before she had her accident. And your mother seemed upset before she left, like she'd been crying or something. Weird, huh?

Well, I need to get going, Alex. Please write and tell me all about your new life and how you're doing.
Sincerely,
Kitty

Alex stared at the letter, thinking about Kitty's words. He wondered what influenced Father Francis to leave St. Andrew's and take a job with the bishop. Was it ambition, or had someone in the bishop's office heard about the priest's affairs with women? If it was ambition, what was Father Francis setting his sights on? If it was his affairs, why wouldn't the bishop just fire him and be done with it? No, the bishop probably doesn't know about the women. So it's pure ambition driving this change.

He thought of Miss Windom's comments about his mother. He understood now why she was driving that route to work that day. But why did she stop to see Father Francis in the first place? And why was she so upset when she left his office? Did she tell him she was pregnant with his child? What did he say that upset her?

Alex turned the letter over and back again. *Too many questions that will never be answered.* He felt his frustration and resentment toward the priest bubble to the surface, and he crumbled the letter into a ball and threw it to the floor just as Brother Paul was walking by.

"You seem a little upset, young man."

"Oh . . . sorry, sir . . . I mean Brother Paul . . . I mean . . . I just read a letter that bothered me, that's all."

"By the look of it, I would say you were a little more than bothered by what you read. You know, we prefer that our students learn to handle their emotions without throwing things. You're new to Drexler Academy aren't you?"

"Yes, sir. Today is my first day."

"I remember seeing you in chapel this morning. What's your name, son?"

"Alex Spencer."

"Alex. That's a strong name. I like it. Alex, the next time something upsets you so much you want to throw things, I want you to come and talk with me about it. Deal?"

"Yes, sir."

"Good. I'm looking forward to getting to know you, Alex."

"Thank you, sir."

The man smiled and nodded and then walked away, humming softly to himself. Alex noticed that Brother Paul walked with a humble, yet confident, stride. And he wore soft-sole shoes that didn't make a sound.

§

Steven Roberts strolled into Walker Hall with no fanfare. The politician was of average height, dressed in black slacks, a white shirt, and dark tie. He wore a black rain coat and carried a dark gray fedora. He shook hands with Mr. Pearson, and the two exchanged small talk for a few minutes. Then Mr. Pearson cleared his throat and addressed the volunteers.

"Okay folks, let me have your attention. I'd like you all to meet the man we're going to help become Boston's newest city council member, Mr. Steven Roberts."

The workers applauded the smiling candidate, who waved his hat in response. Roberts gave his heartfelt thanks to all who had given up their Saturday morning to help him. He said he was sending them out in twos, so they could get as much coverage as possible in the shortest amount of time. Mr. Pearson suggested that Roberts have Alex accompany him. The candidate agreed. After everyone grabbed their campaign placards and pamphlets, the group dispersed.

§

"This is why I'm running for office, Alex." Steven Roberts gestured with his hand toward the dilapidated houses lining the street they were canvassing. "Neighborhoods like this are a blemish on our city. Our communities should reflect Boston's rich history and heritage, not these . . . these shacks with rotted wood and weed-filled yards."

"But these people are poor . . ." Alex said.

"This is beyond just being poor. These people lack vision for their lives. They've never had anyone tell them they could make something of themselves. I want to be a politician who leads them toward better opportunities through education and hard work."

They continued walking from house to house, knocking on doors, but Alex noticed a distinct change in the atmosphere that made him uneasy. On the streets they visited earlier, people at least opened their doors and listened to some of the candidate's spiel. Now when the candidate knocked, people reluctantly pulled back a corner of their drapes, peeked through their windows, and shook their heads.

The streets were deserted. There was an eerie silence in the air. Alex sensed they were being followed. He turned around, only to see a rat, the size of a housecat, scurry into the bushes. He and Roberts continued walking. Alex couldn't shake his uneasiness. He turned around again. This time there were two young men in dark clothes, trailing them. They looked to be in their late teens or early twenties. One stood about average height, the other about a half-foot taller. Both had broad shoulders and wore leather jackets.

"Mr. Roberts, don't turn around. I think we're being followed."

The candidate slowed his pace and began to turn, then checked himself.

"How many are there?"

"Two men."

"How far away?"

"About fifty feet."

"Keep walking like nothing's happening. I need to think."

Alex could hear the sounds of the men's boots tramping on the sidewalk. He felt a rush of fear when he realized they were getting closer. Though the air was cold, he felt perspiration beading on his forehead. He imagined the two men quickening their pace until they got right behind him and Mr. Roberts and plunged knives into their backs. He shivered at the thought.

Mr. Roberts resumed talking about the campaign as if everything was fine, and he casually leaned into Alex and said, "After we pass the white house coming up on our left—not before, but after—turn around and tell me what you see."

Once past the house, Alex looked over his shoulder. The two men following were less than twenty feet away. Then they stopped cold in front of the white house. They had knives in their hands. Alex heard a metallic click and saw the blades retract.

"They stopped following us." Alex said, wiping his brow.

"I thought they might. Keep walking."

"I don't get it."

Once they got a safe distance away, Roberts explained.

"Alex, Boston is divided into political wards, but inside this ward are invisible borders that gangs have set up to define their turf. Not long ago I rode on patrol with a friend of mine who's a policeman. This area is his beat. He pointed out where the different invisible boundaries are located and why. I knew if we could get off their turf, these guys would stop following us. I just had to remember where the border was."

"So if we're off their turf, Mr. Roberts, whose turf are we on now?"

"We're safe here. Of course, I parked my car back there. I should've known better. Let's try to find a pay phone and see if we can get somebody to give us a lift."

"You know, Mr. Roberts, I never thought politics could be so scary and so exciting all at the same time."

"Yeah, and just think, I haven't even been elected yet."

Chapter 8

"Well, have you learned anything at Drexler Academy?" Jack Davidson asked his grandson.

"Yes, sir. I think so."

"You think so? Don't you know if you have?"

Jack had picked up Alex at the school late Friday afternoon and was driving him home for the holidays. A heavy wet snow was falling, making the roads sloppy and visibility limited, yet Jack drove like even nature had to submit to his authority.

"Who's your roommate?"

"His name is Reed Wentworth."

"Wentworth. Now there's a family for you. Old money. Made a small fortune during the Civil War selling overpriced, shoddy goods to the Northern Army. Then turned their profits into real wealth as slumlords. Rented run-down tenements to the immigrants who flooded Boston after the war. The mighty Wentworths . . . Now one of the most prominent families and developers in the Boston area. In less than 100 years, they went from sleaze to big cheese. And do you think anybody cares how they got there? No sir."

"How do you know all that?"

"I'm an attorney, boy. It's my business to know all about the power brokers in this city."

The snow was falling harder now, and Alex was beginning to grow concerned about the speed Jack was driving. But he didn't dare say anything. Jack, however, was in a talkative mood.

"We don't make a big deal out of Christmas around our place. Just another day to Doris and me. I suppose your mother made a big deal out of it when you were little . . ."

"It was the one time of year everyone seemed happy at home," Alex said. "My dad used to take my mother and me to this place that had tons of Christmas trees. We'd pick the one we wanted, and my dad would cut it down and drag it to our car. Then when we got home, my mother would put on Christmas music and make hot cocoa. We'd all decorate the tree and drink hot cocoa. It was fun."

"I remember getting your mother a bicycle one Christmas. I think she was . . . ten or something. What a deal I got on that bike. She wanted this silly little pink thing she'd seen in the store, but they were asking a small fortune for it. And it was junk. I found this nice blue Schwinn marked down on clearance. Darn good bike. And what did my daughter do when she saw it? She cried because it was a boy's bike. I mean, a bike's a bike. And this was a Schwinn for crying out loud—"

"Jack!"

A deer had jumped into the road ahead and was paralyzed by Jack's headlights. Jack pumped the brakes frantically, but he was driving too fast to react in time. He swerved to the right and slammed into the right front quarter of the deer, flinging the animal to the other side of the road. The impact threw Jack forward, his head smashing the windshield. Alex was wearing a lap belt, which left him sore but otherwise unscathed. The car slid down into the ditch and came to a stop, but the wheels kept spinning in the snow. Alex unsnapped his belt, reached over, and turned off the ignition. Except for the sporadic popping sounds from under the hood as the engine cooled and contracted, all was deathly silent.

Jack wasn't moving. Fear began to grip Alex. He thought about his mother's accident. Was this to be his lot in life?

"Jack! Jack! Wake up!"

No response.

Alex saw an amber light flashing around him and heard what sounded like tiny stones pelting the car, then the dull grinding sound of metal studs gripping asphalt. It was the city salt truck. The driver had seen the remains of the deer on the road and then spotted the Lincoln in the ditch.

"Are you folks all right?" the driver yelled through the closed driver's window.

"My grandfather's hurt. I think he needs an ambulance."

"I'll have one here in no time. Sit tight."

Jack began to groan and started to stir.

"Sit . . . tight?" he muttered. "Where . . . the blazes . . . does he think . . . we're gonna go?"

Alex sighed and smiled, realizing it would take more than a deer staring into the headlights to take this old man out.

§

A small fire was crackling in the bedroom fireplace, and the warmth was comforting to Alex, who was propped up on his side in bed, feeling some relief from the bruises he received in the accident. Jack was not as fortunate. The emergency room doctor insisted on keeping him overnight for observation. The blow to his head left him with a tremendous headache and a disposition more crotchety than normal. The doctor, who knew Jack, told Doris he felt confident Jack's headache would subside, but he could make no such promise about her husband's temperament. It was the first time Alex saw Doris crack a smile.

Alex felt good to be back in his room now. He gazed at the picture of the Davidson house on the blank sheet of stationary in his hand while nibbling on the end of a pen, thinking about what to write to Kitty. When he finally put pen to paper, he second guessed every jot and tittle.

> *December 20, 1962*
> ~~*Dear*~~ *Hi Kitty,*
> ~~*Thank you for*~~ *I got your letter the other day.* ~~*It was nice hearing from you*~~

"This is ridiculous. It's just Kitty." He crumbled the stationary into a ball and was ready to toss it onto the floor when he heard the voice of Brother Paul in his head: *"We prefer that our students learn to handle their emotions without throwing things."* Alex un-crumbled the paper and set it aside. He took another clean sheet off the pile next to him and started again. "All right just write like you were talking to her," he instructed himself.

> *December 20, 1962*
>
> *Hi Kitty,*
>
> *I got your letter the other day. Thanks. I'm glad you didn't forget about me. How is school? Tell Wally he's a flake for not writing. I go to an all-boys school, so you're the only girl I talk to these days. Come to think of it, you were the only girl I ever really wanted to talk to. My teachers are good, especially Mr. Pearson (he teaches history) and Brother Paul (he teaches religion).*
>
> *My grandfather and I were in an accident tonight. He hit a deer with his car. We're okay, but the car is pretty banged up. The deer died.*
>
> *My grandparents are important people. They seem to know lots of other important people too. My grandfather wants me to be a lawyer, so I guess that's what I'll be. Lawyers have lots of power, right?*

You'd like my grandparents' house. It's huge. My bedroom has a fireplace. My bedroom at school is small. I share it with an idiot named Reed Wentworth. He's a spoiled rich kid and drives me nuts. Oh yeah, I probably didn't tell you that I live at school during the school year, except for certain holidays.

I was surprised about Father Francis. Are people glad or sad he's leaving? Every time I think about what he did to my mother, I get mad. Real mad. He's worse than I thought he was, Kitty. I know you probably think I just made it all up, but I didn't. I swear. I'm not exactly sure why my mother went to see him before her accident, but I plan on finding out someday. And then he'll have to answer to me. You'll see.

Well I hope you have a nice Christmas, Kitty. Write and tell me what you got.
Sincerely,
Alex

While Alex was re-reading the letter for the third time, he heard a firm knock on his door. He tried to sit upright, but his body instantly reminded him of the accident, and he relaxed back onto his side.

"Come in," he said, groaning faintly.

The door opened slowly, revealing Doris standing rigid in the hallway, her usual impassive look revealing a hint of concern. The smell of her perfume drifted into the room, a fragrance Alex associated with old women.

"I came to see how you were doing before I retired for the evening," she said.

"A little sore, but I'll be fine, thanks."

"Jack can be a wild driver at times. Even at his age he only knows one speed. Slow is not in his vocabulary. But I suppose that's what attracted me to him all those years ago. I don't think I'd like it any other way."

"How did you and Jack meet, Doris?" After posing his question, Alex noticed Doris relax her posture slightly, and the tension in her face seemed to soften.

"Oh, that was another lifetime . . . Yet, sometimes, it seems like just yesterday. We met in college. Jack attended Harvard, and I attended Radcliffe. We were both juniors. Jack was the star quarterback for the football team, one of the Crimson eleven. I used to go to the home games with some of the other girls from Radcliffe. After a game one afternoon, I saw him walking across Harvard Yard. He was quite full of himself, so I didn't want to act interested, even though I was. He came right up to me and asked me how I liked the game. I told him I thought the quarterback missed a lot of good opportunities. Oh, did his face drop when I said that. But he recovered quickly and asked me if I'd like to get a bite to eat, so I could tell him what else he needed to improve upon. One thing led to another, and two years later we were married."

"So, when did you have my mother?"

Tension seemed to return to Doris's face after Alex posed the question. "That's a story for another time," she said. "I think we both need some rest."

She pulled the door closed, and Alex could hear her footsteps as she walked across the hall to her bedroom. He heard her bedroom door close, and the house was quiet. He rolled onto his back and stared at the ceiling. The pattern of swirls in the plaster began to take on the appearance of faces from the past. One resembled his father. Alex wasn't sure if he was smiling or frowning.

§

"I want you to pack your suitcase this morning," Doris said to Alex, who was sitting adjacent to her in the dining room, eating his breakfast. Alex tensed in reaction to her sudden edict and tried to hide his rapid, shallow breathing. He realized his mouth was agape when he felt cold milk dribbling down his chin.

"Where am I going?" he asked.

"You and I are taking the train to Washington this afternoon. I see no reason for you to sit around doing nothing during the holidays. I'm going to show you where I used to work, where the seat of real power is. Now wipe that milk off your mouth."

"Yes ma'am." Alex released a quiet sigh, then grabbed his napkin and dabbed his chin. "What about Jack?"

"Howard will bring Jack home from the hospital tomorrow. I expect he'll be ornery as ever. I prefer to give him his space when he's like that. We'll be back the following evening."

Alex nodded and then smiled when he thought about where they were going. "I've never been to Washington before."

"Then this will be the first of many visits for you. It was my second home for twenty-five years. Even now I get homesick if I'm away too long. Washington is a city where history is made, and I loved being in the thick of it. You will too."

"Jack says I need to become a lawyer . . ."

"And Jack's right. Law is your foundation. But politics is where the action is. Law will be your springboard for getting elected. Oh, I know voters say they want to elect real people into office, people who aren't part of the system, but that's a bunch of hogwash. They want people in office who know the system and can manipulate it to their constituents' advantage."

"I guess it'll be awhile before I need to think about all of that—"

"Well you're wrong," Doris admonished. "You need to start thinking about it now if you expect to make something of your life. Make no mistake; this is not a pleasure trip I'm taking you on."

§

Doris and Alex stepped out of their taxi on Summer Street and faced the bowed granite façade of Boston's South Station. The clock embedded in the pediment above the doorway showed one-thirty.

"Exactly one hour before we leave," Doris said, looking up.

"Plenty of time."

A porter grabbed their bags, and Doris and Alex followed him through the entryway into the Great Room, which was packed with travelers coming and going for the holidays. Doris pointed to the ticket counter for the Atlantic Coast Line where the queue was at least twenty people long.

"That's where we're headed," she said to the porter.

"Looks like it's going to be a long wait," Alex said.

"You don't wait in line when you're a Davidson." Doris said. She led the porter past the ticket line for coach and directly to the front counter. Alex followed, feeling the nasty looks from the customers they were passing in the line on their left. Once he got closer to the counter, he saw a smiling ticket agent standing under a sign marked PULLMAN PASSENGERS ONLY. She was motioning them forward. When Doris was within six feet of the counter, Alex noticed a shadowy movement to his right. He saw the shape dart in front of Doris, make a quick snap, and plunge through the coach queue where it appeared to be swallowed up. Before Alex could grasp what he had seen, Doris yelled, "My purse!"

Instinctively, Alex turned and leaped through the coach line then looked to his left and right. He noticed someone pointing toward the front door, and he looked to see a young boy in a dark, tattered jacket running toward the exit with a white purse tucked under his arm, running like he was determined to score the final touchdown in a championship game. The thief wove between the crowd with the deftness of a halfback, and it looked like he was going to make his escape. Alex trailed closely behind, colliding with one shoulder after another as he plowed his way through the crowd to catch the culprit. Just as the purse snatcher reached for the door, it flung open, knocking him off balance. He dropped the purse and tumbled to the floor, landing hard on his shoulder and providing Alex enough time to catch up.

The thief was writhing in pain when Alex arrived and bent

over to pick up his grandmother's purse. A crowd was quickly gathering, and Alex could see two policemen moving toward the scene. Doris followed closely behind, her face glowing a bright red. Alex turned and glared at the young boy. Pointing to the white purse now under his own arm, he asked,

"Why'd you steal this?"

The boy, curled in a fetal position on the floor, mumbled, "Hungry."

Alex looked at the boy's disheveled hair and dirty face with its sunken cheekbones and realized it could easily be him lying there if his grandparents had not taken him in. He was about to reach down to help the boy up when the police arrived.

"C'mon, get up now, Mickey," one of the policeman said. "How many times have I told you to stay out of this station? You've done it now, trying to steal this fine lady's belongings. What do ya have to say for yourself?"

"Sorry, ma'am."

"Sorry? I should say so." Doris said.

"You care to press charges, ma'am?" the policeman asked.

"Well . . . I certainly should." Doris hesitated. The thief looked at her with fear and rubbed his sore shoulder.

"Where are the boy's parents, Officer?" Doris asked.

"Gone, ma'am. Deserted the boy and left him in the care of his aunt, who's having a time of it herself. A rather hopeless case, it is."

"Hopeless. That's a word used too often in this city," Doris said. She then took her purse from Alex and looked inside. "Since nothing seems to be missing, I'll not press charges." She gave the young boy her sternest look and said, "But should you ever try this again, I'll tan your hide. Do I make myself clear?"

The boy nodded.

"C'mon, Mickey," the policeman said. "Let's get that shoulder looked at. Then I'll take you home. Good day to you, ma'am."

Alex looked at Doris, threw his shoulders back, and puffed

out his chest.

Doris gave Alex a cold glare and a frosty reply. "You and I will talk on the train."

§

Dismal gray skies overhanging a landscape of barren trees and empty fields spotted with half-melted snow passed outside the window of the Pullman Sleeper as it traveled south to New York City, the first of several stops en route to DC. Alex had been gazing at the emptiness for nearly an hour, dreading his inevitable talk with Doris, who assured him they would meet before dinner. Her sleeper room was next door to Alex's, and the two shared a bathroom. Other than hearing the toilet flush once shortly after they boarded, Alex had neither seen nor heard from Doris. He racked his brain trying to figure out what he had done to displease her. If anything, he figured he would've scored points for being aggressive with the purse snatcher, for being her protector.

Two sharp raps on the sleeper door startled the boy, who now felt like a death row inmate being summoned to his execution. He slowly opened the door to find a smiling porter dressed in a crisp white suit and black bow tie.

"Mrs. Davidson has requested that you join her in the lounge car, sir."

"Okay. Thanks."

Alex shuffled down the hallway, shoulders sagging, and crossed over to the next car. Through the swirling blue-gray haze of cigarette smoke, he spotted Doris sitting in a booth and sipping a drink. He immediately straightened his back, walked over, and sat down across the table from her. She showed no signs of softening since he last saw her.

"Have you given any thought to what you did today in the station?" Doris asked.

"Yes, ma'am, I've given it a lot of thought."

"And?"

"And I'm not sure why you're upset with me."

"Did you think you were in the Wild West back there at the station? And you were the heroic sheriff who was going to save the day by catching the bad guy?"

Alex winced. "I don't understand—"

"Precisely. You don't understand. You don't understand that you're a Davidson now and that a Davidson doesn't make knee-jerk reactions. Because a Davidson knows what's at stake if he does. Because a Davidson thinks with his head, not with his emotions."

Doris, whose intensity did not escalate or waver, took a brief pause to allow her words to soak in. Alex shifted in his seat, his eyes blinking rapidly.

"And what if the purse snatcher had a gun? What would you have gained if he had shot you or an innocent bystander? Goods can be replaced. Your life cannot. And reputations can seldom be salvaged once they're ruined by foolhardy stunts.

"Life is like a chess game. It's a series of strategic moves. Your opponents will always be looking for ways to trip you up. If you operate with your emotions, you'll fall right into their hands every time. You let that happen once, you might get away with it. Twice, and your reputation for being a person of influence and power is shot. And you will never get it back. Do you understand what I'm telling you?"

Alex nodded.

"You need to begin cultivating, right now, the practice of thinking before you act. When you enter the political arena, you'll not have the luxury of learning on the job."

Doris paused briefly, again, before continuing.

"Jack told me you kept a cool head the night of the accident. That's commendable."

Alex felt himself blush and hated himself for not being able to control it.

"The purpose of keeping a cool head is so you can think straight and strategize. That's how you gain power over your enemies, and that's how you keep power. I'm giving you a wealth of knowledge and advice right now. I hope you have the sense to heed it."

Doris picked up her glass and sipped her drink. Her words hung in the air.

Outside the window, dusk was settling. Inside, the porter walked around the lounge lighting candles on the center of the tables. He then pulled the chain on an exhaust fan, and the smoke in the room began to dissipate. Alex looked around the lounge car, amazed at how much clearer everything looked to him now.

§

A black and white Checker Cab pulled along the curb on Independence Avenue in front of the newly named Cannon House Office Building. Doris stepped out and looked approvingly at the imposing marble and limestone structure. Alex followed and stood next to her, wondering if he was in the presence of some hallowed monument.

"Well, this is it," Doris said.

"This is what?"

"This is where I spent twenty-five years of my life helping the wheels of government turn."

"This is where you worked?"

Doris nodded, still lost in her memories.

"Can we go in and see your office?" Alex asked.

"No, the person occupying that office now is a Democrat. I'm quite sure I'm the last person he wants to see crossing his threshold. Besides, most representatives are gone for the holidays. Though there is someone here today who will meet with us."

The two visitors took the elevator to the second floor. On the way, Doris told Alex about the man they were going to see: R. Branson Morris, a congressman from Boston who was in the second year of his first term. Doris helped him get elected in

1960 and felt sure he was a rising star in the Republican Party.

When they exited the elevator, they walked to office #235 and stepped inside, where the representative greeted them warmly.

"Doris, it's so good to see you."

"Congressman Morris, the pleasure is mine. This is the young man I was telling you about, Alex Spencer."

Morris smiled and extended his hand to Alex.

"So your grandmother tells me you're going to be a politician one day."

"That's what Doris tells me, sir."

"She has an eye for winners, so if she told you that, bank on it my boy."

"Congressman, what kind of progress is being made on the equal pay legislation these days?" Doris asked.

"I should have known you didn't come just to say hello and introduce me to your grandson, Doris."

"You know me better than that, Branson. Let's not forget the promise you made to me when I stuck my neck out to get you elected. You assured me you'd do everything in your power to get this passed. I was underpaid for twenty-five years because of the simple fact I'm a woman. I don't expect another generation of women to be subjected to the same inequities. Not if I can help it."

"I haven't forgotten my promise. Frankly, I think the bill stands a good chance of passing once we get the language cleared up. We still have a lot of old codgers in the House who don't think women should even be in the workplace."

"I expect you'll change their minds about that. And of course Jack and I will look forward to sending a sizable donation to your campaign coffers once this legislation passes."

"And I'll look forward to receiving it."

The congressman ushered his guests into his inner office where he showed Alex pictures of former President Eisenhower posing with the congressional candidate during the 1960 campaign. He let Alex sit in his desk chair and pretend he was signing Doris's beloved Equal Pay Act into law. It wasn't long before Doris started glancing at the wall clock.

"Thank you for your time, Congressman Morris," she said.

"Leaving already?"

"I know you have lots to do, and I want to show the boy some of the sites around town."

"You know I would join you if I could."

"What makes you think I want you to join us, Congressman?"

Morris smiled and extended his hand. "Always a pleasure, Doris. Give my regards to Jack."

The politician turned to Alex and winked. "Learn everything you can from this woman, Alex. Nobody knows how to grease the wheels of government better than your grandmother."

"I'll take that as a compliment," Doris said.

"So it was meant, Doris. So it was meant."

§

Doris spent the rest of the day showing Alex the buildings she wanted him to remember: the US Capitol, the Library of Congress, and the Supreme Court Building. Inside each, she relived some monumental event that occurred during her tenure with Congressman Walters.

"Can we visit the White House now?" Alex asked.

"Not while Kennedy is president," Doris sneered.

Alex knew better than to press the issue.

"There is one more place I want you to see," Doris said. "I haven't been there in years." She hailed a cab, and within minutes they were in front of Ford's Theatre. They walked inside to the empty, dimly lit auditorium and were surrounded by a somber silence. Doris pointed up to the balcony, stage left, at the presidential box, its balustrade festooned with a 36-star US flag.

"That is where the blood of the first and greatest Republican president was spilled."

Alex had never seen Doris melodramatic, but for the first time sensed she had the capacity to be so. He felt it was probably best to remain silent when she was like this. Better to just listen.

"The preservation of this Union was sealed by his blood," Doris said reverently, as though reading a devotional.

Alex nodded.

"I've done my best over the years to live up to the ideals he espoused," she continued, as though speaking to herself now.

Alex continued nodding.

"And soon, very soon, it will be your turn to preserve the same ideals of freedom and self-government. That's what we raised you to do."

Alex looked up at her. Was she serious? He hadn't been with his grandparents much more than a month. What could she possibly mean by that statement? Still, he felt like he needed to respond.

"I'll do my best, Doris."

The sound of Alex's voice snapped Doris out of her short-lived trance. She looked perplexed and rubbed her temples.

"Do your best at what?"

"What you just said . . . you know . . . preserving the ideals of freedom and self-government."

"Oh . . . yes . . . of course . . ."

"Are you all right, Doris?"

She stiffened up, and her stoic look returned. "Of course I'm all right. Why would you ask such a thing? It's time to head back to the hotel. We have an early train tomorrow."

§

"Your buddy, Reed Wentworth, called while you and Doris were gallivanting around the nation's capital," Jack said in his usual wry manner, which confirmed there were no long-term effects from the bump he had taken on his head.

"Reed called here?" Alex replied. "He's hardly my buddy, Jack. We can't stand each other. Wonder why he's calling me?"

"Said something about wanting to know if you'd like to come over and visit him during the holidays. Sure sounds like a buddy to me."

"Visit him? I couldn't wait to get a break from him. What's he up to?"

"Why don't you go over and find out. Nothing wrong with seeing how the really rich folks live."

"I thought you and Doris were really rich, Jack."

"We've done all right. But nothing compares with the wealth of the Wentworths, not in Boston anyway. It'd do you good to pay a visit. If for nothing else than to see what real money can buy."

Alex wondered how much more a person could need beyond what his grandparents possessed. What they owned surpassed anything he had ever imagined. And yet he found himself growing curious about the Wentworths. Surely someone of their rank would know something about wielding power. And since his personal quest was to accumulate power and the wisdom to use it, maybe a visit to the Wentworths was in order.

§

Howard pulled the Davidson's '59 Cadillac to a stop under the portico to pick up Alex. Always particular about how his employers were represented in good society, Howard questioned Jack about the appropriateness of driving Alex to the Wentworths in the "older automobile."

"I don't give a flip what the Wentworths think of me," Jack said. "Till the Lincoln is replaced, the Cadillac will do just fine. So it's almost four years old, big deal. Not going to buy myself a Bentley just to impress the likes of them. Utility, Howard. Nothing to be ashamed of."

"Yes, sir."

Alex thought he saw Howard cringe when Jack used the word *utility*.

Wentworth Estate was about five miles away, as the crow

flies. Of course, the streets of Boston and its surrounding sub-urbs were not set up to serve as avian flight paths, so it was al-most thirty-five minutes before they spotted the private drive marked with a black sign emblazoned with a gold letter *W*.

Howard slowed the Cadillac and made a left turn, stopping in front of an imposing wrought iron gate that was flanked by a guardhouse manned by a lone security guard who looked like a caricature of a Civil War general.

The man wore a navy blue uniform with brass buttons and gold epaulettes on his undersized frame. A navy blue slouch hat covered his oversized head, and a set of slightly graying mutton chops adorned his face. A sheathed saber hanging from his side swayed as he marched toward the car, with a clipboard in hand.

"What is your business, sir?" the guard asked Howard.

"I am here to drop off Master Alex Spencer for a visit with Master Reed Wentworth."

The guard examined his clipboard, running his finger down the attached list and stopping about half way down.

"Hmm . . . yes. And your name, sir?"

"My name is Howard Chester, sir."

The guard licked the tip of his pencil and wrote on a yellow slip of paper he had pulled from his pocket. He then handed the paper to Howard.

"This is your pass. Make sure it is visible at all times on the left side of your dashboard. And return it when you leave. Fol-low the drive to the next sentry station. You can drop the boy off there."

With that, the guard stepped back from the car, marched over to the gate, and pushed it open. He turned and made a sweeping movement with his right arm, motioning Howard on.

"I do believe the Wentworths think we are still at war, Mas-ter Alex," Howard said as he pulled away.

"Well, I'm beginning to understand now why Reed is so weird."

§

97

Alex followed the cobblestone walkway from the second guardhouse to a set of red brick stairs leading to an expansive patio and a three-tiered granite fountain topped with a bronze replica of Donatello's *David*. Reed Wentworth, wrapped in a camel's hair coat and wool scarf, was lying on a bench next to the fountain, spinning his yo-yo and looking down on Alex.

"I see you made it, kid."

"The name's Alex, Reed."

"Whatever."

Alex trudged up the stairs, trying to remember why he decided to come here in the first place. When he got to the patio, he stopped to catch his breath, and looked around at the view.

"Nice place your family has."

"I know."

"So why did you ask me to come over?"

"I was bored."

"You were bored. That's it? What am I, your entertainment committee?"

"Sure. Why not?"

"Look, I've got four hours before Howard comes back to pick me up. I don't plan on spending them keeping you amused. I came over to see what's so great about the Wentworths and all their supposed riches."

"There's nothing *supposed* about it," Reed replied. "As you can see, the Wentworths have the goods."

"So, show me around the place."

Reed spent the next half-hour ushering Alex around the Wentworth mansion. Alex observed that the estate had many of the same amenities as the Davidson's, just on a much larger scale. There was one feature on the Wentworth grounds that Alex would not find at Woodland Hills.

Reed led him to a concrete bunker built into a hill several hundred yards behind the main house. The side-door entrance was padlocked. Reed bent down and lifted the rubber entry mat and pulled out a tarnished key dangling from a thin, rusty chain.

He slipped the key into the lock, turned, and popped the shackle off the clasp. He pulled open the door, and a smell like rotten eggs drifted out. Alex plugged his nose.

"What is this place?" he asked with a nasally sound to his voice.

"Shooting range. I don't suppose you've ever done any shooting?"

"Can't say that I have. Why does it smell so bad?"

"Sulfur from the gunpowder. You'll get used to it."

Reed switched on the lights as they walked in. To their left was a pine wall that stood about three feet high and ran the width of the room, which was about as wide as Alex's bedroom. On the other side of the wall, the room stretched for about fifty feet and looked like a cave with dirt walls on the sides and the end. Suspended from the ceiling and running from the pine wall to the back of the room was a clothesline that wound around two pulleys.

To the boys' right was a concrete block wall with a hinged wooden cabinet hanging on it, both the wall and cabinet covered with soot and grime.

"What's in there?" Alex asked, pointing to the cabinet.

Without answering, Reed walked over and opened the cabinet door. Inside, neatly arranged on wooden dowel pins, hung six handguns of assorted shapes and sizes. Below the guns were two shelves full of ammunition, each type boxed and labeled for its corresponding usage. Reed pulled out a short-barreled revolver with a black handle and grabbed a box of bullets, setting them on top of the pine wall. "Better start you off small," he said, reaching for a cardboard target on a shelf next to the gun cabinet.

He clipped the target to the rope and ran it out about half the length of the room. Alex watched closely as Reed tipped the gun down and loaded six bullets into the cylinder.

"These are .22 caliber bullets, so even a runt like you should be able to handle the kick," Reed said, pressing up on the chamber until it clicked. "Watch me, kid."

Reed positioned himself in front of the pine wall, spread his feet, and steadied his right hand with his left as he aimed at the target. Holding his breath, he pulled the trigger. Alex instinctively reached for his ears when he heard the report of the pistol. He looked in amazement at the target as Reed reeled it back. The bullet had pierced dead center.

"Where'd you learn to shoot like that?"

"Been shooting like that since I was six. It's a rite of passage in the Wentworth family. Or so my old man says, anyway." Reed turned around and reached into the wall cabinet. "It's the one thing I seem to do right in his eyes—shooting holes in cardboard."

He pulled out a covered metal canister, removed the lid, and ripped off a couple of pieces of cotton. After shoving them in his ears, he handed the can to Alex.

"Forgot about this. It'll keep you from going deaf."

After Alex filled his ears with cotton, Reed showed him how to hold the gun, aim it, and shoot. He clipped a new target on the clothesline and reeled it out the same distance.

"Now picture that target as your worst enemy. This is your chance to get even."

Alex positioned himself in front of the wall. Staring at the target, he imagined it being the face of Father Francis. The thought of shooting him made him shutter. Reed noticed.

"What's the matter, kid? Not afraid to shoot a gun are you?"

Alex glanced at Reed and then turned back toward the target. It was just a bunch of concentric circles now. He spread his feet, aimed, and pulled the trigger. His arm jerked back, and he staggered to regain his footing. Reed pointed at him and laughed. His laughing increased when he reeled back the target and saw it was as clean as when he sent it out.

"Missed completely, kid. No cigar this time." Smirking, Reed turned and reached into the gun cabinet. "Let's see what you can do with a Colt .38."

§

The cold, fresh air was a welcome relief to Alex as he and Reed walked back to the main house from the shooting range. The smell of gunpowder after thirty minutes of shooting made him nauseated. He felt his stomach settling down while he walked, and he was able to appreciate the expanse and beauty of the property.

"Outside of the shooting range, where do you spend your time in a place this big, Reed?"

"Where I can be by myself and do what I want."

"And where is that?"

"When we get to the house, I'll show you."

Once inside, the two headed toward a door at the end of a long hallway on the first floor. Reed opened the door and led Alex up a narrow winding staircase that connected all three floors and ended in an unfinished attic cluttered with dust-covered crates and chests. The only light entered through the octagonal gable window, which looked out on a dreary New England sky.

Reed stepped onto a crate and reached up to pull open the window. He stood still for a moment, allowing the rush of cold air to tousle his thin black hair and part it down the middle.

"Aahh . . . that's more like it," he said.

After stepping down, he bent over, and lifted a corner of the crate. He reached his hand under and pulled out a pack of cigarettes and a box of matches. He plumped down on the crate and lit a cigarette. After taking a drag, he held out the pack to Alex.

"None for me," Alex said.

"Don't know what you're missing."

"Yeah, I think I do." Alex walked over to a small chest that caught his eye. With his hand, he brushed off a layer of dust on the lid, revealing a faded tole painting of pink, white, and violet flowers. "What's in here?"

"Just some junk that belonged to my older sister."

"You didn't tell me you had an older . . . an older—" Alex

sneezed from the dust. "An older sister."

"You didn't ask. Anyway, she's dead."

Alex paused for a second or two, and then continued slowly brushing the rest of the dust off the lid.

"Were you close to her, Reed?"

"Never knew her. She died a few weeks after I was born."

"How'd she die?"

"Not sure. Nobody talks about it. I remember hearing she drowned."

"Oh . . . Ever looked inside this chest?"

"Don't think anybody has. Been sitting up here for fifteen years."

"Can I open it?"

Reed shrugged his shoulders and blew a puff of smoke up toward the window. Alex carefully pulled the pin securing the hasp and lifted the latch. He eased the lid up on its hinges, and the weak light from the window crept in as the pungent smell of moth balls leaked out. Stuffed down between two stacks of neatly folded clothing was a bundle of letters bound with a strand of dried and faded blue ribbon.

Alex gently lifted the letters from the chest and turned them so he could read the handwriting. He froze when he saw the mailing address on the first letter in the bundle.

"What the . . ."

He turned the envelope to catch more light and looked at the return address. "Was your sister's name Carolyn?"

"Yeah."

"Did she know a priest named Father Francis?"

"Beats me. Why?"

"Because this letter is addressed to the priest from my church back in Stonebridge, New York. What are the odds of that?" Alex looked at the postmark, which was faded but legible. "And it looks like she wrote it in 1947. What year did she die?"

"Same year; the year I was born."

"Looks like she never sent it. It's sealed and has a stamp . . .

but no postmark . . . that's weird."

Alex flipped through all the letters, being careful not to snap the ribbon. He counted ten letters in the pile. He sorted through them again and found a letter to Miss Carolyn Wentworth with Father M.D. Francis in the return address section of the envelope. Carefully, he slipped the envelope from the stack, lifted the unsealed flap, and pulled out the letter. The paper had traces of mildew, but the writing was legible, and the letterhead showed it came from St. Andrew's.

June 28, 1946

Dear Miss Wentworth,

What a privilege it was to meet you at my cousin's wedding last week. It was wonderful to be back in my hometown after all these years. Meeting you made the experience all the more delightful. As I mentioned when we spoke, I am returning to the area next month to attend a week-long symposium at St. John's Seminary (July 22-26). If you are free during that week, I would love to set aside time to see samples of your artwork. Of course I still have the contact information you gave me, so I will call you when I arrive in town.

Sincerely,

Fr. Michael Francis

"Your sister was an artist?"

"Yeah. She was going to the Art Institute of Boston when she died. That's her painting on the chest."

"She was going to school to learn folk art?"

"Not just folk art, idiot. She knew all kinds of art. Some of her best stuff is hanging up in her bedroom."

"Can I see them?"

"Yeah, but put everything back in the chest first." Reed climbed onto the crate he was sitting on, flicked his cigarette butt out the window, and pushed the window closed.

Alex looked at the unopened letter to Father Francis at the

top of the bound stack in his hand. He was aching to know what it said, but sensed Reed was getting restless now that his smoke was over. He slid the open letter to Carolyn back into the stack, carefully wedged the stack between the clothes in the chest, and closed the lid. While he slid the pin back into the hasp, he noticed Reed walking over to one of the roof trusses. He brushed dust off the truss into his cupped hand, carried it over to the chest, and sprinkled it over the lid.

"Like to leave things just the way they were," Reed said. "Don't want to give anybody any clues this is my hangout."

"Oh, you mean like cigarettes and a lighter under a crate . . . those kinds of clues?"

"Somebody'd have to lift the crate to see 'em, Nimrod."

Alex rolled his eyes and shook his head.

§

Carolyn Wentworth's bedroom looked like a cross between a museum and an art gallery. The furniture was Art Deco style—blond maple with rounded shoulders on the headboard, bureaus, and vanity, and brushed silver knobs on all the drawers. An oval mirror was mounted atop the vanity and was flanked by two single-candle brass lamps with fringed scalloped lampshades. Paintings of assorted sizes, types, and colors filled the walls from floor to ceiling. The visual assault left Alex feeling dizzy when he first entered the room. Slowly, he scanned the walls, starting at the top and working his way down.

Carolyn's subjects were varied, and each wall of the room showed a unique theme. On one wall, the theme was religious: peasant women praying with their children, variations of the Madonna and Christ child, heavenly scenes with angelic beings, and a bishop wearing a purple and gold sleeveless vestment over a pure white robe, with a white linen miter on his head. His arms were outstretched as if bestowing a blessing. And a bishop's ring adorned his right ring finger.

Alex moved closer to the picture and saw the object of the

man's invocation. The corpse of a beautiful young woman, her hands folded and holding a rose, lay in a gold coffin near the bottom of the canvas. Affixed to the mahogany picture frame was a bronze label engraved with the words *The Last Sacrament*.

Alex lifted his eyes toward the face of the bishop and marveled at the meticulous attention to detail given by the artist. As he studied the bishop's face, he sensed a familiarity that he couldn't quite understand at first. Then it dawned on him. The strong nose, determined mouth, and penetrating gray eyes were unmistakably the same. He was looking at a younger version of Father Francis.

"Reed, this bishop looks just like the priest I was telling you about. Do you know anything about this painting?"

"Just that it's the last one my sister painted. That's her in the coffin."

"That's your sister? Why would she paint herself dead?"

"How would I know? Maybe she had a premonition or something. It's just a painting."

Alex could see that Reed was uncomfortable talking about his sister. And yet he seemed captivated by the artwork the minute he and Alex stepped into the room. He stood in front of *The Last Sacrament* gazing at the corpse of his sister with a look of subdued admiration. The juxtaposition of Reed's face next to the painting allowed Alex to notice that his roommate's features were not at all unlike those of the beneficent bishop peering out ominously from the canvas.

Chapter 9

"Well, Father Francis, it is a new year full of new beginnings and new adventures. Are you ready to start phase one of the building program for the bishop?"

"I was born ready, Father Vincenzo. You know how I thrive on adventure."

The two priests were meeting in Father Vincenzo's office, down the hall from Bishop O'Keane's. It was Father Francis's first day as episcopal vicar.

"What you see as an adventure would be a calamity for me," Father Vincenzo said, chuckling.

"And that is why I am your man for this job."

Father Vincenzo smiled. "Michael, you do not have to sell me anymore. The job is yours, remember?"

Father Francis readjusted his position in his chair. "I trust that nothing more was heard from Mrs. Bartell."

"If there had been, it would be highly unlikely you would be sitting here today."

"Then the bishop knows nothing about her allegations?"

"As I said before, the woman did not provide her name in her letter about you, so I treated it like one of the many anonymous complaints that come to my attention. The bishop appointed me to this position so he does not have to be bothered by such things. I trust you had nothing more to do with her after you and I last spoke about this?"

"That is correct."

"Then we can focus on the work at hand and not be sidetracked by those things that are behind us."

"I would like nothing more, Thomas." Father Francis shifted again in his chair. "We have not discussed my staffing needs."

"This position allows for one full-time secretary to assist you, Michael."

"Yes, thank you, I am aware of that. I would like to hire a very capable young woman from St. Andrew's to fill that position. Her name is Mrs. Thornton. She is a single mother, and very skillful and responsible."

Father Vincenzo arched his eyebrows.

"The diocese has already selected the young priest who will assist you. Father Kaseman is his name. He, too, is very capable and responsible. And more importantly, for your sake, he does not where a skirt."

"I was simply trying to help a young mother in need, Thomas. Will you forever hold my one misjudgment against me?"

"Not forever . . ."

Father Francis stared at his friend.

Father Vincenzo leaned forward, rested his elbows on his desk, and settled his chin on top of his folded hands.

"Michael, when I questioned your wisdom in responding to Mrs. Bartell the way you did, you told me you were a pastor as well as a counselor, and that your pastoral compassion overrode your judgment as a counselor. Do you remember saying that?"

"I recall saying something to that effect."

"I do not have the luxury of permitting my friendship with you to cloud my better judgment as your superior, which I am in this office. Everything we do must be with the view of making Bishop O'Keane look good. Everything. Until I am sure you have that same mindset, I will filter my decisions through my awareness of your . . . weaknesses, shall we say. Women seem to be your Achilles' heel, Michael. And until you have convinced me otherwise, well . . ."

"I understand your position, Thomas, and I appreciate your frankness. I will just have to show you that your trust in me was not misplaced, that I am still the man of good judgment and self-control you have always known me to be."

"I trust that you will, my friend."

Chapter 10

"I was thinking about you over the holidays, Mr. Spencer." Brother Paul spoke in a loud voice to Alex, who was heading out of the chapel after morning service the first day back from Christmas break. Alex turned around, surprised.

"Me, Brother Paul?"

The teacher motioned Alex forward.

"I was reading a paper one of my students turned in for religion class," Brother Paul said with a playful look in his eyes. Lowering his voice, he continued, "And it was so bad I wanted to crumble it into a ball and throw it on the floor. Then I remembered my council to you and realized I better practice what I preach." He smiled at Alex and winked.

"Well, I'm glad you're getting control of your temper, Brother Paul."

"And how about you, Alex? Any more temptations to throw things?"

"None that I can't handle, sir."

"Good. I'm glad to hear that." The man's expression suddenly became serious. "I understand from Mr. Pearson you lost your mother recently."

"Just before Thanksgiving, sir; killed in a car accident."

"I'm sorry to hear that. And your father?"

"He died over a year ago; heart attack."

Brother Paul pressed his lips together and shook his head. "That's more than a young man your age should have to go through. And who is caring for you now?"

"My mother's parents, sir."

"Well, Alex, we share some common life experiences then."

"Sir?"

"My parents died when I was thirteen years old. My maternal grandparents took me for a while, but they were so poor they couldn't provide for themselves and me. They put me in an orphanage, where I lived until I was sixteen. I was a bitter young man when I got out of that place . . . until God got a hold of me."

"I'm not sure God even thinks about me, Brother Paul. And I'm not sure if I care anymore."

"Oh, I can assure you, Alex, He cares for you very much, and He is always thinking about you."

"Well, it just seems like He's got a funny way of showing it, sir."

"I understand how you could feel that way, Alex."

"Why do they call you Brother Paul? Are you a priest?"

"I'm a Franciscan friar. Although some are priests, I'm considered a layman."

"My mother wanted me to be a priest. My grandfather wants me to be a lawyer, and my grandmother expects me to go into politics."

"All are honorable professions. Although I suppose there are those who would not classify politics as such. But what do you want to be?"

"I want to be somebody with power, Brother Paul."

"What kind of power?"

"Power to get back at people who treat others like they're nothing."

"Hmm . . . Sounds like you've got an ax to grind. Care to talk about it?"

Alex hesitated. "I watched a priest, a priest who was supposed to represent God, misuse certain people for his own pleasure. And he got away with it. Nobody did anything about it. I want to be the one who does something about people like him."

"I see. I'm sorry you had such a poor example of the priesthood in that man. I can assure you, not all priests are like that. And I'm not making excuses for the man, but I always ask myself if I'd be the same way if I was exposed to the same life experiences. You know, try to walk in his shoes."

Alex wasn't buying into Brother Paul's reasoning, and noticed the man seemed to change his tack.

"You say you want to do something about people like this priest. Do you intend to accomplish this within the confines of the law? Or do you intend to take the law into your own hands?"

"Whatever it takes, I guess."

"You'd better be sure because the consequences can be vastly different. Have you ever heard the phrase, 'Vengeance is mine, I will repay, says the Lord'?"

"I think so."

"Do you think you can put this situation in God's hands and let Him take care of that person who wronged others?"

"How can I trust Him to repay when He didn't care enough to stop the priest in the first place? Seems to me God just turned a blind eye to all this."

"Have you ever done anything wrong, Alex?"

"Sure, who hasn't?"

"Why didn't God stop you from doing it?"

"I don't know."

"Because you have a free will. It's up to us to choose to do right. He won't make us do it. Funny thing about pursuing revenge, Alex, you just may get it and find it was not as gratifying as you thought it would be."

§

Nearly two hundred jubilant supporters gathered in the assembly room of Faneuil Hall to join candidate Steven Roberts in awaiting the results of the ballot for city council. The election was big news in Boston, since the winner would be filling the spot vacated after the scandalous demise of the city's most endearing councilman.

Candidate Roberts milled about the room, smiling at his supporters, shaking their hands and slapping their backs. A reporter and a cameraman from the Boston Globe—the only local media present—shadowed Roberts, taking notes and snapping pictures, in the longshot that the underdog candidate would experience a miraculous upset over the favored Democratic challenger.

Alex sat next to Mr. Pearson in the front row. Though energized by the buzz in the room and by the confident, indefatigable Roberts, Alex found himself getting anxious as the clock moved its way toward ten with still no word of victory or concession from the other candidate.

"How late will this go, Mr. Pearson?"

"As long as it needs to, Alex. Contrary to what the press has been saying, I think this is going to be a close race. The people of this district are tired of politics as usual. They're tired of their district being known as the combat zone of Boston. I think they're ready to take a chance on a newcomer like Roberts."

A campaign worker came over and tapped Mr. Pearson on the shoulder, then bent down to speak into his ear. The teacher's face lit up. He turned and smiled at Alex.

"I think we may have the answer to your question very soon."

Pearson stood up and walked over to Roberts, and after a brief exchange, the two men left the room. Five minutes later they returned, and a beaming Steven Roberts climbed the stairs to the stage and walked over to the podium. The standing crowd began to chant victory as soon as they saw his expression. It was almost five minutes before the candidate could quiet them down to speak.

"I just got off the phone with my opponent, Mr. Reilly. He called to congratulate me—" Sporadic shouts erupted from different quarters of the room. Roberts used hand gestures to quell the crowd. The cameraman from the globe was now onstage, clicking his shutter rapidly as he moved about the speaker. "To congratulate me on my victory as Boston's newest member of the city council."

The crowd applauded and shouted, throwing confetti into the air. Alex pulled a noisemaker from his pocket and blew until he was dizzy. The euphoria of the moment was unlike anything he had experienced before, and it struck him that he was in his element. It was as though he had slipped on the glove of politics, and it fit perfectly. He had found his calling.

§

The afternoon sun beamed through the dorm window onto Alex, who was stretched out on his bed, with his head propped up on two pillows. Reed Wentworth had stepped out earlier to participate in a yo-yo competition at Walker Hall, so Alex had the room to himself to savor the letter he received from Kitty that day. He opened the envelope with his usual careful attention. As he pulled out the letter, a feather dropped out. He picked it up by the quill, sniffed it, and pulled the dark brown vane between his thumb and forefinger, enjoying its soft, smooth texture. Rubbing the feather back and forth across his chin, he picked up the letter and started reading.

January 7, 1963

Dear Alex,

You really thought I'd forget about you? We've known each other since we were kids, silly. And you're the one boy I've always enjoyed talking to. I like that you've never been afraid to tell me what you're feeling.

I found this Canada goose feather the other day, lodged under a bush in my backyard. I thought about you and our visit to Simms Park and wondered if it came from the flock we saw that day. I'm sending it to remind you I haven't forgotten about you. I also hope it'll encourage you to put this stuff with Father Francis behind you.

I know he disappointed you, Alex, but you've been given such great opportunities with your grandparents now—your new home and school. Think about all you can do with your life. Think about what you can be. You scare me when you talk about getting revenge. Don't you think it's time to let it go and let your mother rest in peace? I hope you will. I know I have. There are good leaders out there, Alex. I think you can be one of them.

I hope your Christmas wasn't too sad. I told Dan that you called him a flake, and he laughed and said you're a rat fink. Please keep writing.
Your friend,
Kitty

Alex opened his hand, and the letter glided down onto his chest. He turned his head and stared out the window, pinching the feather as he drew it between his fingers.

"I'm so glad you were able to let it go, Kitty," he said to the empty room. "I mean that must've been really hard. Let's see . . . what did Father Francis do to you or your family? Um . . . I know . . . absolutely nothing!" He snapped the feather in two and flicked it to the floor, then sat up on the side of the bed. He picked up the letter and glared at it.

"You're naïve, Kitty. You don't have a clue about this man. *I* scare you? Let it *go*? I'll let it go when he pays the price for what he did to my mother."

The door opened, and Reed stood in the doorway looking around the room.

"Who you talking to, man?" he asked.

"What's it to you?"

Reed looked behind the door before closing it, and then looked at Alex again.

"And people say I'm weird." He dropped his duffle bag onto the floor and flung himself onto his bed. With an arrogant smirk he said, "You're looking at the 1963 Drexler Academy Yo-Yo Champion."

Alex hated to encourage his roommate's gloating, but there was no doubt about Reed's prowess in performing with a spool on a string.

"Congratulations," he sputtered.

"Thanks, kid. What's that letter in your hand? From that girlfriend of yours?"

"She's not my girlfriend, all right? I'm not even sure she's my friend." Alex set the letter on his pillow.

"Sounds like the lovers had a little spat."

"Reed . . . y'know, sometimes . . ." Alex stopped himself, realizing he might as well be talking to the wall. Then he remembered Reed's sister and her connection with Father Francis. Maybe, just maybe, he could find a sympathizer in Reed Wentworth. "You remember that priest I was telling you about when I visited your house?"

"You mean the one my sister knew? What about him?"

"My friend Kitty thinks I'm obsessed with getting revenge on him."

"For what?"

"For the way he treated my mother and some other ladies in the church."

"Are you?"

"Am I what?"

"Obsessed with getting revenge, idiot."

"I hadn't really thought I was until I read her letter."

"Kitty really said you were obsessed?"

"Yeah . . . well, in so many words."

"That girl doesn't hold back does she? So what do you plan on doing to this priest?"

"Not really sure. Guess I haven't thought about that yet. But I want him to pay for what he did."

Reed rolled over on his side to face Alex, and propped himself up on his elbow. "You're one of those who likes to play by the book and thinks everyone should, aren't you, Spencer?"

"What's that supposed to mean?"

"It means you think if you play fair with people, life will play fair with you."

"Life has been far from fair with me, Reed. I lost my father over a year ago, lost my mother a few months ago, and now I'm stuck sharing a room with you. What's fair about that?"

"You go ahead and waste your life trying to balance the scales of justice, kid. As for me, I'm going to make sure they tip in my favor. That's the Wentworth way."

"Was that the way for your sister, too?"

"What's my sister got to do with this?"

"You don't think it's just a little odd that your sister painted a picture of herself dead with Father Francis standing over her, blessing her? This, after she shares letters with the priest, maybe even has a relationship with him? And right before she dies mysteriously?"

"So maybe they had a fling. Big deal. They were both

adults. And nobody said she died mysteriously."

"You said nobody talked about it, that maybe she drowned. What if something happened between her and the priest that led to her death?"

"What're you saying, he killed her? You're nuts, Spencer."

"What if he got her pregnant, like he did my mother?"

"My sister never had a baby."

"How do you know she didn't?"

Reed's face started to show anguish. Alex sensed he was stirring thoughts that had lain undisturbed in the back of Reed's mind.

"What color are your eyes, Reed?"

"You can see for yourself."

"They're gray. Not a common eye color is it? What color are your parents' eyes?"

"Y'know, you're beginning to really annoy me now. You trying to tell me I'm some bastard? I know who my parents are. I'm not some orphan who had to be taken in by his grandparents."

Alex winced, as though hit by a left jab. He got up from the bed, grabbed Kitty's letter, and stuffed it into his pocket. He pulled his coat off the wall hook and stalked out of the room, slamming the door behind him.

Once outside, Alex felt the bitter cold air stinging his face and upper body, instantly clearing his mind of all its clutter. As he struggled to put on his coat, he realized how foolish he'd been to goad Reed like he did. He'd allowed his emotions to influence his strategy, the very thing Doris warned him against doing. He felt miserable, wondering if he would ever learn the art of restraint.

§

Mr. Pearson walked into his classroom, looking more focused than usual. He set his books on his desk and went straight to the blackboard. He picked up a piece of chalk and wrote in bold letters: RESEARCH PROJECT. Then he turned and faced the students.

"Many of you are here at Drexler Academy because of its strong reputation as a prep school for the law profession. How many of you plan on becoming attorneys someday?"

Two thirds of the class raised their hands.

"The reality is maybe ten percent of you will make it into a prestigious law school. An even smaller percentage of you will earn big money. Those who will stand out from the pack are those who know how to conduct research and use what they find. So, I'm going to help you get an edge on your competition by giving you a team research project to work on."

Several of the students groaned.

"Before you convince yourselves this is going to be some dry, unexciting exercise, let me give you the guidelines. I want you to find a partner from this class to work with. Between the two of you, select a person—known or unknown by the public, alive or dead—whom you want to research and write about.

"For example, let's say your subject is the current president. I want you to use reliable sources to dig into his past and see if you can determine what shaped him into the individual he became. You'll write a five-page essay describing your findings, which is due six weeks from today. That essay should help me connect your research to your conclusions. Any questions?"

"How are we supposed to know if we're using reliable sources, Mr. Pearson?"

"Good question, Alex. I want you to use primary sources for most of your research. We talked about these a few weeks ago. Primary sources can include material written by the individual you're researching or written by someone from that same era. If you can, you might want to interview your subject or people who knew your subject. I would consider those interviews to be primary sources also. Make sure your sources are trustworthy.

"All right, I want you to take the rest of the class time to find your partner for this project and start discussing who you'll be researching and how you'll do it."

Alex knew immediately who he wanted his subject to be. He also knew Reed could be a valuable partner for this project. But he wasn't sure if he could convince his roommate to team up with him after their heated exchange a few days earlier. Walking over toward Reed, Alex formulated a strategy in his mind.

"Reed, listen, I'm sorry about the way I came across the other day. I said some things I shouldn't have. Can we put it behind us and team up for this research project?"

"You saying you want me for your partner?"

"Yeah, how about it?"

"And who do you plan on researching, this priest you're so obsessed with?"

"I thought it might be a good use of our time."

"And you want me . . . why? So you can prove my sister was a tramp, and that I was the product of her little affair with the priest?"

"I was just thinking the bundle of letters between your sister and Father Francis could be a good primary source, that's all. And I thought maybe you'd be interested in finding out more about how he influenced your sister. Listen, I said I was sorry. Y'know, just forget it. This was a stupid idea."

Alex turned to walk away, and Reed grabbed his sleeve.

"Not so fast, Spencer. I've got questions about my sister I need answered. And if this project can help me find those answers, then I'm in."

"And what if those answers aren't what you want to hear?"

"I'll take that chance."

"All right . . . let's put together a plan, partner."

§

The doors of the city bus swung open, and Alex and Reed got off, stepping onto the curb in front of the main entrance to the Boston Public Library. They looked up at the bronze sisters of literature flanking the entrance to the building. A light dusting of snow covered both statues. Alex fixed his gaze on the statue of Art while Reed stood mesmerized, looking at the statue of Science.

"There's only one thing missing from that Science statue," Reed said.

"What could be missing? It's supposed to be a masterpiece."

Reed pulled out a yo-yo from his pocket and tied a wide loop at the end of the string. He gave Alex a mischievous grin and started up the stairs to the entrance.

"What are you up to, Reed?" Alex followed behind reluctantly. Once Reed reached the top of the stairs, he looked around and strutted over to the statue. Stretching out his arms, he hooked the string of the yo-yo over the right hand of the statue and let the spool unwind. He stepped back and eyed his handiwork.

"*Now* it's a masterpiece."

"Are you through? Can we go in now?"

"Lead the way, Nimrod."

From the library's staircase corridor, Alex entered Bates Hall, before Reed, and instantly felt small. The barrel vaulted ceiling of the reading room rose fifty feet from the pink terrazzo floor and spanned the length of the room for more than two-hundred feet. Natural light flooded in through fifteen arched windows—equally spaced along the east and south walls—creating a heavenly aura within. Thirty-three oak trestle tables, each surrounded with eight Windsor chairs, sat neatly aligned along both sides of the room. Oak bookshelves, each standing nearly ten-feet high on a base of red marble, lined the east, west, and north walls of the room. They were stocked full of thousands of reference books that spoke a discomforting welcome to the two unseasoned researchers entering the room.

Alex and Reed stood frozen, but for their heads turning in unison as they scanned the multitude of volumes surrounding them.

"If we can't find what we're looking for here, kid, we ain't gonna find it anywhere," Reed said, muffling his voice with his hand over his mouth.

"Yeah, but the question is how do we find it?"

They spotted a librarian, who helped them locate a copy of the 1920 Boston census and showed them how to read it. With the census tucked under his arm, Alex walked over to a table guarded by the bust of some famous Bostonian, long dead, and set the census down. He and Reed huddled around it, as though they had found the Holy Grail. They spoke in hushed tones.

"So, this should help us find out just where Michael Francis lived in Boston the first year of his life," Alex said.

"And you're sure this is the right year?"

"Three years ago, my old church had a big celebration for his fortieth birthday. I remember it was in December. That was 1959, so that means he was born in 1919. The 1920 census should show him as a member of some household."

"You're not as dumb as you look, kid."

"Wish I could say the same about you, Wentworth. Now why don't you start looking at the names on the right, and I'll look at the names on the left. I didn't figure there'd be this many people in Boston with the name Francis."

"What am I looking for?"

Alex sighed. "I thought we talked about this on the bus coming over. You're looking for any families named Francis who have a kid named Michael."

"I knew that . . ."

After about fifteen minutes Reed found something.

"Hey, here's one: 'Francis, William M. – Head; Edna B. – Wife; Michael D. – Son.'"

"Let's see." Alex shoved his way over to look at the entry. "William was a salesman. Edna a housewife. Just one kid. Lived on Avondale Street; what ward is that in?" He moved his finger across the row and found the number. "This is the same neighborhood Mr. Roberts and I were in last month and almost got stabbed."

"Okay, so we found out where he lived, can we leave now? All these books give me the creeps."

"Not so fast, Reed. We need to get the 1930 census and see if he still lived at the same address."

"Why?"

"Because that'll help us narrow down what neighborhood school he attended. My bet is there's a Catholic school nearby."

After securing the 1930 census, they searched again for William Francis on Avondale Street but found nothing.

"They must've moved," Alex said. "Now we're back to square one."

"What if the old man died? Or deserted the family?" Reed asked. "They could still be at the same place—"

"But they'd be listed under Edna's name. Why didn't I think of that?"

"Because maybe you are as dumb as you look."

They looked through the names again, and there it was: "Francis, Edna B. – Head; Michael D. – Son." Same address.

"Bingo!" Alex shouted.

A dozen voices nearby all responded, "Shh!"

"We've got what we need, Reed," Alex whispered. "Let's catch the bus back to school. I need to call Mr. Roberts and see if he can help us find the next piece to the puzzle."

§

Steven Roberts eased his sedan into the parking lot at St. Gregory's School, swerving to avoid the countless potholes and crumbling asphalt. Alex, sitting in the back seat with Reed, felt like a pendulum swinging from side to side. He noticed the chipped paint along the fascia of the school building and the sagging overhang at the front entrance, and was beginning to wonder if anyone even occupied the school. Once inside, though, he and his companions found a simple but well-kept interior of freshly painted walls and shiny linoleum floors. A tiny nun, who looked to be in her seventies, walked sprightly toward the visitors, with a broad smile and outstretched hands.

"Councilman Roberts, I am so glad you came to visit us," she said, taking his hand between hers. "I'm Sister Mary Martha. And who are these handsome young men with you?"

"Sister, this is Alex Spencer and Reed Wentworth." Roberts put his hand on the shoulder of each boy as he called his name. "They came along, hoping you might be able to help them with a research project they're working on."

"A research project? I always loved doing research when I was a student. What are you investigating boys?"

Alex perked up. "A priest who I think used to be a student here a long time ago, Sister. His name is Father Francis."

"Michael David Francis, class of 1933?"

"You remember him, Sister?" Alex asked.

"I've taught here over forty years, Alex, and only three boys from St. Gregory's ever went on to the priesthood. Michael Francis was one of them. We tend to remember those things. They remind us we're doing God's work, even when it doesn't feel like it sometimes. So why the interest in Father Francis?"

"He was my pastor in my hometown—Stonebridge, NY—when I was growing up. I just thought . . . y'know . . . he'd be a good person to research." Alex glanced at Reed, who looked like he was getting ready to open his mouth. Alex cut him off. "So, what was he like, Sister?"

"He was a quiet boy. Kept to himself a lot. He loved to read. Always had some adventure story he was caught up in. I think that was his way of coping."

"Coping?" Alex asked.

"Yes, his father was killed in a car accident when Michael was in fifth grade. He was a traveling salesman and lived a rather loose life. I don't like to speak ill of the dead, but the man was not a good example for his son. Michael worshipped the ground he walked on, though. And after the accident, the boy seemed to go into a shell of sorts. Kept to his books, like I said."

"Did he have any girlfriends, Sister?" Reed blurted. Alex

winced and felt his face grow warm.

"Girlfriends? No, no, I don't think so. Though that's to be expected for someone called to the priesthood. He adored his mother, though."

"Was there anything else about him you remember, Sister?" Alex asked.

"Like did he ever get in trouble?" Reed added.

"Well, he was a boy, so he probably got himself into some kind of trouble during his eight years at St. Gregory's." The nun winked at Mr. Roberts and smiled.

"Okay, one more question gentlemen," Mr. Roberts said. "Then Sister Mary Martha is going to give us a short tour of the school."

"Do you know where he went to high school, Sister?" Alex asked.

The nun thought for a moment. "If I remember correctly, he went to St. Thomas Aquinas. Several of our graduates did. But that's been closed for nearly ten years. Like so many of our Catholic schools, their parishes couldn't support them anymore." She turned toward Mr. Roberts: "How did you like our parking lot when you drove in, Councilman?"

"Seems like it could use some work, Sister."

"We do our best on our limited budget to keep the interior of the school spic and span. The students are inside most of the day, so it's important for their surroundings to be clean and up-lifting. But you can only make money stretch so far, as you know. So things like painting the building and fixing the parking lot don't get done."

Roberts nodded.

"I understand you're a visionary, Councilman," the nun continued, her brown eyes riveted on Roberts, like a hunter sizing up its prey.

"I see this city ward as what it can be, not what it's become," Roberts replied. "And I'm not afraid to use unconventional means to help it realize its potential."

A soft smile broke across Sister Mary Martha's face. "I believe you and I are kindred spirits, Councilman. Shall we share some unconventional ideas as we tour the school? Let me start by telling you how the city can fix our parking lot for us. I'm guessing some overflow parking space for the neighborhood subway station during the work week might appeal to you?"

The Councilman's face brightened.

"Walk with me, sir . . ."

§

Back in their dorm room, Reed and Alex reviewed their research findings.

"Okay, so we know where the priest lived as a boy," Reed said. "We know he was probably poor. We know he was in fifth grade when his old man croaked, which means he was about ten years old, maybe eleven. We've got a pretty good idea where he went to high school, but the school is closed, so that's not gonna do us any good. So, we've got diddly."

"Where's your imagination? We've got a lot. This project is about finding out what influenced our man to become who he is, right? Okay, so let's look at the obvious. He was poor. Maybe that's what made him want to become a priest, so he could help the poor. His old man died. Maybe that got him thinking about life after death and spiritual stuff. That could lead him to becoming a priest. The nun said his old man was not a good influence. What if the father hit on women and his son knew this? The boy looks up to his father, so he may think this is normal behavior for a man."

"Give me a break, Spencer. You telling me that even as a priest he's gonna think this is normal behavior for a husband? I thought a priest's job was to preach against that kind of thing."

"I'm just saying, What if? That's all. The nun also said he liked to read adventure stories. What does that tell us?"

"If he's reading books when he doesn't have to, that tells me he's messed up."

"Not everybody's like you, Reed. Some people want to read more than comic books. I think if he likes adventure stories, it might mean . . . well, that he's adventurous."

"Brilliant deduction, Sherlock. How do you come up with these things? So if I like reading murder novels, it must mean I'm murderous, right? How about, he likes reading adventure stories because he wants to escape from the reality of the miserable, boring life he's living?"

"Okay . . . okay, you've got a point."

"Yeah, I know, but if I comb my hair just right the point won't show."

Alex looked up at Reed, puzzled.

"It's a joke, idiot. Get a sense of humor, will you."

"Focus, Reed. Think about our plan. We determined we wanted to do our research in the same order things happened in the priest's life. So, we've been to his grammar school. But we can't visit his high school because it doesn't exist. How else can we find out about his high-school years?"

"It'd be nice if we could find someone who went to the same school with him."

"And how do we do that?"

"Am I supposed to think of everything?"

"What we need is a yearbook or something. I wonder if the diocese saves any of that stuff after it closes a school. Who could we ask?"

"What about Brother Paul? Could he help us?"

"Hmm . . . Might be worth a try. We've got no other leads, and we've only got five weeks left to finish this project. I'll see if I can talk to him after religion class tomor—"

A piercing siren suddenly went off in the dorm building, causing Alex to jump. He looked at Reed who was rolling his eyes in disgust and slowly forcing himself onto his feet.

"What's that?" Alex asked.

"Civil defense drill. Like Russia's got its sights set on bombing Drexler Academy."

"Where do we go?"

Reed reached for the doorknob. "Out to the hallway. C'mon, you know the routine: squat down, put your head between your legs, and kiss your butt goodbye."

§

"And so class, research shows that the early Christian church was not as uniform in its methods of worship as we know it today. Tomorrow we'll begin talking about how Catholicism brought structure to the church throughout the world. For now, you're dismissed. Go in peace."

Alex liked the way Brother Paul always ended his classes by speaking peace over his students. It seemed sincere. He wondered if the benediction meant anything to the others in his class. It reminded him of more innocent days, days before he became jaded, days when he listened to a priest's words as if they came straight from God's lips, days when he still believed.

"Brother Paul, do you have a minute?" Alex asked as the teacher turned toward the door to leave.

"For you, Alex, I might even have two. What can I do for you?"

"Well, it's funny you were talking about research this morning. Me and my roommate are doing a research project—"

"My roommate and I," Brother Paul interrupted.

Alex hesitated. "Oh, right, well we're doing some research on my former pastor, and I wanted to ask you a question."

"Shoot."

Alex explained the need to gather information about Father Francis's high school years and asked the teacher if he knew where he could find that information now that the school was closed.

"Thomas Aquinas High School? You just might be in luck. I have a dear friend and mentor who taught there for years. There's a good chance he might have known your priest. He's getting on in years, but his mind's as sharp as a tack. Would you like me to arrange a time for you and your roommate to meet with him?"

"That'd be great."

"This priest you're researching . . . would he happen to be the one you told me about, the one who disappointed you?"

"Yes, sir. You did say something about trying to walk in his shoes. I figured one way to do that is to find out all I can about his life and what influenced him to become the way he is."

Brother Paul looked at Alex for a few seconds, as if gauging the sincerity of his words. "Fair enough, Alex. Let me see what I can do about arranging a meeting between you and my friend, Father McDermott."

"Thank you, sir."

"And, Alex, if you're gleaning this information to use in a vendetta against this priest, well, I'll be disappointed in you."

Alex felt himself blush and averted his eyes.

"Very disappointed, indeed."

§

The weight of almost ninety years of living left Father McDermott's shoulders hunched and his thin, disheveled hair pure white. He shuffled into the visiting room using a cane, and occasionally teetered as he struggled to resist the tireless force of age pressing in on him. Brother Paul, who was sitting at a round table nearby with Alex and Reed, stood up to greet his friend, and introduced him to the boys. The priest's face lit up with a smile so tender it transfigured his appearance. He reminded Alex of a cherub from one of the stained glass windows in St. Andrew's Church. The priest paused, steadied himself with his cane, and stretched out his trembling left hand toward Alex and Reed.

"God bless you, boys," he said with a gentle voice.

Alex felt something stir on the inside at the sound of the priest's blessing, and all he could think was that he was in the presence of a holy man. He felt like he should drop to his knees, but he was afraid he would look foolish. He glanced out the corner of his eye at Reed, to his left, and was surprised to see his roommate's head bowed and hands clasped together in front of him.

Brother Paul pulled out a chair for Father McDermott and helped him sit down. Once seated, the priest slowly lifted his hands and placed them in front of him on the table. He had limited range of head movement, but his deep blue eyes seemed to transcend space and time. Alex felt they were capable of penetrating his very soul.

"I understand you boys need my help," the priest said, his voice soft but steady.

Alex looked at Reed, whose head was still bowed, then glanced at Brother Paul, who gave him an affirmative nod. "We were hoping you could tell us something about a student by the name of Michael Francis. He graduated from Thomas Aquinas High School in 1937. He was my pastor growing up, and Reed and I are doing a research paper about him."

Father McDermott lowered his eyes and began mumbling, "Francis . . . Francis . . . class of '37 . . ." He paused and turned his head slightly. "Brother Paul, would you be so kind to go to my room—number 112—and look on my bookshelf for the 1937 yearbook."

"You have the yearbook from that year, Father?" the teacher asked, surprised.

"I have a yearbook for each year I worked at Aquinas. They remind me of the lives I've touched throughout my time on this earth. The nursing home was a little reluctant to let me bring all forty volumes, but I told them these are the only family I have, and I want them close by me. I still look at the students' pictures, and I pray for each one of them."

Brother Paul excused himself and left to retrieve the book. Father McDermott looked at Reed and smiled.

"Are you always this quiet, young man?"

Reed looked up and stammered, "N-no, sir. I usually can't

keep my mouth shut."

"What is keeping it shut today?" the priest asked.

"Y-you, sir. I-I feel like I'm . . . like I'm sitting next to . . . God."

The priest chuckled. "Well, Reed, I take that as a compliment, but I don't think God shows His age quite like I do. And if you *were* sitting next to God, what would you say to Him?"

"I would ask Him who my parents are," Reed blurted.

"That's an unusual request. Who takes care of you now?"

"I-I'm not sure if they are my parents or grandparents."

"Why are you unsure?"

"I don't know . . . I've always known them as my father and mother, but it just never felt like they were."

"Do they love you?"

"Love is not a word in the Wentworth family vocabulary. It seems to complicate things."

Reed's transparency stunned Alex. The priest was bringing out a human side to his roommate that he had never seen.

"True enough," the priest said. "Love does tend to complicate because it requires something from us. I never knew my parents, Reed. Brother Paul's parents died when he was a young man. But we both found the love of our heavenly Father. And that love compelled us to give our lives to others. I hope you find your parents, son. But more importantly, I hope you find your heavenly Father. It will change your life."

Alex noticed that his roommate was biting his lower lip, and his eyes were moist. Reed looked relieved when he saw Brother Paul enter the room with a dark blue book in hand.

"Found it," Brother Paul said, laying the book in front of the priest.

"Wonderful." Father McDermott slowly opened the book and thoughtfully turned the pages, smiling when he saw a face that triggered a fond memory. When he reached a certain page, he stopped and frowned. "Oh . . . now I remember Michael Francis."

Alex craned his neck to see what the priest was looking at.

"Says here his nickname was 'Fearless Francis,'" the priest said. "I remember him. Star player in football and baseball, excelled in academics, popular with the women. Extremely competitive. But what I most remember about the boy was his lack of humility. I was quite surprised when I heard he went on to become a priest. He seemed too driven for that. I thought him better suited to being a business man or politician." The priest looked at Alex. "But you say he was your pastor . . . for several years? Where is he now?"

"I heard he's working for the bishop's office in Rochester, New York," Alex said.

"Well, God certainly works in mysterious ways, doesn't He? It's not for me to judge whom He chooses."

"What do you mean he lacked humility, Father?" Alex asked.

The priest thought for a moment. "I remember the classroom banter after a big football game. Seems he was always taking credit for bringing the team a win. And it may have been true, but I was taught to never toot my own horn. You boys know what that means don't you?" The priest gestured with his right hand, as if trying to pull the words out. "Letting your actions speak for themselves.

"Mr. Francis was the same way with his grades. His had to be the highest, and they usually were. And he usually made sure everyone knew.

"I recall pulling him aside on one occasion and trying to talk to him about it. What was that line he gave me . . ." He gestured with his right hand again. "Something about, 'If God has given me certain talents, why should I hide them under a basket?' or something along that line. Not what I considered a humble response from a young man." He looked at Alex, again, and smiled. "But that was then. And if he was your pastor, then I'm sure God got a hold of him and took care of those rough edges."

"You said he was popular with the girls, Father?" Alex said, glancing at Reed.

"Oh yes. Well, as you can see, he was a good looking young man." The priest pointed to Michael Francis's senior picture in the yearbook and started to turn the book for Alex and Reed to view. He stopped, squinted, and leaned closer to the picture. Lifting his eyes toward Reed, he resumed turning the book around. "You look like you could be his brother, young man."

Reed's faced turned red. He glanced at the photograph, then slid it over to his roommate. Alex stared at the picture for a moment, amazed at the resemblance but reluctant to make any comments that would add to Reed's discomfort. When he was through, he slid the yearbook back in front of the priest.

"Father, you said you were surprised he became a priest. Do you know what made him choose that vocation?" Alex asked.

"I'd like to say it was the call of God, but I think it was more his mother's influence. From what I understand, she was a very devout woman who was childless for years after her marriage. She apparently told God that if He gave her a baby boy, she would dedicate him to His service. A modern day Hannah and Samuel, I guess. The boy lost his father when he was young, and his devotion to his mother was unwavering. After graduating from Aquinas, he went on to St. John's Seminary. I lost track of him after that. But I continue to pray over his picture, along with all the other students, usually once each year . . ."

The priest was beginning to sound tired. He reached for his cane and then glanced at his visitors. "I'm afraid I wore myself out with all my talking, gentlemen. If you'll excuse me . . . I think it's nap time."

Brother Paul stood and took the priest's arm to help him up. Once standing, the priest steadied himself with his right hand on the cane and left hand on the back of his chair. He slowly turned his head and body toward Reed and said, "You didn't say what your relationship was with Father Francis, young man. Was he your pastor, too?"

"I never knew him, Father, but he was pretty close to my sister once."

"Ah . . . I see." The priest started to turn away, then stopped and looked back at Reed. "It is a wise father that knows his own child."

Reed gave the priest a puzzled look.

"Shakespeare, *Merchant of Venice*," the priest said. "But it is a happy child who knows his own father. I hope you find what you're looking for, son."

Father McDermott leaned on his cane, lifted his trembling left hand, and smiled. "The Lord be with you, boys." He eased himself around and politely waved off Brother Paul's efforts to assist him. The three visitors watched as the priest shuffled back to the hallway leading to his room. Just as the man of God started to turn the corner, the afternoon sun flooded in through a hallway window, transforming his image into an ethereal silhouette for an instant before it disappeared.

Chapter 11

"Please take a seat, Father Kaseman." Father Francis extended his hand toward one of the two burgundy chairs positioned in front of his leather-topped mahogany desk. His new secretary had the look of someone fresh out of seminary— eager to please but oblivious to the difference between head knowledge and practical experience. Father Francis relished the idea of setting his new charge straight, right from the start.

"I think it is important that you know you were not my choice for this position," Father Francis began. "In my opinion, you are too young and inexperienced to be placed in a role that will require the utmost in dedication and confidentiality."

Father Kaseman's face drained of color as he listened to his new boss. He sat perfectly erect, but, as Father Francis noticed, he was squeezing the arms of his chair and shifting himself in the seat. It was just the reaction the elder priest was looking for.

"You may have come highly recommended by Father Vincenzo, but you will be working for me and, therefore, are going to have to prove yourself to me. What do you know about the local building codes?"

The young priest looked as though he was caught off guard with the abrupt question.

"Building codes . . . well, I took an elective class in public administration in my undergraduate studies . . ."

"I asked what you know about the local building codes, not what classes you took in seminary. What experience have you with negotiating contracts?"

The young priest's discomfort was more noticeable now.

"Contracts . . . I . . . I negotiated contracts with customers I cut lawns for during my junior and senior years in high school."

Father Francis glared at the young man with his cold, gray eyes. "And I suppose your lawn enterprise is the limit of your experience managing finances, too?"

"Yes, Father. That's true."

"Well, Father Kaseman, I have just listed the three primary responsibilities that I will need you to assist me with: navigating building codes, negotiating contracts, and managing finances. I believe it is safe to say that, for all intents and purposes, you have no clue about any of them, at least not at the level I require. Tell me then, why do you think Father Vincenzo felt so strongly about you being my secretary?"

"I'm sure it's because of my academic standing in seminary, Father. I ranked first in my class." The young priest looked relieved that he provided a reasonable response to at least one of the questions thrown at him.

"Your family is from this diocese, is it not?" Father Francis asked.

"Yes, Father, they are. In fact, my great grandparents were instrumental in helping found the parish in Feldsport."

"St. Joseph's in Feldsport?"

"Yes, Father."

"I pride myself in understanding the history of this diocese, Father Kaseman. I do not recall a family of your surname being founders of St. Joseph's parish in Feldsport."

"You are correct, Father. It was my mother's family of whom I spoke—the McGarry's of Feldsport. You may have heard of my grandfather, Patrick McGarry. His father, Thomas, was the first deacon in St. Joseph's."

It all made sense to Father Francis now. Patrick McGarry was the largest donor in the diocese. It was no secret to the area priests that he was one of the few who practiced tithing. And ten percent of Patrick's income from McGarry Wholesale Supply was enough to cover the entire administrative budget for St. Joseph's and two smaller churches within the diocese. Clearly, the bishop's office was showing its gratitude by providing a prestigious appointment for the grandson.

Father Francis surmised that the revelation about Father Kaseman's grandfather had the potential of altering his working relationship with his new secretary. But he determined that the young priest was too naïve to realize this. And he had no intention of easing up on him long enough to let him think differently.

"I have heard of your grandfather, though I have not had the privilege of meeting him. He has a stellar reputation throughout the diocese. Did you spend any time working at his wholesale company during your summer breaks?"

"I did, Father. For three days after my sophomore year of high school."

"Only three days?"

"My grandfather didn't think I was a good fit for the wholesale supply business."

"Then I am certain that the last thing he would want to hear is that his grandson was not up to the job graciously awarded him by the bishop's office."

Father Francis could see a look of reverential fear on his secretary's face, and he knew he had found his weak spot. And he would manipulate that to his full advantage, if necessary, to keep the young priest under his control.

"I strongly recommend that you make a trip to the county office as soon as possible, and begin acquainting yourself with the local building codes."

"Yes, Father. I'll get started right away."

"Before you leave, Father Kaseman, I want to make sure it is clear how I will handle visitors to my office. As you know, I was pastor of St. Andrew's Church in Stonebridge for fifteen years, and there are certain parishioners with whom I intend to maintain close ties. They have leaned on me for help over the years, and I want to continue to be there for them. These people are like family to me, do you understand?"

Father Kaseman nodded.

"I want them to feel free to visit me without fear of interruption, from you or anyone else, when they are in my office. As their former pastor, I feel I owe them that respect. And I expect you to honor their visits accordingly. Do I make myself clear?"

"Yes, Father. May I say I think it's admirable to see such a true shepherd's heart in someone of your position. I can only hope that people will say the same about me in the years ahead."

"Your future is charted by what you do today, Father. If you remain teachable and humble, I believe the things you learn while working in this office will have a profound effect on the outcome of your ministry. And think how proud you will make your grandfather."

Father Kaseman's face brightened. He stood up and extended his hand. "It is an honor to be working for you, Father Francis."

Chapter 12

"Y'know . . . we don't have to . . . do this, Reed," Alex said, panting as he neared the top of the stairs to the Wentworth mansion.

"You sound like you're about to keel over, kid. These steps too much for a wimp like you?"

"It's asthma, stupid . . . I've had it since I was little . . . Don't like to talk about it." Alex reached the top of the stairs seconds after Reed. He bent over and grabbed his knees to catch his breath. "This cold air . . . doesn't help any."

"I still think you're a wimp," Reed said.

Continuing to hold his knees but breathing slower, Alex turned his head toward Reed. "Y'know, I liked the side of you I saw with Father McDermott better than the one I'm looking at now."

Reed stiffened and clenched his fists, his usual impudent countenance changing into a scowl. "You ever bring that up again, you'll be sorry."

Alex straightened himself and backed away. "Lighten up, will you. Fine, I won't mention it again." He watched Reed for a few seconds and waited until he relaxed his stance. Once he saw his shoulders go down, Alex asked, "You sure you still want to go through with this?"

"I didn't come this far to stop now. I gotta know what's in that letter. Think you can walk without passing out, Nimrod?"

Alex sighed. "I'm right behind you."

§

The boys reached the top of the winding staircase and stepped into the attic. Reed went through his usual routine of opening the gable window, striking a match, and lighting a smoke. Alex waited for him to shake the match and flick it away. Then he slid the small chest containing the letters over to where he could take full advantage of the sunlight streaming through the window. He knelt down and leaned over and began fumbling with the hasp. After a few seconds, he paused and straightened himself.

"You sure we're doing the right thing? I mean, maybe we

should have tried harder to get into St. John's Seminary before we came here."

Reed, standing with one foot resting on the crate, took a long drag and exhaled toward the window. "Why are you always second guessing everything? You know the people at St. John's weren't going to give us the time of day."

"Yeah, but we could've at least visited the library and read Father Francis's thesis."

"We already talked about this. That thesis wasn't going to tell us anything other than how good he was at dishing out bull. Just open the stinking chest, will you?"

Alex thought for a moment, then bent over and resumed opening the latch. He gently lifted the lid and saw the bundle of letters right where he had placed them. He pinched the blue ribbon between his fingers and started to ease the bundle out when the ribbon snapped.

"Oh great!" he said.

"What?"

"I just broke the ribbon."

"Big deal. We can fix it later."

Alex pulled the broken ribbon away from the letters and lifted the unbound bundle from the chest. He removed the unopened letter to Father Francis from the top of the pile and rested the remaining letters on the top front corner of the chest. Reaching into his pocket, he pulled out a small jackknife and unfolded the blade. He slid it under the envelope flap and eased it down the full length of the envelope. With his thumb, he closed the jackknife and slipped it back into his pocket. He started to pull the letter from the envelope when Reed interrupted.

"Do you smell that?"

"Yeah, they're called moth balls."

"No, idiot. I smell smoke."

Alex sniffed, and then turned his head. Out of the corner of his eye he saw smoke rising from the floor near the attic wall where Reed had flicked his match.

"Over there!" Alex shouted, dropping the letter and racing toward the smoke. He turned to see Reed bending down and grabbing his cigarettes and matches from underneath the crate. Reed then jumped onto the crate and flung them out the gable window.

Alex looked down and saw flames shooting up all around him. He ripped off his jacket and began swatting, but the air from the window and some old newspapers stacked on the dry cedar flooring planks were fueling the fire faster than he could control it.

"Let's get out of here!" Reed yelled, jumping to the floor.

"The letters!"

"Forget the letters, we gotta go!"

Alex swatted the flames once more and turned to find his way back to the doorway. The smoke was so thick now, he could barely see. He walked quickly with his hands in front of him to feel his way out. His foot hit something solid, and he lost his balance, falling forward onto his hands. He was surprised to realize that the smoke was above him, and he could see clearly along the floor. Looking back to see what he tripped on, he saw the chest on its side, the letters strewn next to it. His eyes were beginning to burn, and he could hear Reed screaming his name—his proper name. He felt strangely amused to hear Reed yelling *Alex* and wondered if this would set a precedent.

It was becoming increasingly difficult to breathe if he lifted his head more than a few inches from the floor. Squirming on his belly, he twisted himself around and reached back until he thought his arm would pop out of its socket. But then he felt it. An envelope. He had no idea if it was the one he wanted, but he grabbed it and stuffed it down his pants. He kept hearing his name being called, but it was sounding more distant and distorted. He felt himself getting dizzy, and for the first time he realized he was in danger. He lost all perspective of where he was and how to find the door. He struggled to get to his feet, and the smoke immediately overcame him. His airways became swollen and narrow. He began to panic, gasping to get air into his lungs, but feeling, instead, the painful burning of the acrid smoke he was sucking inside. While thrashing his arms to move the smoke away from his face, he felt something latch firmly onto his right wrist and pull. It was then that he heard a familiar voice.

"C'mon, kid. Follow me."

Alex saw that Reed was holding a handkerchief over his nose and mouth while he led Alex to the doorway. Reed pushed open the door, and the two boys staggered into the winding stairway, coughing uncontrollably. Alex, his eyes still burning, saw a blurred image of two men in dark uniforms, carrying something red and racing up the stairway. As they pushed past, they yelled at the boys to get out of the house. Alex heard the attic door open, followed by a swooshing sound, and he presumed that the men were attempting to extinguish the fire. He and Reed continued to descend the stairs to the first floor, then ran to the patio near the fountain.

Reed balled his hand into a fist and smashed the thin layer of ice in the fountain. He began scooping ice water into his cupped hands and flushing his eyes. Alex did the same, then reached down and grabbed the front of his undershirt to dry his eyes. He looked up at the gable window. The smoke was dissipating. On the ground below the window he saw one of the estate's security guards bending down to pick something off the lawn. It looked like a pack of cigarettes.

Reed saw it, too, and moaned.

A towering man with slicked back silver hair was marching toward them from the house. He was wearing a pin striped navy suit and a severe look. The security guard intercepted him and handed him the pack he had found on the ground.

"I'm dead," Reed groaned. "My old man's gonna kill me."

Mr. Wentworth, his face red and veins popping out on his forehead, stopped and stood within inches of Reed, glaring down with a look of wrath that Alex thought should be reserved for God alone.

"Is this your idea of working on a school project!" he bellowed, holding out the pack of cigarettes and pointing toward the gable window, where smoke was just trickling out now.

"I can—"

"Not a word! To think I envisioned turning the Wentworth fortune over to you someday. You're nothing but a disappointment to me. You and your friend gather your things. You'll be taken back to school immediately, if not sooner."

As the man turned to walk away, sirens could be heard coming up the long drive. Mr. Wentworth yelled to the security guard still standing nearby: "Lieutenant, tell the firemen their services will not be needed."

The master of the estate continued walking toward the house, and Alex could hear the man's leather heel shoes hitting the sidewalk long after he was out of sight.

§

Reed had gone down to use the dormitory shower, leaving Alex alone in the room. The two never shared a word on the ride back to school. Alex couldn't seem to shake the image of Reed's face, pained from the hurt and humiliation inflicted by Mr. Wentworth. His own feelings toward Reed had been altered. Clearly, he could have died in that fire if Reed hadn't helped him to safety. He never pictured Reed as the heroic type, but he certainly proved himself as such in this case.

Alex began to strip off the smoke-filled clothes he was still wearing. He pulled off his sweatshirt and saw how close he came to becoming a human torch. The bottom front of the shirt was charred black. He figured it was probably on fire just before he tripped and fell. The fall, along with crawling on his belly, probably smothered the flame.

Then he remembered the letter.

He unbuckled his belt and unsnapped his slacks, and the letter fell to the floor, face down. He bent over and picked it up.

"Please be the one, please be the one," he murmured as he

turned the envelope over. He blew out a sigh of relief when he recognized the handwriting of Reed's sister and saw it was addressed to Father Michael Francis. He set the envelope on the bed and finished undressing.

After removing his slacks, he slipped into a pair of pajamas. He stuffed his dirty clothes into a laundry bag, tied it up, and threw it toward his closet. Once seated on the edge of the bed, he picked up the letter. *Maybe I should wait for Reed.* No sooner had he entertained that thought when it occurred to him Reed didn't even know he had the letter. A moral dilemma now faced him, much like one Brother Paul had discussed in one of his classes: Is it better to tell someone the truth when you know it might inflict pain, or is it better to withhold the truth to protect another's happiness? Alex determined he would read the letter first and then decide whether to tell Reed about it.

He slowly pulled the folded letter from the envelope, lifted the top and bottom flaps, and began to read.

May 2, 1947

Dearest Michael,

It is with a trembling hand and resolute heart that I write this letter to you. The last ten months we have shared together have been the sweetest of my short, unhappy life. I have felt alive and vibrant whenever we've been together. My art has taken on new meaning, for I now feel as though I am able to allow my soul to speak through my work without any sense of shame. It has been your love and encouragement that has created this change.

That same love has borne fruit of another sort—within my womb. I am pregnant with your child. I wanted to tell you two months ago when we last saw each other, but you seemed so weighted down with cares, I could not bear to add to your load. Nor do I intend to add to it now.

By the time you receive this letter I will be gone from this tragic world. For me to continue to live with this pregnancy would bring untold disgrace on you and to the Wentworth name. It is the former about which I am most concerned, for I know this scandal would destroy your future in the priesthood and prevent you from achieving the glorious destiny to which you are called. For its effects on my family's standing in this god-forsaken city, I would never be forgiven. The only solution I see for removing the problem is to remove myself.

I wish we could have met on different terms, in a different life. How rich our lives would have been together. But, it was not meant to be. I am not afraid for me, but I am afraid for the eternal welfare of our child. Do you think God will forgive me for what I am about to do? If the child was a boy, I dreamed of naming him Reed. I remember you saying it was a name you admired. If it had been a girl, I would have named her Edna, after your mother. I pray you will not hate me but will understand that what I do, I do out of my love for you.

Love,

Carolyn

Alex felt numb. He began to understand why no one talked about Carolyn's death. Suicide would have been as scandalous as the pregnancy. But it would be easier to cover up if only a few people knew about it. And yet Reed was clearly alive, so how did Carolyn hide the pregnancy, and why did she change her mind and decide to have the baby? Was her fear for her child's eternal welfare strong enough to change her mind? Alex hoped that was the case. And why did she take her life after Reed was born? Maybe the disdain of her parents was more than she could bear. And how much did Mr. and Mrs. Wentworth know? Plenty, Alex figured.

With all of these questions swirling in his mind, Alex decided to withhold information about the letter from Reed. He had to strategize, like Doris taught him. Had to think through every move, like a chess game. He placed the letter back into its envelope and slid it under his mattress. Minutes later, Reed returned from the shower.

"You doing okay?" Alex asked.

Reed didn't reply but began drying his hair with a towel.

"Thanks for getting me out of the fire. I don't think I would've made it out alive if you hadn't grabbed my wrist."

"I wish I died in that fire."

"I'm sure it's not that bad, Reed. I'm sure your old man will cool down."

"My old man will cool down when I'm out of his life. You heard him."

"People sometimes say things they don't mean when they're angry."

"Maybe in your world. Listen, kid, I know you mean well, but I really don't want to talk about it right now."

"Sure, Reed. I'm gonna head down and get a shower."

As Alex reached for the door knob, Reed said, "Guess we'll never find out what was in those letters my sister wrote. I heard one of the security guards who passed us on the stairway talking to another guard before we left. He said the stuff near the window was destroyed." Reed paused and then added, "I'm sorta glad."

§

Mr. Pearson stood next to his desk, facing the class with his right hand resting on a stack of papers. "All in all, your research papers were very impressive. Most of you put a lot of thought into your sources. I did not put a lot of weight on grammar and punctuation . . . this time. Your ability to research and connect that research to your conclusions was what I was most interested in. Most of you demonstrated you could do that. And I'm very pleased."

The teacher then began to return the research papers to their respective authors. When Alex received his and Reed's paper, his heart sank. Scrawled at the top was *C+* and a note from Mr. Pearson saying, *Please see me.* Alex held up the paper to Reed, seated next to him. Reed seemed indifferent to the grade.

Following class, the two boys approached Mr. Pearson with their paper.

"That's not the grade I was expecting from you two after you told me your plan for this project," Mr. Pearson said. "Do you know why you received the grade you did?"

"Not really," Alex said. Reed shrugged.

"You did a fine job of showing me snippets of the priest's life: the loss of his father at a young age, his introversion in grammar school and conceitedness in high school, and his inordinate need to be the center of attention. But you failed to connect the dots for me. I mean you conclude by telling me the priest was a great spiritual leader of a small-town parish for fifteen years, how he was a leader in his community, and how he was promoted to a position working for the bishop. But you fail to show me how these life experiences in his youth molded him into that person."

Alex and Reed glanced at each other.

"Something tells me there is more about this priest than what you mentioned in your paper," Mr. Pearson said.

Alex began fidgeting with his pen.

"Whether you gentlemen grow up to become attorneys or not, I want you to know that it's never okay to base your conclusions on anything less than the truth. If the research you provided for your priest is accurate, I would say that, short of a miraculous change of heart, your man is still driven by an insatiable need to satisfy himself. He may be very cunning to make sure his actions appear benevolent toward others, but ultimately, he will do only those things that satisfy some need within.

"I know that's a hard thing to say about a priest. But remember, we're talking about being objective observers. John Adams said, 'Facts are stubborn things; and whatever may be our wishes, our inclinations, or the dictates of our passion, they cannot alter the state of facts and evidence.' Try to remember that when you do your next research project, gentlemen."

Chapter 13

Easter came in mid-April, and Boston's unusually mild and sunny weather provided a welcome respite for Alex. Since the attic fire, Reed had withdrawn more and more until Alex found himself missing the sarcastic wit of his roommate. The cold, dreary weather during the weeks that followed only added to the morose atmosphere within the dorm room.

Alex had not been home since Christmas. He was looking forward to the week off from school and was eager to reconnect with his grandparents. There was still so much he didn't know about Jack and Doris, still so much to learn. He had no illusions about them, no visions of them greeting him with hugs and kisses upon his return for Easter break. But compared to Reed's situation at home, life with the Davidson's was a slice of heaven, and he was increasingly grateful for their care.

"Don't forget, we have to strip our sheets and flip our mattresses before we leave for the holiday," Alex reminded Reed while they were packing their bags.

"Yeah, I know. Spring cleaning time at Drexler Academy."

"Got anything planned for next week?"

"Oh, I don't know. Maybe I'll try torching another room in the Wentworth mansion just so I can see that look on my old man's face again."

Alex pulled the corner of his fitted sheet and yanked it off the bed. "He's probably forgotten all about it by now, Reed."

"Right. If you say so."

"You mind helping me flip my mattress?"

Reed finished latching his suitcase, shuffled over to the end of the bed, and grabbed the mattress handle. Alex was already gripping the handle on the opposite end.

"Ready?" Alex said. "On the count of three: one, two, three." In unison, the two lifted the mattress off the box spring and started to flip it.

They both saw the envelope.

"Got a stash you're hiding there, Spencer?"

"Oh . . . yeah, something like that." Alex balanced the mattress on his shoulder, while stretching to grab the envelope. He could see Reed watching and saw his expression change from casual indifference to surprised recognition.

"Hey, that's my sister's name on that envelope."

"Huh? What are you talking about?"

Reed shoved the mattress up on its side and leaned it against the wall, throwing Alex off balance before he could snatch the envelope. Reed jumped over and grabbed it and rolled onto his side on the box spring. He held the envelope up and saw it was the letter his sister had written to Father Francis. Sitting upright and then jumping to his feet, he faced Alex, waving the envelope frantically in his face.

"How long? How long have you had this?"

Alex backed away with his palms out in front of him. "Now, Reed, calm down. Just calm down."

"Calm down? Calm down?" Reed's face was a deep red. His body was shaking.

"I don't think you're gonna wanna read it. That's why I kept it from you. I grabbed it when I fell down in the fire."

"Who are you to decide what I should read? It belonged to my sister, not you!"

"She's not your sister, Reed." Alex blurted before he could stop himself.

Reed looked like he'd been shot. He lowered his right arm, still holding the envelope in his hand. With his left hand he felt for the edge of the box spring and followed it to the end where he sat down, his back toward Alex.

"Reed?"

Reed held up his left hand to silence Alex. Then he reached into the envelope and pulled out the letter. He unfolded the flaps and began to read to himself. When he finished, he rested his elbows on his knees and leaned forward, looking at the floor.

"Reed? You okay?"

Not a sound.

"Reed . . ."

Not a movement, except the occasional twitch of Reed's shoulders as if he was struggling to keep from sobbing. Alex quietly grabbed his suitcase and duffle bag and left the room. As he pulled the door closed behind him, he whispered, "Sorry, Reed."

§

"Master Alex, this letter arrived two days ago. I felt it best not to forward it to Drexler since you were coming home."

"Thanks, Howard." Alex recognized Kitty's handwriting even before the letter was in his hand.

"And may I say it is good to have you back at Woodland Hills."

"It's good to be back. Jack seemed pretty quiet when he was driving me home earlier. Is he all right?"

"Mr. Davidson has not driven the Lincoln since it was repaired after he hit the deer. The Cadillac has been the automobile of choice for him these last few months." Howard wrinkled his nose. "I was pleased when he said he was taking the Lincoln today. Though I noticed he seemed unusually apprehensive when I brought the automobile up from the carriage house."

"Hard to believe Jack would be afraid of anything."

"Oh not afraid, Master Alex; simply apprehensive. I have never seen Mr. Davidson fearful."

"That's good to know, Howard." Alex admired the valet's loyalty to Jack, and he had to remind himself that no matter how comfortable he felt with Howard, he was still a boy who was more guest than family in this house. "I'm going up to my room for a while."

"Dinner will be served at seven tonight, Master Alex."

"Thanks, Howard. I'll be there."

§

Alex sat at his desk, pulled out the letter opener, and sliced through the envelope from Kitty. He had no desire to stroke the handwriting or sniff the envelope for any trace of her scent. He felt like he was just going through the motions this time. Her last letter changed something in him. What exactly that change was, he wasn't sure. He just knew he felt more sympathy for her than affection. Kitty was someone who always wanted to believe the best about people. In more innocent times, Alex admired that trait. But life had become much more complicated for him over the last year, and he found himself rejecting ideas he formerly embraced. To him, people were guilty until they proved themselves otherwise. Not exactly a good trait to have if he aspired to be an attorney. He realized that. But he figured law school would somehow work that out of him.

He pulled the letter out. She was using pink stationary now, the lacy kind. And it had her name on it. Probably something her mother picked out, he figured.

April 5, 1963

Dear Alex,

I'm surprised I haven't gotten a letter from you since Christmas. You must be really busy. Did you get much snow there this winter? It's been mostly just cold here, bitter cold. The creek behind my house was frozen solid until just a few weeks ago. I was able to do a lot of ice skating, but I couldn't stay out too long or my feet started getting numb. I'm already counting the days until summer.

Speaking of summer, I have some good news. The company my father works for is sending him to Boston

for a week near the end of June. He's going for some kind of training at a school called MIT. Is that far from you? Since I'll be on summer vacation then, my father said he'll take my mother and me with him. He wants me to see the historical sites in Boston. I asked my mother if we could stop and see you while we're there. She said to see if your grandparents would mind. The dates are June 24–28. I hope we can see each other. It feels like it's been a long time. Let me know what your grandparents say.
Your friend,
Kitty

P.S. Do you like my new stationary? My mother got it for me the other day.

Alex wondered how he felt about seeing Kitty again. There was no question how he felt about seeing Mrs. McAlister. He noticed that he got that old butterfly-in-the-stomach sensation when he read that Kitty wanted to see him. Just like he felt when she touched his shoulder at the Halloween party. Just like he felt when she sat next to him at Simms Park. Like he felt so many times when they were together this past year. But why? Then it occurred to him, when he took the stuff about Father Francis out of the equation, he still liked Kitty. No, stronger than like. But love? Did he even know what that was? How does anybody know?

He felt his mind starting to go into overload and decided he had to think about something else or someone else. He glanced at the wall clock and saw that it was almost six-thirty. Enough time to clean up for dinner. It was just the diversion he needed.

§

"I received a letter from Mr. Pearson, saying you were a big help with the campaign for Steven Roberts," Doris said to Alex once the salad was served. Alex noted to himself what a difference a few months made since his first dinner at Woodland Hills with Jack and Doris. Back then, Doris hardly acknowledged his presence. Now she was actually initiating conversation, and Jack seemed less interested in eating and more involved in listening.

"I really liked the campaign," Alex said. "I didn't realize it would be so much fun."

"Fun aside, what did you learn from the experience? What was your opinion of the candidate? What did you think of his campaign promises? How will Boston be better now that he's been elected?" Doris asked with the same seriousness and intensity as when she grilled Alex on the train.

"I think Mr. Roberts is a good man. I think he really wants to make a difference in peoples' lives. When we campaigned, he said how he wanted to help the people in his ward get better educations and better jobs, so they could help themselves. I think if he can do that, Boston will be a better city."

Jack looked at Doris and gave a nod of approval.

"I'm glad to see you're using your head more," Doris said. "I agree with your assessment of Steven Roberts. In fact, I've asked Mr. Pearson to see if he can arrange for you to assist the councilman this summer as an intern. There's no reason for you to sit idle while Jack and I are away."

"Away?" Alex asked.

"We'll be in Europe all of June," Jack said. "Travel there every summer—part business, part pleasure. Tried to talk Doris into letting you go with us, but she said you'd be too fidgety after the first week." Jack looked at Doris and winked.

"You keep your grades up and your nose clean," Doris said, "and I'll consider letting you go with us next summer. I think you'll better appreciate the experience when you're a year older. Anyway, I think it's important that you spend time as an intern this summer, learning from Mr. Roberts."

"Yes, ma'am." Alex could hardly believe his ears. Before moving in with his grandparents, he had never traveled outside of a couple-hundred-mile radius of Stonebridge. On a few occasions when his parents took him to Niagara Falls, they crossed the border into Canada. That was the extent of his international travel. Now his grandparents were handing him the possibility of traveling to Europe next year. What would Kitty think of that? Then he remembered Kitty's letter.

"Doris, I got a letter from a friend of mine from Stonebridge. She's coming to Boston in June with her parents, and she wondered if it would be all right for her and her mother to visit me at Woodland Hills."

Jack smirked. "She, huh? What's her name?"

"Kitty McAlister. We went to school together."

"What days in June?" Doris asked. She looked irritated.

"The twenty-fourth through the twenty-eighth."

Doris thought for a moment. "They may visit on the twenty-sixth between two and four in the afternoon. I'll ask Howard to play host in our stead."

Alex wondered why Doris was being so restrictive about the date and time. "And if they can't come on the twenty-sixth, is there any other day that would be good?"

Doris had just taken a sip of her iced tea. She placed the goblet down on the table, wiped her lips with her napkin, and turned toward Alex. Jack was shaking his head, as if to say *When will you learn boy?*

"Did you, or did you not ask if your friend and her mother could visit you at Woodland Hills?" Doris asked.

"Yes, ma'am, I did."

"Did you, or did you not say they would be here from June twenty-fourth through June twenty-eighth?"

"Yes, ma'am, I did."

"Then what is it you do not understand about my response? The Davidson's are one of the most prestigious families in Massachusetts. Woodland Hills is listed as one of the ten largest estates in the Boston area. People do not visit our home when it is convenient. It is by invitation only. I am overlooking your friend's ignorance of that fact because she clearly does not walk in our circles. But there is no excuse for you to be oblivious of how proper society functions."

"Yes, ma'am." Alex looked over at Jack, who was casually finishing a dish of his favorite ice cream and peeking up periodically at Doris, as if gauging whether she was going to go another round or two. Alex jabbed his spoon into his own dish of ice cream, thoughtlessly moving the frozen clump in circles inside the dish. He wasn't too sure he was ready to spend a month in Europe or anywhere else for that matter where he had to be in close proximity to Doris for too long.

§

After dinner, Alex began thinking how little he knew about Woodland Hills. If what Doris said was true about it being one of the ten largest estates in Boston (and there was no reason for her to exaggerate about something like that), then there was a lot for him to explore.

Before he went to bed, he asked Howard to describe the lay of the land for him. Howard explained that the Davidson's home sat on fifteen acres. The five acres surrounding the home included the sloping lawns and terraced gardens. Beyond these were natural woodlands with a pristine stream on the east side of the property that cascaded peacefully over a fifteen-foot wide bed of slate. Overlooking the falls and spanning the stream was a rustic arched bridge with a bench on each side. Howard remembered the bridge being the place Alex's mother most often escaped to when she lived at Woodland Hills.

The next morning, Alex awoke at sunrise and put on his jeans and sweatshirt. He grabbed his jackknife off the dresser and slipped it into his pocket. He stepped into his sneakers and bent down to lace them up—tying double knots in both, since single knots had a tendency to come loose if he walked any great distance. And this morning, he planned on doing plenty of walking.

After stepping out onto the rear patio, Alex closed his eyes and listened. All of nature was coming alive with the new day. Birds were chirping, squirrels were scampering and squeaking, and a soft, cool breeze whistled through the patio eaves, brushing Alex's face in the passing. He wondered if this was what heaven was like.

He descended the deck stairs and strolled down the field-stone steps to the gardens, through the clusters of yellow, white, blue, and lavender spring blossoms, stopping to breathe in their scent and to pull out his knife and snip a flower before turning right toward the woods. In front of him was the well-worn path Howard had told him to look for. The morning dew was soaking through his sneakers, but the cold dampness made him feel more alive, more a part of his surroundings. Though the trees were still bare, there was a denseness to the woodlands that provided a sense of escape when he pushed past the first straggly branch dangling across the pathway. He felt like he was entering another world.

The air was cooler among the trees and the perfumed scent of the gardens gave way to an earthy smell of decaying leaves and rich topsoil. His wet sneakers were like magnets attracting dirt and twigs with each step, and feeling more like lead boots after a while. He stopped periodically, kicked the side of his feet against a tree to knock the debris off, and continued on.

Before long, he heard a soft bubbling sound. Looking ahead, he could see sunlight filtering through a clearing and glimmering on the ripples of the stream. The path made a bend to the right and continued winding along the bank. As Alex walked on, he heard the bubbling of the stream begin to fade, replaced by a sound like a steady summer rain. He saw the faded rails of the bridge before he saw the waterfalls, and he took the turn on the path that would lead him there.

The weather-beaten bridge looked as natural to the woodlands as the trees and brush. Alex stepped onto it and looked over the rail at the water flowing beneath him. One by one he plucked the petals from the flower he was still holding and watched them float gracefully down to the water and over the falls. He walked over to the bench on the falls side of the bridge and sat down, leaning his right hand on the seat. His fingers detected some irregularities in the wood, and he looked to see initials etched into the bench. The carvings were as weathered as the bridge, and the letters were upside down from where he was sitting. He slid over on the bench and looked to his left to see the initials *JD & BS* encircled by the outline of a heart. It took only a few seconds for him to identify the initials as those of his parents: Jean Davidson and Bill Spencer.

Bending closer to the seat, Alex ran his forefinger along the initials and recognized his father's handiwork. Three years earlier, Bill had taken his son camping in the Adirondacks. One day while they were hiking, Bill showed Alex how to mark a trail. On the first tree, Bill decided to carve his initials, starting the sweep of the *S* under the *B*, like it was on the bench. Alex pictured his mother bringing his father here to her special spot and the two of them looking at the waterfalls, holding hands, maybe even kissing. For the first time in his life, he was able to imagine them loving each other and enjoying each other's company.

Stretching out his right leg, Alex reached into his pocket and pulled out his knife. He opened the blade and leaned forward to position himself over the initials. Digging the point of the blade into the bench seat, inside the heart and below his father's initials, he started etching an ampersand. It took several passes to complete it. Then he started working on the letter *A*. Fifteen minutes later he was finished. He sat up, looked at the heart, and smiled. Its message was now complete: *JD & BS & Alex*.

Alex moved over to the bench on the other side of the bridge and leaned back, stretching his arms out and resting them on the railing. He tipped his head back and closed his eyes, feeling the warmth of the morning sun on his face. He felt that old peace settle on him, the peace that, until now, he had experienced only within the walls of St. Andrew's Church.

It took him by surprise.

He listened and heard the sound of the gentle breeze finding its way through the woodlands, the barren trees offering little resistance. And for the first time in months, Alex opened his heart to God and prayed.

When he finished, he continued sitting quietly with his eyes closed, thinking. Thinking about Reed and wondering what was happening between him and Mr. and Mrs. Wentworth. Wondering if he confronted them about the lie. Wondering if he asked how Carolyn really died.

Thinking about Kitty, always Kitty. Wondering why he could not seem to forget her. Wondering how he could have been so angry with her one minute and eager to see her the next. Wondering if they would ever see eye to eye about Father Francis.

And thinking about Father Francis. Wondering if justice would ever be satisfied. Wondering if the priest would ever pay the penalty for his actions. Wondering if there was enough good in the man to even affect him with a just penalty.

A sudden commotion, which sounded like it was less than thirty feet away, broke Alex's meditative silence. The desperate shrill cry of a small animal targeted for a larger predator's breakfast echoed through the woods. Within seconds, silence returned. And life in the woodlands resumed as if nothing had happened.

Chapter 14

With the start of the last quarter of the school year at Drexler, it was clear life would not resume to normal for Alex and Reed. Too much had happened between them. The new normal for Reed was sitting on his bed for hours spinning his yo-yo or sketching, while smoking cigarettes. The first time he lit up after returning from Easter break, Alex warned him if he got caught he would be expelled. Reed just shrugged it off. It was as if he had set himself on a self-destructive course, and no one was going to talk him out of it.

Alex asked Reed if he had talked to his parents—now his grandparents—about Carolyn but was met with a cold stare. After that, their communication was limited primarily to grunts, shrugs, and nods. And if more than that was required, a fragmented sentence usually sufficed.

Alex noted one improvement in his roommate—the type and quality of drawings he was producing were remarkably more appealing. One by one Reed removed the bizarre animal-creature pencil sketches from the dorm wall and replaced them with portraits and still lifes he had drawn in chalk pastels. The transformation was dramatic.

On one of the rare occasions when Alex and Reed spoke in coherent sentences to each other, Alex complimented his roommate and asked him how he learned to draw with chalk.

"Just started doing it," Reed said. "Found this case of chalks in my sis—, my mother's room when I was home. Figured they're as much mine as anybody's. Like to think she'd be happy I'm using them." And after that, communication reverted to the new normal.

By mid-May, Alex's concerns about Reed had reached the point where he felt like he needed to talk with somebody. At the end of the school day he walked to Brother Paul's office. The door to his office was open, and the aroma of a mild, sweet smoke floated out. Alex knocked on the door jamb. Brother Paul, puffing on a rustic styled pipe with a knobbed bowl and ivory mouthpiece, looked up from his desk and smiled.

"Alex, to what do I owe this pleasure?"

"I was wondering if you had a few minutes to talk, Brother Paul."

"Of course I do. C'mon in and have a seat." He removed the pipe from his mouth, turned it over, and tapped it on a piece of rounded cork in the center of his ashtray.

Alex pulled out the chair and sat down, not knowing where to put his hands and not knowing where to begin.

"What's on your mind?" Brother Paul asked.

"Well . . . it's about Reed."

"Reed Wentworth?"

"Yes, sir." Alex paused, wishing the teacher could read his mind, so he didn't have to talk about it.

"What about Reed, Alex?"

"Well . . . I . . . I'm concerned about him."

"Concerned?"

"Yes, sir."

"Concerned about what?"

Alex looked down at the floor and began squirming in his seat.

"Alex, I like to think you and I have established a good rapport over the last several months. Clearly, you have something on your mind concerning Reed. Why don't you just relax and tell me what it is."

Alex took a deep breath and exhaled. He then proceeded to provide Brother Paul snippets of the story about Carolyn Wentworth and Reed, being cautious not to reveal his own role in Reed's discovery of his mother's identity. He also was careful to leave out any mention of Father Francis. And he was careful not to discuss Reed's new habit of smoking in the dorm room. He figured he'd already caused his roommate enough trouble. When he finished, he let out a sigh and leaned back in his chair.

"That's a very tragic story," Brother Paul said. "You seem relieved to have gotten it off your chest."

"I am, sir."

"And why is that?"

"Sir?"

"Why is it a relief to have gotten it off your chest, Alex?"

Alex felt his face grow warm and looked down at the desk. He could sense Brother Paul's eyes were locked on him.

"Is there more to this story than what you've told me?"

Alex didn't lift his eyes. "Yes, sir, there is."

"Do you care to share it with me?"

"Not really, sir."

"That's your choice, Alex. But if you'd like some advice, be a friend to Reed. I'm sure he's feeling quite empty and lost right now. He may have gained a set of grandparents, but he lost the only set of parents he's known. And he is no doubt struggling to mourn the loss of the mother he never knew. I fear his life may never be the same."

"What if he won't let me be a friend to him right now?"

"Without knowing the whole story, it's hard for me to know why he'd react that way. But I can probably guess. If you feel you've done wrong by Reed, and I sense you do, then you owe him your full support and friendship. As long as it takes to make things right . . . or as right as they can be."

"Yes, sir . . . thank you."

"I'll be praying for you and Reed, Alex. And if you ever decide you want to tell me the rest of the story, you know where to find me."

§

Over the next several weeks, Alex tried everything to act on Brother Paul's advice. His efforts seemed futile. Reed had retreated into his own world and was unwilling to come out for anything but his classes and meals. Alex noticed that Reed's yo-yo sat on his desk untouched while he became totally engrossed in his art. By now, every inch of wall space on Reed's side of the room was filled with his chalk sketches. It reminded Alex of Carolyn's bedroom. And each new sketch showed an improvement from the last. Reed's talent was like a pent up blossom finally released into the sunlight and allowed to fully bloom.

The day before the end of the school year, Reed started taking down his pictures from the wall and stacking them neatly in a binder. Alex was sitting at his desk, reading a note he had received from Kitty that confirmed her visit the following week.

"Still getting letters from your girl . . . what's her name . . . Katie?" Reed asked.

"Huh? . . . Yeah . . . uh, Kitty. Her name's Kitty." Alex had almost forgotten that Reed could talk.

"What kind of pictures does she like?"

"Pictures? I dunno. She likes kittens, I think."

Reed sorted through his binder of pictures and pulled one out from the pile. He held the picture out to Alex. "Don't have a kitten, but I've got this one of a tiger cub. Think she'd like that?"

Alex took the picture and looked at it. "Yeah, sure. Thanks. I'll give it to her next week when I see her."

"Going back to visit her in New York?"

"No, she's coming to Boston with her family. Stopping by with her mother to see me at my grandparents' house."

Reed continued flipping through his binder. "Hope I have a Kitty someday who wants to come and see me."

Alex nodded, unsure what to say.

"You know that priest did my mother wrong," Reed said. "Did your mother wrong. Wonder why he's allowed to be a priest."

"Not sure." Alex wondered what had suddenly gotten into Reed.

"Shouldn't be . . . shouldn't be allowed . . . ." With that, Reed continued pulling the remaining pictures off the wall, storing them in his binder.

Alex shook his head and went back to reading Kitty's note. The next morning when he got up, Reed was gone.

§

"How do I look, Howard?" Alex stood before the full-length mirror, scrutinizing his choice of outfit for Kitty's visit.

"You look splendid, Master Alex. The blue tie will bring out the color of your eyes quite nicely, I think."

Alex looked down at his brushed suede Hush Puppies with their soft crepe soles and cringed when he compared them to Howard's shiny cordovan Oxfords.

"Do you think my shoes look childish?"

Howard pursed his lips. "In the words of Mr. Davidson, I would say your shoes are utilitarian, sir. They serve their purpose efficiently and economically."

"Which is your nice way of saying they're ugly. I get it."

Howard smiled. "This young lady must be very special to you, sir."

"I'm not sure what she is to me, Howard. One minute I'm mad at her, the next I'm . . . well, I'm like I am right now. Know what I mean?" Alex straightened his belt, so the buckle centered perfectly with the tip of his tie.

"I do, sir."

Alex looked up at Howard. "You do? Is there someone special in your life, Howard?"

"There was once, Master Alex. A long time ago . . ."

Alex sat down on a stool next to the mirror. "Tell me about her, Howard . . . please."

Howard smiled shyly. He pulled a side chair over from the wall and sat down, placing his folded hands on his lap. Tilting his head toward the ceiling, he had the look of one who was savoring the moment.

"Well . . . it was just before Britain went to war with Germany in 1939. I was twenty-one at the time, still living in my hometown of Northampton, about an hour or so from London. I was working as a footman for a very wealthy family in town, living a simple life and feeling quite contented, I must say. Then I met Helen, and I was smitten. She was a city girl from London. Her mother had died a few years earlier, and her father was a businessman. His work required him to travel to India, keeping him out of the country for just over a year. So, he sent Helen, who was eighteen at the time, to stay with her grandparents in Northampton while he was away.

"She had been living in town for less than a month when we met at the May Day fair. She was helping her grandmother run a booth for the ladies auxiliary. I cannot recall what she was selling, but when I walked by the booth and saw her, I had to stop, just to have a chance to talk with her. Well, one thing led to the next, and I asked her for a date. We saw each other exclusively throughout the summer. And we fell in love."

Howard looked at Alex as if to be sure the boy understood the next point he wanted to make.

"You understand, most employers at that time preferred their footmen to be unmarried. So for me to wed Helen would have jeopardized my job. But neither she nor I cared. We knew somehow it would work out. But the war changed everything."

Alex was leaning forward with his hands on his knees, engrossed in Howard's story.

"In late August I received my conscription notice, calling me to serve as a militiaman. I was supposed to serve only six months and then be placed on reserve duty. Helen cried when I told her, but I assured her that six months would go by quickly, and we could be married as soon as I finished basic training. Within weeks after I started, Great Britain declared war on Germany. And my six months turned into four years.

"For the first ten months Helen responded to my letters, but then she stopped writing. Friends from town who wrote me said she had gone back to London with her father when he returned from India."

Howard looked at Alex, indicating he was finished with his story. He started to get up when Alex stopped him.

"That's it? That's the end of the story? Did you ever see Helen again?"

Howard sat back down and pulled out his pocket watch. He raised his eyebrows and said, "Your friend will be here in less than twenty minutes, Master Alex. Perhaps we should finish this another time."

"Just tell me how it ended, Howard. Please . . ."

"As you wish . . . When I was given a medical discharge in 1943, I returned to Northampton to recuperate for a few months. When I gathered enough strength, I traveled to London, to her father's home. Only the foundation remained. The home had been destroyed in the Blitz, and the debris cleared away. The neighbors told me Helen died in her bed, sleeping."

Howard paused and swallowed. Folding his arms, he sat back in his chair and stared at the wall for a moment.

"And then I knew why her letters had stopped coming . . . Her father had been gravely wounded in the blast and died a few days later.

"Shortly afterward, I received an invitation from a friend in America to come and visit. With Helen gone, I no longer had a reason to stay in England. So I came to Boston and have been here ever since."

Alex sat up straight on the stool and shook his head. "Was there ever anyone else after Helen, Howard?"

"There could never be anyone else for me, Master Alex. Helen was the one and only."

Alex thought for a moment. "I hope I can feel that way about a woman someday."

Howard stood up and straightened his jacket and tie. "I am sure you have plenty of time for that, sir." He looked at his pocket watch again. "I believe your guests will be arriving any minute."

§

Howard's story affected Alex in a way that left him even more receptive to Kitty's visit, more appreciative of her friendship and their history together. He was looking forward to catching up on the news from Stonebridge and telling her about his life. His only regret was Mrs. McAlister would be coming with her.

Howard and Alex stood side-by-side under the portico as the taxi pulled up. Mrs. McAlister's mouth was running before she even exited the car.

"Oh my! Why, I've never seen such a place! Well, Alex! Look at you, all grown up!"

"Good to see you, Mrs. McAlister," Alex said, stepping forward to shake her hand. But his eyes were drawn to Kitty, who was coming out of the car behind her mother. He saw her white patent leather shoes first as she stuck one leg then the other out the door. Her legs looked like those of a woman—soft and silky. He realized she had stockings on and felt his insides begin to tingle.

When she moved out from behind the car door, he could see she was wearing a soft white sweater over a light blue dress with an embroidered collar and white buttons down the front. Her hair was longer than the last time he saw it—down to her shoulders and curled up on the ends. She combed her bangs to one side like she always had. She moved away from the car, and the breeze coming through the portico blew her bangs across her forehead. Alex noticed her white gloves when she brought her hand up to brush her hair away from her eyes. She looked at him and smiled, lifting her hand in a hesitant wave. Alex smiled back.

Howard stepped forward to greet the mother and daughter. "On behalf of Mr. and Mrs. Davidson, I would like to welcome you to Woodland Hills Estate. The Davidsons send their regrets that they are not able to be here today and have asked me to ensure that your visit is a pleasant one. My name is Howard Chester, and I will be your host this afternoon. If you ladies will kindly follow me, I will show you to the powder room where you may freshen up. And when you are ready, there are refreshments on the patio."

Mrs. McAlister was giddy as a school girl as she followed Howard to the front entrance. Alex walked over to greet Kitty, and she reached up and gave him a hug.

"It's good to see you," she said. "You look good."

"So do you, Kitty. I like your dress."

"Thanks." She blushed. "Dan said to say hi."

"Good ol' Wally. Is he keeping out of trouble?"

"You know Dan." Kitty's eyes widened as she passed

through the front door into the main foyer. She turned her head slowly, gaping at the richness of the décor surrounding her. Alex pointed to the white paneled staircase.

"My room is up there."

"I'd love to see it. I'd love to see the whole house."

"Howard will give you and your mother a tour once you've had something to drink."

"The powder room is right this way, ladies," Howard said, pointing toward the hallway to their left. "First door on the right."

"Thank you, Mr. Chester," Mrs. McAlister said. "I can't get over how lovely it is here. Alex, you are one lucky boy!"

"Yes, ma'am." He looked at Kitty, who had begun turning to follow her mother. "I'll wait here for you, Kitty."

"Okay, thanks." She shrugged her shoulders and smiled.

After the women left, Alex walked over to Howard. "So what do you think of Kitty?"

"She seems to be a very lovely girl, Master Alex."

"I just wish we had a chance to talk without her mother around. There's so much we need to catch up on."

Howard looked straight ahead. "Mrs. McAlister does seem to be a rather animated woman, sir."

"You have a nice way of putting things, Howard."

"Thank you, sir."

After several minutes, the ladies returned, and Howard led them out to the patio. The view overlooking the sloping lawn and terraced gardens was breathtaking. Everything was in full bloom, and Mrs. McAlister remarked how delightful the brilliant blossoms looked under a "sky the color of my swimming pool." She said she always prided herself on having a green thumb, and the gardens were giving her all sorts of new ideas for home.

Howard seemed to relish playing the guide and provided the ladies an authoritative overview of the estate: built in 1895, 18 rooms, 6 bedrooms, 4 baths, 8 fireplaces, adjoining carriage house with 4-car garage and upstairs apartment, all on 15 acres of land. Following the refreshments, he took everyone on a tour of the home and carriage house, and finished up on the patio approximately thirty minutes later.

"Master Alex, perhaps Miss Kitty would enjoy a game of billiards," Howard said.

Mrs. McAlister put her hand to her mouth to quell a giggle when she heard Howard address Alex with the title of *Master*.

Alex looked at Kitty. "Have you ever played pool before?"

"No, but I'd like to try."

"Splendid! I would love to watch you two play." Mrs. McAlister said.

"I thought, Mrs. McAlister, that you might enjoy a special tour of the gardens," Howard said. "Perhaps we can ask the gardener to provide you some cuttings to take with you for your gardens at home."

"Oh my!" Mrs. McAlister put her hand to her bosom. "Well that would be wonderful, Mr. Chester."

"After you, ma'am." Howard stepped back to allow Mrs. McAlister access to the stairs descending from the patio to the gardens.

He turned his head toward Alex and winked.

Grabbing the rail, he stepped down to the first step and followed cautiously behind Mrs. McAlister, who punctuated her theatrical descent with the cry "Oh dear!" with each step she took.

Alex gestured with his arm to Kitty and said, "C'mon, follow me."

§

The window shades to the billiard room were raised, allowing the natural light to fill the room and accentuate the satin sheen of the oak paneled walls. Alex walked over to the wall rack and removed two cue sticks. He handed one to Kitty, who had removed her gloves and set them on a table nearby.

"You really never played this game before?" Alex asked.

"Nope. I watched my father play at my uncle's house but never played it myself. Is it hard?"

"Just like anything, if you know what you're doing, it's pretty easy. You're gonna need to put some of this chalk on the tip of your cue stick, like this." Alex showed her how to apply the chalk and then handed the block to her. While Kitty chalked her stick, Alex began racking the balls for a game of eightball. Kitty held out her cue stick.

"Did I do it right?"

"Looks good to me."

"Now what?"

"Now we start hitting the balls. Let me show you." Alex lifted the rack from the table and rolled the cue ball to the opposite end. He walked around the table toward the cue ball, explaining the objective of the game.

"We're gonna play eightball. There are seven striped balls, seven solid balls, and the eightball, which is that black one in the center. I'll take the first shot; that's called the break shot. If the first ball I hit into a pocket is striped, then that's what I have to hit in the rest of the game. And you have to hit solids. If the first ball is solid, then I hit solids and you hit striped. The first one to get all of their balls in plus the eightball wins. Make sense?"

"I guess . . ."

"Let me show you." Alex lined up the cue ball, leveled his stick, and took his shot. Kitty moved closer to the table to watch, and saw a solid color ball drop into the corner pocket.

"You have solids, right?"

"You got it." Alex took his second shot and missed. "Your turn."

"I'm not sure if I know how to hold the cue stick."

"Okay, watch me." Alex went through the motions without using any ball. "Think you got it?"

"I think so . . ." Kitty leaned over the table. She put her stick next to the cue ball, drew back, and drove the stick under the ball and along the billiard cloth. She looked at Alex and frowned.

"Let me see if I can help you, Kitty." He walked around and stood to Kitty's left. "Now get in position to shoot."

Kitty leaned over and rested her left hand on the table. Alex rested his left hand next to hers, a few inches away. He noticed how soft and delicate her hand looked. He showed her how to position her fingers to guide the cue stick and then told her to try the shot again. The results were the same.

"I'm sorry . . ." Kitty said.

"You mind if I help you hold the cue stick?"

"Okay."

Alex came around behind Kitty and slowly moved closer. Her floral scent hit him when he leaned his chest against her shoulders. He felt his legs get weak. He reached his left arm around her and took her hand. His voice cracked a little when he tried to give her instructions.

"Now let your hand go limp and let me shape it for you." Kitty complied as Alex positioned her fingers around the end of the cue stick. "Now keep your hand just like that. Don't move it."

Kitty nodded.

Keeping his left hand wrapped around Kitty's, Alex reached over with his right hand and placed it over hers on the butt of the stick. Her hair brushed against his face, and the sweet, clean smell left him feeling lightheaded. He wondered what it would feel like to run his fingers through her auburn strands. Where her hair had parted, he could see the pale soft skin of her neck, and he wondered what it would taste like to kiss her there. He felt warm all over and could feel his body start to tremble. He needed to take this shot before he made a fool of himself.

"Ready?" he asked.

"Ready," Kitty answered softly.

He wondered if she was feeling what he was feeling. She seemed in no hurry to have him move away from her. He slowly, purposefully pulled back the stick, still keeping his left hand curled around Kitty's.

"Can you see how level I'm keeping the cue stick before the shot?"

"Uh-huh," she whispered.

"Are you ready?"

She nodded, her hair brushing against his face again. For those few seconds, his whole world was at peace.

Slam! The cue ball rocketed across the table, scattering several balls and knocking a striped one into the side pocket.

They stood motionless. Neither of them seemed willing to come apart. Finally, Alex relaxed his hands from hers and stepped back. Kitty set the stick down and turned toward him, her face only inches away and her brown eyes gazing into his.

"We did it," she said, touching both of his arms lightly.

"Yes we did." Alex rested his hands on her shoulders and noticed every detail of her face: her tiny nose, the faded freckle above her left cheek, and her thin lips, tastefully adorned with pale red lipstick. He felt his heart pounding and, strangely, thought of Poe's *Tell-Tale Heart*, wondering if Kitty could hear its thunderous beating. Everything in him wanted to kiss her, and he thought she felt the same. He tenderly brushed a strand of hair off her forehead. She closed her eyes. He leaned forward and hesitated. Her eyes were still closed. Moving his hand behind her neck, he pulled her gently to him. He felt the warmth of her breath and smelled the richness of her fragrance as his lips touched hers. They felt moist and inviting. He felt her hands wrap around his waist and draw him closer. After several seconds, he pulled his head away and looked at her. Her eyes were open, showing a tenderness that felt new, yet familiar. She began caressing his face.

"Happy birthday," she said softly.

"It's not till Sunday." Alex kissed her hand as it moved past his mouth.

"I know, silly, but I'm not gonna be here Sunday."

"I wish you were . . . ." Alex placed his hands on her waist and pulled her closer.

"Me, too . . ." She rested her head on his chest. "I was afraid you were never going to speak to me after I sent that letter."

"What letter?" Alex asked, kissing her forehead.

"The one I sent after Christmas, telling you to forget about Father Francis."

Alex remembered the letter and felt his passion drain from him. His hands slid from her waist, and he pulled away, suddenly feeling awkward.

"What's the matter, Alex? Did I say something wrong?"

"No . . . I . . . it's nothing . . . Can we sit down or something?"

They walked over to the sofa adjacent to the billiard table and seated themselves at opposite ends. Kitty's face showed anguish even though she seemed to be trying to project an air of calm. She sat erect, hands on her lap, her body angled toward Alex, waiting for him to speak.

Alex wriggled in his seat. He looked at Kitty, started to open his mouth and thought better of it. After squirming some more, he finally stood up and started pacing in front of the sofa, looking at the floor.

"You and I feel differently about Father Francis," he said. "Probably always will. When I got that letter from you, I'd just found out something else about the man that made me hate him even more. I know you don't like to hear this stuff. You like to think the best of people. I get that about you, Kitty. And most times I admire that. But not when it comes to him."

Kitty's expression turned from anguish to irritation. She sat quietly as long as she could.

"My roommate, Reed Wentworth . . . I told you about him in one of my letters . . . he had a sister, who turned out to be his mother. She got pregnant by Father Francis. And she ended up killing herself over it."

"That's very sad, if it's true."

"If it's true? I saw the suicide letter she wrote to Father

168

Francis."

"And how did you come by this letter if she sent it to the priest?"

"That's just it, she never sent it."

"She never sent it. Could it be she wrote it to blackmail Father Francis and never sent it because she chickened out?"

"But she killed herself . . ."

"Do you know that for a fact?"

Alex paused. "Well . . . no, but—"

"Alex, everything you are telling me now and in the past about Father Francis is based on presumptions. Your presumptions. Are you willing to ruin a priest's reputation and hurt all those people who trusted him because of your presumptions?"

Alex felt his face grow warm as his anger and frustration fomented. "Why are you always so willing to ignore reasonable evidence against this priest? Have you ever considered where there's smoke, there's fire?"

"Have you ever considered that your need to get revenge has affected your judgment? People can make things look and sound like whatever they want, Alex. But facts don't lie. And you don't have enough facts to convince me Father Francis is an evil man."

"My mother was pregnant, Kitty. With Father Francis's child. Is that evidence enough for you?"

Kitty's face and voice softened, but her resolve was unchanged. "I know your mother was pregnant, Alex. Dan overheard his father telling his mother about it. Mr. Wallace saw it on the autopsy report."

Alex felt himself go weak. "Who else did Dan tell?"

"Just me, as far as I know."

"And you're not convinced Father Francis got her pregnant?"

"Alex . . . did you know your mother was seeing someone at work?"

"What?"

"I heard my father talking to my mother about it. She hung around a lot with one of the night foreman. They took breaks together, ate dinner in the cafeteria together. My father said most of the people at the plant knew about the two of them. She never talked to you about him?"

Alex stared at Kitty, collecting his thoughts. "If she was so attached to this guy, why did she want us to move back to Boston with her parents? Did you know about that, Kitty?"

"No I didn't, Alex. And I don't know why she wanted to. I just know you can't blame her pregnancy on Father Francis until you know all the facts. I'm sorry."

Alex walked over to the window nearby and stood with his hands in his pockets, looking out at the woodlands. All he wanted right then was to run out and lose himself among the trees, and become invisible to the world.

Chapter 15

"Father Kaseman, bring me the drawings for St. Cecelia's." Father Francis's voice boomed through the intercom on his assistant's desk.

"Yes, Father, right away." When he walked into his boss's office, Father Kaseman lost his hold on one of the four rolls of schematics in his arms. While struggling to prevent the roll from dropping, he lost his balance, and all four drawings tumbled to the floor. The young priest dropped to his knees, scrambling to collect the drawings, while Father Francis stood behind his desk, arms crossed, glaring down at the man.

"I just got off the phone with the architect," Father Francis said. "He informed me that he delivered these drawings to you yesterday."

"Yes, Father. He did."

"I thought I made it clear to you that you were to bring them to me as soon as they arrived, so I had sufficient time to review them before the committee meeting this afternoon."

"You did, Father. Unfortunately, right after the architect left, I received a call from the Central Permitting Office. They were responding to your questions about impact fees. By the time I got off the phone with them, I forgot about the drawings. I'm sorry."

"Father Kaseman, you are aware that this is just the first of five building projects I will be managing over the next five years. The projects will continue to increase in complexity as we progress. I do hope you are up to the task—"

"Hello! Hello! Anybody here?" A woman's voice crackled through the intercom on Father Francis's desk.

"What is that?" Father Francis snapped.

Picking himself off the floor with drawings in hand, the younger priest responded: "It sounds like a woman's voice."

"I am aware it is a woman's voice. Why is it coming through my intercom?"

"I think my talk button must be sticking, Father."

"See that it's fixed. And find out who she is."

"Yes, Father." The young priest left the office, turned right, and walked thirty feet—past the ladies' room, past the drinking fountain and men's room—straight to his desk. Before he released the malfunctioning button on his intercom, Father Kaseman greeted the woman, who introduced herself as Mrs. Thornton from St. Andrew's. She said she was here to see Father Francis.

"I'm afraid Father Francis is not available," he said as he leaned over and released the talk button. Within seconds, he heard the voice of his boss, a voice dramatically transformed from the one he heard just minutes ago.

"Father Kaseman, would you be so kind to show Mrs. Thornton to my office. I always have a few minutes to spare for an old friend."

Chapter 16

Alex walked into his dorm room at Drexler Academy and set his suitcase and duffle bag on top of his bed. He was glad to be back, glad to have summer behind him. He hadn't heard anything from Kitty since her visit in June, except a short, formal thank-you note. Though written in her handwriting, the words seemed more like her mother's.

June 30, 1963

Dear Alex,

Thank you for your warm hospitality during our recent visit. Our tour of Woodland Hills was the highlight of our trip to Boston. Please extend our sincere appreciation to Mr. and Mrs. Davidson for opening their home to us. We are deeply grateful to our host, Mr. Chester, for his enjoyable tour of the estate. His warmth and kindness made us feel right at home.
Sincerely,
Kitty McAlister

P.S. Thank you for the drawing.

He had mailed Reed's sketch to her after she left, with a short explanation that he was sending it on behalf of the artist. After all that happened during Kitty's visit, he forgot to give it to her. About her visit itself, he forgot nothing.

For days he replayed every word, every touch, every smell in his mind. The tumult of his emotions confused him. One minute he was imagining the thrill of his first kiss with Kitty, feeling the same tingling sensations again rising up from within. The next minute he was seething with anger at the thought of the priest and of Kitty's relentless defense of the man. If not for the distraction of his internship with Councilman Roberts, the summer of '63 would likely have been remembered as the summer Alex Spencer almost lost his mind.

The internship was a welcome diversion, even though it proved to be less exciting than Alex had anticipated. His duties were limited primarily to answering phones and stuffing envelopes. Other than accompanying Roberts to a ribbon-cutting ceremony and a public hearing to discuss paving St. Gregory's parking lot, he spent little time with the new councilman. Still, Alex's superiors commended his work and reminded him he was playing an important part in the political process. That was enough to satisfy him.

He started unpacking his suitcase, moving his clothes into his dresser. Reed's side of the room remained the same as he left it almost three months ago, except the walls had received a fresh coat of paint, the standard institutional off-white flat. Alex was eager to get off to a better start with Reed this school year. He was hoping they could move beyond the hurt he had inflicted upon their relationship before summer break. He wanted to make good on his promise to Brother Paul to make things right with Reed, to be a friend to him. His hope was that summer break made his roommate receptive to patching things up.

Two light raps on the door reigned in Alex's meandering thoughts. He closed the dresser drawer and said in a raised voice, "It's open, Reed." There was no response. "Well one thing's for sure, he learned some manners over the summer," he said to himself as he walked over to open the door. "I said it's open, Reed—"

Standing before him was a pimple-faced, red-haired boy dressed in a white shirt and plaid slacks and wearing Coke-bottle glasses with thick black frames resting halfway down the bridge of his freckled nose. With his left index finger he pushed his glasses up and smiled, revealing a gap between his front teeth wide enough to slide a pencil through, or so Alex thought. He stuck out his right hand.

"Eugene Knoll's the name. I guess you and I are roommates." He sniffed when he finished talking.

For a moment, Alex was speechless. Then he said, "You

must have the wrong dorm. I already have a roommate."

The boy looked down at a three by five card in his hand and responded, "Your name Alex? Alex Spencer?" *Sniff.*

"Yeah."

"This room number 120?" *Sniff.*

"Yeah, but—"

The boy held the notecard in front of Alex's face. "Says right here, this is where I belong." *Sniff.*

"Well, I think there's been a mistake. A guy by the name of Reed Wentworth is supposed to be in here." Alex looked down at the blue Oriental carpetbag sitting next to the boy's foot. "You can come in for now, but I wouldn't bother unpacking until I get to the bottom of this." He pulled open the door, and Eugene reached down with both hands and lugged his bag into the room.

Alex walked down to the administration office, wondering if maybe Reed had requested a different dorm room. He couldn't really blame him if he did.

"Mr. Wentworth withdrew Reed from the school over the summer," the clerk said. "It says here Eugene Knoll is your roommate this year."

"Do you know what school Reed transferred to?"

"I'm sorry. That information was not provided." The woman was looking past Alex at the line of students forming behind him. "If that's all, I need to help the next student."

Alex started to turn away, then looked back at the woman. "Wouldn't you need to know where he transferred to, so you could send his school records?"

"That's correct, but as I said, that information was not provided."

"Thank you, ma'am." Alex turned and shuffled back to his dorm room. His mind was struggling to calculate what his roommate's last move was. It seemed likely that he confronted Mr. and Mrs. Wentworth over the summer. Something obviously upset the apple cart. The Wentworths wouldn't have pulled Reed from a prestigious school like Drexler without placing him in a more prominent one. Not when appearances were so important to the family. And they would have been sure the administration at Drexler knew of the upgrade and had Reed's records sent accordingly. And yet, none of that seemingly happened. The Wentworths certainly wouldn't have allowed him to quit school. What would people say about the heir apparent being a high-school dropout? In Alex's mind that left only one option: Reed ran away from home. And only God and Reed knew why and where.

Alex entered his dorm room to find his new roommate on his hands and knees, tape measure and pencil in hand, drawing a line on the floor.

"What are you doing?" Alex asked.

Eugene looked up, pushing the bridge of his glasses with his finger. "Did you know there is exactly 225 square feet of space in this room? That means we each get 112.5 square feet. Since I'm the new guy, I decided to give you 113 square feet and me 112. But you don't have to thank me. This line represents the border. Robert Frost, my favorite poet, says fences make good neighbors. I figure this line can be our fence. You live over there; I live over here." *Sniff.*

Alex felt a sudden urge to pretend Eugene's head was a soccerball and give it a swift kick. Instead, he walked over to his own bed, lay down, and pulled the pillow over his head. His hopes for the new school year were fading rapidly.

§

"How was your summer, Alex?" Brother Paul asked when he spotted Alex sitting at a table in Walker Hall.

"It was . . . memorable, Brother Paul."

"Memorable? That's not a response I usually hear." The teacher set his books on the table but continued standing. "How did things work out between you and Reed Wentworth?"

"They didn't. We ended the school year on a sour note. I was looking forward to getting a fresh start with him this year, but turns out he's not coming to Drexler anymore."

"I heard that news from Mr. Pearson. He called Mr. Wentworth after hearing he withdrew his son."

"Does he know why Mr. Wentworth did that?"

"Mr. Wentworth said it was for personal reasons. He assured Mr. Pearson it had nothing to do with Drexler Academy."

"Did he say where Reed would be going to school?"

"According to Mr. Pearson, he was evasive on that point, too. But Reed is sixteen; by law he doesn't have to attend school anymore."

Alex hadn't thought about that. It opened the slim possibility that Reed was still living at home, just not going to school. But then he remembered the rage and disgust Mr. Wentworth displayed the day of the attic fire. There was no way he would tolerate that lifestyle from Reed. "I'm concerned he may have run away, Brother Paul."

"So am I, Alex. Did he ever talk to you about doing something like that?"

"No . . . not that I can remember."

"There's no telling where he could be." The teacher picked up his books from the table and cradled them in his right arm. He furrowed his brow and patted Alex's shoulder. "The best thing we can do for Reed now is to keep him in our prayers."

Alex nodded.

§

Other than having to put up with Eugene Knoll's eccentricities, Alex enjoyed a freshman year that passed uneventfully. Until November 22, 1963.

If he remembered the summer of '63 as the time he came close to losing his sanity, Alex remembered that Friday in November as the day he and his country lost their innocence. The principal's announcement over the intercom was seared in his memory.

"May I have your attention, please? We just received word

that President Kennedy was shot and killed in Dallas, Texas."

Shot and killed. The words swirled in Alex's head while he slogged down to Walker Hall to catch the news coverage on television. His thoughts drifted back to the first time he shot a gun with Reed, and how he pictured himself shooting Father Francis instead of the target. "Imagine it's your worst enemy," Reed had said. Is that what this assassin was thinking when he pulled the trigger? Was the president truly his worst enemy? He wondered how Doris and Jack were reacting to the news. He wondered if deep down they were relieved, knowing the Kennedys' chances of destroying the country were greatly diminished now. He wondered what the world of politics would be like by the time it was his turn. And he wondered if he would still run as a Republican.

§

Easter break was one of Alex's favorite times of the school year. It usually meant that milder weather had arrived and the gardens at Woodland Hills were coming to life again. He had grown to appreciate his walks around the estate, especially his jaunts to the bridge near the waterfalls. Like it was to his mother, the bridge had become his place of escape when he needed to be alone with his thoughts. Fifteen minutes earlier, he had returned from a late afternoon stroll when Jack snagged him walking by the billiard room and invited him in for a game of pool.

"How'd you like to go on a little business trip with me?" Jack asked, chalking the tip of his cue stick. Alex had just missed a shot and was walking over to the bar to grab his drink.

"Where to, Jack?" He took a sip of iced tea, squinting to adjust to the light of the Tiffany lamps overhead.

"New York City. Looking to expand the law firm's regional boundaries. I've done well in Massachusetts, but the real money is in the Big Apple." Jack leaned over the table and took his shot, knocking a ball into the corner pocket. "Meeting with some people in Manhattan next Friday to discuss the possibilities."

"I've never been to New York City. Will we have time to see any sites?"

"We'll fly in late Thursday afternoon, get a bite to eat, and take in a show. Been itching to see this new musical, *Hello Dolly*." Jack took his second shot and failed to pocket a ball. "Friday morning's yours to explore all you want. Fly home that afternoon."

"Flying . . . I've never done that before."

"Better get used to it. One day it'll be more affordable than a train. Then everybody'll be flying. Mark my words."

"Is Doris going with us?"

"Doris? On an airplane? She'd sooner vote Democrat. No, just you and me. Get to look at the stewardesses all I want without Doris elbowing my side. Feel chipper just thinking about it."

§

Jack and Alex walked out to the tarmac at General Edward Lawrence Logan Airport and climbed the stairs to the awaiting TWA flight to New York. A smiling blonde stewardess wearing a blue pillbox hat and matching jacket and skirt greeted them at the cabin door and showed them to their seats in the front. The other passengers, mostly dour-faced businessmen puffing on their tobacco of choice, followed closely behind, newspapers and briefcases in hand.

Alex, sitting in the window seat, watched in awe as the plane lifted off the runway and all of Boston shrunk below him. When the plane leveled off, he looked out on clouds that resembled soft billows of cotton, and he had an almost irresistible urge to jump into them and roll around like a child. He turned to comment on the clouds to Jack and noticed the man's face was pale, and his hands were gripping the arm rests.

"Always glad when the takeoff's over," Jack said, loosening his grip and trying to maintain his dignity.

"How many times have you flown before, Jack?"

"About a half dozen flights. Love flying. Hate takeoffs,

though."

The stewardess came by and offered Jack a menu. Waving it off, he said, "Scotch and water for me, heavy on the Scotch. A Coke for the young man."

It was a small thing, but Alex noticed. Jack referred to him as "the young man." He wondered if it was a slip, or was Jack starting to see him differently now. In just over two months he would turn fifteen. He started shaving six months ago when he noticed a few whiskers popping through his peach fuzz. And his voice already sounded as deep as his father's, at least as he remembered it. Maybe this trip to New York was Jack's equivalent of a bar mitzvah, his secular celebration of Alex reaching manhood. Alex smiled, discovered the button to recline his seat, and stretched out his manly frame to its full five-foot-five-inch length.

The wheels of the Boeing 707 touched down at Idlewild Airport exactly thirty minutes after takeoff. Alex spotted the Statue of Liberty as the plane circled the runway, and he remembered one of Mr. Pearson's history lessons, the one about the flood of immigrants who passed the statue on their way to Ellis Island at the turn of the century. Seeing the statue changed Alex's view of history—from a collection of dry facts to a palpable reality.

Jack hailed a taxi outside the airport, and within a half-hour, he and Alex were checking in at the Waldorf-Astoria. After dinner at the hotel, they grabbed a cab to St. James Theater to watch the play. With Jack there was no down time. He approached everything in life as a mission to be accomplished. As soon as he checked one thing off his list, he immediately moved to the next. He lived fully aware that his time on earth was finite, and he expected to make the most of every second allotted him. It surprised Alex, then, that Jack insisted they walk the mile back to the hotel.

It was an unusually mild evening for early April in New York, and the sidewalks were full of people of all ages, ambling about. Jack had been thoroughly pleased with the musical and was showing an unusually agreeable disposition. Alex decided it was a good time to discuss his future.

"Jack, do you mind if I ask you a question?"

"Depends on what it is."

"Well, when I first came to Woodland Hills, you told me I was going to become a lawyer. You even implied I'd be working for your firm one day."

"Go on . . ."

"Doris thinks I should go into politics."

"So what's your question?"

"Doris says law is my springboard into politics. But I don't get why I have to go through all that schooling if I'm going to be a politician."

Jack continued to look straight ahead, but Alex could see his countenance had taken on the look of a trial attorney.

"Still haven't asked a question. Just told me what you think. First of all, you don't *have* to go through all that schooling, you *get* to go. And it'll be Harvard for you—college and law school—just like it was for me. Secondly, Doris and I think differently about politics as a career. She was unique to have a long run in Washington with Congressman Walters. Most times, that city chews people up and spits them out every few years. It's called democracy. And what's the average schmuck going to do when the voters kick him out on his rump? If he's smart, he's going to parlay his small investment of time in public service into a lucrative and lasting career in the private sector. The people who do this best are the lawyers. Been doing it for decades."

"What if I want to have a long career in politics like Doris?"

"It's not a question of what *you* want, young man. It's a question of what the fickle voter wants."

The sign for the hotel was visible now, and they walked the last block in silence. The doorman opened the door when they approached the front entry. After they stepped inside Jack pulled out his wallet and gave Alex a twenty-dollar bill.

"Heading into the bar for a nightcap. You'll probably be asleep when I get back to the room. Won't have time to talk in the morning. Use this to see the city tomorrow. Be back here no later than one. Any questions about getting around," Jack tipped his head toward the concierge, "ask him."

"Thanks, Jack."

§

"Good morning, sir. Marcel at your service." The smiling doorman opened the door for Alex when he approached from the lobby.

"Morning to you, Marcel. Thank you." He stepped outside into the shadows of skyscrapers, which looked like behemoths of glass and steel, standing shoulder to shoulder and shredding the sunlight into slivers of gold. The chorus of jack hammers, car horns, and pedestrian chatter made him feel alive and free. One of the greatest cities in the world was open to him, and he had twenty dollars to burn. It just didn't get much better than this.

He strolled over to a newsstand nearby and perused the wide assortment of tawdry tabloids and dignified dailies, all screaming for the attention and resources of passing readers. Amidst the clutter of print and paper, two words on an unassuming gazette, shoved to the side on the second shelf, grabbed Alex's attention: *YO-YO ARTIST*. He picked up the paper, a community weekly called *The Village Herald*, and started reading.

"Dat'll be ten cents, pal," the newsstand vendor said. Alex looked up, then reached into his pants pocket and pulled out the $20 bill. "Ya gotta be kiddin' me. Dat da smallest ya got?" Alex reached into his jacket pocket and felt something metallic. He pulled out a quarter and handed it to the vendor. "I'll keep da change for da trouble," the vendor said, flipping the coin in the air. Alex started to say something, then shook his head and walked away.

Walking past a few store fronts, he found a bench and sat

down. He turned the paper up and read the story:

YO-YO ARTIST ATTRACTS CROWDS IN EAST VILLAGE

A street artist who goes only by the name of Row has been captivating residents and tourists in East Village with his unique blend of talent. Using colored chalk, Row recreates the works of master artists on the sidewalks of St. Mark's Place. Once a work is completed, he stands next to it, performing expert tricks on a Duncan yo-yo to draw the attention of people walking by. He is quickly becoming one of the highlight attractions among the street artists in East Village. (Picture on page 2.)

Alex quickly turned the page and found a small picture of the artist named Row. He was standing next to a sidewalk chalk drawing and performing what looked like Rock the Cradle on his yo-yo. The artist had a full beard and thin black hair that almost reached his shoulders. A cigarette dangled from the side of his mouth.

How many other people can draw with chalks like that and do fancy tricks with a yo-yo? Could that be who I think it is?

He strained his eyes to make out the details of the chalk drawing. Something about it looked familiar. There were onlookers in the newspaper picture, leaning over the drawing and blocking portions of the lower half. But he could see what looked like outstretched hands above the viewers' heads. Below the hands was something golden, but most of it was obstructed by the onlookers. He wished he had a magnifying glass. *I wonder if the concierge can find me one.* He stood, rolled up the paper, and stuffed it into his pocket, then headed back to the hotel.

After securing a reading glass, Alex unrolled the newspaper on a table in the lobby and began examining the picture. The beard covered too much of the artist's face to identify any familiar features, even with the magnification. But he noticed something in the chalk drawing that made him gasp. The hands were shaped as if bestowing a blessing. And on the right ring finger was a bejeweled ring. He moved his eyes down the picture. Where there was a gap between two onlookers, he saw the letters *Sacr.* Alex slapped the table. "It's him! That's *The Last Sacrament.* Only Reed would know about that."

Alex gathered the paper and reading glass and hurried back to the concierge. Handing him the glass, he asked, "Can you tell me how to get to St. Mark's Place in East Village?"

The man frowned. "East Village, sir? That's not a place for respectable people."

"I need to get there. I need to see this artist." Alex showed him the article in the paper.

The concierge shrugged his shoulders and handed Alex a subway map. He explained how to purchase a ticket and showed him how to find the station near the hotel. He circled his final stop on the map and told him to get off at First Avenue Station. Alex had the man change his twenty-dollar bill into two fives and ten singles and hurried to the Lexington Avenue station two blocks away.

§

Alex squinted when he came up out of First Avenue Station, adjusting his eyes to the sunlight. The sky was cloudless and there was a cool, gentle breeze now that he was away from the taller buildings. He walked down East Fourteenth Street to First Avenue and turned left. When he reached St. Mark's Place, he began to feel like he was in a foreign country. The names on the buildings could have come off the Ellis Island rosters. Italian-, Spanish-, Polish-, German-sounding names were plastered on the signage above the shops and restaurants. Equally strange and varied were the scents wafting out from these establishments. The conglomerate smells of spices, fried sausage, soaps, and sewage left Alex feeling queasy.

St. Mark's Place stretched for several blocks, but most of the action appeared centered near First Avenue. The sounds of poets reading and musicians strumming, beating, and singing created a carnival atmosphere on the street. Alex felt certain Reed would be close by. He walked east along the north side of the street, scanning the crowds for any sign of the man he saw in the picture. When he reached Avenue A, he crossed to the other side of St. Mark's Place and continued his search in the opposite direction.

"Hey, man, ya wanna buy some ganja?" A disheveled man with ragged clothes held out a plastic bag toward Alex and waved it in his face. Alex thought it was a type of pipe tobacco and wondered if Brother Paul would enjoy it. Remembering he was too young to buy tobacco products, he thought better of it and shook his head at the man. Looking ahead, he saw a small gathering of people—some squatting, some standing—all engrossed in watching a man drawing on the sidewalk. Alex felt his heart begin to race as he approached.

Standing behind a taller man in the crowd of onlookers, Alex periodically leaned to the side to look at the artist. He was sketching a basket of flowers on the sidewalk. A couple of young boys in the crowd started horsing around, and one of them lost his balance, bumping into the artist. The man turned his head, covered with long black hair, and snapped, "Hey Nimrod, watch it." His voice was unmistakable, and his eyes were gray.

Alex eased himself out from behind the tall spectator, and Reed saw him.

"Hey, kid! What're you doing here?"

Alex pulled the newspaper from his pocket and held it up. "Came to see the famous yo-yo artist—Row."

Reed shook his head. "Looks like you found him."

The crowd began to disperse when Reed started gathering his chalks and putting them in his case. When he was finished, he stood up and brushed his hands on his pants.

"I hope you're not mad at me for coming here, Reed. Can

we go somewhere and talk?"

Reed glanced around, looking uneasy. "Did anybody come with you?"

"No, just me. My grandfather brought me with him to New York on business. He's got a meeting this morning and told me I could see the city for a while." Alex patted his pocket. "He gave me a few bucks to spend. What do you say we get something to eat?"

Reed nodded and pointed to a small café. "They got pretty good grub in there."

§

Alex and Reed found an empty table in the rear of the restaurant and placed their order. Alex felt awkward and waited a few minutes to give Reed a chance to start the conversation, but he didn't say a word. Finally, Alex broke the silence.

"I didn't recognize you with that beard."

"That's the whole point. I don't want to be recognized."

"Has anyone come looking for you?"

"My grandparents haven't if that's what you mean. Didn't expect they would, not without pressure from the law."

"So why change your name and disguise yourself?"

"Because I'm a runaway who's not eighteen, and cops think it's their duty to bring people like me back home."

"Why the name Row?"

"Reed Oliver Wentworth. My initials." Reed picked up the copy of *The Village Herald* Alex had set on the table. "They never asked me if they could take this picture or write the story about me. Journalists are scumbags."

The waitress brought the food and two Cokes to the table and left the check with Alex. Reed devoured both halves of his tuna on rye and guzzled all his soda, then wiped his mouth on the sleeve of his jacket, which also served to partially muffle a short but tremulous burp. Alex, who hadn't finished the first half of his ham and cheese sandwich, looked on in surprise.

"So, why'd you leave, Reed?"

Reed held up his empty glass and said, "Sorta tough to talk when my mouth is dry."

Alex signaled the waitress, who came over and refilled both glasses. Reed took a gulp and set the glass down, running his finger along the Coca Cola etching.

"A short time after I got home for summer break, I confronted my parents—or grandparents, whoever they are—and showed them the letter. They denied Carolyn was my mother. Said she was a sick woman; delusional is the word they used. I asked how she died. They both looked uncomfortable with the question. Said as far as they were concerned, she was dead. But they didn't know for sure. Said she took off shortly after I was born. I asked why she left. They just looked at each other. Then the old man said he figured she was jealous now that there was a son in the family. Didn't add up, y'know?"

Alex nodded while chewing his sandwich. Reed chugged the rest of his soda, then continued.

"The old man said he hired a private investigator. Took the guy a couple years, but he traced her to East Village. That was about fifteen years ago. They never asked her to come back and never tracked her after that."

"So, you came here to find your sister?"

"No, I came here to find my mother."

"But your parents said—"

"I don't care what they said. They're lying. Look at my eyes, Spencer. You said it yourself: who has gray eyes in my family? Even that priest we met said I looked like Father Francis. I want to find my mother; find the truth."

Alex took one last sip of his drink. He wiped his face with a napkin and set the napkin on his plate.

"I take it you haven't had any luck finding Carolyn."

"Not yet."

"Where you living?"

"A cold-water tenement a few blocks from here. Share it

with ten other guys."

"Runaways?"

"Some."

"You able to make it on the money from your sidewalk art?"

"I get by."

"What do you do in the winter?"

Reed looked away and mumbled, "Whatever it takes."

Alex reached into his pocket and pulled out his cash. He took two singles for the lunch bill and another single for his trip back to the hotel. The rest he set on the table in front of Reed.

"What's this for?" Reed asked.

"Consider it my investment in one of the highlight attractions in East Village."

"I owe ya, kid."

"You don't owe me anything, Reed. But I hope you keep in touch and let me know if you find Carolyn."

Reed stood, picked up the money, and stuffed it into his coat pocket. He picked up his chalk case from the floor and rested it on the table. "You know that priest started all this. Father Francis. He ruins people's lives and goes on his merry way . . ."

Alex nodded, then stood and pushed his chair in. "I think we've both got a score to settle with him."

Reed's face took on a cold, sinister expression. "Well, if I get to him first, there won't be anything left for you to settle."

Alex felt chilled by the implication of Reed's words. He rolled up the newspaper in his right hand. He felt awkward and wasn't sure how to say goodbye. He stood there tapping the paper against the palm of his left hand, looking at the table. Finally, he said, "Good seeing you, Reed."

"Likewise, kid."

Alex tapped Reed on the arm with the paper, turned, and walked away.

On the subway ride back to the hotel, Alex kept replaying Reed's comments about Father Francis in his mind. Though he was surprised at the intensity of Reed's hate for the priest, he derived an element of pleasure from knowing that someone else despised the man as much as he did.

He wondered what he would say to Jack if he asked where he went. He hoped the concierge didn't say anything about him going to East Village. He needed to have a good story, so he didn't give anything away about Reed's whereabouts. If Jack asked him how he spent his money, he would tell him the truth: he bought a paper, rode the subway, bought some lunch, and gave the rest to a poor man. He smiled when he imagined Jack shaking his head and saying, "You're starting to act just like a Democrat." Maybe that wasn't so bad anymore.

PART 2

Chapter 17

"How much longer, Thomas? Can you tell me that? How much longer will Bishop O'Keane prolong his decision?"

"Patience, Michael, patience. All good things come to those who wait." Father Vincenzo looked around the restaurant. "Including our dinner, I hope."

"Save your platitudes for the likes of my assistant. He lives on such banalities."

"Come now, Michael, Father Kaseman has served you well these years. And having him in the diocesan office has certainly kept his grandfather happy. When Patrick McGarry is happy, his financial support keeps flowing. These are not trivial things."

Father Francis took a sip of wine and dripped some on the white tablecloth, fueling his frustration. Dabbing the spill with his napkin, he said, "Eight and a half years. Has it occurred to you that it has been eight and a half years since I started working as episcopal vicar? And if Father Kaseman has done any good during those years, it is because of my influence over him."

"Always taking the credit."

"As I should, when it is due. Need I remind you that I completed the building projects assigned me, on schedule and under budget? The new grammar schools I built are thriving at nearly full enrollment. And with only one year before registration begins for St. Vincent College, the bishop has still not appointed its chancellor."

"You do remember that technically the appointment must be made by the Board of Trustees?"

"Oh, save your breath, Thomas. We both know that the Board will honor the bishop's wishes for this appointment. And I cannot for the life of me understand what is taking him so long to make a decision."

"Ah, finally." Father Vincenzo saw the waiter approaching with their food.

"My apologies, gentlemen," the waiter said. "We have a table of sports celebrities dining with us this evening who've been getting a lot of attention from our patrons. Unfortunately, it has disrupted our serving process." He removed a bottle of wine from his tray and set it in front of the priests. "This bottle of Merlot is compliments of the manager for any inconvenience the wait has caused you."

"That is very kind," Father Vincenzo said, lifting the bottle and looking at its label. The waiter placed the food on the table, and the priest inhaled deeply and sighed. "This reminds me of the fine meal your housekeeper at St. Andrew's made for us that day I visited. What was her name?"

"Miss Windom," Father Francis said. "May she rest in peace."

"Oh my, when did she pass?"

"Last fall, shortly before Thanksgiving. From what I understand, she had a heart attack. I was unable to attend the funeral because I was out of the country at the time on another one of Bishop O'Keane's fact-finding missions."

"That is sad news, indeed." Father Vincenzo gave a nod of thanks to the waiter, who was leaving, and then lifted his glass. "To Miss Windom: may the fragrance of her culinary delicacies fill the atmosphere of her heavenly abode."

Father Francis raised his glass and shook his head. "Your gift for waxing poetic never ceases to fascinate me."

Father Vincenzo smiled and began cutting his food.

"I wonder if you took note of something our waiter mentioned," Father Francis said.

"To what are you referring?"

"The fact that they have a table of visiting sports celebrities who have attracted the notice of the patrons, to the point it has disrupted the workflow."

Father Vincenzo took a bite of food and looked at the priest for clarification.

"The quickest way to put St. Vincent College on the roadmap," Father Francis said, "is to attract and enroll the best athletes we can get. Back when you and I were in school, what was the first thing people thought of when they heard the name Thomas Aquinas High School? You smile, Thomas, but you know it was football. We were one of the best in Boston. And what do you think of when you hear Notre Dame University? Fighting Irish football. I want people to hear the name St. Vincent College and think Crusaders football, or Crusaders basketball, or Crusaders baseball. Nothing will increase public awareness of our school and increase its coffers better than a winning sport's team."

"I haven't seen you this animated since we were teenagers. Perhaps Bishop O'Keane would be better served by making you head coach."

"You and I both know that would be beneath me."

"Are you certain that being chancellor of the college isn't beneath you, Michael? Perhaps Bishop O'Keane should just step aside altogether and relinquish his role to you."

"In due time, Thomas. You did say all good things come to those who wait."

Chapter 18

Jack leaned his head back and blew a cloud of cigar smoke toward the ceiling of the library. "A shame Doris won't let me smoke these anywhere else in the house. Hates the smell of them. Says they remind her too much of fat cat politicians." Jack snickered. "What other kind are there? Sure I can't interest you in one? You've earned it."

"No thanks, Jack," Alex said. "No offense, but they never appealed to me either."

"Suit yourself." Jack took another puff and exhaled. "Got a Harvard College degree now. How's it feel?"

"I guess it hasn't really sunk in yet, especially since I have another three years of law school ahead of me."

"Three years. That's nothing. Fly by before you know it."

"I hope so. I'm anxious to make something of my life."

Jack leaned over and tapped his cigar on the ash tray. He grabbed his glass of Scotch and water and leaned back in his chair. "Doris won't tell you herself, but she's mighty proud of you, Alex. You've come a long way since you came to live with us. When was it . . . eight years ago, or so? Wanted the same for your mother, but . . . well, that's water under the bridge. Important thing is you did it. Commend you for that." Jack lifted his glass in salute and took a sip.

"Thanks, Jack. That means a lot to me. I wish my mother and father were alive to see it." Alex paused and took a sip of coffee. "I sometimes forget what they looked like, how they sounded. I wonder if I'll eventually lose them from my memory all together."

"You won't. Life has a way of reminding you. Sometimes when you least expect it. Something you see, something you hear, something you smell. Just like that, you'll remember."

Alex was sitting with his legs crossed. He reached forward and grabbed his ankle and stared at the floor, thinking.

"If our New York office continues to grow like it is," Jack said, "there'll be a place for you there when you're finished with law school."

Alex looked up. "Why not the Boston office?"

"Need young blood in New York. New money requires fresh ideas. Boston's old money. Probably get bored here."

"And what about politics? You know that's where my heart is."

"You'll know when the time is right to throw your hat into the ring. Just hope you'll know when it's time to pick it up and walk away."

"Jack, I appreciate everything you and Doris have done for me. The new car for graduation. Drexler and Harvard. Woodland Hills. You didn't have to take me in when Mother died, but you did. I'm grateful."

Jack stood and lifted his glass, again, in salute. Alex noticed that his grandfather's eyes looked moist before he turned away to look out the window.

Alex stood, took another sip of coffee, and set the mug down. "Think I'll take a walk over to the falls before it gets dark."

Jack lifted his hand in acknowledgement and continued facing the window. As Alex turned, he saw Jack's reflection. He was wiping his eye.

§

Alex could hear the familiar sound of the falls as he approached the rustic bridge. Several afternoons of heavy rain at Woodland Hills had swelled the stream to the top of its banks, accelerating its lazy flow to a torrent of water slapping and sloshing its way over the falls. He sat down on the bench where he had carved his name. His etching was as weathered now as his parents' initials. While he watched the water rushing beneath the slats of the bridge, he thought about the years that had passed.

Suddenly the stream became for him a metaphor of time and of life. Some days pass untroubled, void of disruptions, allowing the steady rhythms of life to play their pleasant and peaceful tunes. Other days are met with storms, some mild, some so severe they jostle you and hurtle you uncontrollably toward an abyss where you drop with gut-wrenching speed to a depth never before plumbed, not knowing if you will smash against the rocks or splash into a new reservoir that promises an altered life with unfamiliar rhythms but the same placid tunes in a different key.

He considered himself fortunate that his life had brought him to Woodland Hills, although he realized he had never lived here long enough to discover its rhythms. Much of the last eight and a half years, he was away at either Drexler or Harvard. During most summers, he spent a month in Europe with Jack and Doris. The remaining weeks he was busy acquiring a political education: from 1963–1967, in the office of Councilman Roberts, and in subsequent years, in the office of Senator Roberts. Steven Roberts had handily won his election to the Massachusetts state legislature in the fall of 1967 and continued to mentor Alex in the ways of government.

With his acceptance at Harvard Law School, Alex would finally have a chance to experience Woodland Hills as home. Having grown weary of dorm life and of roommates who wandered in at all hours, drunk, stoned, or both, he had asked Jack and Doris if he could live on the estate and drive the half-hour commute each way to school. He shied away from the political activism rampant on the campus and the trust-fund brats who failed to appreciate the opportunities life had given them. Sometimes, he wondered if he was too old for his age.

Kitty had told him that once, years ago. She said it teasingly after she found a single, wiry gray hair sprouting among his brown wavy locks when he was thirteen. He remembered it hurting when she pulled it, but he enjoyed feeling her fingers in his hair. That seemed like another lifetime.

They had lost touch after her visit to Woodland Hills, though she always remembered to send him a Christmas card—the generic kind that usually had a religious sentiment, and often included a photo of her. She always signed the card simply "Kitty." He almost reciprocated one year, actually bought her a Christmas card. But he labored so much over how she would interpret his actions that he finally ripped it up and threw it away.

He had no serious relationships with any girls throughout his years at Harvard. There were certainly plenty of girls he found attractive, but when he measured them against Kitty, he found them wanting. After taking relentless ribbing from his Harvard friends about his ineptness with the opposite sex, he decided to attend a party one Friday night and pick up the first girl who seemed interested. He drank three beers that evening. As unconditioned as he was to alcohol, it might as well have been a keg.

Though much of his memory of the night is clouded, he will forever remember the attempted kiss.

She was a Radcliffe girl, slender with short blonde hair and an alluring smile. He wished he could remember her name. She really didn't deserve what happened to her that night.

Alex noticed she had been eyeing him since he arrived. By his second beer, he found the confidence to approach her. She looked even better up close. Her eyes were almond shaped, giving her an exotic look. Her teeth were flawless and her lips were full and sexy. She wore a loose-fitting white blouse that hung down past her waist and a skin-tight leather skirt that stopped halfway between her waist and her knees.

The music was deafening, so Alex motioned for her to go outside with him, so they could talk. She smiled and followed while he chugged his last beer of the evening. Once outside, Alex's head was spinning. The girl was leaning against a tree, looking very provocative as she drew her finger across her lips. Alex took her hands, wrapped them around his waist and leaned forward to kiss her.

That's when he felt it.

A sudden gurgling deep in his stomach was working its way up. Before he could stop it, the remains of half-digested pizza pickled in ale erupted from his mouth and splattered all over the front of the girl. What happened after that remains a blur, but it was then he made the commitment to avoid any substance that took away his control.

Over the noise of the stream, Alex heard the sounds of twigs breaking and turned to see someone walking along the path toward the bridge.

"Oh, Master Alex. I'm so sorry. I thought you were in the library with Mr. Davidson." Howard stopped and began turning back.

"No, no, that's okay, Howard. Please, join me." Alex pointed to the empty bench on the opposite side of the bridge.

Howard stepped onto the bridge and sat down, resting his

hands on his knees. "I certainly don't want to intrude on your quiet time, sir."

"You're not intruding, Howard. I was just thinking about my life and how much it's changed since coming to Woodland Hills. I'm looking forward to getting to know the place better over the next three years."

"Well, I know Mr. and Mrs. Davidson are pleased that you have chosen to live here while finishing your law studies, sir."

"I figured Jack was. He even offered the full use of his library while I'm home. I wasn't sure about Doris, though. She's seemed more reserved than usual these few days I've been back."

Howard looked uncomfortable and diverted his attention toward the trees.

"What are you not telling me, Howard? I've seen that look before. You'd make a lousy poker player."

Howard folded his hands and rested his arms on his thighs. He began rocking his feet when he turned toward Alex. "I really should not say, sir. I can tell you that I overheard Mrs. Davidson telling her husband that it will be a great comfort to her having you nearby during this time."

Alex squinted. "During what time, Howard? Is something wrong with Doris that you're not telling me?"

"I really should not say, sir. I believe Mrs. Davidson plans to tell you herself."

Alex stood and began pacing the bridge, his mind thinking the worst. Death was present too often in his life. He had tricked himself into believing it had been appeased after the death of his mother. Was it time to brace himself for a fresh encounter? "Is she dying, Howard?"

"Not that I know of, sir." Howard stood and straightened his slacks and adjusted his jacket. "I'm sorry if I've caused you any concern, Master Alex. You do understand my need to respect Mrs. Davidson's wishes."

"Yes, of course. You're just doing your job. I'm sure Doris

will tell me when she's ready."

"If you will excuse me, sir. I should return to the house."

"Certainly, Howard. Thank you." Howard bowed slightly and walked away. Alex continued pacing the bridge, trying to force any fearful thoughts about Doris's condition out of his mind.

What filled the mental void was a sudden image of Reed Wentworth. It surprised Alex. He hadn't thought about him for some time. He had hoped his former roommate would have dropped him a line at some point, but he never did. Alex had kicked himself for not getting Reed's address when he saw him that summer in '63. But in all likelihood he had moved on. The life he had chosen was bound to be transient until he found Carolyn. If he found Carolyn. He remembered the look of hate on Reed's face when he talked about Father Francis. That's the look he was seeing in his mind's eye now.

Alex thought about his own feelings toward the priest. It had been relatively easy to suppress them over the last eight years. The sheer busyness of school life helped. But he was always aware they lingered just below the surface, ready to emerge at the sight of someone in a clerical collar or at the sound of church bells ringing. And he liked it that way. There were times he would purposely expose himself to such triggering mechanisms so he wouldn't forget. He told himself he was ripping the scab to keep the wound from healing. As long as he could still feel the pain, he knew he had it in him to exact revenge. And he was closer to that now than he had ever been.

§

The next morning Alex had breakfast with Doris on the patio. The sun was already warm peeking over the top of the trees, and the mist hovering above the grounds was beginning to dissipate. A hummingbird fluttered nearby, sucking nectar from the potted flowers on the patio. Doris was quiet and seemed preoccupied with her thoughts as she ate her ham and cheese omelet. Alex read the morning newspaper while he ate a bowl of oatmeal. He wished he hadn't prodded Howard about Doris's condition. Scant information was worse than none at all. He realized ignorance can be bliss. He struggled to conceal his anxiety by focusing his attention on the news of the day.

"Anything good in there this morning?" Doris asked, breaking her silence.

"It says that 500,000 people marched on the capital yesterday to protest the Vietnam War."

Doris shook her head. "That war is tearing this nation apart. We can thank Kennedy for getting us into that. I'm glad you didn't have to go."

"You can thank my asthma for that." Alex wanted to remind her that Eisenhower was the one who first got the country involved in Vietnam, but he thought better of it.

"Have you had any problems with your asthma lately?" Doris asked.

"Not really." Alex set the paper aside. He thought this would be a great time to segue to the topic of her health. "How have you been feeling, Doris? You haven't seemed your normal feisty self since I've been home."

Doris looked up; she had a serious look on her face. "I'm glad you brought that up. I went to the doctor for my annual physical last month, and they discovered a lump. The biopsy showed I have cancer. I'm scheduled to have a mastectomy."

"Does that mean they'll have to . . ." Alex placed his hand on his chest.

"Remove a breast? Yes. That's exactly what that means."

"When?"

"Next Thursday. I'll be in the hospital for about a week. The doctor tells me it will be two to three months before I'm back to feeling normal. Though I suppose it will be a different kind of normal than I'm accustomed to."

"So . . . this is not life threatening?"

"The doctor thinks he caught it soon enough, but he won't

know for certain until he operates."

Alex took a moment to process Doris's news. "Are you scared?"

Doris threw her shoulders back, took a deep breath, and exhaled with a nervous laugh. "I have stood up to some of the most cantankerous, contentious, stubborn, and self-absorbed politicians you would ever want to meet, and I never once flinched. I'm not about to cower over some six-letter disease. Besides, I need to stick around to see you get elected someday."

Alex nodded and smiled. He was relieved to see there was still fight in his grandmother. He felt certain if she could maintain her pugnacity, there was nothing she couldn't overcome.

Chapter 19

The brown 1970 Camaro took a right onto Oxford Street and another right into the parking lot, only a stone's throw from Langdell Hall and three hundred feet from the gates of Harvard College Yard. Alex was closer now to his destiny than to his past.

Dressed in a blue Oxford shirt, khaki slacks, and loafers, he grabbed his brief case and strolled into Langdell Hall for his first class on criminal law. The lecture hall was only half full, but he was early. The class didn't begin for another fifteen minutes. Walking to the center section, he found a seat in the middle of the fifth row—close enough to see the whites of his professor's eyes, but far enough away that he wasn't singled out.

He flipped the latches on his brief case, sitting on his lap, and lifted the top. Everything inside was neatly arranged: notebook on the left, hornbook and casebook on the right, pens and pencils poked inside leather loops in ordered fashion, and a package of breath mints stuffed inside a cloth pouch sewn into the lid. He pulled out the mints and popped one into his mouth, then started flipping through his hornbook to review the basic premises of criminal law.

"Mind if I sit here?" It was the voice of a young lady, and she sounded vaguely familiar.

Alex looked up and almost choked on his mint. "Uh . . . no, of course not," he sputtered, his face feeling like it was on fire.

"Looks like you're wearing the school's crimson colors today," she teased, patting her cheek. She sat down and extended her hand to Alex. "I'm Marcia Stillman."

Alex reached over and shook her hand. "Alex, Alex Spencer." He was hoping she might not remember his face. It had been at least three years . . . The room at the party that night was dimly lit . . . When they stepped outside it had been dark—

"I believe you and I met at a party once," she said. "You may remember; I was wearing an unusual designer outfit of cotton, leather, and puke."

Alex cringed. "I was hoping you wouldn't recognize me."

"Trust me, yours is a face I'll probably remember for the rest of my life." She laughed as she pulled her notebook from her bag.

"You're certainly being a good sport about it."

"It's been three years . . . and at least a year since I've stopped going to counseling for the trauma you caused me."

She had a playful smile that Alex liked. "Well that was my one and only drinking binge," he said. "I'm just sorry your memory of me is tainted by that moment of insanity."

She smiled. "Well maybe I'll give you a chance to redeem yourself, Alex Spencer."

Just then, Professor Stanley Pinkerton walked into the room, and all extraneous chatter faded to a few desperate whispers from those who realized they forgot to bring pen or paper. With his sullen face and dark attire, the professor looked more like a mortician. In fact, many of the students referred to him as The Undertaker, behind his back of course. Rumor had it when Pinkerton was a young attorney in Albany he had once advised Franklin Delano Roosevelt on some property matters. Upon see-

ing the dour young man, FDR told him a smile would do won-
ders for his business. Pinkerton looked up and replied to the future president, "My dear sir, I am a lawyer not a dentist."

Standing in front of his lectern, the professor looked out on
one hundred sets of eyes staring at him like hungry little birds
eager to swallow any morsel dropped into their open and waiting
beaks. Each student was poised, pen in hand, and ready to capture his every word. Shaking his head, the man began his dis-
course: "So you think you've got what it takes to become a
lawyer . . ."

§

"Can I buy you lunch, Marcia?" Alex asked while packing
his books into his briefcase after the lecture. "It's the least I can
do after . . . you know . . ."

Marcia smiled as she slung the strap of her book bag over
her shoulder. "As long as it's not pizza."

"I know a nice little French sandwich shop on Chauncy
Street. I can take us there."

"*Café des Amis*? I love that place." Marcia looked out the
window at the clear, sunny sky. "It's such a nice day. Let's
walk."

They stowed their books in Alex's trunk and strolled up
Massachusetts Avenue toward Chauncy Street. Alex initiated an
exchange of casual small talk: Where are you from? (She grew
up near Albany.) What brought you to Harvard? (It seemed the
logical choice after Radcliffe.) How do you like it? (It's everything she hoped it would be.)

Soon, Alex's angst subsided, and he was allowing himself to
relax next to Marcia. She was still as attractive as the night he
first met her. Her hair was a little longer, and she ran her fingers
through it whenever the breeze would tousle her thin blond
strands. Her style of clothing was more conservative now, and
he attributed that to entering the grown-up world of law school.

"What got you interested in studying law?" Alex asked. He

noticed her expression became more serious, and she used her hands when she talked.

"Because I don't like standing by watching bad people get away with things they shouldn't. I've got this silly notion that as an attorney I can play some small part in affecting justice in this crazy world." She looked at Alex and shrugged.

"Sounds like there's a story behind all that," Alex said.

"A story? Yeah, you might say that."

"I'd love to hear it."

"You might not feel that way afterward."

"Try me."

Marcia gazed at Alex for a moment. "Ten years ago, my sister and two-year old niece were murdered by my sister's husband. He was her high-school sweetheart. Everybody loved him. Happy-go-lucky Hank we called him. Until he started drinking. Shannon, my sister, got pregnant right after they got married. Once she had Emily, the pressures of family responsibilities started building on Hank, and he coped with the stress inside a bottle.

"After a while, we began to sense they were having their troubles. One time Shannon came over to the house with a big bruise near her eye. She just laughed it off saying she wasn't paying attention when she opened the refrigerator. A few months later, she had a broken arm. Supposedly tripped when she was walking down the stairs.

"My parents finally confronted her. That's when she broke down and told them what was going on. My parents tried to convince her to leave Hank, but she insisted she could work things out with him. When he broke her nose after a drinking binge, she decided she'd had enough. She and Emily moved back home with my parents, and my father helped her find an attorney to begin filing for divorce.

"My dad was concerned about what Hank would do once he knew Shannon was ending the marriage. He insisted the attorney obtain a restraining order before serving Hank. The jackleg failed to send the papers for the restraining order to the court clerk when he sent the petition for divorce. By the time the attorney realized his mistake, it was too late.

"Hank knew my parents always made it to my volleyball games. He sometimes went to watch them himself in earlier years. He waited until he knew we were out of the house, and then came to have it out with Shannon. We found out later from the police that she had called asking for help, saying her husband was outside the house, pounding on the door. Without a restraining order, though, they had no immediate need to respond.

"When we came home . . ." Marcia choked up and inhaled a few short faltering breaths before letting out a sigh. "Sorry. Still gets to me after all these years . . . When we came home, we found Shannon and Emily dead, strangled by the hands of the man who was supposed to protect them."

Marcia finished her story just as she and Alex reached the corner of Massachusetts and Chauncy, about a block from *Café des Amis*. She stopped and grabbed the pole of the street sign, balancing herself on one leg while bending the other behind her to adjust the strap on her sandal.

Alex stopped, clasped his hands behind his head and let out a long sigh. "I'm so sorry you had to go through all that."

After putting her foot back down, Marcia looked over and said, "And that is why I want to be a lawyer, Alex Spencer. Are you sorry you asked?"

"No, not at all. It's refreshing to find someone who shares the same passion for justice."

"Oh, it's more than a passion for me. It's an obsession."

Alex considered her response. "I've been accused of being obsessive, myself."

"Then it looks like I'm in good company."

"Still hungry?" Alex asked.

"Starving."

Alex crooked his arm and extended it to Marcia. "Shall we?"

Marcia grinned and locked her arm with his while they

strolled to the sandwich shop.

§

Café des Amis was buzzing with the afternoon lunch crowd, mostly older students and a few professors dining at a table near the bar, looking somewhat less scholarly with frothy mugs of ale in their hands. Alex and Marcia squeezed past a couple waiting for indoor seating and headed toward the patio in the rear. They saw some people getting up to leave from the table near the fountain and snagged it. After placing their orders, Marcia sat quietly for a moment, staring into the fountain and smiling.

"In all the times I've come here," she said, "I've never been able to get this table."

"I must be your lucky charm, then."

"I think you still have some proving to do in the charm department."

"I can see I'm going to have to work hard to erase that image of me from your mind."

Marcia played with the straw in her drink. "How come you came over to talk to me that night at the dance?"

"Well, I don't remember a whole lot about that evening, but I do remember you were staring at me from the time I came into the room."

"Guilty as charged."

"And you looked attractive, so I thought I would . . .well, hit on you."

"And you did, literally."

Alex hung his head, feigning shame. Looking up, he asked, "So why were you staring at me that night?"

"Honestly?"

"Yeah."

"Well, I thought you were cute. But mostly I wondered if it was your first time drinking. Drunk didn't look normal on you. And I was curious, sort of like when you're passing an accident; you can't help but slow down and look."

"I see. I was just a curiosity to you?"

"That's about it." Marcia said, chuckling.

The waiter brought their food and refilled their glasses with iced tea. Marcia dipped her spoon into her soup, brought it to her lips, and blew softly before sipping it. After taking a drink of iced tea, she looked at Alex. "So why did you decide to become a lawyer?"

"It was decided for me. My parents both died when I was young, and I moved in with my grandparents. Jack, my grandfather, runs his own law firm, Davidson and Associates, and insisted I study law."

"I've heard of that firm. Mostly corporate law, right?"

Alex nodded. "Funny thing is my grandmother wants me to go into politics. She worked for former Congressman Walters for twenty-five years."

"But what do you want to do, Alex?"

"I want to be in a position where I can influence good, where I can wield power over those who mistreat the little guy and helpless women and innocent children. For me, that place is in politics." Alex felt energized talking about it.

"I admire your goals," Marcia said. "My guess is you've got your own story, too."

"It's a long one."

Marcia looked at her watch. "My next class is not until three."

Alex took another sip of tea. He shifted in his seat and then began telling his story about Father Francis, about his mother, and about Kitty. Marcia listened attentively for the next fifteen minutes, sometimes leaning forward and asking questions to make sure she understood the facts. When Alex finished, he leaned back in his chair and looked at Marcia, trying to gauge her reaction. He wasn't expecting her first question.

"So, are you in love with Kitty?"

"In love? Where is that coming from? You heard me say how frustrated she is with me because of my feelings toward the priest."

"I heard your words, Alex, but I also heard your heart. It's important to you what Kitty thinks."

"Well, we've been friends since we were kids. I guess it is important to me what she thinks. But love?"

Marcia gazed pensively at the ice cube swirling in her glass as she moved her straw in a circular motion. After a moment, she looked up, smiling. "I think you'll make a great politician. The Democratic Party can use someone with your passion."

"Democratic Party, huh?"

"Well I can't imagine you would run as a Republican . . . Oh, wait a minute. Congressman Walters, corporate law . . . Your grandparents are Republicans, aren't they?"

"With a capital *R*."

Marcia rested her chin in her hand. "Hmm . . . Looks like I've got my work cut out for me."

"Think you can change me into a Democrat?"

"Oh, Alex. You already are one. You just don't know it yet."

§

If ever there was a model for consistency, it was Stanley Pinkerton. The immutable pedagogue came to class every day sporting a black suit, white shirt, and black bow tie. His leather Oxfords, also black, were always lustrously polished. On a clear, sunny day, if Professor Pinkerton moved just a few inches to the side of the podium, the sunlight pouring in through the east windows reflected off his shoes, giving the illusion his feet were afire.

Everyone knew that during the second week of Pinkerton's first-year criminal law class, the professor introduced the casebook method of study he would use throughout the semester. In anticipation, Alex and Marcia had their casebooks and notepads in front of them, pens in hand.

"*Stare Decisis*," Pinkerton began from behind his lectern, while one hundred hands began scribbling. "A Latin term meaning to stand by that which is decided. In the practice of law, it is the policy by which judges are generally obligated to adhere to a principle of law established by a previous ruling of the court. And they are generally obligated to apply that precedent to future cases that are substantially the same. A key word here, ladies and gentlemen, is *generally*. Precedents can be overturned, but not without much effort. And why is that?"

Hands went up throughout the room, but Pinkerton ignored them all. He stepped to the side of the podium, where the sun's rays hit his shoes and radiated a bright white glow near the floor. It looked as if his feet were touching holy ground. "It is because," he continued, "the major objectives of the legal system are predictability and stability."

Pinkerton stepped back behind the podium and looked around the room. "We meet here today in Langdell Hall. Does anyone know the contribution of this building's namesake?" Again, hands shot up around the room, and again, Pinkerton ignored them. "Christopher Langdell brought us the case method for studying law. This is the method we will be using in this class because it will teach you how to reason between facts and principles of the law. In short, it will teach you how to think like a lawyer."

The law professor spent the remainder of the class explaining the case method and reviewing the first three cases in the case book. When the class was dismissed, Alex had fifteen pages of notes, and his fingers felt numb. He shook his writing hand before closing his briefcase.

"Have you looked at case twenty-two in our casebook, Alex?" Marcia asked.

"Case twenty-two, are you kidding me? I read the first three for this class. You're already that far?"

"What can I say? I'm curious. Case twenty-two may interest you. It reminded me of the things you told me about that priest, Father Francis."

Alex's ears perked up. "Really . . . Care to talk about it over some lunch?"

Marcia gave Alex a sheepish look. "Yesterday I noticed some trees in Cambridge Common that were just starting to show their fall colors. I made a picnic lunch for us this morning, hoping I could talk you into going there. You wouldn't mind stretching out with me on a blanket under an elm tree, would you?"

"Marcia Stillman, am I seeing things, or are you batting your eyes at me?"

"I know you don't like hanging around undergrads. And I know the Common is full of them this time of day. I figured I'd need to work a little harder to sell you on the idea." Marcia's hands gyrated as she talked and came to rest with both hands on her cheeks. "Guess I need to work on my flirtation, huh?"

Alex grinned. "So who's bringing the blanket?"

Marcia smiled coyly and winked.

§

Alex spread Marcia's blanket under a tree near the Civil War monument, then sat down and watched as Marcia removed the contents of her picnic basket. They ate stretched out on their sides, facing each other, nibbling on baguettes and fresh fruit and vegetables. Alex began thumbing through his case book to find case twenty-two. Once he found it, he was silent for several minutes while he carefully studied the summary of *Commonwealth v. McNulty*. When he finished, he looked up at Marcia and shook his head.

"This is sort of eerie," he said. "Father Francis must have borrowed from this guy's playbook: same story, different names." He tapped the page of the book with his finger. "This jerk, Father McNulty, counseled women from his church and had sex with them during their counseling sessions. Big difference is one of these women had the courage to come forward. Accused McNulty of rape.

"Says here her attorney tried to make the case that 'the

priest's position of spiritual authority was equivalent to physical force in its ability to pressure the victim into having sex.' Of course the court acquitted him because the woman was old enough to consent, and because the law and precedent cases require that physical force be used to constitute rape. So, the priest is let off the hook and probably gets a cushy job in the bishop's office or some other church until the smoke clears." Alex slammed the book closed and rolled onto his back, staring up at the tree and fuming.

After a few minutes, Marcia stretched her arm just past the edge of the blanket to scoop up a handful of fallen leaves near his head. She lifted her hand over Alex and let the leaves fall a few at a time.

"What are you doing?" he asked, brushing the leaves from his face and chest.

"Trying to pull you out of your mood."

Alex rolled over onto his side. "It just infuriates me, Marcia. Since I was thirteen I've been carrying this animosity inside me. I thought when I got older, I could get revenge for the way Father Francis treated my mother and the other women at St. Andrew's. Thought I could balance the scales of justice. And then I look at this case about Father McNulty, and I feel like that helpless teenager again. What good is it to know the law if I can't use that knowledge to help others?" He picked up a few of the leaves around him and started rubbing them between his fingers. Without looking up at Marcia, he said, "I suppose you're thinking I have an unhealthy obsession with Father Francis and need to move on with my life."

Marcia sat up. "No, that's not what I was thinking at all. And I resent your presumption. I am not Kitty, Alex."

Alex looked up, astonished. He continued to rub the leaves between his fingers, more slowly now.

"And even if I did think that," Marcia continued, "why should that matter? Are your convictions so weak you'll change them just so you don't offend somebody? You've got every right to be angry over what that priest did to your mother and those other women. But you act as though you're unsure of what to do with that anger. So you complain about how helpless you feel, how unfair life is. You're only as helpless as you allow yourself to be, Alex.

"Anger can be a great motivator for change. Why would you want to lessen it when it can be the very thing that drives you to action? I'm angry at all the Hanks in the world who abuse women and children. I feed on that anger because it's what drives me to read ahead to case twenty-two when I only need to read to case three. It's what makes me want to be a great lawyer instead of a good lawyer.

"You're ready to throw in the towel because you think knowing the law is useless if you're bound to abide by precedent cases. You heard Pinkerton today. Precedents can be overturned with effort. I can pretty much guarantee you won't be able to do that being ignorant of the law. And how do you intend to legislate new laws as a politician if you're clueless about the legal process?

"You say you've been carrying animosity since you were thirteen. Big deal. All that tells me is you know how to hold a grudge. But if you tell me you've allowed that animosity to shape you so you're better equipped to handle adversity down the road, well then I'd say you're on to something. So far I hear a lot of spite, Alex, but I don't hear how you plan on making things right."

Alex sat up slowly and leaned back on his right arm, looking at Marcia, whose face was flushed and neck covered with faint red blotches.

"Ouch . . . that cut," Alex said.

"Would you have preferred a scratch instead?"

Alex tipped his head back and closed his eyes. "No, I think a scratch would've only irritated."

"Alex, you're an intelligent man, a compassionate man, but I'm not sure you've learned to be your own man."

He opened his eyes and looked at Marcia. "You're not going to sew up the first cut before you start the second?"

"It's all part of the same surgery."

Alex smiled weakly. "I see. And how do you suppose the patient will fare?"

"I think that's up to the patient."

Alex thought for a moment. There were other questions he wanted to ask her, but he was reluctant to steer the conversation. Her words had erupted as if they'd been stirring inside of her for days. He would much rather be sure she emptied herself of all of her concerns and misgivings now, once and for all. "Well, Dr. Stillman, you've given me a lot to think about today. Is there anything else you'd like to prescribe for your patient?"

A faint smile appeared on Marcia's face. "Just this." She leaned over and kissed Alex on the cheek. "My mother always mixed something sweet with my medicine. It made it go down easier."

§

"Thanks for taking the time to see me, Senator." Alex reached out his hand to Steven Roberts and shook it.

"Alex, it's always good to see you. Sit down. How's your grandmother recovering?"

"She's doing well, sir. Doctors didn't find any other cancer when they operated, so they've given her a clean bill of health. When I told her I was coming to see you, she insisted I tell you to make sure the governor is re-elected this November."

"Sounds like she's as spunky as ever," Roberts said, chuckling. "Tell her I'll do my best."

Alex leaned forward in his chair. "Senator, you've been my mentor since I first worked on your campaign for city councilman. I've watched you behind the scenes and in front of the cameras, and you've always seemed true to your beliefs. You've never wavered. I respect that about you."

"Thank you, Alex."

"Now that I'm studying law, I find myself wondering about what I believe. I want more than anything to serve in politics on a national level . . . but . . ."

"But what?"

"I'm not sure I want to run as a Republican."

Roberts smiled. "And you're wondering why I chose to run on the Republican ticket?"

"Yes, sir. I am."

Roberts tilted back in his chair and loosened his tie. "It may surprise you to know that most of my ancestors on the Roberts side, going as far back as the Civil War, were dyed-in-the-wool Democrats. My mother's family was all over the map politically, but she was a Republican through and through. She was a student of history and a staunch believer in the rights of individuals rather than the rights of groups. She believed in pulling herself up by her own bootstraps rather than relying on the government to help her out. And she resented my father's hard-earned tax money being used for social programs. Matilda Roberts was a bit unusual for the women of her time, but her influence left an indelible mark on me.

"I think you'll find, Alex, most people choose their political affiliation based on what their parents believe. Very few take the time to actually think through the political process: how it works and how it affects them. I think it's critical you're thinking about this now, before you enter politics. I'm sure you realize you'll have quite a battle on your hands with Jack and Doris if you run as a Democrat."

"I've thought about that, sir. Quite a bit, actually. I owe a lot to my grandparents. They've given me opportunities in life I never would have had without them. And though I respect them, I don't always agree with them. Jack's all about business. I'm inclined to think he's a Republican not because of the party's core values but because its policies are good for his law firm. Doris supports the party with almost a religious fervor. She believes the Republicans can do no wrong." Alex paused for a moment. "Do you think I'm just an idealist, Senator?"

"An idealist is someone who's unrealistic and impractical. I don't see you as that, Alex. If anything, I see you as someone who's not comfortable with any gray areas in his life. You see things as black and white, right and wrong. I'm afraid life, and especially politics, is not that way. Someone once said politics is the art of compromise. Compromise requires you to make concessions that may not exactly fall on your scale of what is right."

"So have I been wasting my time thinking I stand a chance in politics?"

"No, I don't think so. Study the lives of the politicians you most admire and see how they practiced compromise. And then decide which party affiliation will permit you to operate closest to your core beliefs. Both parties need honest people like you, Alex. But only you can decide which one is right for Alex Spencer."

Alex nodded slowly, thinking about the senator's words as he pushed himself up from the chair. "Thank you for your time, sir."

His mind seemed more muddled than ever. He came in hoping for answers but was leaving only with options and another sober assessment of his insufficiencies to add to Marcia's list. He was beginning to feel symptoms of the Peter Pan syndrome and wondered why he ever had to grow up.

§

Balancing the pizza box in one hand, he slipped the key in the lock and turned it. He knocked as he slowly pushed the door open with his shoulder. "Hello?"

"I'll be right out, Alex," Marcia shouted from her bedroom. "While you're waiting, take a look at that paper on the table."

For the two months he had known Marcia, Alex always felt uneasy walking into her apartment. She had given him a copy of her key, so he could have a quiet place to study near school. She shared the apartment with another law student, Mary Griswold, who was the sovereign of sloppiness. It wasn't that Mary was slothful. She carried a full load at school and worked at least twenty hours a week, waiting tables at a nearby Denny's. She argued that she just didn't have time to put things away. Alex tried to reason with Marcia that a cluttered apartment was the sign of a cluttered mind. Marcia countered that brilliant minds are too busy thinking elevated thoughts to waste time with things as mundane as cleaning and organizing. He concluded it was a topic best left alone.

The path from the entryway to the kitchen was strewn with clothing, shoes, and wrappers, and Alex felt like he was negotiating a mine field. He made it to the kitchen table where he found the one-page document lying next to a pair of lace panties. He plucked the underpants with his thumb and forefinger and set them aside, far enough so they weren't a distraction. For a moment he pondered why the panties would be on the kitchen table in the first place, but quickly pushed the thought from his mind.

The document looked like a case study copied from a microfiche machine. The heading said: *Commonwealth v. McNulty*. At first Alex was puzzled, thinking it was a copy of case twenty-two from his criminal law casebook. Further reading showed it was the same priest, but this time the charge was embezzlement. He was accused of misappropriating funds received for the purchase of burial plots in his church's cemetery. Over a three-year period, he spent over $3,000 of that money renovating a hunting lodge he inherited from his uncle. This time he was found guilty. Though not required to serve prison time, he had to make full restitution and was on probation for one year.

"What do you think?" Marcia walked up behind Alex and placed her hands on his shoulders. Alex tipped his head back to acknowledge her, and she kissed him on the forehead. He felt her damp hair brush against his face and breathed in her herbal after-shower fragrance.

"Where'd you find this?" he asked.

"I stumbled across it when I was doing some research in the

library the other day. The name *McNulty* jumped out at me when I was scanning the microfiche."

"Well at least he was convicted on this one."

"That's why I xeroxed it. Don't you see? This guy got off on the earlier rape charge. But eventually the law caught up with him, and he paid the price."

"Somehow I don't see how paying back the money he stole and being on probation for one year constitute paying the price for embezzlement *and* rape."

"Didn't you read the story I xeroxed on the other side?"

Alex turned the page over and saw a copy of an article from the Boston Globe. The story was about Father McNulty and his defrocking from the priesthood after his conviction for embezzlement. The article quoted the remorseful cleric as saying, "The only thing I know how to be is a priest. I've given thirty years of my life to my calling. I feel like a man without an identity, now."

A man without an identity. Alex pondered the words. He could think of no greater punishment for Father Francis than to strip him of his identity. His arrogance and hubris stemmed from his perception of himself as a spiritual leader above reproach and owing deference to know man unless it was expedient.

Alex slapped his hand on the table. "That's it!" He looked at Marcia, who jumped when he hit the table. "My focus has been all wrong. I've been so obsessed with wanting an eye for an eye that I overlooked other possibilities for nailing Father Francis. So maybe I don't have any hard evidence against him that proves his infidelity. But someone as pompous as him is bound to screw up somewhere else, just like this McNulty guy. I want to be the one who catches him when he does."

Marcia was sitting across from him now, opening the pizza box. "I had hoped those stories would help. Though I certainly didn't expect that strong of a reaction." She pulled out a slice of pizza, took a bite, and looked for a place to set it on the table. "There's way too much clutter here," she mumbled. She stretched her arm across the table and swept it to her left, brushing everything to the floor. Alex looked on in astonishment.

He reached over tentatively and pulled a slice from the box, brought it back and rested it in his hand.

Marcia laughed. "I remember a time when I thought I'd never want to be within a mile of you when you ate pizza."

Alex rolled his eyes. "You ever going to let that go?"

"What's the matter with you?"

"Nothing, it's just that you keep bringing up something I'm ashamed of and would rather put behind me."

"I'm . . . sorry?"

"You sound as if you're not sure that's the right thing to say."

"It's because I'm not sure if it's what you want to hear."

"Am I that difficult to understand?"

"Sometimes. Yes, sometimes you are."

Alex thought for a moment, then reached his hand over and placed it on top of hers. "I don't mean to be. I'm sorry."

"Thank you." Marcia placed her other hand on top of Alex's and began rubbing it gently. "You know, Mary's working an all-nighter tonight at Denny's. You could stay if you want . . ."

Alex rubbed his neck, his brow furrowed. "Marcia, we've talked about this before . . ."

This was the second time she had asked. If she had been Kitty, it would've taken every ounce of his strength and willpower to turn her down. But she wasn't Kitty. With Marcia, it was awkward but easier to say no. It's not that Marcia was unattractive. By all measures she was beautiful and provocative. Any man would have killed to get the invitation she was presenting. But Alex couldn't get past seeing her as a friend, a kindred spirit. Maybe over time they could become lovers. But would she wait that long?

"I know," Marcia said. "You don't want to worry Jack and Doris by not coming home. Am I ever going to get a chance to meet your illustrious grandparents?"

"As a matter of fact . . ." Alex reached into his back pocket, pulled out a crumpled envelope, and handed it to Marcia. "Excuse the wear and tear. I've been carrying it in my pocket for a few days and kept forgetting to give it to you."

Marcia ripped open the envelope and pulled out a red tri-fold card with a Christmas wreath in the upper corners of both flaps. The flaps opened to reveal a single white card inviting the recipient to the annual Christmas gala of Davidson and Associates Law Office on December 10, 1971, at the Parker House in Boston. Marcia tipped her head with a look of approval.

"I would be honored to accept, Mr. Spencer. Who else will be there besides your grandparents?"

"Attorneys and staff from the Boston office and some of its high-end clients. I want to warn you, though, most of them are Republicans. So you'll have to behave yourself."

"Oh, Alex. I'll be the model of decorum."

§

From a block away, the Parker House glimmered with elegance, its marquee illuminated with the colors of the season. Alex pulled up to the valet parking area, left the keys with the attendant, and walked around the car to open the door for Marcia. She looked stunning in her black and beige dress. The rhinestone trim of its heart-shaped velvet bodice accented her full and shapely bosom, and the glittering choker collar of the sheer long-sleeved top gave her a regal appearance. She stepped out of the car and pulled her cashmere shawl tight around her shoulders. Her layered silky skirt flowed to its full length, leaving just the tips of her resplendent silver pumps visible. She was a picture of style and grace, and Alex was pleased to have her by his side.

They passed through a set of bronze-plated doors and stepped into the expansive mahogany-paneled lobby where the concierge directed them to the Dickens Room.

"How exciting to think Charles Dickens stayed here when he

toured America," Marcia said as they walked toward their banquet room.

"I can't say I'm a big fan of Mr. Dickens," Alex replied.

"Not a fan of Dickens? How can you not like all those fanciful characters he brings to life in his stories? And his depictions of squalor in Victorian London are heart wrenching."

"I'm more interested in reading biographies—studying the lives of great people, how they thought, how they made decisions. Especially the lives of those who've been dead for a while. They've got nothing left to prove and can be judged accurately for what they did or didn't accomplish."

"Will people study your life someday, Alex?"

"I've never thought about that. Why do you ask?"

"Because I think you have the potential to live a life someone would want to read about. You're intelligent, compassionate, and darn good-looking in a tux." Marcia had a smirk on her face when she turned toward Alex and winked.

"Here it is: The Dickens Room," Alex said. He stopped and pulled open the door.

The sounds of big-band music, laughing, and chatter spilled out to the hallway but were quickly corralled when the door closed behind Alex. He stood, holding Marcia's hand and gazing around the banquet room at the hundred or so guests, all bedecked and bejeweled in the finest accouterments Boston could offer. He spotted Jack and Doris on the other side of the room and leaned over to tell Marcia he wanted to introduce her to his grandparents. Marcia took a deep breath and sighed.

"Let's do it," she said.

Jack spotted them walking over, and his eyes seemed to be assessing Marcia from head to toe. He looked up at Alex and gave a wink of approval.

"Jack, Doris, I'd like to introduce you to Marcia Stillman," Alex said.

Jack extended his hand. "Nice to meet you, Marcia."

Marcia gave Jack a firm handshake and smiled, saying what

an honor it was to be a guest at the law firm's party. Doris showed no inclination to shake hands with Marcia, but she did manage to muster a warm smile and greeting.

"Is this your first time at the Parker House?" Doris asked.

"Yes, ma'am, it is. And doesn't it have a rich history? I understand JFK announced his run for Congress here and proposed to Jackie in the main dining room."

Alex felt his heart skip when he looked at Doris. Though she maintained her smile, her expression changed from courteous to contemptuous in an instant. Alex took Marcia's arm and said, "How about we get ourselves something to drink?" Marcia looked puzzled, then smiled at Jack and Doris.

"It's a pleasure to meet you both," she said. Jack nodded and smirked. Doris just stared, her plastered smile beginning to crack and give way to a look of scorn.

On the way to the punch bowl Marcia asked, "What was that all about?"

"You brought up Kennedy."

"I simply mentioned he was part of the history of the hotel."

"Doris hates the Kennedys. I should've told you."

"Well she probably hates me, now, too. Are there any other quirks about your grandmother you want to tell me about before I make a total fool of myself?"

Alex was beginning to see a pattern whenever he was with Marcia. The first few minutes they were together, he was glad to see her, glad to touch her and hear her voice. After about a half-hour, sometimes less, he began to feel tense and anxious around her, defensive and uncomfortable. He looked at his watch. It had been twenty-five minutes since he picked her up. The pattern was holding steady.

"Which one of the punch bowls has alcohol?" Marcia asked the attendant, who pointed out the English Christmas Punch spiked with rum and red wine. "I'll have a glass of that, please. What about you, Alex?"

"Well, seeing I'm driving, I'll take the other, please. Be

careful of that stuff, Marcia. My grandfather has them mix it so it's pretty potent."

"I hardly think one little glass is going to do more than help me relax. I'm mortified that I offended your grandmother. You weren't kidding about them being staunch Republicans." Marcia took a sip of her punch and relaxed her shoulders after she swallowed. "Who's that tall old guy over there talking with the brunette?" she asked, pointing with her glass. "He looks familiar."

Alex stretched his neck to look. "Oh, that's Congressman Walters."

"The one your grandmother worked for?"

"Yep, that's the guy. He's one of Jack's biggest clients."

"Hmm . . . that's convenient."

"What's that supposed to mean?"

"Nothing, it just seems like a cozy little world, politics and business. You know, you scratch my back, I'll scratch yours."

"How's that different from any other relationships?"

Marcia looked astonished. "Is that how you see us and our relationship?"

"I didn't say that."

"But you implied that every relationship functions on the premise of what's in it for me."

"Maybe that's true, maybe it isn't . . ."

"Equivocating, Counselor?"

"Just trying to keep the peace."

Marcia held out her empty glass and grinned. "You can start by being a doll and getting me another glass of punch."

"And that'll keep the peace?"

"For now . . ."

Halfway through her third glass of punch, Marcia appeared much more relaxed. Holding Alex's right arm with both her hands, she nuzzled her head against his shoulder. "Aren't you gonna ask me to dance?" she asked. "They're playing a slow song."

Alex turned and bowed. "May I have the pleasure of this

dance, Miss Stillman?"

"Certainly, sir." She guzzled the remainder of her punch and set the glass down. Alex put his arm around her waist and walked her to the dance floor, relieved to have a respite from conversation. The band was playing an old ballad. He remembered the melody, but the words seemed more poignant with Marcia's arms snuggled closely around his neck and his thoughts as far from her as Kitty was from Boston.

Once there was a time
When life had not a care
The sky was always blue
And the breeze blew through her hair

Once there was a time
Her eyes looked into mine
Her lips were soft and warm
And her skin was pale and fine

Once there was a time
But that time was long ago

"What are you thinking about?" Marcia asked softly in his ear.

"Nothing much."

"Where'd you learn to dance so well?"

"Doris made me take dance lessons one summer when we were in Europe. Said it was necessary if I wanted to be cultured."

Marcia snuggled closer. "You know, Mary won't be home tonight . . ."

Alex's mind raced, searching for excuses. "Let's see how the night goes."

Marcia laid her head on Alex's chest until the end of the song.

"I thought that was you dancing. Hello, Alex."

"Senator Roberts, Mrs. Roberts. I didn't know you were going to be here." Alex shook hands with the couple.

"I think your grandmother invited me in appreciation for the governor getting re-elected. I guess she thinks I had something to do with his landslide victory. Who's your lovely dance partner?"

"This is Marcia Stillman. She and I are . . . classmates at Harvard."

Marcia smiled and greeted the senator and his wife. "I understand you've been a political mentor for Alex, Senator."

"I think Alex and I have learned from each other over the years."

Marcia plopped her hand on Alex's shoulder. "Maybe you could help me convince him he's more Democrat than Republican."

Roberts looked nervously at Alex, who was suddenly feeling sweat pouring from his armpits.

"Marcia has this crazy notion that I should become a Democrat," Alex said, trying to diffuse the conversation.

Marcia became indignant, her hands gyrating and voice beginning to slur as it escalated. "What do you mean 'crazy notion?' You're as anti-big business as I am. How many times have you said you want to help the underdog instead of some self-serving capitalist? That's what the Democrats do, not the Republicans. Am I right, Senator?"

By now, guests standing nearby were listening to Marcia's tirade and becoming incensed. Alex was wide-eyed with shock. "Senator, maybe you could help me escort Miss Stillman to my car. I think she's had a little too much to drink."

"I don't need any escort," Marcia argued. "And I only had two glasses of punch. Or was it three? I dunno . . . Why are we going to your car? The party just started."

"Because, I said so." Alex could feel himself beginning to tremble, but he was determined to maintain his composure. Senator Roberts assisted Alex with taking Marcia out to the valet pickup area.

"Do you want me to wait until the car comes around?" Roberts asked.

"That's not necessary. Thank you."

As he turned to leave, Roberts patted Alex on the shoulder and said quietly, "I'm beginning to understand more clearly the dilemma you talked to me about."

"I feel quite certain that dilemma was resolved tonight, sir."

Marcia slept for most of the ride back to her apartment. She leaned heavily on Alex once she got out of the car and began walking toward the building. Alex pulled out his key and unlocked the door. Flipping on the light switch, he stepped inside and walked Marcia back to her bedroom, tripping over the debris littering the floor along the way. He rolled back the sheets of Marcia's bed and helped her lay down. When he started to cover her, she mumbled something about Mary working the all-night shift. He kissed her on the forehead, turned, and walked out of the room. When he reached the front door, he pulled out the key from his pocket and hung it on the wall hook. He quietly opened the door, engaged the inside lock, and reached over to turn off the lights. After glancing back into the dark room, he stepped over the threshold, pulling the door closed behind him. Hearing the latch click, he lifted his head and sighed.

Chapter 20

All two hundred seats in the chapel at St. Vincent College were filled with students and dignitaries, and nearly two dozen additional guests stood along the back and side walls. It was a sweltering late summer day, and even with the windows and rear doors open, the room was oppressive. Those fortunate enough to hold programs listing the order of events were busy fanning them back and forth to find a whisper of relief in the stifling atmosphere.

Facing the wilting assembly was Bishop O'Keane, who was

concluding the celebration of the Mass of Blessing for the new college. After kissing the altar, he walked over to the bishop's chair and sat down. This was the cue for the new chancellor of the college to come forward and officially open the school.

Father Francis strode to the podium, hands folded reverently in front of him, his face beaming with pride. He had no notes to rely on, no poems, no stories, no scripted prayers. But from the time he opened his mouth until the time he finished thirty minutes later, he held his listeners spellbound, believing they were witnessing the dawning of an institution that would impact the Church and the world for eternity. He reminded them to not despise small beginnings. Though the college was starting with only one hundred students, he envisioned the day when St. Vincent College would become St. Vincent University, with thousands of students walking through its hallowed halls each year. The timing of his gestures, the variance of his intonations were flawless, and his words flowed like honey to the enraptured audience.

After concluding his final statement, the priest waited, slowly scanning the room. When he was certain his pregnant pause had reached its climax, he lifted his voice and said, "As Chancellor of St. Vincent College, I declare to you this day— Thursday, August 31, 1972—the doors of this school are now open." Applause erupted from the students and visitors, who, after the dismissal, quickly exited to get some fresh air. After thanking the bishop, Father Francis joined Father Vincenzo, who was waiting in the first row.

"Very impressive speech, Chancellor," Father Vincenzo said. "And what is more remarkable is that it was given extemporaneously."

"One does not need notes, Thomas, when he has been thinking about the same speech for nearly a year."

"You sounded like you believed every word of it."

"Because I do believe it. I am not one to go through the motions, as you well know. I intend to make this college second to none in this state. If I am still chancellor after that, I will strive to make it a university that attracts the most gifted students in this country."

"I have no doubt you will, Michael. You have done a remarkable job since you were appointed chancellor last year. I doubt if anyone else could have gotten this school up and running on such a tight schedule."

"The bishop does seem to enjoy working people under pressure."

"Speaking of pressure, how is Father Kaseman handling his responsibilities as director of administrations? I was rather surprised you insisted on hiring him for that position. Especially in light of your earlier frustrations with him."

"I admit Father Kaseman was not the most qualified for the job, but his years as my assistant showed me he is someone I can trust to ensure my directives are carried out."

"Of course it didn't hurt that his grandfather donated a hundred thousand dollars to the college athletic department after Father Kaseman was promoted."

"A pleasant coincidence, Thomas, I am sure."

§

"Father Kaseman, now that the college is up and running I would like us to look at what we will do to develop our football team." Father Francis tilted his desk chair back and folded his arms, watching the perplexed look on Father Kaseman's face.

"Isn't that something you should discuss with the athletic director, Father?"

"I have discussed it with Coach Hart, and he assures me he is doing everything he can with the players he has. But without more promising raw material to work with, he cannot deliver a winning team to me anytime in the foreseeable future. Of course, that is unacceptable."

"And what can I do to change that?"

"I am glad you asked, Father. Coach Hart tells me that we

were unable to enroll two all-star football players from one of our inner-city high schools because we could not help them find a way to pay for tuition."

"Yes, Father. I am aware of that."

"Are you also aware that the federal government has just passed the Higher Education Amendments, which makes more grant money available to colleges like St. Vincent?"

"Yes, Father."

"And are you aware that those two all-star football players are now using that grant money to attend another private college in the state?"

"Father, those young men didn't qualify for that grant money. I saw the numbers. I helped them complete their applications when they were interested in St. Vincent."

"I strongly suggest you learn how to complete these grant applications so our students do qualify, Father. Do I make myself clear?"

"What are you saying, Father?"

Father Francis slowly leaned forward, his cold penetrating eyes glaring at the priest. "I should not need to remind you of a certain agreement we made three years ago, Father Kaseman. I would hate to have to sully your reputation by making your private indiscretions known to your grandfather and the bishop's office. Your grandfather has donated a substantial amount of money to help us establish our athletic department. I would like you to do your part in assuring his investment was not in vain. "

"I understand perfectly, Father."

Chapter 21

Alex felt the case slamming his thigh with each thrust of his leg. Sweat was soaking his undershirt—under the arms, across the shoulders, in the small of his back. His heart was pounding its way up to his throat. His chest felt tight, lungs constricting, breathing difficult. It wouldn't be too much longer now. People were a blur in his peripheral vision. He was amazed he hadn't clipped anyone yet. His focus was forward, watching the signs. *Almost there*. For a split second he focused on a clock on the wall. *One minute to six*. He increased his stride when he saw the sign for Gate 17. The gate attendant was turning to close the door to the jet bridge, and Alex shouted, "Wait!"

"I'm sorry sir," the attendant said. "The cabin door is already closed. You'll have to re-schedule your flight."

Breathless, Alex looked at his watch. "But . . . I had . . . ten more seconds . . ."

"Sorry, sir. We have another flight to New York City leaving at seven-thirty."

Alex re-scheduled for the next flight, the last of the evening, and looked for somewhere to get a cup of coffee and a bite to eat. The crowd had begun to thin, and he could hear the sound of his new Bostonian wingtips clicking on the floor. He looked down at his shoes and smiled. *You cost me my flight, but you sure do look nice.*

Howard had taken him to a shoe store in Cambridge on the way to the airport. Alex was determined he was going to begin his law career in New York with a new pair of leather heel shoes. Once in the store, he had trouble making up his mind. The floor was carpeted, so he couldn't judge the sounds of the shoes, only their comfort and appearance.

He was drawn to the wingtips for their classic styling. The salesman invited him to slip the shoes on and get acquainted with them, as if they were to become his new friends. It was love at first fitting. He asked if he could walk around the back storage room, so he could see how they felt walking on concrete, since he'd be treading city sidewalks frequently. When he heard the sound, the sale was clinched.

By the time Alex and Howard left the shoe store, rush-hour traffic was inching its way out of the city, eliminating any chance of making the six o'clock flight.

McGinnity's Pub looked like the typical airport watering hole, cramped and nondescript, but it was close to his gate, and Alex was exhausted. He found a small table with two chairs, set his briefcase on one and sat in the other. A waitress who looked like she was just finishing up a twelve-hour shift and had only one nerve left to fray shuffled over to Alex's table, coffee carafe in hand.

"Yeah?" she said.

"I'll take a cup of coffee and the turkey club, please."

"That it?"

"Yep, that'll do it."

The woman reached over, filled Alex's cup halfway, and shuffled off. Alex looked at the half-filled cup and wondered if the sandwich would come with one slice of bread or two. He took a sip of coffee and noticed a man sitting at the bar who'd been glancing his way while the waitress was taking his order. The man looked familiar. When he looked toward Alex again, it was as though he, too, was trying to remember. The man started to get up, then hesitated, and resumed sipping his drink. Then he reached into his pocket, pulled out a coin, and began flipping it. That's when Alex remembered.

Alex got up from the table and walked over to the bar. The man turned toward him.

"Dan Wallace?" Alex said.

"Alex Spencer?" the man responded as he stood up. Both men grinned and gave each other a bear hug.

"What are you doing in Boston?" Alex asked.

"Here on business."

"Can you join me at my table? Man, how many years has it been?"

Dan grabbed his drink and followed Alex.

"I wondered if that was you," Dan said, sitting down after Alex moved his briefcase. "Same wavy brown hair, just a bit of gray in there now."

"I could always count on you to keep me humble, Wally. So

you're here on business. What are you doing these days?"

"Working for GM. I got a job at the plant near Stonebridge after I finished community college. Came to Boston to get some management training at the plant in Framingham. Moving me up to a supervisor position back home." Dan beamed when he announced his promotion.

"That's great, Dan. Congratulations. Next thing you know, you'll find some lucky girl, get hitched, and start a family."

"Not hitched yet, but I found the girl, and we're engaged."

Alex reached over to shake Dan's hand. "Congratulations, again. Do I know the lucky girl?"

"You sure do. It's Kitty McAlister."

Alex couldn't have felt more dazed if Dan had knocked him on the head with a board. He tried to recover his composure, but he knew Dan noticed his reaction.

"You looked surprised," Dan said.

"Yeah, yeah, I guess I am. I just never pictured you and Kitty together. Not that that's bad, it's . . . I . . . I'm happy for you, Dan. For you both."

"When we were kids, I always thought you and Kitty would end up together."

Alex laughed nervously. "Me and Kitty? C'mon."

"No, I'm serious. You two were always doing things together. Even after you moved away, Kitty was always talking about you. Wondering what Alex would think about this or what Alex would think about that. It wasn't until after she and her mother visited you in Boston that she seemed to be able to forget about you. How many years ago was that?"

"Eleven. Or so . . . Have you set a date for the wedding?"

"If it was up to me, I'd say let's do it now and get it over with. But Mrs. McAlister wants her daughter to have a summer wedding, and she needs plenty of time to plan everything. You know how she is."

Alex nodded and rolled his eyes. "What does Kitty want?"

"Oh, she'll go along with her mother. Even though we've

been dating over a year, we've only been engaged for a couple of months, and I think she's still getting used to the idea of getting married. So what about you, Alex? I'm doing all the talking. Haven't asked what you've been up to."

"Keeping busy. Just finished law school and going to work at my grandfather's law office in New York. In fact, I'm flying there to find an apartment this weekend, providing I don't miss another flight."

"Sounds like you're doing all right for yourself. I'm sure it helps having grandparents with money."

Alex sensed that Dan felt insecure and was looking for some way to level the playing field between them. "I don't know where I'd be right now if it weren't for my grandparents," he said. "I owe a lot to them."

"So will there be a Mrs. Spencer any time soon?"

"Haven't had a lot of time for dating and all that. Well . . . there was a girl . . . We went to law school together. I thought she might be the one, but it turned out we were better as friends than we were as a couple. We stay in touch. She just recently got engaged, too. Man, Wally, I'm starting to feel old. I'm surprised Kitty didn't mention anything in her Christmas cards about you and her dating."

"Christmas cards?"

"Yeah, she sends me a card every Christmas. Been doing it for years."

Dan shifted in his chair. "I didn't know that."

"They're pretty generic, just a card and her picture. I figured I was part of some mass mailing she sends out for the holidays."

"That's news to me." Dan stared at his drink, tapping his fingers.

Alex tried to change the subject. "How are your parents doing? I still miss your mom's Sunday dinners."

Dan worked up a smile. "Mom and Dad are fine. Kitty and I go over every Sunday. You should stop in and visit them if you're ever in Stonebridge. I'm sure they'd love to see you."

"I'd like that."

Dan glanced at his watch and reached in his back pocket for his wallet. "I better start heading for my gate." He placed a tip on the table and stood up. "It was good seeing you, Alex."

"Great seeing you, too, Dan." Alex pushed himself up from the table. "I'm glad I missed my plane. Say hi to your parents for me. And please convey my best wishes to Kitty. I'm happy for you both."

The two men shook hands. After Dan left, Alex sat down and slumped in his chair. He reached for his coffee, took a sip, and spit it back into the cup. It was cold. He looked around for the waitress and realized he was no longer hungry. His appetite vanished along with his chances of ever having a future with Kitty. Why had he fostered this fantasy about Kitty all these years, the fantasy that one day all of his issues with Father Francis would be resolved, the fantasy that he and Kitty would then pick up where they left off when they were teenagers, the fantasy that he could actually be in control of his destiny?

After fumbling for his wallet in his jacket, he pulled out a five dollar bill and dropped it on the table. He started to put his wallet away but then thought about the harried waitress, wondering if the same hand of fate set the parameters for her life. He pulled out a ten dollar bill and laid it on top of the five. Slipping his wallet into his breast pocket, he grabbed his briefcase, and turned to leave when he saw the waitress shuffling toward him with his sandwich.

"Want this?" she asked, her eyes bloodshot, shoulders sagging.

"I want you to keep that for yourself. It's on me." He pointed to the cash on the table. The woman's pale face kept the same lifeless expression, but Alex noticed her shoulders lift.

"Thanks," she said.

Alex turned and started back to Gate 17. He was in no hurry this time.

§

Park Avenue seemed endless if one looked north from the steps of the office building housing the New York branch of Davidson and Associates. The building, located between East Forty-seventh and East Forty-eighth Streets, was also home to two of the firm's largest clients. Alex would be plying his newly acquired law skills to help protect the intellectual property of the smaller of the two—Dengler Publishers—a thriving mid-sized publishing house.

It was three in the afternoon, and Alex had just finished viewing his new office. He wanted to get a feel for the place on a Saturday when it was relatively empty. The last thing he needed on Monday morning was to look like a dumb newbie, especially when it would be common knowledge that he was the grandson of the owner.

Earlier in the morning, he had signed a six-month lease for an apartment, two blocks from the office. It was the first one he looked at—a furnished one-bedroom on the third floor of a five-story brownstone—and it was affordable. Like Jack, he didn't like prolonging a process. Why view ten different apartments if the first one met his requirements?

Jack insisted Alex was to live off his own income in New York. There would be no subsidies, and Alex was fine with that. He was ready to become his own man. But he was also beginning to realize that his starting salary, which seemed generous to him at first, was not going to stretch as far as he thought in the most expensive city in the country.

He stepped down onto the sidewalk and turned left. Towering in front of him was the Pan Am building. He could see a helicopter lifting from the roof and banking toward JFK. On the other side of the skyscraper lay his destination—Grand Central Station. From there he would pick up the subway to East Village and find the answer to a question that had plagued him for over a decade.

For a long time after his last meeting with Reed Wentworth, he felt guilty for not following Brother Paul's admonition to be a friend to Reed. But time and distance had a way of assuaging his conscience of much of that guilt. Now that he was back in the city, he couldn't seem to get Reed out of his mind. He didn't know if it was the old guilt re-surfacing or just curiosity. Whatever the motivation, he had to find out for himself if his former roommate was still in East Village and if he was still alive.

§

East Village was not as Alex remembered. St. Mark's Place, once the throbbing center of a flowering counterculture, looked more like a patient on life support, its vital signs barely visible. Everywhere Alex looked he saw vacant shops, their once colorful storefronts faded and peeling around shattered, disfigured windows. Gone were the artisans and musicians who skirted the sidewalks and filled the area with vitality. Replacing them were seedy characters, crouching in the shadows and offering a moment of ecstasy to those willing to part with a few greenbacks and their sanity.

Near the spot where Alex remembered seeing Reed drawing on the sidewalk was a small bookstore, still open. Alex walked in and was met by a leery stare from a woman sitting on a stool behind the counter, her long gray hair and wrinkled skin evincing a life hard lived. She had one hand on her lap and another underneath her faded floral shop apron, and she never moved as Alex approached.

"Good afternoon, ma'am," Alex said. The woman nodded. "I'm trying to find an old friend who lived here about eleven years ago. He was a street artist."

The woman sneered. "Lots of street artists come and gone in eleven years."

"This guy was different. He not only drew well with chalks, but he was exceptionally good at performing tricks on the yo-yo. Went by the name of Row."

The woman shook her head.

"Were you here in '63?" Alex asked.

"Been here since '57. Seen lots of artists and musicians. All thought they were something special. All gone."

"Where'd they go?"

"Some died, some went to California. Who knows where they all went."

"And you're sure you don't remember an artist who did tricks with a yo-yo?" Alex leaned forward and rested his hands on the counter. That's when he noticed the outline of a handgun underneath the apron.

"Said I don't remember. Means I don't remember."

Alex backed away from the counter slowly. "Well thank you anyway, ma'am. I appreciate your time." He turned to walk away and noticed a set of eyes peeking through from the other side of the bookshelf to his left. They seemed to follow him as he walked past. Once outside, he turned and looked through the barred front display window and saw an old woman of short stature in a drab gray dress, walking slowly toward the front door. Her head, covered with what looked like a linen doily, twisted from side to side as she walked, and she was wringing her hands. Alex waited for her at the foot of the entryway.

Outside in the daylight, the woman's features were more pronounced. Her faded blue hair was drawn up in a tight bun underneath the doily, pulling the skin of her temples upward and lending a demonic quality to her glazed and darting eyes. Liver spots dotted her pale, rutted face, and stubs of gray whiskers sprouted indiscriminately on her chin and above her upper lip. She looked at Alex with a malicious grin, revealing small, yellowed teeth spaced unevenly in a set of inflamed gums.

"You are looking for one called Row?" she asked Alex in a quavering voice, her eyes flitting from left to right.

"Yes, ma'am. Do you know him?"

"I might." She looked up and down the street. "But we mustn't talk here. They may hear us."

"Who will hear us?"

The woman put her finger to her lips and motioned Alex to

David Moore

follow her. She led him to the backdoor of a vacant shop facing southwest on St. Mark's Place. She walked up three steps, grabbed the door handle, and looked around before opening the door. With the creaking of the hinges, Alex could hear a light scurrying on the wooden floor of the room, and when he stepped inside behind the woman, he saw a long, thin tail disappear through a hole in the wall.

The room looked like it had been used as a kitchen during more prosperous times. Black cabinet bases, topped with faded red laminate, lined two walls. A chipped, free-standing porcelain sink, stained with rust, divided one set of cabinets underneath a window covered with soot and graffiti. In the middle of the room stood a small wooden table, cracked along a joint and scarred by the cuts of a sharp blade. Two chairs sat on each side of the table, and the haggard woman slid one out and sat down.

Alex found himself mimicking the woman, looking around before sitting down.

"Can you tell me now where I can find Row?" he asked.

"He's not here."

"I can see that. But I thought you brought me in here to tell me where I can find him."

"You're an impatient one . . . He moved away several years ago. To find a woman named Carolyn."

"Yes. That's his sister . . . or mother . . . Do you know where he went to find her?"

The woman looked around before continuing. "I moved to East Village from San Francisco in '67. Shortly after I was here, I noticed the street artist named Row who drew just like a woman I knew in Haight-Ashbury. Her name was Carolyn."

The woman tipped her head back and rolled her eyes, then glanced around the room and wrung her hands before continuing.

"I told Row all about Carolyn one day when I was watching him draw. He was convinced it was the Carolyn he was looking for, and within days he was gone. Gone."

236

The woman tipped her head back and rolled her eyes, again. Then she started snickering. When she brought her head forward, she put her finger to her lips. "Shh . . . Do you hear? They're coming."

Alex was feeling very uneasy and started to get up to leave.

"You mustn't go yet. I have a message for you. They have told me to tell you."

"Who are these people you keep talking about?"

"You don't know? They are all around us. Listening, watching, speaking. Give me your hands."

Alex figured he would play along, let this lunatic have her fun, and then hightail it out of there as soon as she was finished. He stretched his hands across the table. The woman started to take hold of them and then jumped back as though jolted by electricity. She pressed her hands against the sides of her head. A look of fear was on her face.

"The vengeance of man worketh not the righteousness of God," she cried.

She tipped her head back, again, and rolled her eyes, taking short, quick breaths. When she finished, she rested the backs of her hands on the table, her fingers moving as tentacles tickling the air. She glared into Alex's eyes and spoke a foreboding rhyme:

Like the wind, you have shaken a reed
To where blown only known by a marge
On hate for a father doth feed
Whose guilt will be laid to your charge

Alex jumped up from the table, knocking his chair over. As he turned and ran toward the door, the woman began screaming: "The day of vengeance is coming! The day of vengeance is coming! Ha-ha-ha-ha-ha!" He shoved open the door and stumbled down the stairs, her sinister laugh following closely behind him. Scrambling to his feet, Alex broke into a full run, determined he wouldn't stop until he reached First Avenue Station . . . or died.

§

The day of vengeance is coming! THE DAY OF VENGE-ANCE IS COMING! HA-HA-HA! Alex shot up in his bed, cold sweat soaking through his pajama top. It was the second night in a row he had dreamed about his visit to East Village. Each time he woke up, he hoped it was all just a nightmare.

But then he remembered it really happened.

Until Saturday afternoon, he had never experienced the macabre side of life, and he hoped he never would again. During almost every waking moment since his encounter with the crazed woman, Alex mulled over the lines of her ominous verse. Now that the dream had roused him to full consciousness, he lay in bed brooding, once again, over their full meaning.

Like the wind you have shaken a reed. He remembered a story from his childhood catechism class about a reed shaken in the wind. But the crazy woman altered the line to say he was the wind that had shaken Reed. How did she know Row's real name was Reed? Maybe he revealed it to the woman before he left for California. Or maybe she knew it supernaturally. And if she knew that supernaturally, what else did she know? And in what way did he shake Reed? By telling him about Father Francis? By keeping the suicide letter from Carolyn? Maybe.

To where blown only known by a marge. Alex had no clue what this line of the verse meant, and gave up trying to figure it out.

On hate for a father doth feed. Alex had no doubt that when he saw Reed last there was hate in his eyes for Father Francis. But that was eleven years ago. Had Reed allowed that hatred to foment all this time? Or had he found Carolyn and been able to bury his animosity toward the priest? Alex wondered if there was anything that could alter his own feelings toward Father Francis. Certainly Kitty had tried and failed. Marcia, on the other hand, had commended his righteous indignation. She knew it was not hate he felt but, rather, an insatiable drive to right a wrong. Yes, he had nurtured emotional wounds all this time, to remind himself an injustice had occurred and had to be rectified. But he didn't think himself capable of hatred.

Whose guilt will be laid to your charge. These words troubled him more than any of the other lines of the verse. Was he to believe that he would be held accountable for the hate in Reed's heart? How could he be responsible for choices Reed made? Aren't human beings free moral agents, liable for their own choices?

While Alex wrestled with these ethical conundrums, his alarm went off, signaling an end to his prospect of getting a good night's sleep before his first day on the job.

§

"Good morning, Alex. I've been looking forward to finally meeting you." Scott Decker, lead attorney for the New York office of Davidson and Associates, stepped out from behind his desk to shake Alex's hand. "Jack's been saying a lot of good things about you."

"Thank you, Mr. Decker. It's a pleasure to meet you, sir."

"Please, have a seat."

Alex set his briefcase on the floor, unbuttoned his jacket, and sat down in one of the two brown tweed upholstered chairs in the office. Decker continued to stand, leaning against his desk.

"I know Jack has already let you know you'll be assigned to our legal team representing Dengler Publishers. I'll introduce you shortly to the two attorneys you'll be working with: Kevin Littlejohn and Fred Stannos. Both are seasoned practitioners in the field of contract, trademark, and publishing law. Ruth Kowalski is the team's legal secretary.

"One of your first projects on the team is to assure Dengler that the new book they're publishing for Governor Bechtold is not going to come back to bite them with lawsuits for liable or copyright infringement. From what I understand, Bechtold doesn't pull any punches when he writes about some of the clowns he's worked with in New York State politics. He's nearing the end of his second term and doesn't plan on running again, so he's got nothing to lose, politically speaking that is. He also pulls from a lot of primary sources, so we need to verify the accuracy of what he's quoting and the context in which he's using it. You'll be getting some face time with the governor during this process. Jack tells me you two have already become acquainted."

"I don't know if acquainted is the right word. I met him when I was thirteen years old. I was with my grandparents, and we had dinner with him. I can't imagine he even remembers me."

"I wouldn't be too sure about that. When he heard Jack's grandson was coming to work at this office, he insisted you be part of the Dengler team. He's looking forward to seeing you."

Alex nodded at Decker and smiled. He wasn't sure why the governor would be looking forward to seeing him, but it pleased him to hear it. He relished the idea of talking with someone who had been in politics as long as Bechtold, someone who had attained his level of power and influence without losing his integrity along the way.

"Well, that's an overview of what you'll be doing, Alex. Any questions?"

"I'm sure I'll have a few for the team, but none that I can think of right now."

"Before I introduce you to Kevin and Fred, I need to make you aware of something. Kevin was pushing hard to get a friend of his hired for this position, a friend who has ten years of experience practicing law in the publishing field. When Kevin found out the team was getting the owner's grandson instead, and that you were fresh out of law school, he wasn't too pleased. I'm sure he'll continue to act like the professional he's always been. It just might take a little while for him to warm up to you."

"I understand, sir." Alex heard himself say the words, but in truth, he didn't understand. Why would Jack choose a rookie like him over an experienced professional? Was Jack becoming more sentimental than practical as he got older? Suddenly he felt the pressure to perform bearing down on him, the same oppressive weight he thought he shed when he left Harvard. He was beginning to understand that this pressure—like his three-piece suit, silk tie, and wingtips—was part of the attorney's attire, and he was expected to come to work every day fully dressed.

§

By the third mid-week meeting of the Dengler team, Alex was beginning to grasp his role and responsibilities more clearly. As the novice, his primary function was to perform the grunt work of securing permissions to use any published material quoted in the governor's book. Typically, this would have been Ruth's responsibility, but she was already overloaded with additional work from another secretary, who was out on leave. Alex found the work boring and monotonous, but he figured it was all part of paying his dues.

Eager to make a good impression on Kevin, Alex told him in his first team meeting that he was happy to do whatever the team needed. And Kevin was glad to oblige by assigning him any menial task he could find. Alex was expecting a new allotment of mundane activities when he entered the room for his third team meeting. He was pleasantly surprised to discover that the governor of New York had given him a reprieve.

When the whole team was in the meeting room, Kevin began: "Alex, you'll be going with Fred on Friday to meet with Governor Bechtold at the Roosevelt Hotel between eleven and noon. He's in town to address the Chamber of Commerce. We had some difficulty scheduling this hour with him, so let's make sure we make the most of it.

"This meeting is to review the accuracy of some statements the governor made in his book. Your job, Alex, is to listen, observe, and take notes. Fred will be responsible for directing the discussion. It's critical that we get this information, so Dengler can stay on target with their release date for the book.

"All right, let's move on to contracts in progress . . ."

§

Alex and Fred Stannos stepped out of the cab in front of the Roosevelt Hotel, walked through the revolving door, and climbed the steps into the expansive lobby decorated in 1920s elegance. They grabbed the first available elevator and began the slow ascent to the fifteenth floor.

"Remember, let me do the talking," Fred said. "I've been trying to meet with the governor for two weeks to validate these last three inflammatory statements in his manuscript. If we can't substantiate them today, our recommendation to the publisher will be to pull them from the book to avoid any libel suits."

"How many have you validated so far?" Alex asked.

"I've counted ten different statements that have the potential to be defamatory. I've validated seven of those statements as being factually accurate. Many of them were stated by others before the governor and never challenged. The last three instances appear to be the governor's opinions, unless he can provide me evidence that proves otherwise."

The elevator stopped on the eighth floor, and two men wearing matching light blue leisure suits with open-collared white shirts and white patent leather shoes stepped in and punched the button for the twelfth floor. They were carrying what looked like props for a sales demonstration. Fred looked at his watch.

"Might have been quicker to take the stairs," he grumbled.

When they finally reached the fifteenth floor, Fred and Alex stepped off the elevator and followed the room signs toward suite 1527. They approached the door to the suite, and noticed a tall man in a black suit standing guard at the door. He turned his head toward them and stared as they approached.

"We're here for an eleven o'clock meeting with Governor Bechtold. My name is Fred Stannos, and this is Alex Spencer. We're attorneys representing Dengler Publishing."

"Just a minute," the guard said. He cracked open the door enough to stick his head in, and spoke to someone sitting at a desk nearby. "Attorneys from the boss's publisher here." Within seconds the man opened the door fully and motioned Fred and Alex to come inside.

The two men stepped into the living room of a spacious suite set up like an office. A woman sat at a small desk by the door, typing. And two men in dark three-piece suits sat in green up-holstered easy chairs in the far corner of the room. They were puffing on cigars and reviewing paperwork spread out on a small table in front of them. One of the men looked up briefly and then knocked the ashes from his cigar into a brass spittoon on the floor between the chairs. Alex could hear a phone ringing in an-other room and the voice of a woman responding to the call. Without looking up from her typing, the secretary near the door said, "Please take a seat, gentlemen. The governor should be here shortly."

Fred looked at his watch, and Alex could see frustration on his face. The two sank into a well-worn couch located kitty-corner from the men in the easy chairs. And then they waited, listening to the tedious rhythm of clacking and ringing from the manual typewriter. Five minutes passed, and Fred began fidget-ing. Five minutes later he stood up and started pacing in front of the couch. Finally, at a quarter past eleven they heard some commotion out in the hallway. The secretary stopped typing, and the two men in the corner reached down simultaneously and stubbed out their cigars on the insides of the spittoon.

The door opened, and the booming voice of the governor filled the room.

"Gentlemen, gentlemen. I hope I haven't kept you waiting long." He strode over toward the couch where Fred was standing with his hand extended. The governor shook Fred's hand, but his eyes were on Alex, who was struggling to extract himself from the deeply creviced cushion. The governor laughed and reached out his hand. "Here, grab hold," he said, pulling Alex up to his feet. "This couch's been here since ol' Tom Dewey lost to Truman in '48." Looking over his shoulder toward the secretary at the door, he said, "Betty, tell that tight-wad manager if he wants the state to continue paying rent on this place, he's got to get me a new couch."

"Yes, sir," Betty responded mechanically.

The governor looked at Alex. "You must be Alex Spencer. All grown up since the last time I saw you. How're Jack and Doris doing?"

"They're doing well, sir."

"Good, good. Glad to hear it." The governor turned his head toward Fred. "You fellas here to talk about my book?"

"Yes, sir, there are a few—"

"Good, good. Follow me back to my office." The governor glanced over toward the two men sitting in the corner chairs. "You crockheads haven't been smoking cigars in here have you?"

The two men put on their best choir-boy faces and shook their heads. The governor grunted and started down the hallway. His office was at the end, just past the bathroom. He waved the two men to go into the office ahead of him. "I'll be right in boys. Gotta pee like a race horse."

Alex and Fred pulled two chairs over in front of the governor's desk and sat down. Fred looked nervously at his watch and twisted his arm to show Alex. It was 11:22. After a few minutes they heard the toilet flush and the sound of water running in the sink. A few seconds later the governor walked in smiling and zipping his fly. As he walked toward his desk he said, "How'd you like Drexler Academy, Alex? Helped Jack get you in there, if I recall." Fred glanced at Alex with a look that said *Keep it brief.*

"I liked it very much, sir. I appreciate your help with that." Alex glanced at Fred for his approval. Fred looked like he was about to say something to the governor to steer him toward the topic of his book.

"Drexler shaped me into the man I am today," the governor continued. He was tilted back in his chair now, feet up on his desk. "One of the finest schools in the country for preparing young men for public service. Far cry from what our public schools are turning out these days, I'm here to tell ya."

The governor paused and looked like he was remembering something. Fred sat up straight and opened one of the documents on his lap. "Gov—"

"Jack ever tell you about the time he and I strung up a Yale player on the Harvard flag pole?" the governor asked, chuckling.

Alex was stunned and curious. "No sir, I'm sure he hasn't." He glanced at Fred out of the corner of his eye and saw him hang his head.

"Well, it was the last game of the 1923 season. We were playing Yale at home. Jack and I paid some kid to go into the Yale locker room during the game to try to steal a uniform. The kid found a duffle bag sitting unattended on the locker room bench. It had everything in it—navy jersey and socks, gray pants, helmet and cleats. Probably belonged to an injured player, hoping he might get to suit up that night.

"Well, we whipped Yale big-time. To celebrate, Jack and I stuffed that uniform with hay, shoved the helmet on a pumpkin painted beige with red streaks for the head, and hoisted that sucker up the flagpole. Next morning when the president came strolling on campus, he saw this bloody-looking Yale player hanging on the flagpole and he passed out on the spot. When he came to he called the cops. He was madder than a hornet when he figured out he'd been pranked. Jack and I about wet ourselves laughing so hard. Yesirree, Bob!"

Alex couldn't help but smile, picturing Jack involved in something juvenile and fun. Fred kept looking at his watch the whole time the governor was telling his story. He looked like he was ready to pounce on the first opportunity to speak. The governor, still chuckling, glanced over at Fred.

"You look like you're wound tighter than a drum, Mr. . . . ."

"Stannos, sir. Fred Stannos. Governor Bechtold, if I don't get validation on these statements from your book," Fred held up the paperwork he brought, "then I'm afraid we'll have no choice but to recommend they be removed before publishing."

Governor Bechtold gave Fred a puzzled look. "Why didn't you say so?" He picked up the phone. "Betty, I'm sending Mr. Sandnose up front to talk to you. Give him the supporting documents he needs for the book, will ya?" The governor hung up the phone and looked at Fred. "Go on up front and Betty will fix you up with everything you need. She's the one who did all the background research for me. She'll be able to answer your questions better than I can."

Fred stood up, looking relieved. "Thank you, Governor Bechtold. We appreciate your time." He turned and motioned to Alex with his head to follow him from the room.

"Alex, why don't you and I chat a little longer while Mr. Samhose gets the information he needs from Betty."

"Stannos," Fred said.

"What's that?"

"Nothing, sir." Fred glared at Alex, then turned toward the governor and nodded. He closed the door gently as he left.

Governor Bechtold shook his head. "That boy needs to get him some looser fitting briefs. I've never seen a man so uptight."

Alex smiled. He was able to relax now that Fred was out of the room. And he was beginning to understand why Jack liked Frank Bechtold so much. The governor was a man who was comfortable in his own skin. Someone who was very easy to like.

"Jack tells me you want to get into politics someday."

"Yes, sir. I'd like to run for Congress."

"Congress, huh? Why not something at the state level?"

"With all due respect, sir, there's not enough power at the state level. Not to influence to the degree I want."

"So you want power? What're you going to do with it when you get it?"

"I want to help the little guy. The guy who feels like he's getting stepped on and abused and doesn't think he can do anything about it."

"Sounds a bit idealistic, don't you think?"

"Someone once told me that an idealist is someone who's unrealistic and impractical. I believe my goal of using power to help others is realistic. If I pass laws that expand rights for those who have none, I'm using power to help others. If I pass laws that help businesses grow and create more jobs, I'm using that power to help people who need jobs and businesses that want to prosper and grow."

"You talk like a Democrat one minute, a Republican the next. How old are you, son?"

"I'll be twenty-five on June thirtieth."

"End of this month, huh? Well, technically you'll be old enough to run then, but that doesn't mean you'll be ready."

"Do you think the voters would accept someone my age?"

"Hard to say. Right now with this Watergate fiasco going on, the only sure thing is that voters are going to run into the arms of the Democrats in droves. No telling how long it'll take Republicans to recover from this scandal."

Alex hesitated to ask his next question, but then threw caution to the wind. "What are my chances if I run as a Democrat?"

Bechtold didn't flinch. "If you mean your chances of winning, I'd say fifty-fifty. If you mean your chances of being killed by Doris once she found out, I'd say pretty good. No, you stick with the Republican Party, son. I think the winds of change are blowing, and the party is going to need fresh new ideas from young folks like you. If JFK did nothing else for this country, he whetted voters' appetite for youthful leaders."

The governor looked up at the clock on the wall and saw that it was noon. Sliding his feet off the desk he said, "Looks like it's about time for my next appointment, Alex. Let's take a walk up front and see if Mr. Stubnose got what he needed."

Chapter 22

By September, Alex had found his stride. He settled into a comfortable routine of waking at twenty after six each morning, making himself a cup of coffee or tea, and spending the first half-hour of the day reading, almost always a biography. By seven he was in the shower, and by seven-thirty he was dressed and out the door, briefcase in hand, strolling to Steve's Place—a small diner on East Forty-eighth Street—where he ordered his usual breakfast of two eggs (over easy), a slice of toast (lightly buttered), a small bowl of oatmeal (with a dash of brown sugar), and a medium glass of orange juice. Over breakfast he perused the Wall Street Journal and New York Times, focusing on the headlines and editorials. By eight-fifteen, he was on his way to the office, arriving precisely at eight twenty-five.

His evenings were no less predictable. At seven o'clock he packed his briefcase, took the elevator down to the lobby, strolled out the front doors, turned left along Park Avenue, another left on East Forty-seventh Street, and arrived at Gino's at ten after seven. His dinner selections varied but usually centered around three of the many Italian and American offerings listed on the menu. By eight-fifteen he was walking back to his apartment, a block and a half away, and arrived at eight-thirty. The remainder of his evening was spent reading or watching mindless TV on a small black and white set, which got terrible reception even with the upgraded rabbit ears.

For someone accustomed to having change thrust upon him, Alex appreciated the consistency of his new life. What he was increasingly aware of, though, was how lonely he had become. Up until now he had always been surrounded by other people. At Drexler he had Reed and a plethora of other students and teachers to keep him company. At Harvard College he had his dorm and fraternity buddies. At law school he had Marcia. For even though their romantic attachment ended, their friendship continued, and they spent countless hours together studying, debating, and theorizing about the intricacies of the legal system.

Now he spent ten hours a day, five days a week with a team of people he knew little about outside the realm of their legal expertise. Conversations, when they did occur, seldom broached topics more personal than Do you think the Yankees will make it to the Series this year? He needed a deeper level of human interaction, but wasn't sure how to find it.

On Saturdays he took long walks in Central Park, watching couples holding hands and parents playing with their kids. One time he tried to strike up a conversation with an attractive young woman sitting on a park bench. She looked to be in her mid-twenties and approachable, and she had no ring on her finger.

"Hi, mind if I sit here?" Alex said.

The woman forced a smile but continued looking straight ahead without speaking.

Alex sat down, leaving a comfortable distance between them. "I noticed you watching the kids playing. Sort of makes you wish you were that age again, doesn't it? Carefree, uninhibited . . ."

The woman smiled and nodded, continuing her gaze straight ahead.

"I grew up in a small town where life was slow and simple," Alex continued. "When I look at those kids it reminds me of those innocent times. No worries, no cares . . ."

The woman jumped up, pulled a gun from underneath her jacket, and shouted, "NYPD! Freeze!" She was pointing the gun at a man in a blue sweat suit who was kneeling down and rifling through a purse someone left unattended on a blanket. The man started to get up, like he was going to make a run for it, but then dropped to his knees and put his hands behind his head as the undercover cop approached. By the time the policewoman had the man cuffed, two uniformed officers rode up in a squad car to relieve her of her quarry. The woman cop came back to the bench to pick up her dummy purse, so she could move on to another observation point.

"Nice talking with you," she said to Alex as she grabbed the purse and turned to walk away. Alex gave her a pained smile. Once she was out of sight, he stood and began wending his way home, mentally crossing Central Park off his list of places to make acquaintances.

In subsequent weeks and months, he attended the theater and wandered through countless museums. Though the experiences entertained and enlightened, they did nothing to relieve the emptiness gnawing away on the inside. Beyond his desire for companionship, he needed the peace he experienced as a boy, sitting quietly alone in the sanctuary of St. Andrew's Church. The peace he felt when sitting by the waterfalls at Woodland Hills. One cool Sunday morning in December while he was out walking, and thinking about that peace again, he wondered if there was anywhere in this city called Gotham where he could find it.

And that's when he heard them.

They were faint at first, but the further north he went on Fifth Avenue, the more pronounced they became. Church bells. Pealing in several different octaves and calling the faithful to worship. For some reason the sound was not affecting him the way it had for years. It wasn't ripping at the scab of bitterness and resentment he had so diligently allowed to fester. Instead the sound of the bells was drawing him to follow. He continued walking and saw the twin Gothic spires of St. Patrick's Cathedral jutting into the cloudless azure sky. He followed a cluster of people through the front entrance and slid into an empty pew in the rear.

Alex sat with his eyes closed throughout much of the Mass. It was the first time he had stepped inside of a church since his mother died. So much was different. The sweeping changes approved by the Second Vatican Council were quickly apparent to him. Gone was the Latin liturgy he struggled to learn as an altar boy. The priest, who was now facing the people, was speaking in English. Alex listened intently. The words he used to recite by rote suddenly conveyed meaning.

When the Mass concluded, Alex remained seated until all but a few stragglers had gone. He looked around now and tried to absorb the beauty of his surroundings. The massive columns, the vaulted ceilings, and the oak seating reminded him of the reading room in Boston library, which he and Reed had visited so many years ago. But the similarities ended there.

Maybe it was the stained glass windows or maybe it was the linen-draped altar with the golden cross rising up from the center. Or maybe it was the amber hue from the lights suspended from the ceiling. Whatever it was, there was a splendor about this place, a majesty that hinted of God's presence. And to his wonderment, Alex no longer felt alone.

Chapter 23

The Dengler team of Davidson and Associates held its first meeting of the New Year on the sixth of January—one day before Alex's dreams began coming true. Kevin Littlejohn led the meeting and was reviewing the team's accomplishments for 1974. He stated that Dengler Publishing had released Governor Bechtold's book in mid-September, and it had proved to be as controversial as anticipated. To date, there had been no legal challenges to the validity of his statements, no accusations of libel. The team had proved its worth to the publisher.

Littlejohn had begun discussing the strategy for the team's upcoming projects when the office receptionist peeked her head inside the door.

"Governor Bechtold's office is on line four," she said.

"I'll take it in my office, Jenny," Littlejohn said, starting to get up.

"Uh . . . they asked to speak with Mr. Spencer, sir."

Littlejohn looked at Alex as though struggling to hide his contempt. Sitting back down, he motioned to Alex with his hand. "Guess you'd better take that."

Alex excused himself and hurried to his cubicle to take the call.

"Hello. Alex Spencer speaking."

"Good morning, Mr. Spencer. This is Betty Webster from Governor Bechtold's office. The governor will be in New York City tomorrow and would like to know if you could meet him at his Roosevelt Hotel office for lunch at noon."

"Sure . . . yes, I'd be happy to join him for lunch. Room 1527, right?"

"That's correct. I'll tell the governor you'll be there."

"Thank you." Alex hung up the phone and smiled. *Lunch with the governor. Now that's the way to start the new year.*

§

Alex gazed at himself in the elevator mirror, primping between the twelfth and fifteenth floors—pushing back a lock of hair, straightening his tie, adjusting the silk handkerchief in his breast pocket. The elevator bell rang at the fifteenth floor, and he stepped off, confident he looked his best. Striding up the hallway to the governor's suite, he saw the guard in front of the door, a different man from his last visit but equally intimidating.

"Alex Spencer to see Governor Bechtold," Alex said.

The man stuck his head inside and repeated the same phrase to someone nearby, presumably Betty Webster. The guard then opened the door and stepped aside for Alex to enter. Betty was busy typing, this time on a smaller, quieter electric typewriter. Without looking up, she told Alex to have a seat.

Alex walked over to the couch, reluctant to sit down again on the time-worn cushions. As he got closer, he realized the sofa had been replaced with something similar yet firmer. He no sooner sat down when he heard Betty's phone ring. She looked toward Alex and said, "The governor will see you now." He stood up and took a deep breath. He exhaled and began walking down the hallway toward the last door on the left, just past the bathroom.

"Alex Spencer," the governor said, standing up. "Come in, come in. Good to see you, son." He came around his desk and slapped Alex on the back. "How've you been?"

"Very well, sir."

"Good, good. Have a seat. Hope you're hungry. Betty's having the kitchen bring us up some soup and sandwiches." The governor walked around to his desk chair and sat down. He leaned back with his hands folded and resting on his protuberant belly.

"Sounds good, sir. And may I congratulate you on your book. I understand it's selling faster than Dengler can print them."

The governor laughed and slapped his desk. "Amazes me that folks are interested in the ramblings of an old fart like me. You fellas did a bang-up job covering my keister on the legal side. Appreciate it."

"Thank you, sir."

"But I didn't bring you here so we could jabber about my book. Been keeping up with the news lately?"

"I try. What news are you referring to?"

"The news about Congressman Hellman blowing his brains out."

Alex nodded and squeezed his lips together. "Sad story . . ."

"Tragic, tragic. Ol' Hapless Harold gets caught taking kickbacks and figures the shame is too much to live with. Always baffles me how these crockheads never feel shame in committing the act, only when they get caught."

Alex shook his head.

"Important thing is I got a vacancy to fill in the thirty-seventh district. If I'm not mistaken, that's where you grew up. Am I right?"

Alex could see now where the conversation was heading, and felt his heart racing. "Yes, sir. I lived in Stonebridge until I was thirteen."

"Plan on calling for a special primary in early August. I'd

like to see your name on the ballot for the Republican Party. How do you feel about that?"

"August? I mean . . . that's not much time. Nobody knows me . . . How would I begin? Who would I be running against?"

"Doesn't matter nobody knows you. Probably work to your advantage. Listen, thanks to Watergate and Nixon's resignation last August, the Republicans took a beating in the November mid-terms. We lost forty-nine seats in the House. Can't afford to lose any more."

The governor leaned forward in his chair, resting his elbows on his desk. "There's only one guy I know of who could be a serious contender in the Republican primary. That's Louis Pagani. He's a home-grown boy from the thirty-seventh, and lots of those folks love him as their assemblyman. To me, he's nothing but a royal pain in the backside. Kicks against the party line whenever it suits him. He carries some baggage, too. Rumors about him having ties to the mafia have followed him like a shadow. Voters tend to look the other way when it comes to that stuff on the state level. But you start talking national politics, they get all puritanical."

"You think I can beat him?"

The governor sat back and slapped the desk again. "Well if I didn't, I wouldn't be wasting my time talking to you right now. You're too young to have any serious kind of baggage, and you come from good stock. Jack and Doris aren't known in New York like they are in Massachusetts, but most folks remember Congressman Walters fondly. If you can help the voters make the connection, that'll go a long way."

"Who do you think will run on the Democratic ticket?"

The governor leaned back, again, looking pensive. "Hard to say, hard to say. The clown who ran against Hellman in '72 has already said he has no interest, and the congressman ran unopposed in '74. I'm sure within the next few weeks we'll see some folks testing the waters. The sooner you get your campaign started, the quicker your chances of gaining name recognition and building support for your candidacy. Once the fishbowl starts filling up with other goldfish, it's not as easy to stand out."

"I'd like to discuss this with Jack and Doris before I commit to anything, sir."

"Of course, of course. But I wouldn't sit on this too long. You've got paperwork to submit, fees to pay, and money to raise before you can start your campaign. I'm sure Doris can help you get started when you're ready. She's got plenty of campaign experience under her belt. As for me, I can't look like I'm trying to influence the ticket. So, for the record, you and I talked about my book in this meeting, which we did. And we enjoyed a nice lunch together, which we will, if it ever gets here." The governor glanced at the wall clock. "There are plenty of vultures out there who'd like to rip a piece of my hide if they could, especially since my book's been published. I'd prefer we didn't ring the dinner bell for 'em, if you know what I mean."

"I understand, sir."

"Good, good." The governor reached for his phone and dialed. "Betty, can you see where our lunch is? They take much longer, it'll be time for supper." He hung up the phone and leaned forward, resting his left elbow on the desk and cradling his chin in his hand between his thumb and forefinger. "Now, Mr. Spencer, let's talk about what you're going to do for the people in the thirty-seventh district . . ."

§

Friday evening, Alex took a TWA flight out of JFK and touched down at Boston Logan at 8:05. Twenty minutes later he slid into the front seat of Jack's '74 Lincoln, glad to see Howard's familiar smile.

"Thanks for picking me up, Howard."

"My pleasure, sir. I trust you had an enjoyable flight."

"Hit some turbulence coming in. I hope it's not prescient of what awaits me at Woodland Hills."

"Sir?"

"I've come home to talk to Jack and Doris about running for Congress."

Howard glanced at Alex with a perplexed look. "But you only recently started working for Mr. Davidson's law firm, sir."

"I know, I know. That's what worries me about telling Jack. I mean, he knew entering politics was my ultimate goal. Though he probably hoped once I started practicing law, I'd forget about it. But I haven't, Howard." Alex explained to Howard about the opening in his home district and about his meeting with Governor Bechtold.

"The governor and Mr. Davidson have been friends for years," Howard said. "Perhaps the two of them have already discussed this with each other."

"No, I asked the governor before I left our meeting if he had spoken to Jack or Doris. He hadn't. He said he thought it best for me to discuss it with them."

"I see. Might I ask when you plan on speaking with Mr. and Mrs. Davidson about this, sir?"

"Tonight. I want to give them plenty of time during the weekend to mull this over."

Howard raised his eyebrows and pursed his lips, but didn't say a word.

"Is tonight not a good time, Howard?"

"Might I suggest you wait until morning, sir? The weather system that no doubt caused your flight turbulence has given Mr. Davidson a terrible migraine. I'm not sure he would receive your news . . . amenably . . . in his current condition."

"No, I'm sure he wouldn't." Alex said. He was beginning to feel his own head starting to throb.

§

Jack was still in his pajamas and robe when Alex joined him in the dining room for breakfast. He had a copy of the Wall Street Journal open in front of him and was rubbing his temples.

"Head still bothering you, Jack?" Alex asked.

"Not as much as yesterday. Felt like my head was in a vice. Now just feels like I'm wearing a hat one size too tight. Big improvement, though."

"Glad to hear it. Where's Doris this morning?"

"She's coming. Morning constitutional. When you get to be our age, moving your bowels takes precedence over just about anything."

Alex grimaced. "Too much information for me, Jack."

"Decker tells me you're getting along fine at the office," Jack said.

"Not sure if Kevin Littlejohn would give you the same report."

"Ah, he's just a sorehead. Better watch himself. He'll be working for you one day."

Alex cringed on the inside. The last thing he wanted was to have Jack thinking about his grandson's bright future at Davidson and Associates. Just then Doris opened the door and stepped into the room, wearing a sage colored bathrobe and carrying a copy of the Boston Globe. A pair of bifocals rested on the bridge of her nose, and she was reading the headlines as she scuffed along the floor in her house shoes. A woman from the kitchen staff followed closely behind with a carafe of coffee. When Doris reached the breakfast table, the woman set the carafe down and pulled the chair out for her. She then walked around and filled each person's coffee cup. Before leaving, the woman announced she would be serving breakfast in about ten minutes.

When Doris finished perusing the front page, she set the paper down and took a sip of coffee, glancing over her bifocals toward Alex, who was sitting to her left.

"What brings you here from the big city?" she asked, setting her cup down.

Alex took a sip of coffee and wiped his mouth with his napkin. "Governor Bechtold invited me to have lunch with him earlier this week."

Jack looked up from his newspaper. "In Albany?"

"No, at the Roosevelt Hotel in New York."

"Why would Frank Bechtold invite you to lunch?" Doris asked.

"To talk politics. A congressman from the thirty-seventh district killed himself last week. The governor wants me to run as a candidate to fill that position."

Jack's lips thinned in disapproval. Doris removed her bifocals and set them on the table, her attention riveted on Alex. Her voice had a tone of urgency.

"Did he say if he set a date for the primary?"

"Sometime in early August. He didn't have a specific date yet." Alex could see Doris calculating in her head.

"Did you give Bechtold an answer?" Jack asked.

"I told him I wanted to talk to you two before I gave him my decision."

"I turned down a very qualified attorney to give you that position at the New York office. Expected I'd get more than a few months out of you." The tips of Jack's fingers were white from the pressure he was placing on his temples.

"Jack, you knew full well he intended to go into politics one day," Doris said. "Why are you acting like this is such a big surprise?"

"Because I didn't expect 'one day' to be six months after I hired him for a job at the office."

"You've been around politics long enough to know that one has to be ready to jump when opportunity presents itself. And that is seldom when it's convenient."

Jack glared at Doris. "Don't need to talk to me about the inconvenience of politics. Lived with it all my life."

"And may I remind you," Doris said, "that my political connections are what enabled your law office to prosper and make you a very wealthy man."

Jack pushed himself up from the table and folded his paper. He squeezed it in his right hand, tapping it slowly against the edge of the table. "And not a day goes by I don't wonder if the cost was worth it." He turned and started to walk away.

"What is that supposed to mean? Where are you going? You haven't eaten breakfast."

"Lost my appetite."

Alex sat benumbed as he watched Jack leave the room. Doris immediately switched into political strategizing mode.

"You'll need to file your paperwork on Monday. There's no time to waste. I'll contact Congressman Walters to see if he'd be willing to endorse your candidacy. You're going to need a campaign manager—"

"Doris . . . I can't do this without Jack's support. Right now, it's clear I don't have it. He stuck his neck out for me when he hired me. I can't bear the thought of letting him down." Doris turned and faced Alex squarely. She had a steely glint in her eyes, and began thumping the table with her forefinger.

"If you ever intend to survive a congressional campaign, you are going to have to stop worrying about offending people, and become dogmatic about winning. Voters aren't looking for some back-peddler who's going to change his position every time someone squeals. You've been talking for years about running for office. And now that you've been handed this golden opportunity—and trust me, it is golden—are you going to begin dithering because Jack is not happy with it?"

Alex pushed his bottom lip out and blew while tapping his fingers on the table. "This is going to take money, Doris. Lots of it. Governor Bechtold said I'll need to raise at least $50,000 just for advertising alone."

"So we'll get it."

"Campaign finance laws have changed since Congressman Walters last ran for office. It's not like Jack or you can just write me a check for $50,000."

"You let me worry about the money. Now who's going to run your campaign?"

"I'd like to see if Mr. Pearson would be willing. He's had

plenty of experience running campaigns for Senator Roberts."

"But only at the state level."

"And now he'll get experience on the federal level."

"Let me ask Congressman Walters who he would recommend."

"I need someone who knows me, Doris, someone I can trust. Mr. Pearson meets both those requirements."

"And if he says no?"

"*Then* we'll talk to Congressman Walters."

The door to the dining room opened and the same woman from the kitchen staff stepped in, carrying a tray laden with hot breakfast food and a pitcher of orange juice. She looked puzzled when she saw Jack's empty seat.

"Mr. Davidson is not feeling well and decided to skip breakfast," Doris said. The woman nodded and continued serving Doris and Alex. Once the woman left the room, Alex looked at Doris.

"I can't leave things hanging like this with Jack," he said.

"Jack will be fine. He just needs some time to process all of this."

"I've never seen him so angry."

Doris laughed. "Then you've missed a lot over the years."

§

Doris knocked softly on the library door and heard Jack's gruff response to come in. He was sitting in his easy chair, puffing on a cigar. When he saw it was Doris, he instinctively reached for the ashtray to stub it out, but paused. Doris noticed his hesitation and decided to leverage his smoking to her advantage.

"Don't put that out on my account," she said, walking into the room. "This is your library. We always agreed you could smoke your cigars in here."

Jack pulled his hand back from the ashtray, brought the cigar to his mouth, and took a puff. It looked like he was going to blow the smoke in her direction, but at the last second, he turned and blew it away. Doris walked up to the easy chair across from him and sat down.

"What's bothering you, Jack?"

"Who said anything's bothering me?"

"Your words and actions out there said you're upset. Did you think Alex was going to work at Davidson and Associates forever?"

"Thought he'd give me more than a few months."

"You thought you could hand the business over to him."

"Maybe I did. I'm nearly seventy-three. Worked all my life to build this law firm. Course I'd love to keep it in the family. Leave a legacy. Feel a sense of immortality. What's wrong with that?"

"What's wrong is that's not what he wants to do with his life. He wants to enter politics."

"That what he wants or what you want, Doris?"

"Do you see me twisting his arm?"

"Like you tried to do with Jean? No. But I think you've been grooming him for this since he first came here. And he doesn't have the backbone his mother had. Wouldn't dare oppose you."

"After all these years, you're still blaming me for Jean leaving."

"Think all three of us can take some of the blame for that. Not like we didn't try to reconcile with her after Alex was born. But I don't remember you showing the same openness to what Jean wanted for her life that you're showing Alex. Can't help wondering if you'd feel the same way if he wanted to practice law instead of run for office."

Doris sat quietly. Her back was erect, her hands gripping the arms of the chair. She hated when Jack brought up anything about Jean, which was seldom. Motherhood was one part of Doris's life she was unable to reconcile, so she kept its memories locked away in a mental file labeled *Unresolved*. And she only ventured into that file when she had to retrieve some specific data, never just to ruminate. There was that one exception when she took Alex to Ford's Theater and inadvertently delved into that subconscious repository, dredging up bitter memories better left forgotten.

"Do you ever think about Jean, Doris?"

"That seems rather fruitless to me."

"One time Alex said he was concerned that he'd forget what his mother and father looked like. I told him he wouldn't. Told him things in life would remind him when he least expected it. Happens to me sometimes. I'll see some little girl sassing her mother in a store, and I think of Jean. She could be a pistol at times . . ."

"Jack, it's important to Alex you support him in this campaign." Doris's words snapped Jack from his thoughts, and he looked up briefly. Then he dropped his gaze to the floor and stared for a moment before looking up again.

"What's he need me to do?"

"I think he just wants to know you're behind him."

Jack took a puff from his cigar, held it for a few seconds, and blew the smoke off to his side. "Have been for years. Won't change now."

"I'm glad to hear that."

The two sat in silence for a moment. Finally, Doris tried pushing herself up from the chair, but struggled to get to her feet. Jack, still seated, reached over, and grabbed her hand. He pulled until she stood upright.

"We aren't spring chickens any more, Doris. If Alex is going to make politics his career, might be time I thought about selling the business."

"Why don't you hold off until we see how his campaign goes. It's one thing to want a career in politics; it's another to get elected."

"You sound pessimistic."

"No, just pragmatic."

"You know, ever since you told me how I needed to improve as a Harvard quarterback, you've been giving me pretty good advice. How many years has that been?"

"More than I can count. And my advice has been better than pretty good."

"Guess I'll continue to listen to you, then," Jack said, sticking his cigar in his mouth.

Doris strolled to the door and opened it. Before she stepped out of the room, she turned toward her husband. "You're a good old codger," she said, grinning.

Jack pulled his cigar out and lifted it toward Doris, blowing a ring of smoke in her direction.

§

By early February of '75, Alex was campaigning in earnest throughout the thirty-seventh district of New York State. With the assurance that Jack and Doris would cover his lost income, James Pearson took a sabbatical from Drexler Academy to run the campaign. Traveling in Pearson's '73 Chevelle Malibu, Alex and his campaign manager logged thousands of miles each week, traversing six counties between Rochester and Buffalo.

Their days began early with meet and greets in sub-freezing temperatures outside Kodak, Xerox, and General Motors factories, shaking hands with first-shift workers going in and third-shift workers coming out. Alex's greeting seldom varied for each three-second exchange: "Hi, I'm Alex Spencer. I'd appreciate your vote for Congress." From the factories, they drove to shopping plazas, civic associations, radio and television studios, wherever Alex was provided a platform for getting his name and message out.

His message was simple: voters could count on his integrity, and voters could count on him to support policies that would create jobs, fuel the economy, and reduce inflation. With the country in the wake of Watergate and in the throes of recession, Alex's message slowly began to resonate with the voters of Western New York.

One segment of voters he struggled to reach was women. Polls showed most women in the thirty-seventh district thought he was cute but out of touch with the challenges they faced stretching their family budgets. Pearson decided a campaign stop with a homespun message at the nation's first indoor shopping mall would go a long way toward countering these misperceptions.

Midtown Plaza sat in the heart of downtown Rochester in the county where most of Alex's constituents lived. On Saturday afternoons, the mall bustled with shoppers escaping the bitter cold to enjoy the comfort of its spring-like atmosphere, tropical plants, and fountains.

Mr. Pearson had a small platform set up for Alex near the center of the mall underneath the Clock of Nations—a clock tower surrounded by twelve colorful cylinders that rotated around the tower and opened on the hour, displaying animated pageantry from the major cultures of the world. Alex would speak after the noon chime, when the crowds would be the largest.

Thirty seconds before noon, people began streaming in from every corner of the mall. By twelve o'clock, a group of over a hundred men, women, and children surrounded the Clock of Nations, standing shoulder to shoulder, entranced by its mechanical magic. By the time the last cylinder closed, Alex was standing on his platform, microphone in hand, introducing himself to onlookers as the next Congressional Representative from the thirty-seventh district.

Most stayed for the first few minutes and listened out of curiosity to his story of being raised by a widowed mother who worked in one of the local factories and struggled to make ends meet. One by one, the crowd began to thin out. When Alex finished speaking ten minutes later, there were about fifty people still listening and watching, but only one who caught his eye.

He could see her auburn hair peeking out from beneath her ivory woolen cap. She was standing near the back of the crowd, holding her winter jacket in her arms and clutching a shopping bag with the name McCurdy's in bold white letters. She looked the same as she did in her last Christmas card. Alex watched her while the crowd dissipated and she inched her way toward the platform. She was smiling and appeared to be alone. When she was sure that Alex saw her, she raised her hand to shoulder level, close to her chest, and waved. Alex stepped down from the platform to greet her.

"Kitty, what a nice surprise," he said as she approached. Kitty stopped about two feet from him, looking unsure of herself. Alex stepped forward, gave her a quick hug, and stepped back. "You look terrific."

"So do you, Alex," she said, blushing. "I saw your campaign signs along the road, but I didn't know you were going to be here today."

"I go wherever people gather these days. Got to get folks to remember this sorry puss long enough to vote for me."

"Yours is a face I would never forget." She looked uncomfortable as soon as she heard herself say the words.

Alex looked around. "Are you here alone?"

"Yeah." She lifted her shopping bag so he could see it. "Just came to pick up a new outfit for work."

"Have you had lunch yet?" Kitty shook her head. "I heard they have a nice restaurant on the top floor. Will you join me?"

"Top of the Plaza . . . I'm not sure if I'm dressed appropriately . . ."

"I think you look perfect." Alex turned toward Mr. Pearson, who was winding up the microphone cord. "Jim, I'd like to introduce you to a good friend of mine, Kitty McAlister."

Mr. Pearson set the cord down, then brushed off his hands while walking over toward Alex and Kitty. "Pleased to meet you, Kitty. Maybe you can tell us how to get the women of Western New York interested in this character."

"Kitty, this is James Pearson, the finest history teacher at Boston's Drexler Academy. He also happens to be my campaign manager. But it's too early in the campaign to assign him a superlative for that role."

Pearson punched Alex in the arm playfully. "How about hardest working, most intelligent, best looking . . ."

"We'll see about that . . . Listen, I'm going to take Kitty to lunch upstairs. Can you spare me for about an hour?"

"As long as we're out of here by two-fifteen, we'll have plenty of time to make it to the civic association in Pittsford. Enjoy."

"Thanks, Jim. Let's plan on meeting here under the clock at two."

Pearson nodded. "It was a pleasure meeting you, Kitty. And I was serious about the women of this district."

"Well, we are a rather discriminating lot," Kitty said, "but I'll see what suggestions I can offer your candidate."

"Fair enough," Pearson said, waving his hand.

§

"Right this way, please." The maître d' escorted Alex and Kitty to a window table, seated them, and handed each a lunch menu. "Your waiter will serve you shortly," he said before leaving.

Kitty seemed more relaxed, even bubbly, as she looked out the window of the sumptuous restaurant. "I've always wanted to eat up here just to see the view of the city."

"It is a nice view," Alex admitted, but he was looking at Kitty when he said it. He quickly turned his gaze out the window when she seemed to sense he was staring and glanced over.

"It's been a long time," Kitty said.

"Too long." Alex began fidgeting with his silverware. "I ran into Dan in Boston last summer. He told me the good news. Have you set a date yet?"

Kitty lowered her head. "No."

"I have to admit I was surprised when he told me. I never pictured you and Dan as a couple. But, I'm happy for you."

"You are?"

"Why wouldn't I be? My two favorite friends from child-hood finding happiness with each other . . . I mean that's the stuff of fairy tales, right?"

"Is it?"

"You don't sound too happy about getting married."

Kitty brought her hands to her lap and looked out the window. "Dan and I aren't getting married, Alex."

Alex looked at her reflection in the window and saw that she was looking at him.

"What happened?" he asked.

"You told Dan about the Christmas cards I sent you."

Alex felt his face grow warm. "I . . . I didn't know it would be a problem."

"Dan was insecure. He thought I had stronger feelings for you than I did for him."

"Just because you sent me a Christmas card each year?"

Kitty turned her head and looked at Alex. "Yes."

"Couldn't you convince him he was overreacting, that send-ing the cards was just a friendly gesture, that you sent them to other people too?"

"That's just it—" Kitty stopped when the waiter approached the table.

"We're going to need a few more minutes, please," Alex said, opening the menu in front of him.

"Certainly sir. May I get you something to drink?"

"Iced tea for me," Alex said, glancing at Kitty.

"Iced tea sounds fine," Kitty said, forcing a smile.

Once the waiter had gone, Alex looked up from his menu. "You were starting to say something . . ."

"Maybe we'd better figure out what we want to eat before the waiter comes back."

"Sure." Alex could see she was uncomfortable, and he didn't want to push her for a response if she wasn't ready.

For the next few minutes they studied their lunch menus in

silence. Occasionally, Alex peered over the top of his menu to steal a glance at her. He was awed by her simple, yet elegant, beauty. Her Christmas photos—usually black and white Polaroids, which some family member probably snapped—didn't do her justice. They failed to capture the pale softness of her skin and the deep tenderness of her brown eyes. He noticed her sparkling snowflake earrings just below the edge of her ivory cap and the faint lines beneath her eyes, giving her a refined womanly charm that he found alluring. He noticed her delicate fingers holding her menu, their manicured nails painted red. He noticed the ring finger that would never be fettered with a gold band from Dan Wallace. And he smiled.

"You seem pleased about something," Kitty said with a questioning look.

Alex reached across the table and took her hand. "I am very pleased to see you again."

"You are? Why?"

"Because—ugh, I see our pesky waiter coming back. Let's order our food, so he'll leave us alone."

While Alex and Kitty finished placing their order, the house musician sat down at the baby grand on the bandstand and began tickling the keys. After warming up with some jazz scales, the piano player eased into a melancholy melody that sounded familiar to Alex. He tilted his head and listened, listened until he remembered.

Until he remembered the Parker House. And remembered dancing with Marcia. And remembered dreaming of another place, another time, another girl. And remembered thinking that he lost that girl. That girl who loved him for his tenderness. He remembered that that girl became a woman. A woman with auburn hair, soft skin, and delicate fingers.

He slid his hand across the table and caressed those fingers. And she let him. She was smiling. And her eyes were bright, and her face was flushed. And for the moment, she was his again.

"Would you care to dance with me, Kitty McAlister?"

Kitty looked uneasily around the room. "But nobody else is dancing . . ."

Alex stood up, offering his hand and a winsome smile. "It's because they're all waiting for us to take the lead."

Kitty reluctantly took his hand. "I'm not a good dancer," she said as she walked with him to the dance floor.

"Just follow me."

Alex faced her, holding her right hand extended in his left, with his right arm across her back. "Now rest your left hand on my shoulder." Kitty obliged, her face tense with concentration. "Relax," he said, "this is supposed to be fun." He felt her arms loosen, and she gave him a nervous smile. "Ready?" She nodded. "Here we go . . ." With that, Alex began dancing the basic steps of a slow fox trot, leading Kitty with long, smooth movements across the floor. Her eyes were fixed on his, trying to anticipate his moves. After a few stumbles, she got the hang of it, and her face looked calm and confident.

"I remember learning this dance in high school," she said, beaming. "It's all coming back to me, now."

"You're doing great."

Alex couldn't remember when he ever felt so light and free. Her hand felt like it was molded to fit his. The small of her back felt warm and familiar. Her scent, which drifted across the dance floor, was enchanting. It was different from the floral fragrance she used when they were younger. This was the woman's version, not a lusty aroma evoking raw sexuality, but, rather, a comforting scent kindling affection and endearment.

By the time the pianist was playing the first few bars of the chorus, there were two other couples on the dance floor. Alex looked at Kitty and motioned with his head. "I told you they were just waiting for us to lead." She grinned and shook her head. At the end of the song, while the musician sustained the last note, Alex lifted his hand and gently spun Kitty around. She brushed her bangs with her fingers and laughed.

"That was fun," she said.

"And looks like our timing's perfect. There's our food."

When they reached their table and sat down, they could see a light snow falling outside the window.

"Oh, isn't that pretty?" Kitty said. "It reminds me of Christmas."

Alex looked out the window toward the river and pointed to some people ice skating. "I always looked forward to your Christmas cards, you know."

"I often wondered if you even got them."

"Howard was always very good about forwarding mail to me, wherever I was living." Alex opened his napkin and spread it over his lap. "How come you kept sending them to me?"

"Because I told you at your mother's funeral I would write to you."

"That was more than twelve years ago. Your faithfulness puts me to shame, Kitty."

"I didn't send the cards to make you feel ashamed. I sent them so you knew I hadn't forgotten about you. I sent the pictures because I didn't want you to forget about me."

"And I never have. Never." He paused a moment before continuing. "Tell me what you've been doing with your life all these years. I feel I know so little."

"There's not much to know. After I graduated from St. Bartholomew's, I went to community college. Then got a job at the General Motor's plant, along with Dan and a dozen or so other kids from our graduating class. I worked as a secretary for one of the managers. The pay was decent, but I hated the job. After two years, there was an opening at the diocesan office for a secretary, and I've been working there ever since. I rent a small one-bedroom apartment close to work. And I drive a Chevy Vega."

After hearing her mention the diocesan office, Alex shifted uncomfortably in his chair. He was reluctant to ask but desperately wanted to know.

"If you're wondering if Father Francis still works for the diocese," Kitty said, "the answer is no. He's now chancellor of the new Catholic college in Feldsport, St. Vincent's. I work for his successor, Father Domenici."

Alex nodded. He was afraid they were treading very close to forbidden turf, and he was determined not to make the same mistake twice. "You like the work, then?"

"Very much. For me, it's more rewarding than building parts for cars. I feel like the work I do in some small way impacts others for good. Does that sound corny?"

"Not at all. I hope to do the same when I'm a congressman."

"What are your chances of winning?"

"I've got to win the primary first. That means I've got to defeat Louis Pagani. I understand he's pretty popular around here."

"Not with me he isn't. I don't trust the guy."

"Do you trust his opponent?"

Kitty paused and considered his question. "I want to."

It wasn't the response he wanted to hear, but he covered his disappointment with a smile. "Spoken like a true Western New York woman," he said.

Kitty glanced outside where the snow was coming down now in large, fluffy flakes. "If this keeps up there'll be good skiing tomorrow." She turned toward Alex. "Ever done any snow skiing?"

"No, I'm afraid my grandparents were only interested in me learning activities that would help me in my career. That limited me to dancing and golf."

"I know a great place to ski if you can free up some time tomorrow."

"The only campaign stops on my schedule are some meet and greets at a few local churches. After that, I'm free. But I don't have the clothes for skiing, let alone the equipment."

"Stand up."

Alex gave her a puzzled look.

Kitty motioned with her hand. "Stand up, please." When Alex stood up, she said, "You're about the same size as my fa-

David Moore

ther. We can stop by and ask him if you can borrow his ski pants and jacket. You can rent skis at the resort. Tell me where and when to pick you up, and I'll drive."

"Sounds like a date, then."

Kitty grinned. "Tomorrow, I lead, Mr. Fox Trot."

§

Bristol Mountain Ski Resort was packed with snow and skiers when Alex and Kitty arrived at mid-afternoon. Once Alex was fitted for some rental skis, Kitty took him to a flat, open area of snow where she could show him the basics.

"First, I'm going to show you how to walk with your skis. Place your feet shoulder-width apart with your knees slightly bent, so you're feeling pressure on your shins."

Alex followed Kitty's instructions and started falling forward.

"Use your poles to balance." Kitty said.

He checked his fall with his poles, and soon he was in the proper position.

"Now slide your right ski forward along the inner edge of your ski. Make sure you're moving your right pole forward at the same time."

Alex started out nicely but forgot to bring his left ski forward, assumed a split position, and toppled over. Kitty laughed. "I'm pretty sure I didn't look this foolish when we were dancing yesterday," she said.

Alex lifted his hand. "Just help me up, smarty pants."

After about thirty minutes, Alex was demonstrating enough control to venture onto a ski slope. Kitty pointed to the beginner's slope she was taking him to, and Alex asked, "How do we get up there?"

She pointed to the chairlifts. "We ride on one of those."

Alex shook his head.

Kitty nodded.

Alex placed his hands on his hips and shook his head.

272

Kitty placed her hands on her hips and nodded.

Ten minutes later they were sitting on the chairlift, riding up four hundred feet to the top of the beginner's slope.

"When the chair gets to that sign, point the tip of your skis up, hop off the chair, and ski away from the lift, to the right," Kitty said.

"Are you kidding me?"

"You can do it. Get ready . . ."

"I can barely stand up with these—"

"C'mon. Get ready . . . Now." Kitty executed the move gracefully and turned her head quickly to see the chair smacking Alex on his backside and propelling him forward toward a group of unsuspecting skiers standing nearby.

"Point your tips!" Kitty yelled.

Alex remembered just in time and stopped within inches of slamming into a young girl standing with her parents. He lifted each ski one at a time, and maneuvered himself awkwardly around toward Kitty. He looked at her with wide eyes and a big grin and gave her a thumbs-up. Kitty pressed her lips together and made the sign of the cross.

"Okay, so this is the hill we're gonna go down," Kitty said, when Alex had caught up with her. "Point your skis sideways, like this."

Alex finessed his skis into the position Kitty was showing him.

"Now turn your shoulders and move your poles so they're pointing downhill, without moving your skis yet."

Alex began twisting his torso and broke out into song: "C'mon, baby. Let's do the twist."

Kitty shook her head and rolled her eyes. "All right, silly, taking small steps, move your skis around so they're pointing downhill. Keep your poles in the snow, so you don't start sliding."

Seconds later, Alex was in position for his first downhill run. Following Kitty's final instructions, he bent his knees, leaned forward, and pushed off his poles. He felt the cold air whipping his face as he picked up speed. He heard the swishing of the snow against his skis and felt exhilarated. Kitty was tagging along, just to his right, beaming.

"YEEE-HAH!" Alex yelled.

He saw Kitty laugh, then her expression quickly changed to one of alarm. Alex faced forward and saw another inexperienced skier drifting into his pathway, oblivious to his quick approach. Like a flash, Alex remembered what Kitty had told him about turning. He took pressure off his left ski and transferred his weight to his right, adjusting his course to the left of the skier. When he was safely past, Alex looked to his right and saw Kitty smiling, giving him a thumbs-up. This time, he wanted to make the sign of the cross but was afraid he'd lose his balance. Instead, he just looked heavenward, figuring she'd understand.

When they reached the bottom of the slope, Kitty glided over to Alex and patted him on the back. "I'm impressed."

"Well, I had a great instructor. I can't believe how much fun I'm having. I felt like I was flying down that hill."

Kitty pointed to the intermediate slope, which was steeper than the beginner and two-hundred feet longer. "That one will make you feel like you've been launched from a rocket."

"You think I'm ready for it?"

"Not yet. But a few more times down the beginner's slope, and I think we can give it a try."

"Let's keep going then."

When dusk began to settle over the ski resort, Alex and Kitty finished their last run down the intermediate slope and headed in. After returning the rented equipment and stowing Kitty's gear, they strolled to the lodge to warm up with some hot cocoa and dinner. They found a vacant table close to a rustic fireplace that took up nearly a third of the wall. A slow-burning fire was crackling in the firebox, casting an orange-red glow over that section of the room.

Alex helped Kitty remove her ski jacket and pulled her chair out for her, hanging her coat across the chair back after she sat down. He draped his jacket over the back of his chair and sat down across from her. The server brought a carafe of hot cocoa to the table and left after taking their order for dinner. Alex gazed at Kitty. Her face looked radiant with the scarlet glow of her cheeks bathed in the warm hues of the firelight. She noticed him staring and put on her bashful girl face.

"What are you looking at?" she asked.

"The prettiest girl in this room."

She gave him an amused expression and turned her head to scan the room. "Prettier than that girl sitting over there wearing the pink top?" She motioned with her head.

Alex turned his head to look. "Much prettier."

Kitty continued the game. "Prettier than that blond with the blue turtleneck?"

Alex looked and hesitated. "Hmm . . ." She kicked him under the table. "Yes, prettier than that blond."

Kitty continued cautiously. "Prettier than the girl you told Dan about?"

Alex paused and pondered her question. "The girl I told Dan about is pretty. She is also intelligent, funny, and kind."

Kitty shifted in her chair and looked away. "I'm sorry. That was wrong of me to put you on the spot like that."

"Don't be sorry, Kitty. I'm glad you brought her up. Her name is Marcia Stillman, and we met at law school." He looked up at the ceiling briefly, rubbing the nape of his neck. "Well, we actually met one time before then, but that's inconsequential. We started dating in law school. I believe she loved me, and I liked her very much."

"Did you ever talk about getting married?"

"We talked around the subject, but never discussed it direct-ly."

"How long did you see each other?"

"We dated for about four months."

"What happened?"

Alex thought for a moment and then shrugged. "There was just something that kept coming between us . . ."

Kitty leaned forward, expecting him to continue. When he didn't, she asked, "Do you know what that something was?"

Alex glanced at her and thinned his lips. "Actually, I should have said *someone* kept coming between us. You see, every time I tried to see Marcia as someone more than a friend, I kept comparing her to you. And she never measured up."

He noticed Kitty's head tilt slightly, like she was wondering *Why would you do something like that?*

"I feel a little foolish telling you all this," he said.

Kitty looked at him now with the same accepting eyes he remembered as a boy. The look that always made him feel safe to be himself with her. She was smiling softly.

"Please don't ever feel foolish around me, Alex. We've known each other too long for that. I know exactly what you felt with Marcia. Why do you think Dan and I aren't getting married?"

"I thought it was because of the Christmas card issue."

"The Christmas cards were just a symptom of the real issue. You see, I couldn't love Dan because he wasn't you. You asked me yesterday why I couldn't just explain to Dan that sending the cards was just a friendly gesture. Why I didn't remind him that I send cards to other people too. I couldn't because it would have been a lie on both counts. Dan knew I hated sending cards to people. I'd always rather tell someone face-to-face how I feel. He tried to encourage me to send them because he wanted me to be more like his mother. But you're the only one I've sent a Christmas card to each year. Just you.

"And it wasn't just a friendly gesture. I didn't want to lose you. You remember that day at your grandparents' house when you kissed me? . . ." Kitty started to choke up and paused to compose herself. "I told myself I wasn't going to cry," she said, laughing through her tears. "When you kissed me that day, it was the first time I thought you felt the same way about me that

I felt about you . . . the way I have felt about you since I was ten years old."

Alex sighed. "And then I blew it by getting upset about Father Francis."

"I always figured at some point you'd put that priest behind you. All these years I've prayed for that very thing. And I've held onto the hope that when you did, you'd have room in your heart for me."

Alex handed her a clean napkin to dry her tears. He watched her quietly as she dabbed her eyes. He felt as though their conversation had cleared the air, as though they had been immersed in a cleansing fountain, and the misunderstandings between them had been washed away. Maybe Kitty was right. Maybe it was time. Time to move beyond the hurt of the past and try to forget about the priest. Alex wasn't sure if he'd be elected to Congress, but he was sure that no matter what direction his life took, he wanted to live it with Kitty by his side.

"You know," Alex said, "the next several months are going to be pretty hectic with this campaign. There's not going to be much free time. But I'll be in the area quite a bit, and I'd really like to see you whenever I can."

Kitty smiled. Her eyes were still moist. "I'd like that very much, Alex. Very much, indeed."

Chapter 24

"Pagani is killing us in the polls," James Pearson said to Alex. They were driving to their fifth campaign stop of the day—a meeting with the League of Women Voters—and if the previous stops were reliable indicators, Alex would be spending most of the evening with this irascible group defending himself against the attacks of Louis Pagani.

"I'm tired of being on the defensive all the time," Alex said. "Isn't there anything we can pin on this guy? To hear the press, you'd think he was up for canonization."

"It's not so much that the press loves Pagani, they just don't like you, Alex. You're an outsider. An outsider from a rich, powerful New England family. They're going to make you fight for every inch of political ground you get."

"And what ground have we gained so far? We got the Catholic vote largely because of Pagani's divorce from his wife two years ago. So it's a vote *against* Pagani more than a vote *for* Spencer."

"Your showing well with the younger demographic."

"Sure, as long as they're white collar. The blue-collar workers are leaning heavily toward Pagani. And let's face it, this is a blue-collar district. What about Pagani's mafia connections? Any substance there?"

"Nothing but rumors. Rumors that have been floating around for years. I'm inclined to think when rumors dog someone for that long, there has to be some substance that will surface sooner or later. Let's hope it's sooner. In the meantime, take heart that the papers say, 'Mr. Spencer is likeable and explains his positions on the issues in an easy-to-understand manner.'"

Alex grunted.

§

By mid-July, Louis Pagani's dominance in the grueling campaign leading up to the August fifth primary was firmly established. Of those Republicans polled, sixty-five percent favored the hometown candidate, while only thirty percent said they planned on voting for Alex. The remaining five percent were undecided. Short of a miracle, Pagani was certain to become the Republican nominee for November's general election.

During the early weeks of July, Alex picked up his pace dramatically, surviving on four to five hours of sleep a night. He focused most of his energy on winning supporters in Rochester and its closest suburbs. James Pearson, who was more than twice Alex's age, kept the same arduous schedule and showed no signs of letting up. The only down-time for either of them came on Sunday afternoons. For Alex, those were the times he spent with Kitty.

The second Sunday in July found Alex as far from the political fray as possible. He and Kitty escaped to the Genesee River, lazily paddling their wooden canoe past stately oaks and craggy maples lining the grassy river banks. The quiet of nature was soothing to Alex. The sweet music of songbirds provided a melodic backdrop to the slow rhythmic sloshing of the paddles as they dipped into the water. Kitty sat in the front, paddling on the port side, while Alex paddled on the starboard from the rear.

"Why don't you take a break and turn around, so we can talk?" Alex said.

"If you insist . . ." Kitty set her paddle on the floor of the canoe. "Don't you dare try to tip me," she warned as she gingerly maneuvered herself around on the seat.

Kitty was wearing a pair of khaki shorts with a light blue pullover and a white baseball cap. The outfit highlighted her summer tan, and Alex had trouble keeping his eyes off of her.

"This is much better than looking at your back all afternoon," he said.

"As long as you don't mind doing all the paddling."

"It's the best exercise I've gotten all week."

"I'm concerned about the stress you're under with this campaign."

"It's only a few more weeks until the primary. I've got to feel like I've given it my best shot." Alex paddled silently for a moment, thinking of the right words to convey his next thoughts. "I'm thinking about starting up my own law practice after the primary."

"You don't think you have a chance of winning the nomination?"

"The polls are lopsided in Pagani's favor, Kitty. I've got to face reality."

Kitty looked down at the passing water and leaned over to

dip her fingers in. "Where would you set up your law office?"

"Not Stonebridge. Too many memories there to haunt me. Somewhere close to you, though. Would you like that?"

Kitty smiled. "You know I would. But won't your grandfather expect you to take over his firm?"

"I have no desire to live in New York City. It's too hectic for me. A quiet, peaceful life is what I'm after."

"And you'd just throw away your dream of entering politics?"

"I think Jack was right when he tried to discourage me from a career in politics. He said my longevity hinges on the whims of the voters. And right now the voters in the thirty-seventh district are saying, 'Thanks, but no thanks, Alex Spencer.'"

"But that's now, and a lot can change between now and the primary. I don't know how to explain it, Alex. Call it woman's intuition. But I think you're going to win this primary and the general election too."

Alex's face brightened. "You really believe that?"

"I do. And I know you're exhausted and feel like it's pointless, but now, more than ever, is when you need to give it everything you've got. Pagani's going down, Alex. I know it like . . . like I know your favorite color."

Alex grinned. "And what is my favorite color?"

Kitty pointed to her shirt. "Hel-lo!"

§

Over the next several days, Alex struggled to hold on to Kitty's optimistic outlook. His campaign continued to show signs of floundering, with the coffers being depleted faster than they could be replenished. On the last Friday of July, Alex and James Pearson huddled around a table in the campaign office, a small storefront in downtown Rochester, and discussed their strategy for the next ten days leading up to the primary. A few minutes before noon, the phone rang, and the lone volunteer in the office took the call.

"It's for you, Mr. Pearson. County GOP Chairman."

Pearson looked at Alex and raised his eyebrows as if bracing himself for more bad news. Pearson picked up the phone. "Richard, how are you doing, my friend? No we haven't . . ." He motioned for Alex to turn on the television. "We've got it on now, Richard. Thanks for the call." Pearson hung up the phone and hurried over to the TV. "The chairman said there's going to be some breaking news about Pagani. Turn it up, Alex."

> "A source within the Monroe County District Attorney's Office has confirmed that a grand jury was convened yesterday to investigate claims that Assemblyman Louis Pagani used his influence to benefit a sign company with reputed ties to organized crime. There are allegations that the assemblyman convinced the Chairman of the Department of Transportation to cut down more than a thousand trees along Interstate 90. This cleared the way for Select City Signs to erect billboards and avoid paying any cost for removing the trees—a charge normally incurred by companies erecting signage on state property.
>
> "Yesterday, the grand jury heard testimonies from at least six individuals connected to the case. When interviewed moments ago, Assemblyman Pagani said he declined an invitation to participate in the hearing because, and I quote, 'It is nothing more than a witch hunt initiated by Governor Bechtold to aid the failed campaign of my opponent, Alex Spencer.'
>
> "Pagani has been leading by a wide margin in the race to win the Republican nomination for Congressional Representative of the thirty-seventh district. With the primary only days away, it's unclear how this latest development will impact his lead in the polls. In other news . . ."

"Yes!" Alex shouted, slapping the table. James Pearson was

wearing a broad grin as he reached over to turn down the volume on the TV.

"The press will be calling any minute," Pearson said. "We've got to prepare a statement right now. We'll schedule a press conference for one o'clock."

"We want to say something that's respectful of the legal process but raises questions about Pagani's innocence."

"Exactly."

"This is a gift from heaven, Jim."

"Let's just be sure we make the most of it."

§

By one o'clock, a crowd of twenty reporters and photographers had gathered outside the campaign office, awaiting Alex's comments. After putting the finishing touches on his response, Alex walked outside to greet the press.

"I have a brief statement," he began, "and then I'll take your questions." He opened his sheet of notes and looked around to gauge where the television cameras were located. After repositioning himself, so the cameras were getting his best angle, he began.

"Like most of you, I just heard the news about the grand jury investigation concerning Assemblyman Pagani. As an attorney, I think it's important that the public understands that this is simply an investigation to determine whether any crime has been committed. Assemblyman Pagani has not been indicted as of yet, so it would be unfair of me to make this an issue of the campaign.

"That said, I deeply resent the assemblyman's allegations that this is a witch hunt initiated by Governor Bechtold for my benefit. The governor has gone out of his way to avoid endorsing either candidate, so I find it rather disingenuous of Mr. Pagani to make such a brazen assertion. I can only presume that the assemblyman's offhand comments were simply a knee-jerk reaction to some very unwelcome and stressful news. Of course, this raises the question of how the assemblyman would handle the stress of being a congressman, where one's words resonate beyond the local level. But I'll leave it to the sensible voters of the thirty-seventh district to make that determination. I'll be happy to take any of your questions now."

For the next ten minutes, the press peppered Alex with questions about the investigation and how he thought it would affect him in the polls. When the press conference was winding down, a smiling female reporter shouted one last question that Alex hadn't anticipated.

"Mr. Spencer, you were spotted canoeing on the Genesee River last week with an attractive young woman. Do you care to tell us who she is?"

Alex felt himself blushing and tried to cover it up with a warm smile. "You folks don't miss a thing, do you? She's a very dear friend. We grew up together in Stonebridge. And that's all I'm going to say about it for now." With that Alex waved his hand to signal the end, and several reporters groaned as he turned and walked back inside the campaign office, with James Pearson following.

"Excellent job." Pearson said, patting Alex on the back once they were inside. "I'd be very surprised if the polls didn't start turning in our favor."

"I need to let Kitty know the press is on to us," Alex said, flushed with excitement. "Jim, I think we've still got a chance of pulling this off."

"Best chance we've had yet."

§

By Monday of the following week, the polls had made an abrupt turn, showing Alex neck and neck with his challenger. On Tuesday, the Times Union—Rochester's afternoon daily newspaper—endorsed Alex as the most promising candidate and least likely to bring further scandal to the district. By the end of the week, he was leading in the polls for the first time. On August fifth, Alex won the Republican primary with fifty-two percent of the vote. Two weeks later, the grand jury investigating Louis Pagani returned a no-bill, saying there was not enough evidence to indict the assemblyman.

With only three months to the general election, Alex had no time to savor the primary victory. The following day, he was back on the campaign trail contending with his Democratic challenger, Daniel Brumfeld—a college professor and first-time candidate from the thirty-seventh district. Brumfeld, who was in his mid-fifties, taught political science at one of the local colleges and came across as a stodgy, snobbish pedagogue whenever he spoke. Alex, with his youth and vitality, was a welcome contrast to the wearisome professor.

Interest in the Republican candidate's secret woman had mounted since the primary, and Kitty agreed to accompany Alex on the stump during the weekend. He always introduced Kitty as his dear friend. And to demonstrate just how dear she was, he gave her a kiss before launching into his speech. The crowds loved it and called them the Republican Jack and Jackie. Alex only hoped Doris would understand if she ever got wind of the comparison.

Daniel Brumfeld never really stood a chance. Throughout the campaign, Alex maintained a healthy lead over his contender. When the votes were counted on the second Tuesday in November, Alex won by a fifteen percent margin. Although he wouldn't be sworn in until January, he was now a member of the United States Congress. He had finally attained a position of power and influence. Now he hoped he knew how to wield it.

Chapter 25

On January 5, 1976, Alex Michael Spencer was sworn into the Ninety-fourth Congress of the United States by Speaker Carl Albert. Looking on from the House gallery were the family and friends who helped him get there: Jack and Doris, James Pearson, Steven Roberts, and Kitty. Following the ceremony and lunch in the Congressional dining room, Alex said his goodbyes and began the work of learning how to be a congressman.

On the walk back to his office in the Cannon Building, he met another junior representative who had just enough knowledge to be helpful. And for Alex, the man couldn't have come at a better time.

"I'm Ted Holbrook," the man said, "Congressman from Ohio." He extended his hand to Alex. "Saw you getting sworn in earlier."

Alex shook the man's hand. "Alex Spencer from New York."

"City?"

"No, western part of the state. Just elected in November."

"Have you been assigned to any committees yet?"

"I submitted my preferences. Still waiting to hear from the chairman. At this point I'm just eager to learn as much as I can as quickly as possible."

"There are a few of us who started meeting for breakfast during the first session. All freshmen, sworn-in last January. You're welcome to join us. Gives us a chance to discuss policy issues. We meet in the Cannon Cafeteria at 7:30 every weekday."

"I appreciate that. Is this a bipartisan group?"

"No, all Republicans. Easier on the digestive system."

§

The following morning at 7:35, Alex stepped into the Cannon Cafeteria and gazed across rows of tables filled with men and a few women, all wearing dark suits and chattering. While trying to remember if there were any distinguishing features about Ted Holbrook that would stand out in this conglomeration of statesmen, Alex heard someone call his name. Looking to his right, he saw Holbrook standing and waving him over.

"Welcome to our holy convocation, Alex," Holbrook said, smiling. "This is Glen Baldwin and John Harrison."

"Nice to meet you, gentlemen." Alex shook hands and sat down.

"I saw that overwhelmed look on your face when you walked in." Baldwin said. "You'll be wearing that look for most of your first year here." The other two men laughed and nodded in agreement.

"Looks like dark colors are in fashion in the House," Alex quipped.

"You'll find that the House has its own unique customs and traditions," Harrison said.

"And unique ways of punishing those who don't conform," Baldwin added.

"Dark suits it is, then," Alex said. "Any other advice for a novice like me?"

"Just remember the members with most seniority run the House," Baldwin said. "And if you think you're here to be an agent of change, forget about it. The big decisions are made by those who lead committees. The sooner you can get a committee assignment, the sooner you can start climbing the ladder."

"Well, I hope to get my assignment today," Alex said.

Holbrook looked at his watch and elbowed Harrison. "We'd better get started if we're going to swing by my office before that 8:30 meeting. Excuse us gentlemen. Alex, glad to have you with us."

Alex stood and shook both men's hands.

"You learn a lot in these committee meetings," Baldwin continued when Alex sat down. "About things you wouldn't have thought you were even interested in. Last session, I sat in on some open Senate hearings just out of curiosity. Senator Nunn was chair. They were investigating financial aid fraud within colleges. I had no idea how much federal money was being used to fund college educations in this country. And how much was unaccounted for by the Department of Health, Education, and Welfare. My girlfriend works for HEW's student loan program, and she said the crap is going to hit the fan when the committee's final report is issued."

"I've got a few colleges in my district. I wonder how this could affect them." Alex said.

"Right now, my girlfriend has a list of hundreds of colleges that have been flagged for possible financial-aid fraud. No doubt, HEW will want to make examples of some of them."

"Is there any way I could find out if any of my colleges are on that list?"

"I can ask, but I doubt very much that's information she'll release."

"I understand. I'm sure you can appreciate my concerns, though."

"I'll see what I can do for you. But I guarantee once you get a committee assignment, you're not going to have time to worry about your constituents." Baldwin chuckled and slapped Alex on the back.

§

Following Friday morning's breakfast of champions, Glenn Baldwin told Alex to stop by his office sometime that afternoon. He had something for him. At three o'clock, Alex stepped into Baldwin's office, and the congressman motioned for him to close the door behind him. Baldwin then pulled out a document and invited Alex to sit down.

"My girlfriend could probably get fired for this. But I told her I was just going to show you this list; I can't let you take it out of my office." Baldwin slid the document across his desk to Alex. "This is the list of colleges in New York State that have been flagged by HEW for possible financial-aid fraud. It's organized alphabetically."

Alex picked up the two-page document from the desk and began to scan the names. Reading through all of the first page and two-thirds of the second page, he stopped when he saw *St.*

Vincent College: Feldsport, NY. He resumed scanning until he reached the bottom of the page and then went back up the list and put his finger on the line for St. Vincent College.

"What does the ratio 90/10 signify next to St. Vincent College?" Alex asked.

"It means ninety percent of the school's revenue is coming from federal aid programs. Only ten percent is coming from the school or students. The Higher Education Act of 1965 limits that ratio to 85/15. So the school is exceeding that by five percent."

"So what could happen to a school that exceeds that limit?"

"I suppose they could disqualify themselves from receiving further federal aid money."

"Which means they would likely have to close their doors."

"Worst-case scenario, I would say you're correct."

Thoughts began swirling in Alex's head. He had information that could finally put Father Francis on the defensive. Information that could conceivably cost the priest his job. Perhaps he could still balance the scales of justice in his own way, like he and Marcia discussed a few years ago. He laid the document back on the desk and pushed it gently toward Baldwin.

"Thank you, Congressman. This has been very informative."

"Just remember, however you use this information, you didn't get it from me."

Alex smiled and nodded.

Chapter 26

Two weeks after meeting with Congressman Baldwin, Alex was back in Rochester for a weekend visit with his constituents and for some much needed time with Kitty. He had mulled over the information he received about St. Vincent College and decided that while he was in town he would speak to Father Francis.

Kitty met Alex at the airport on Friday evening. With temperatures in the mid-teens, it was one of the coldest nights since the winter season began. After stopping to pick up a pizza, they drove straight to his local congressional office to begin organizing for a town-hall meeting scheduled for the next morning.

"I've missed you," Kitty said after they sat down at a table in the office and started eating.

"You said that a few times in the car," Alex said, smiling.

"Yeah, I guess I did, didn't I?"

"I missed you, too." Alex began flipping through a stack of papers in front of him and sighed. "Looks like everybody and their brother wants me to do something for them."

"Isn't that why you ran for office, to help people?"

"Yeah, it's just a little overwhelming right now."

"What else do you have planned for this weekend besides the town-hall meeting?"

Alex noticed a scheming look on Kitty's face. "Why do you ask?"

"My mother wants us to come for dinner Sunday afternoon. But if you're too busy . . ."

Alex's shoulders sagged. "Is that really how you want to spend the few hours we have together this weekend?"

"We'll have all tomorrow afternoon and evening. I didn't think a few hours with my parents would be asking too much. I mean we have to eat, right? And my parents are really proud of you. What's the matter? Don't you like them?"

"I like your dad, Kitty. He's a good man."

"But not my mother?"

"I didn't say that. It's just . . . you know how your mother can be."

"No, Alex. How can my mother be?"

"Come on, Kitty. Let's not fight. We don't get nearly enough time to spend together as it is." Alex pushed his papers aside and looked into Kitty's eyes. "If it's important to you that we have dinner with your parents, we'll go."

"Thank you."

"We won't have all of tomorrow afternoon to ourselves, though. I have an appointment at three o'clock."

"Really? Where?"

"St. Vincent College."

"With whom?"

Alex shifted uneasily in his chair. "Father Francis." He glanced at Kitty, a frown now eclipsing her bewildered look.

"What business do you have with him? Or is that none of *my* business?"

Alex hesitated. "The truth is I can't give you any specifics, Kitty. What I can tell you is that some issues concerning the college were brought to my attention, and I need to discuss them with Father Francis."

"Were these issues brought to your attention, or did you go looking for them?"

"What difference does it make? The issues need to be addressed."

"Are these legitimate issues, or is this a witch hunt?"

Alex straightened his back. "How do you know I'm not meeting with him to give him a heads up on something . . . something that could be detrimental to the school if it isn't addressed?"

"Are you?"

Alex said nothing.

Kitty shook her head. "When will you get over this obsession with Father Francis?"

"It's not an obsession. I'm doing my job."

"I think it is. And I think it has been for years."

"I can't help what you think."

Kitty looked at Alex and sighed. "I have hoped and prayed you would get beyond the hurt you experienced. Instead, you continue to allow it to poison you. Getting revenge is more important to you than finding happiness. It's more important to you than me. I love you, Alex. I have always loved you. But I don't like what you've allowed yourself to become. I won't stand by, watching you give in to this bitterness. I can't."

"What are you saying, Kitty?"

"I'm saying you need to make a choice. You can grow old and bitter, nursing this wound you believe Father Francis inflicted, or you can find a way to heal the hurt and forgive him. Until you can forgive, we have no future."

"I'm not ready to do that."

She stood up and pulled her car keys from her purse.

Alex felt the blood drain from his face. "Kitty . . . wait . . ."

Kitty held up her hand. "I'm sorry for you, Alex. I'm sorry for us. I think we could have a great life together, but this thing with Father Francis keeps getting in the way." She turned and started walking toward the door when Alex jumped up in her path to stop her.

"Kitty, please . . . don't give up on me. Not now."

Kitty drew back, tears running down her cheeks. "I'm not giving up on you. I don't want to give up on us. But you need to make a choice." She walked past Alex and opened the door, letting in a blast of arctic air. When it closed, Alex stood shivering. He heard her walk to her car. Heard her open and close her door. Heard her engine struggle to turn over. Heard her rev the engine once it started. Heard her drive away. And then he heard nothing.

He walked over to the table where they had been sitting and smiling at each other only moments ago, and he slumped into his chair. In front of him lay a slice of pizza, cold and lifeless on a flimsy paper plate. He picked it up, hesitated, and then flung it against the wall. After sitting motionless for several minutes, he forced himself up and walked over to the closet, pulling out a cot and blanket. After setting up the cot, he stretched out on it and pulled the blanket over him, wondering if it was possible to feel any more alone than he felt now.

§

After waking early from a fitful night's sleep, Alex took a

taxi to the nearest car rental office and rented a four-wheel drive Blazer for the weekend. Weather forecasters were calling for heavy snow over the next twenty-four hours, and he didn't want to risk getting stranded. He drove to a nearby Marriott and rented a room. After a hot bath, he felt marginally better. He struggled to keep his mind free from thoughts of Kitty as he finished preparing for his town-hall meeting. The people braving the frigid weather to attend the morning gathering would be expecting something more than trite tidings from a melancholy messenger.

Even after seeing Kitty's anguish, Alex never considered canceling his meeting with Father Francis. Deep down, he knew she was right, but he had carried his bitterness too long to throw away an opportunity to see the priest squirm. And with Kitty gone, Alex had no constraints keeping him from carrying his plan to its conclusion.

§

Following the town-hall meeting, which ended at noon, Alex drove back to his hotel to freshen up. The meeting had gone better than expected, his constituents clearly cutting him some slack until his congressional honeymoon ended. Alex had once asked his breakfast group how long the honeymoon lasted for freshman congressman, and one of them responded, "There's no set time—could be weeks or months—but you'll know for sure when it's over."

After grabbing some lunch, Alex took a short nap. When he awoke, he sat down and reviewed his notes for his meeting with Father Francis. He was surprised at how calm he felt. Confident that he was prepared, he put on a fresh shirt, grabbed his briefcase, and headed toward the town of Feldsport and his first encounter with Father Francis since becoming a grown man.

§

Halfway to Feldsport, a heavy snow began falling, so Alex switched to four-wheel drive. By the time he reached St. Vincent

College, he found the campus road covered with a few inches of snow. His Blazer moved effortlessly toward the administration building, and he parked it in a visitor space near the main door. Grabbing his briefcase, he stepped out of the vehicle, pulled his collar close around his neck, and walked to the door.

Once inside, he spotted a young woman behind a counter along the wall. Assuming she was a receptionist, he walked over and announced his arrival.

"Father Francis will be available to see you shortly, Congressman Spencer," the woman said. "He's just finishing up with a two o'clock counseling session."

"The chancellor of the university has time to counsel students?" Alex asked incredulously.

"He likes to squeeze one or two sessions into his weekend schedule for those students struggling with their spiritual walk. He says it allows him to stir up his ministry gifts, which don't get used much in his role as chancellor."

"I'm curious, are most of those appointments with female students?"

The receptionist looked at Alex wide-eyed. "Why yes. How did you know?"

"Lucky guess."

Alex looked at his watch. It was two minutes before three. He spotted a display case off to his right with trophies lining its shelves, and he walked over to look. His eyes scanned the dates on the trophies. The school, which was only four-years old, won championships in football and basketball for the last three years. Additionally, the school won championships in baseball for the last two years. Alex leaned over to view a trophy on the middle shelf. Then he heard the sound of footsteps. And a strong voice, which he recognized immediately.

"Quite the winning record, would you agree, Congressman?"

Alex straightened himself and turned to see the face he'd been loathing for years, smiling at him and looking much older than he remembered. Returning a polite smile, Alex extended his hand to the priest.

"Father Francis, it's been a very long time."

"Yes it has, Alex." The priest shook Alex's hand, then stepped back, folded his arms, and appraised his former altar boy.

"I remember when you were just this high," he said, moving his leveled right hand to his chest. "Now look at you. You are a grown man and a congressman, no less. It is inspiring to see an alumnus from St. Andrew's doing so well for himself."

"Thank you, Father."

Alex thought how much smaller the priest looked to him now. He calculated that the cleric would be in his late fifties—around fifty-six or seven. His body appeared well-toned, but his face, while still handsome, was creased in spots, and his hair was more salt than pepper. But he still carried himself with the same regal bearing that could make people around him feel insignificant. Alex had to keep reminding himself he was no longer the teen-aged altar boy who withered in this man's presence. He was a Harvard-educated attorney and an elected federal official who had the power of the United States government backing him. He motioned toward the trophy case.

"It looks as though St. Vincent's has done well for itself, too. Your winning record is extraordinary."

"I am sure that is the result of much prayer," the priest said with a smile.

"I certainly don't want to negate the power of prayer, Father, but don't you think much of the school's success on the field can be attributed to your ability to recruit so many star athletes?"

"We have been blessed to have attracted some of New York's finest athletes and scholars to St. Vincent College. I believe the culture of excellence that prevails at our school is what draws them."

Alex chuckled. "That may be what draws them, Father, but it's federal financial aid that keeps them. Am I right? I mean this is a private school. I can't imagine tuition is within the reach of the average student."

"Perhaps we can take this conversation to my office where we can be more comfortable," Father Francis said, motioning Alex toward the hallway.

"Certainly. Lead the way, Father."

The two men walked down a short corridor lined with pictures of smiling students involved in various campus activities. Stretched along the top of one wall was an elegant white banner with the words HALL OF EXCELLENCE in large, bold type in the official school color of royal purple. Approaching a door on the left, the priest motioned for Alex to step inside before him.

The spacious office was oval shaped with raised-panel mahogany wainscoting on the bottom half of the walls and traditional tan wallpaper on the top. An "L" shaped mahogany desk sat centered along the end wall to the right and was flanked by four upholstered office chairs.

"Please have a seat," the priest said as he walked behind his desk to sit down. Alex took the chair nearest the priest, and set his briefcase on the seat to his left.

"Very nice office, Father. Looks like the college is taking good care of its chancellor."

"The Board has been very gracious. They understand that a man's office must be suitable to the work with which he's been entrusted."

"I wish the US government felt the same way. You should see the average representative's office."

Father Francis showed a congenial smile. "So, is this a social visit, Congressman, or do you have some specific business to discuss?"

"A little of both, Father. As the new representative of this district, I want to become acquainted with the various institutions within my jurisdiction and the people who run them. Of course in our case, this visit is a chance for you and me to become *re-acquainted*, isn't it?"

The chancellor lifted his eyebrows and nodded.

"You probably aren't aware of it," Alex continued, "but you made quite an impression on me when I was an altar boy. I used to watch you say Mass, and I thought, 'I want to be just like him someday.' I seriously considered entering the priesthood."

"I think you would have made a fine priest."

"Well thank you, Father. That's kind of you to say that. My mother—you remember her, Jean Spencer—she wanted me to be a priest. She used to say, 'When you become a priest, Alex, be a good one.' And I'd think, aren't they all good?" Alex chuckled when he said it.

The priest continued smiling, but narrowed his eyes.

"Mother used to get a lot out of her counseling sessions with you, Father. Said they helped her cope with the loss of my father. I never thanked you for helping her."

"It was my pleasure. Your mother was a dear woman."

"I guess I didn't appreciate her until after she was gone." Alex paused and started scratching his head. "You know, Father, a few questions have haunted me since my mother died. First of all, what was she doing at the rectory before going to work that day . . . before her accident?"

Alex waited for a response.

"And what is the second question, Congressman?"

"Why was she crying when she left the rectory?"

Father Francis sat straight in his chair and placed his hands in front of him on the desk. "Well, Alex . . . Do you mind if I call you Alex?"

"Yes, I do mind, Father. I am an elected representative of the United States Congress and am due the honor associated with that position."

The priest stared for a moment, only a faint smile remaining. "Congressman Spencer . . . if I am not mistaken, your mother died thirteen years ago, shortly before I left St. Andrew's. Much has happened since then to occupy my thoughts. I regret to say I cannot remember why your mother visited the rectory or why she might have been crying."

"I see . . . I see. You know, there was something else I used to enjoy doing when I was an altar boy. I enjoyed walking over to the church after school and praying near the altar. Did you know there was a heat vent right near the kneeler? A heat vent that apparently connected to the duct feeding into your office. I heard things I shouldn't have heard, Father. Coming from your office. When my mother was supposed to be counseling with you. Shocking things . . ." Alex shook his head slowly.

The priest's smile faded, and his expression became cold. "Shall I presume you have moved beyond the social nature of this visit?"

"Yes. Yes I have, Father."

"Then what is the business you would like to discuss?"

"Where do I begin? My primary business is to invite you to resign from your position as Chancellor of St. Vincent College."

Father Francis gave Alex a scornful grin. "And what is your secondary business?"

Alex leaned forward and looked directly into the priest's eyes. "To drive you out of the priesthood."

"That is a rather ambitious agenda for your first term, Congressman. One that has no chance of succeeding, I am afraid."

"You seem rather confident about that, Father."

"Clearly, you have no other witnesses to what you purport to have heard. Otherwise you would have come after me long before now."

"Maybe so, Father. Maybe so." Alex leaned back in his chair. "By the way, does the name Carolyn Wentworth mean anything to you?"

"Does it mean anything to me? No. Do I recognize it? Yes."

"I'm surprised it doesn't mean anything to you, Father. I understand you and Carolyn were very close at one time. Very close, indeed. In fact . . . didn't she give birth to your son?"

Father Francis narrowed his eyes. "I resent your tawdry accusations, Congressman. And unless you have some proof that these charges are true, this conversation is over."

Alex looked at the priest and raised his shoulders with a sign of indifference. He stood up slowly, reached over to grab his briefcase, and then turned back toward the priest.

"You know, I'd hate to leave before discussing one more thing, Father. You don't mind if I sit down again . . ."

Without waiting for a response, Alex sat back in the chair and looked at the ceiling for a moment.

"We haven't discussed the issue of federal financial aid. You see, as a congressman, I'm privy to certain information. And it has come to my attention that the Department of Health, Education, and Welfare is launching an investigation as to why St. Vincent College has exceeded its quota of federal aid. I'm sure in that investigation they'll be taking a close look at the grant applications from the star athletes you've recruited, just to make sure none of the numbers were padded. This could certainly jeopardize your role as chancellor, don't you think, Father? And if the diocese was to hear of the other . . . tawdry accusations . . . on top of the college's financial discrepancies, well, they just might think it's time for you to hang up your cassock."

The priest glowered at Alex. "You will regret the day you stepped into my office, Congressman Spencer."

Alex stood and grabbed his briefcase. "My only regret, Father, is that I didn't step in sooner."

§

Once Alex left the office, Father Francis got up from his desk, walked over, and closed the door. Returning to his desk, he flipped through his Rolodex, then picked up the phone and dialed. "Senator Blake. This is Father Michael Francis. I have a favor to ask of you, my friend . . ."

§

"So how was your first weekend back to see the voters, Alex?" Ted Holbrook asked at the Monday breakfast gathering.

"Anybody throw tomatoes at you?" John Harrison asked, teasing.

"It went surprisingly well, actually," Alex said. "The biggest concern, of course, is the cost of fuel. The farmers are feeling the pinch with gas at sixty cents a gallon and climbing. I think my appointment to the agriculture subcommittee gave them a sense that someone was on the inside looking out for them."

"That's why they sent us here," Holbrook said.

"I remember my first visit back to my district last February," Glenn Baldwin said. "I won my election by a slim margin; in fact, it was so close, we had to have a recount. A few die-hard supporters of my opponent, Bernie Trott, refused to accept his defeat. When I arrived at the town hall for my constituent meeting, I saw several bumper stickers in the parking lot that said *Trott for Congress*, and I knew it was going to be an interesting morning.

"When I walked into the building, I saw them. All six were lined up along the back wall, wearing their *Trott for Congress* campaign pins and holding placards picturing their candidate's smiling face. I walked over and said, 'I don't know if you gentlemen heard or not, but the election's over, and I won.'

"They all glared at me. 'We heard,' one of them spoke up. 'Doesn't mean we have to believe it.' I just shook my head and walked away. I mean, could you imagine people acting that way if it was a presidential election? Sure makes for an uphill battle at the beginning of your term."

"Well, thankfully, I didn't see any Daniel Brumfeld bumper stickers on the cars at my meeting," Alex joked. "Of course, most of the bumpers were covered with snow."

The men around the table chuckled.

"Not to change the subject," Alex said, "but I had an unexpected message on my answering machine when I got to the office this morning. From Senator Blake."

All three men set their silverware down in unison and looked at Alex. "Senator Jeffrey Blake?" Holbrook asked.

"Chairman of the Senate Ethics Committee?"

Alex nodded.

"What did he want?" Baldwin asked.

"Said he wanted me to meet with him in his office today at five o'clock."

Baldwin looked at Holbrook, who raised his eyebrows. Harrison dropped his head and mumbled, "Uh-oh."

"What'd you do wrong?" Baldwin asked Alex.

"I didn't do anything wrong. And if I had, I'd be having a meeting with the chairman of the House Ethics Committee, not Senator Blake."

"Maybe so, but it doesn't bode well, Alex," Baldwin said.

"I've done nothing to be ashamed of. Maybe he just wants my advice on some ethics case he's laboring over." Alex's lighthearted comment was met with somber expressions from his three breakfast companions. "Guys, will you lighten up. I'm confident when we meet tomorrow for breakfast, I'll be able to tell you it was nothing more than a perfunctory visit."

Baldwin shook his head. "Alex, Alex. You can be so naïve at times. Senator Blake doesn't make routine visits with freshman congressmen. And, I'm afraid you'll have little appetite for breakfast tomorrow morning once he's through with you."

Alex felt himself growing weak.

§

As Alex approached the Russell Building, he recalled an earlier visit to the Senate offices with Doris during one of their trips to Washington. Back then he was simply a curious, carefree teenager, tagging along with his grandmother on a fieldtrip. Now he was a responsible public figure, entering the building because one of the most powerful chairmen in the US Senate summoned him. Although still unsure what prompted the senator's invitation, Alex felt himself resisting an urge to turn around and run, an urge that increased with each ascending step he took to the main door.

Once inside the building, he took the elevator to the second floor, stepped off, and began walking down a stately arched corridor, looking for room 259. The sound of his leather heels tapping against the polished parquet floor reverberated down the long, empty corridor. It was a sound void of any authoritative resonance, and, as Alex slowed his pace, it resembled the diminishing tick of a clock running out of time. When he saw the bronze plaque with the name Senator Jeffrey Blake, he stopped, took a deep breath, and exhaled as he opened the door. After several minutes, he was ushered from the reception area to the Senator's office door, which was ajar. Alex rapped twice.

"Come in!" a voice bellowed.

Alex pushed open the door and stepped into a rectangular room with mauve colored walls crowned with wide ornate molding. A large cherry desk butted up to the left wall, with a US flag standing beside it. Senator Blake stood with his back to Alex in front of a granite fireplace centered on the end wall. He held a brass poker in his hand and was forcing a smoldering log into place, sending sparks flying out onto the hearth.

"Close the door, and sit down," Blake said, still facing the fireplace. His cold reception erased any thoughts that this would be a cordial visit.

Two chairs, with a round cherry table between them, faced the fireplace and sat atop a red Oriental carpet. Walking timorously on the balls of his feet, Alex made his way to the chair on the right and sat down. Blake continued prodding the log.

"I understand you're a Harvard graduate, Congressman," Blake started.

"Yes sir. College and law school."

Blake shook his head, while jabbing the poker at the log. "Hard to believe such ineptitude can come out of a school of that caliber."

Alex began to squirm. "Sir?"

Senator Blake turned slowly away from the fire and glared at Alex. His right hand was wrapped around the handle of the fireplace poker, and he began tapping it against the wooden floor.

"I received a call this weekend from a dear friend of mine, Father Michael Francis. Said you were threatening to use information you gathered from HEW to tarnish his reputation."

Alex tried to swallow, but all moisture had left his mouth. The senator lifted his voice and the poker, leveling both in the direction of the freshman congressman.

"With one call, I can bring your misconduct to the attention of the House Ethics Committee. And they will begin an inquiry into why you interfered with an ongoing investigation by a cabinet-level department of this government. Why you disclosed confidential information. And why you used your official influence to bully a constituent. I can assure you, everything you've said behind closed doors will come to light. Anyone who provided you information will be called to account. By the time the Committee and the press are through with you, you'll regret the day you were born. Your influence as a congressman will evaporate overnight. Your political career will end before you can blink an eye. You'll be lucky if you can find a job shining shoes on Capitol Hill."

Senator Blake paused briefly and lowered the poker, his gaze fixed on Alex, who was sitting rigid and motionless. Alex felt a bead of sweat running down his left temple but couldn't find the strength to wipe it.

"There is only one thing saving your sorry hide right now," Blake continued, tapping the poker against the floor to accentuate his words. "One thing keeping me from bringing your name before the House Ethics Committee. And that's my respect for Jack Davidson."

Blake lowered the poker, then turned around and leaned it against the leg of the fireplace. He reached up, and grabbed a cigar and matchstick off the mantel. He struck the match and lit his cigar, taking three quick puffs before turning back toward Alex.

"Your grandfather helped me years ago during one of my darkest hours. Represented my company in a trademark infringement case when I was a young businessman in Boston. His legal savvy not only helped us win the case but protected us from future damages. Enabled me to grow that company and sell it at a terrific profit. I'd hate to think what it would do to him to see his only grandson under investigation. Hate to think what it would do to his business."

Blake sucked on his cigar and blew a cloud of smoke toward Alex.

"There're lots of Democrats in Congress who remember and loath your grandmother and her former boss. They'd love to make an example of you just to settle some old scores. They wouldn't hesitate to drag Jack's law firm into the investigation. Just to be sure you weren't using your influence to help the family business. Your one thoughtless and stupid action could open a Pandora's box, Congressman."

Blake walked over in front of Alex and leaned forward, his face only inches away. Jabbing the air with his cigar, he continued.

"I don't know what your vendetta is with Father Francis. But it stops right now. Is that clear?"

"Yes, sir."

Alex barely found his voice to respond. Hot ashes from Blake's cigar dropped onto his leg. He could feel them smoldering on his pant leg but didn't dare move. Blake hovered in front of his face, glaring, for a few seconds before straightening himself and turning back toward the fireplace. Alex quickly brushed the ashes off his leg and saw a hole in his pants the size of a pencil eraser.

"Michael Francis has been a friend of mine since we played football together at Thomas Aquinas High School. He performed my daughter's wedding. And he's likely to be the next bishop of his diocese when the current bishop retires this year. In fact, the apostolic nuncio has already submitted his name to the Congregation for Bishops. From there it goes to the pope for his decision." Blake turned toward Alex and resumed jabbing his cigar into the air. "I won't allow you or anyone else to jeopardize my friend's chances of attaining this position. You understand me, Congressman?"

Alex nodded.

Blake took one more drag from his cigar and tossed it into the fire. He turned and walked slowly to his desk, sitting down in his executive swivel chair. Leaning back, the senator fixed his eyes on Alex.

"Let me tell you what you're going to do, Congressman. There's an ethics conference coming up in San Francisco in late February. My secretary can provide you the details before you leave. I expect you to attend all three days at your own expense. You're to report back to me when you return. Then, I'll decide if we can put this issue behind us." The senator glared at Alex for a moment longer, then jerked his head toward the door. "Now get out of my office."

With that, the senator spun around in his chair and began perusing a document on his desk. Alex stood and paused awkwardly before turning and walking out. The clothes beneath his suit were soaked in sweat, and his skin felt cold and clammy. But inside he felt dead, as though the senator had pulled the plug on his life support and left nothing to sustain him.

§

For the next few weeks, Alex kept a low profile. He stopped attending the breakfast meetings. After a few days, Ted Holbrook called to see if he was all right. Alex explained that it would probably be best for the group if he distanced himself from them for now. Holbrook understood. Word had leaked out shortly after the meeting with Senator Blake that Alex had been called on the carpet for something. Nobody seemed to know the details, but most of his fellow representatives looked at him like he was contagious.

When he wasn't in committee meetings, Alex spent much of his time in his congressional office in Washington. He had purchased a cot and spent most nights working late and sleeping in his office, showering in the congressional gym in the morning. Work was the only thing that kept him from sinking into despair. If he had any down time, he spent it torturing himself, mentally replaying his meeting with Senator Blake and his last meeting with Kitty. He was anxious to get the ethics conference behind him and meet with Blake again. At least then, he would have some idea if he'd still have a future in politics. He hated uncertainty. And he hated himself for creating it.

To say he wished he'd taken Kitty's advice and put Father Francis behind him was an understatement. Hardly a day went by since his meeting with Senator Blake that he hadn't thought about her words. Certainly he experienced a brief euphoria following his confrontation with Father Francis. To release thirteen years of pent-up hostility with the measured calm of a prosecuting attorney and to see the look of spite on the priest's face was exhilarating. But within forty-eight hours, Father Francis was back in control, and, according to Blake, stood a good chance of becoming a bishop. Once again, Alex was powerless to stop the priest.

Kitty was right. He had wanted revenge more than happiness. But not anymore. He was tired of the struggle. In the summer, he would turn twenty-six. He didn't want to spend another year of his life being a lonely crusader on an elusive chase for justice. He wanted happiness. And he wanted Kitty. He only hoped she would believe him this time.

Chapter 27

"Thank you for meeting with me on such short notice, Father Vincenzo."

"I can always find time for our next bishop, Father Francis.

And I haven't been on campus since St. Vincent College opened. It's remarkable what you've accomplished here."

"Thank you. Though it may be a bit premature to call me the next bishop. My sources tell me that the Congregation for Bishops has not sent its final selections to the Holy Father yet. We could still be months away from knowing who he will select."

"Well, there is no one more suited to filling Bishop O'Keane's shoes than you, Michael."

"If you were not taking the position with the archbishop of Boston, I doubt whether my nomination would be as certain. But I am thankful for such blessings."

"And I'm thankful to be going home to Boston. Mother is eighty-two now. She's in wonderful health, but she won't live forever. It will be nice to live close to her and my siblings after all these years."

"I am truly happy for you, Thomas. Is Bishop O'Keane showing any improvement?"

"I'm afraid not. The tremor in his right arm is very pronounced, which, of course, affects his writing. His balance is becoming more unstable. I know he's determined to keep working until the pope selects his replacement, but the sooner, the better."

Father Francis nodded at Father Vincenzo, who was sitting to the left of his desk in the chancellor's office. After a moment of awkward silence, Father Francis sat back in his chair and said, "I have asked you here to discuss something that must remain confidential, Thomas. As I am so close to being nominated for bishop, I cannot afford to have any information leaked that could endanger my chances of being selected."

Father Vincenzo folded his hands on his lap and tilted his head slightly, his eyes questioning. "You have my confidence, Michael."

"Thank you." Father Francis leaned forward and rested his elbows on his desk. "I received an unpleasant visit from our new representative, Congressman Spencer, two weeks ago. According to him, the Department of Health, Education, and Welfare will soon be investigating St. Vincent's to see if there are any improprieties in our students' applications for financial aid. It seems we have an inordinate amount of federal grant money coming to the college.

"I spoke with Senator Jeffrey Blake, our old friend from Aquinas, and he assured me this could just be a routine process. HEW was recently under heavy scrutiny by a Senate Committee, and is looking to clear its name by playing tough with schools that are not adhering to the rules."

"Then you may have nothing to worry about . . ."

"So I thought until I met with Father Kaseman, my director of administrations. Apparently my trust in him was misplaced. It appears he may have padded some of the numbers on some students' applications, so they could get enough grant money to attend St. Vincent College."

"Did you tell the senator this?"

"Yes, I did. He felt certain I should dismiss Father Kaseman. Then we could explain to HEW that we became aware of the discrepancies and took the appropriate remedial actions. He was confident that any investigation would then be dropped quietly."

"Have you acted on his advice?"

"I dismissed Father Kaseman two days ago. He did not take it well. I told him I would provide a glowing recommendation to you, and I was sure you could find a parish for him to serve in."

Father Vincenzo leaned back and sighed while shaking his head. "And you expect me to do this without any disciplinary action first? The man knowingly misrepresented information on government documents, Michael."

"And, of course, you will put that in his personnel file, Thomas. You and I both know that will prevent him from ever securing a parish of his own, which should be punishment enough, wouldn't you say?"

"I don't know . . ."

"Would you rather discipline him through the formal process and take the chance of infuriating his grandfather when he finds out? Can the diocese afford to lose any of Mr. McGarry's support?"

Father Vincenzo considered Father Francis's argument. "I know of an opening for an associate at a small church in the Adirondacks. I can contact the Ogdensburg diocese. But what's to keep his grandfather from seeing this as a demotion for his grandson?"

Father Francis smiled. "I feel quite confident that Father Kaseman will be able to convince him that this is the Lord's will for his ministry."

"You seem rather sure about all of this, Michael."

"Father Kaseman has been quite predictable over the years." Father Francis cleared his throat. "There is one other matter to discuss . . ."

Father Vincenzo shifted uneasily in his chair.

"With Father Kaseman gone, I have had to move my staff around to fill the gaps. This has left me without a secretary. I understand Congressman Spencer's girlfriend works in the diocesan office."

"Yes, Kitty McAlister, a sweet girl. She works for your successor Father Domenici."

"What is the chance of me stealing her from Father Domenici?"

"I don't understand . . ."

"Have you never heard the adage *Keep your friends close and your enemies closer*? For whatever reason, Congressman Spencer appears to have ill will toward me. Unfortunately, he is in a position of power, now, and could cause me an immeasurable amount of trouble if he so chooses. I believe Senator Blake has already reprimanded him for threatening me about the financial aid issue, but the congressman lacks wisdom. I do not trust him. I would feel much better having someone who is close to him, like Miss McAlister, working closely with me. Perhaps it will enable me to anticipate his next move, should there be one."

"I'll see what I can do, but I can't make any promises. What if Miss McAlister prefers to stay where she is?"

"Do you really think she will pass up an opportunity to work for the future bishop?"

Father Vincenzo lifted his hands and shrugged.

Father Francis shook his head slowly and smirked. "Thomas, Thomas . . . wherefore dost thou doubt?"

Chapter 28

When United flight 201 touched down at San Francisco International Airport on the morning of February 21, Alex set his watch back three hours to eleven-thirty. He peered out the window at the sky, which looked like a blue canvas overlaid with random brushstrokes of white. The pilot announced that the current temperature was fifty. It would be a perfect day for biking.

Alex had been planning for this day ever since Senator Blake mandated he attend the ethics conference, which didn't begin until Monday. Coming in early on Saturday allowed him nearly two days to search the city. Though he realized it would be like finding a flea on an elephant, he was determined to try. He considered it a part of his retribution. He had to find Reed and tell him that he failed.

Taking a taxi to the Hotel Majestic, Alex checked into his room and donned his riding clothes: a pair of jeans, a sweatshirt, and a light jacket. He slipped into his sneakers and headed back down to the lobby to secure a map and rent a bicycle. Shortly afterwards, he was at the corner of Haight and Ashbury Streets, flipping a coin to decide which direction to take first.

Slowly pedaling west on Haight Street, Alex scanned the tired faces of those idling along the sidewalks, casualties of the street party that erupted nearly nine years earlier during the Summer of Love. The party had long since sputtered out, and most of its youthful participants had moved on to responsible lives. What remained was this disheveled, bedraggled long-haired remnant that never escaped from the delusion that their poverty was fashionable. Alex strained to see something familiar in their faces, in their eyes, in their movements that would remind him of Reed. Yet there was very little to distinguish one from the other as they lingered largely unnoticed among the crowds of locals and tourists.

Alex slowed his bike when he saw a patron exiting a shop in front of him to his left. She was carrying an easel in her arms and walking to her car, parked along the curb. The sweet smell of burning incense wafted out through the shop door before the breeze forced it closed. Alex looked up at the sign above the shop and read *Ziggy's Art Supplies*. He parked his bike in a stand in front of the store, locked it, and stuffed the key into his pocket. When he opened the door, he heard a familiar jingle, which reminded him of Beaman's grocery store in Stonebridge. The smell of incense was much stronger now that he was inside, and the soft mystic sound of Eastern music emanated from the front of the store.

A woman stepped out from behind a display to the left of Alex. She had black hair and dark skin, with a red dot in the center of her forehead, close to her eyebrows. Her pale lips parted when she smiled, revealing a glistening set of straight teeth. Her deep brown eyes glowed with an innocent vitality that contrasted sharply with the cold stares on the street.

"May I help you?" she asked.

"Well, I hope you can," Alex said, smiling. "I'm visiting from Washington, DC, and I'm looking for an old school mate who moved here about nine years ago. The last I knew he was a street artist, drew pictures on the sidewalk with chalks, and went by the name of Row. Do you have many street artists come in for supplies?"

"Most of our customers are residents in the neighborhood. We do get an occasional street artist, but most have left the area. Those who are still here usually can't afford to shop at Ziggy's."

Alex pursed his lips. "I understand . . . The man I'm looking for was also very talented with the yo-yo."

The woman smile politely and shook her head. "I'm sorry."

"Is there any particular place where poor, struggling artists hang out around here?"

"Some who've been here since the sixties are homeless. You'll see them on the street and in Golden Gate Park, living in the groves and bushes. They keep to themselves. Others, who can afford it, rent rooms in Upper Haight."

"That narrows it down some. But it sounds like this could be quite a challenge . . . Thanks for your help, Miss—"

"Ziggy. People just call me Ziggy," she said with a pleasant grin.

"Thank you, Ziggy."

He turned to leave, and when he reached the door Ziggy added, "There is one other place you might look: the free clinic on Clayton Street. If your friend has been sick and has no money, that's where he would go."

Alex smiled and turned his thumb up. "Thank you, again."

Once back on his bike, he continued down Haight to the next intersection and turned right onto Clayton Street. The Haight Ashbury Free Clinic was on the corner, on the second floor of a drab gray building with steps leading up from the sidewalk. Alex locked his bike and trudged up the stairs, not quite sure who he should talk to or what he should say.

After getting nowhere with the receptionist, he decided to inform her he was a congressman visiting the area and would appreciate any help she could give him in finding his friend. This opened the door for him to speak with the physician on duty, who then authorized the receptionist to check the records for the names Row, Row Wentworth, or Reed Wentworth. None of the names were found. Alex thanked her and moved on.

He spent the rest of the afternoon riding tirelessly around the neighborhood, up and down the rolling side streets lined with stately trees and bright Victorian homes, in and out of shops and cafes, asking clerks and servers if they'd ever seen an artist who stood around six feet tall, had gray eyes, and who did tricks with a yo-yo. Sometimes he received hopeful leads that never panned out. Most times he was met with a puzzled but sympathetic look, followed by a slow shaking of the head.

At five-thirty, the sun began to fade into the horizon, and Alex felt his stomach growling. It was the first time he thought about food since he arrived in the city. And now it was all he could think about. He was back where he started over four hours ago—at the corner of Haight and Ashbury. He spotted a little diner called Herbie's just east of the intersection and rode over to check it out. The menu was posted on the window and consisted of standard American fare, including hamburgers and hot dogs.

But not just any hot dogs.

These were Herbie's Hots, made from the finest pork and lathered with Herbie's Hot Sauce. "Guaranteed to make you scream, 'Fire!'" For the timid, there was the one-alarm sauce. For the daring, the two-alarm sauce. And for the fearless, there was the three-alarm sauce, which came with a pitcher of water shaped like a fire extinguisher.

Alex peeked into the window. The place was crowded, and everyone seemed to be having a great time. Through the window he heard a bell ring three times, followed by shouts of "Fire!" He chuckled to himself and thought, *Why not.*

He pulled open the door and walked into a room electrified with the sounds of laughter and chatter and silverware clinking against glass plates. The distinctive smells of fried grease and onions, mixed with the pungent odor of tobacco smoke, gave the place a state-fair ambience, minus the manure. A sign at the door said SEAT YOURSELF. Spotting an empty chair at the counter, Alex walked over and sat down.

Pulling a menu from a metal rack in front of him, Alex glanced toward the open kitchen beyond the counter. A dwarfish man with a large head faced him, standing over a grill. His hands were in constant motion—flipping burgers with the spatula in his right hand and turning hot dogs with the tongs in his left. And he barked orders non-stop to the other kitchen staff, which consisted of two gangling teen-age boys, tripping over themselves and hustling to keep up.

The short man wore a white double-breasted chef uniform and a white toque that sat low on his forehead and drooped over his left ear. Both the uniform and cap were stained with grease. He had an irascible disposition, a leathery face, and a grating voice. He spewed expletives frequently when he was annoyed, and the patrons seemed to enjoy egging him on just to hear his high-pitched obscenities or watch his vulgar gestures.

Alex watched in amusement when a customer sitting at the end of the counter yelled, "Hey Herbie! Still waiting for my dog. Trying to starve me to death?" Without missing a beat, the little cook, still holding the spatula, cocked his right arm up at the elbow, stuck up his middle finger, and rolled his hips, then brought the spatula down to flip the next burger. Alex looked down at his menu and smirked, wondering how Herbie's act would play in Stonebridge.

"What'll it be, Big Boy?" a woman asked.

Alex looked around to see where the voice was coming from, but saw no one.

"Down here, Goliath."

Alex turned around to his right and looked down to see a woman standing no taller than his belly. She wore a blue waitress uniform—with blue and white checker trim on the sleeves and collar—a white apron, and a starched cap. Pinned above her chest on the left was a white plastic tag with the name Marge engraved in black letters. She had a curmudgeonly look but a twinkle in her eye that said she enjoyed being mischievous.

Alex swiveled his head to look at the cook then back at the waitress.

"Yeah, that's right, Bozo. You're in munchkin land, where the little people rule."

"Are you two related?" Alex asked, gesturing back and forth with his finger.

"That's my husband Herbie. We run this joint. You're not from around here are you?"

"I'm visiting from the East Coast. My name is Alex Spencer. I'm a congressman from New York State."

"I won't hold that against ya, Mr. Congressman."

"That I'm a politician or that I'm from New York?"

"Both. Have you figured out what you want to eat?"

"I think I'll try two Herbie's Hots with the three-alarm sauce."

"Feeling pretty brave tonight, huh, Tiger?"

"Brave or foolish, not sure which." Alex had forgotten the woman's name already and looked at her tag again. "So tell me, Marge, what does it mean when people scream "Fire!" after the bell rings?"

"When the bell rings three times, that means somebody's order for a three-alarm Herbie's Hot is done and ready. Some dummy started yelling "Fire!" years ago when he heard the bell ring, and it just sorta caught on with the customers."

"Got it. But only with the three-alarm?"

Marge nodded. "Only with the three-alarm. Now, you having anything else with your hots?"

"How about some onion rings and a Coke."

"Comin' right up, Bigfoot."

Alex smiled as Marge left with his order. He was glad he decided to eat here. His frustrations about his fruitless afternoon had all but disappeared. There was still tomorrow. There were still a few places he hadn't checked out in Upper Haight. And he had yet to search in Golden Gate Park. He didn't want to think Reed was homeless, but he wasn't going to rule it out. A lot could have gone wrong for his old friend since their last visit together.

The bell rang three times, and Alex cupped his hands around his mouth and shouted, "Fire!" along with several other raucous regulars.

Glancing up, he saw a sign above the opening to the kitchen. He hadn't noticed it earlier when his attention was riveted on Herbie. The sign read CASH ONLY! NO CHECKS OR CREDIT CARDS ACCEPTED! He felt for his wallet in his back pocket and pulled it out to see if he had any small bills. He planned on using his American Express card for any expenses he incurred on this trip but brought a few hundred in cash for backup. He didn't relish the idea of whipping out a hundred-dollar bill and asking his prone-to-sarcasm hosts to break it for a three-dollar meal.

Opening his billfold, he saw he had a ten folded in with the other cash, and he relaxed. His eye caught sight of a piece of folded paper wedged in the corner crevice of his billfold, and he pulled it out. As he unfolded the tattered note, he remembered. His eyes scanned the four lines he had written down nearly two years ago:

> *Like the wind, you have shaken a reed*
> *To where blown only known by a marge*
> *On hate for a father doth feed*
> *Whose guilt will be laid to your charge*

He was drawn to the second line, the line he was never able to decipher. Reaching into the inside pocket of his jacket, he pulled out a ballpoint pen and clicked the end. Tracing over the letter *m* in the word *marge*, he changed it to an uppercase letter. When he was through, he re-read the first two lines. He set the paper down on the counter and swallowed hard. *Is this the Marge that will lead me to Reed?*

While Alex was still thinking, Marge returned with his Coke. She was on the other side of the counter now, and had climbed up onto a step that ran the length of the counter, enabling her to stand at eye-level with her customers.

"You look like somebody just stepped on your grave, Congressman," Marge said.

"Huh . . . Oh, sorry. Just thinking about something."

"Didn't think you politicians could do stuff like that."

Alex forced a smile. "Marge, would you mind if I ask you a question?"

"Can ask all the questions you want, Stretch. Don't mean I'm gonna answer 'em."

"I'm trying to locate an old friend of mine who moved out here in '67 to find his mother. He was a street artist named Row; drew with chalks on the sidewalks. Stands about six feet tall. When I last saw him, he had long black hair and a beard. Anybody like that ever come into your diner?"

Marge gave Alex a skeptic look. "This ain't some undercover investigation your doin', is it? Cause we pay our taxes and everything . . ."

Alex put his palms out toward her. "No, no, not at all, Marge. I really am looking for my friend. I spent the whole afternoon asking around Haight-Ashbury to see if anyone might have run into him somewhere. I'm beginning to fear he's homeless, gone, or dead."

While Marge stared at Alex, the bell rang three times, and the shout of "Fire!" rang out. Alex didn't join in this time.

"That'll be your dogs," Marge said, stepping down and turning to get them. Watching her waddle away, Alex thought about the look in her eyes when he asked her about Reed. *She knows something. I'm sure of it.*

A few minutes later, Marge returned with Alex's hot dogs and onion rings and placed them on the counter. She started to leave and then hesitated. "Anything about this friend of yours that's . . . peculiar?"

Alex laughed. "I used to think a lot was peculiar about him when we shared the same dorm room. Did I mention he's good with a yo-yo?"

"No, you didn't." Marge looked like she was calculating something in her head. "Is his old man religious?"

"Well . . . that all depends on who his father is." Alex felt like he was playing a guessing game with the woman. "If it is who I think it is, then yes, he is a religious person; he's a priest."

Marge's eyes widened. "Does your friend go by any other name than Row?"

"His real name is Reed, Reed Wentworth. Row is an acronym formed from his initials."

Marge held her hand up, signaling she needed a moment. She turned and jumped down from the step and scurried out to the kitchen, where she motioned to her husband. He stepped down to the floor from his platform and faced his wife. Alex could just see their heads above the top of the stove, and Marge was talking fast. Occasionally she turned her head toward Alex, and Herbie turned also. After a minute or so, Marge nodded her head, and Herbie seemed to nod in agreement. Marge gave him a peck on the cheek, and Herbie started to blush, his face momentarily softening. But the second he climbed back onto his platform and resumed cooking, the sour puss returned.

When Marge stepped back up to the counter to face Alex, she was panting, and made a gesture indicating she needed to catch her breath. After a moment she said, "Every Sunday I pack up the leftovers I've saved from the restaurant all week. Bring it to the homeless in Golden Gate Park. Been doing it for years. There's a homeless man lives there by the name of Reed. Sounds like he might be your guy. Goes by the name of Reed Francis, though. But that don't mean nothing. People over there change their names to suit their fancy. If you wanna meet me here tomorrow morning at 11:30, you can come with me. I'll show you where he stays."

"Thank you. I'll be here," Alex said, his voice wavering. He saw the tattered paper from his wallet sitting on the counter and held it up. "I've been waiting nearly two years for you, Marge." Just then the bell rang three times. This time, Alex shouted.

§

At 11:25 the next morning, Alex stepped out of a cab in

front of Herbie's and saw a sign that said CLOSED hanging on the front door. He tried the door handle. It was locked. Pressing his face to the window and cupping his hands along his temples, Alex peeked in and saw some movement in the kitchen area. He rapped on the window three times and saw a tall, skinny figure moving toward the door. When the person got closer, Alex recognized him as one of the boys working in the kitchen the night before. After fumbling with the lock for a few seconds, the boy unlocked the door and opened it, smiling self-consciously at Alex.

"I'm looking for Marge," Alex said.

"My mother's in the back, loading the car."

Alex stepped inside, and the boy locked the door and led the way to the rear of the store.

"Marge is your mother?" Alex asked as they walked.

"Yes, sir."

"I didn't know . . . little people . . . could have children as tall as you."

"It happens."

"Was that other young man working with you last night your brother?"

"No, just a friend from school."

"My name is Alex Spencer, by the way." Alex extended his hand. "What's yours?"

"Tommy, Tommy Reicher." The boy gave Alex a flimsy handshake and a smile that revealed silver braces across his top teeth.

"Good to meet you, Tommy."

At the back of the store, the rear door was propped open, and Marge and Herbie were loading the last few boxes of food into the back of a rusted blue Ford Falcon station wagon. The rear bench seat was folded down, and the back of the car was packed with boxes.

"Good morning, folks," Alex said, smiling.

"Mornin' to you, Mr. Congressman," Marge replied. "I

don't believe you met my husband."

Alex introduced himself to Herbie and was surprised at how docile and bashful the little man was when he wasn't working in his kitchen. He showed a tenderness toward his wife and son that contrasted sharply with his bristly cook persona. And after witnessing their genuine devotion and affection for one another, Alex found himself liking the Reicher family more and more.

"Ready when you are, Mr. Congressman" Marge said, wiping her hands as her son closed the tailgate of the station wagon. "Tommy'll get in first."

Tommy came around from behind the car, opened the passenger door, and slid to the middle of the bench seat. Alex stepped in after him and closed the door. The scent of food and cold cardboard filled the car. Marge got in on the driver's side and sat down on a thick cushion, which lifted her to the appropriate height. Her feet rested on modified brake and gas pedals that extended from the floorboard nearly a foot higher than standard pedals. She closed her door, pulled the shift lever on the steering column, and proceeded out onto the service road to Ashbury Street. From Ashbury, she took a left onto Haight and drove west to Golden Gate Park.

Marge parked the Falcon close to the east side of the park and pointed to a dense growth of bushes and trees. "Your man lives in the clearing behind those bushes. About six or eight more with him. All harmless and hungry. Tommy and I'll take you there. Then we'll go on to the other spots. Pick you up in about an hour if you want."

"That'd be great," Alex said as he started to open his door.

"Mr. Spencer," Marge said, her tone suddenly serious, "I wanna warn you, these men are not what your kind is used to seeing. Lots of them sick from drugs and booze. Some just down on their luck. They can be dirty and smelly. But they're human beings. Precious fruit of God's earth. Looking for some kindness from somebody, just like the rest of us."

Alex pressed his lips together and nodded. "Marge, what

motivates you to do this for these people?"

Marge placed her hand on her son's knee and looked up at Alex. "Cause there was a time when Tommy and I were in the same boat with these folks. Why don't you let Tommy out to start unloading, and I'll tell you the story."

Alex stepped out of the car, and Tommy slid over on the seat and stepped out behind him. When Alex was back in the car, Marge continued in a low voice.

"See, a long time ago, fifteen years to be exact, I was raped by a man who thought it would be a big joke to 'hump a midget,' as he put it. I got pregnant. Nine months later I had Tommy. I lost my job near the end of my pregnancy. Had no kin to help. Stayed in some charity shelters as long as I could, but they're not for taking care of folks long-term. When our welcome ran out, Tommy and me ended up on the streets. Eventually found our way to this park. The homeless folks here treated us like we were family. Made sure we were safe and fed.

"After a while, I picked up a waitressing job at a place that let me keep Tommy in a back room when I worked. That's where I met Herbie. He took a liking to Tommy and me. When he married me, he became my savior. But I never forgot my time here. And bringing this food is my way of saying thanks."

Alex shook his head slowly. "You're quite a remarkable woman, Marge."

"Just a survivor, Mr. Congressman."

Tommy stuck his head underneath the tailgate and said the boxes were ready to go.

The three each grabbed a box of food and began walking along a footpath into the park. When they reached a break in the stand of bushes to their right, Marge turned off the path and walked through into the clearing, with Tommy and Alex following.

Around the northern quadrant of the clearing's perimeter was a scattering of blankets, tarps, and cardboard, loosely assembled to provide a veneer of shelter and privacy for the inhabitants. Smoke arose from a circle of stacked rocks in front of one of the more prosperous shelters, which looked like an old green army tent. Marge looked back at Alex and smiled.

"They got the fire ready cause they know I'm coming with some cold burgers and dogs to warm up."

As the three got closer to the camp, Alex smelled the musty scent of damp, dirty blankets mixed with campfire smoke. And he heard snoring, coughing, and chattering coming from various shelters. A few heads popped out from underneath makeshift awnings to observe the approaching visitors.

"Hey, it's Marge," one man said.

"Marge is here," another said, louder.

"Hi Margie!" another cried.

Marge turned toward Alex; her face was beaming. "Your man is over here," she said, motioning with her head toward a black plastic tarp strung over a rope between two trees and staked to the ground. Alex could see the back of a man seated in a webbed lawn chair. Three of the webs were frayed, and two others had already snapped and were dangling down the back of the chair. The man had long, uncombed hair—black with a trace of gray—and his shoulders were of average span and slightly stooped. He turned his head slowly to his left when he heard Marge's approach.

"How you doing today, Big Boy?" Marge asked the man.

"Livin' the dream, Margie. Livin' the dream."

"Brought a visitor for you today."

Alex, who had been standing behind Tommy, walked around next to Marge. He struggled to hide his reaction when he saw Reed, but his involuntary gasp gave him away. With his sagging, emaciated face and protruding cheekbones; and his drooping gray eyes with their constricted pupils; and his filthy, disheveled hair and overgrown beard, Reed looked like a corpse that was still breathing. He stared at Alex with an unknowing, apathetic look, while scratching his arms with shaking hands.

"Hi, Reed . . . It's me, Alex Spencer."

Reed squinted for a few seconds and then smirked. "That you, kid? What're you doing here?"

"Came to see you. How you doing?"

"Livin' the dream, kid. Livin' the dream."

Marge touched Alex's sleeve. "Tommy and I will leave you two alone. We got folks waiting for lunch." She motioned her head toward a group of men standing outside Reed's tent.

"I'll meet you back at the car in an hour," Alex said. Tommy took Alex's box of food and followed his mother and the waiting men toward the fire pit.

"Welcome to my humble abode, kid. Pull up a chair, and make yourself comfortable."

Alex eyed another beat-up lawn chair near the back of the tent, dragged it over across from Reed, and sat down.

"You're a long way from home, aren't you?" Reed asked, still scratching.

"Out here on business. I'm a congressman now, Reed."

Reed let out an impressed whistle. "A congressman all the way from Washington paying me a visit at Camp Golden Gate. How about that."

"I ran into a crazy woman in East Village two years ago. She told me you came out here in '67 to find Carolyn. Did you ever find her?"

A slight smile parted Reed's whiskers. "Yeah, I found her."

Alex leaned forward in his chair. "Can you tell me about it?"

Reed started to respond but went into a coughing jag that sounded deep and painful. Alex reached toward him with concern, but Reed waved him off. When he finished coughing, he hacked up a wad of phlegm and spit it out toward the entrance to his tent.

"Sorry, kid. Comes on all of a sudden." He reached for a dented metal thermos, unscrewed the top, and guzzled something. After wiping his mouth on his sleeve, he screwed the top back on and set the thermos down.

"Have you seen a doctor about that?"

Reed raised his eyebrow and smirked. "Thought you wanted to hear how I found Carolyn."

Alex sat back and nodded.

"When I got to Haight-Ashbury that summer, the place was like one big party. Kids came from all over. I found a crash pad to live in and started doing my sidewalk drawings for a while. Some guy told me about a woman who had a small studio on Cole Street where she taught art. Said the woman drew just like me. So I visited the shop and saw the lady. It was Carolyn. Much older and thinner than the pictures I'd seen of her, but definitely her. She went by the name Carolyn Francis.

"I didn't want to just blurt out who I was, so I figured I'd sign up for a class and get to know her a bit. She noticed the similarities in our techniques and began asking me questions about my background and training. At first, I lied to her and told her I attended the Art Institute of Boston. Her face lit up, and she told me she'd attended the same school. I asked her what year she graduated, and her face suddenly looked sad. She told me she didn't graduate because some things happened in her life that forced her to drop out—"

Reed suddenly had another coughing spurt, but it was less severe than earlier. When he was finished, he took another swig from the thermos and wiped his mouth on his sleeve.

"I told her it was too bad she didn't finish, and she just sighed. Then I got bold and asked her if she got pregnant or something. At first, her eyes opened wide, like I'd just read her mind. Then she got defensive and said her reasons for dropping out were personal. So I let it go.

"One day, shortly after that, we were alone in her studio, drawing and talking. She commented about the color of my eyes. She asked me if either of my parents had gray eyes. I told her I thought my father did. She looked at me funny and asked, 'Don't you *know* if your father has gray eyes?' I told her I didn't know for sure who my father was. She said that was sad and asked me if I knew who my mother was. That's when I decided to tell her the truth—at least as I knew it to be.

"I said my mother came from a wealthy family in Boston. She attended the Art Institute of Boston but didn't finish because she got pregnant by a priest she met at a wedding.

"By this point, Carolyn's face was white, and she had to sit down. So I waited before continuing.

"I told her my mother had considered killing herself when she was pregnant, just to protect the priest's reputation. But she changed her mind for some reason and gave birth to her baby, her son, Reed, before leaving him with her parents to raise. I then looked directly into her eyes, which were filled with tears, and told her I was Reed Wentworth, her son. She fainted."

Reed reached again for his thermos and took a drink, looking over at Alex, who was sitting rigid and waiting for Reed to continue. "You sure you want to hear all this, kid?" Reed asked, setting the thermos down.

"Are you kidding me? I've been waiting thirteen years to hear this story."

Smirking, Reed wiped his mouth and continued. "When she came to, she was crying and laughing, wanting to look at me and ask me all sorts of questions. After that she told me her story.

"She said she fell in love with the priest and thought he loved her. For several months after meeting her at the wedding, Father Francis visited Boston every chance he could get, just to see Carolyn. In late January of '47, they spent an afternoon alone together in a friend's chalet after skiing. That's when she got pregnant. She realized her condition in early March, but she didn't tell anyone at first. She knew her parents (my grandparents, now) would be furious, and she was concerned about ruining the priest's reputation. Sometime in the spring, she thought about killing herself.

"She remembered writing the suicide letter to the priest. Said she hesitated to send it for a few days because she was so afraid. She hid the letter in the chest—the one with the tole painting on the lid. That same week, the priest surprised her with a visit, and she told him she was pregnant. And you know what advice that great spiritual leader gave my mother?"

Alex shook his head.

"He said, 'Make it go away.'"

Alex thought for a moment. "You mean abortion?"

Reed nodded. "Yeah, he even gave her the name of some people who would do it for her. What a guy, huh? My mother said she had always been real religious up to then. She decided to have the baby and not tell anyone who the father was."

"Why didn't she want to reveal who the father was?" Alex asked. "She probably could've gotten Father Francis kicked out of the priesthood."

"And that's why she didn't. Even though she lost respect for the priest, she still revered the priesthood and, as she put it, didn't want to lift her finger against God's anointed.

"She made the mistake of telling her parents she was pregnant. You can probably guess how that went over. The old man sent Carolyn and her mother to Europe for the rest of the pregnancy, so she wouldn't bring scandal on the sacred Wentworth name. When they returned home from Europe with me, the old man decided to tell folks I was his and my grandmother's son. He had my birth certificate changed, so I became the son and heir he never had.

"My mother was so disgusted that she ran away from it all and went to East Village to start a new life. Eventually, she worked her way across the country to get as far away from the Wentworth shadow as she could. Ended up out here in the early sixties. Never married. Never had another kid."

"Where is she now, Reed?"

Reed dropped his head and sat quietly for a moment. "Died two years ago. Heroin overdose. But she left me something to remember her by . . ." Reed slowly rolled up his right sleeve. The crook of his arm was black and blue and riddled with needle marks. "Betcha never seen the arms of a heroin addict have you, kid?" With a glint of humor, he moved his arm closer to Alex, who drew back with a start. Reed began laughing himself into another coughing jag that lasted for several seconds. When it subsided, he took another drink from his thermos. This time he wiped his mouth with his hand.

"Reed, let me get you help," Alex pleaded. "You don't need to live like this."

"Don't I?" Reed's face suddenly took on a sadistic look. "Did you ever stop to think if you'd never told me about Father Francis, if you'd never taken my mother's suicide letter that I might be living some normal life somewhere? And now you think you can help me?"

Reed's words were like blades piercing Alex's conscience.

"And tell me, Spencer, what happened to all your great plans to get even with the priest? Let me guess, you've been too busy building a cushy career for yourself to worry about it."

Reed started hacking again, harder than before. His face turned red and the veins were bulging on his neck and forehead. He spit another wad of phlegm toward the entrance to his tent and took another drink. This time he didn't bother to wipe his mouth. Spittle and liquid ran down, and some of it sprayed on Alex as Reed continued his diatribe.

"I hate that priest. For what he did to my mother. For stealing her life. For going on with his life like nothing happened. For treating me like I was disposable . . ." Reed hung his head and breathed heavily. After a moment he started shaking his head slowly from side to side and began snickering. "And that's exactly what I've become . . . disposable."

"I did try, Reed," Alex said. "I tried to get even, but it backfired." He told him about his attempt to disgrace the priest, how it went wrong, and how an ethics committee might investigate him for his actions. He told him about the ethics convention that brought him out to San Francisco. He told him about his decision to forget about the priest and move on with his life. And he told him about Father Francis's chances of becoming the next bishop of Rochester.

"A bishop," Reed said, sounding drowsy. "He told my mother it was his dream to become a bishop. And you're going to sit by and let that happen, knowing all you know about him?"

"It's out of my hands, Reed. There's nothing else I can do."

"Nothing else you *can* do? Or nothing else you *will* do?"

Alex didn't respond.

"And when is the good father to be made bishop, if he's selected?" Reed asked.

"Not sure, could be weeks or months away."

"Do me a favor, Spencer. Let Margie know when the date's been set, and have her tell me. I'd like to know. Maybe in some deranged way it would bring an end to this for me— y'know, the priest achieves his dream; game over; I lost. Maybe then I could move on. I'll never forgive him, but I'd like to forget him."

"Sure, I can do that for you, Reed. I hope you can move past this. You're still young. You've got a lot of life to live. I wish you'd let me get you some medical help."

Reed pointed to a shoebox sitting on top of layers of blankets covering the ground to his right. "All the medical help I need is in there. And I think it's about time for my medicine. So, if you don't mind, I'll say goodbye."

Alex pushed himself up from the chair and brushed off the back of his pants. His mind was racing. Had he said everything he'd come to say? Was there anything else he could do to convince Reed to get help? Was this visit sufficient penance to atone for ruining Reed's life? Then he saw Reed getting up and extending his trembling hand toward him. Alex clasped it and helped him up, feeling his own hand shudder with his.

"Good seeing you, kid," Reed said, wearing his incessant smirk. "Don't stay away so long next time."

Alex gazed into his friend's tired gray eyes, eyes that only minutes ago were alive with bitterness and hatred but now disclosed a mood of languid sadness. And he wondered if he was looking at those eyes for the last time. He wrapped his arms around Reed's shoulders in a bear hug, feeling more bone than flesh and choking back the overwhelming urge to retch. Alex said the one thing that came to his mind: "I'll be praying for you, Reed." When Alex stepped back, he noticed the smirk was momentarily gone, and Reed was biting his lip. Alex turned and started walking out of the tent, conscious of avoiding the areas where Reed had spit.

"Don't forget to let Margie know about the priest," Reed said.

Alex lifted his hand and nodded. When he reached the edge of the clearing, he looked back and saw Reed on his knees over the open shoebox, wrapping a strap around his upper arm. Alex turned away and kept walking.

§

Reed set the empty, dripping syringe in the shoebox and released the rubber strap from around his bicep. He set the strap in the box and fumbled around until he felt the familiar smooth lines of the short metal barrel, the machined grooves in the rotating cylinder, and the warm textured grips of the contoured handle. When he pulled his hand from the box, he was cradling the only thing in his world he could rely on—his Colt .38. He kissed the barrel and muttered, "I think it's time we touched God's anointed."

Chapter 29

Alex pulled open the oak door leading into the rear of the sanctuary at St. Andrew's Church in Stonebridge. It had been a little over two weeks since he returned from the ethics conference in San Francisco, and he had much for which to be thankful. In his follow-up meeting with Senator Blake in DC, Alex was told by the Senator that he would not push for an investigation of the congressman by the House Ethics Committee. He had decided to chalk up the freshman representative's careless actions to bad judgment, stemming from his youth and inexperience. But Blake left Alex with the stern warning that should he ever use his position of authority so recklessly again, the senator would personally do everything within his power to have Alex ousted from office.

The trip back to Stonebridge was for both business and personal reasons. Alex met with a community leader the day before, on Friday, to discuss federal funding for summer programs to assist minority children. But today, during the quiet of Saturday morning, it was his time to reconcile with God.

The oak door to the sanctuary still made the same creaking sound it did the last time he visited thirteen years ago. Alex stepped inside the vacant chamber and looked around. Nothing had changed. The traditional altar remained, in spite of Vatican II. Golden hues of sunlight still filtered through the same stained glass windows. Votive candles burned softly near the altar, mixing the scent of melting beeswax with the sweet fragrance of incense that lingered in the air. The crucifix hanging over the center of the altar wasn't as large as he remembered it, but it was clearly the same. Alex felt like he had come home.

He turned, walked toward the holy water font, and dipped the tips of his fingers into the reservoir. Making the sign of the cross, he felt the familiar cool dampness on the center of his forehead. He walked toward the front pew and sat on the side close to the center aisle. To his right he saw the heat vent. Remaining silent all these years, he hoped. How he wished he never sat next to it that cold October day. How much different life would have been without those memories to haunt him, without all those years of frustration from wanting justice and having it elude him. But today was not about justice. It was about mercy. Mercy he needed to receive and mercy he needed to give.

A man, his shoulders slightly hunched, limped out from the vestry with a broom and dustpan in his hands. Alex recognized it was Mr. Knapp, the janitor, still busy with the work of cleaning the Lord's house. Alex smiled when he saw the man, and it occurred to him that time seemed to have passed St. Andrews by, leaving much unchanged. Mr. Knapp, looking around the room, nodded when he saw Alex, and walked over in front of the heat vent, where he began to sweep the floor. He glanced at Alex a few times, as though he wanted to say something, but then seemed to think better of it and continued his work. After Mr. Knapp left the room, Alex made his way to the kneeler to pray.

Sinking his knees into the cushion, Alex looked up at the crucifix over the altar. He remembered the Christmas story about a host of angels appearing to shepherds on a hillside, saying, "Peace on earth, goodwill to men." He was finally ready to have peace in his life. And ready to show goodwill by forgiving the priest he'd despised for too long and by praying for the man whose life he'd shipwrecked. He bowed his head, closed his eyes, and talked to God.

When he was finished, Alex lifted himself from his knees. He took a deep breath and let it out slowly. It felt like a weight had lifted from him. And he felt clean. Walking toward the center aisle, he turned toward the altar and dropped to one knee, then stood up, making the sign of the cross. He walked out the side door of the church into a sunny, mild early March morning. He looked at his watch and smiled, then started down the sidewalk for a stroll into downtown Stonebridge.

When Alex reached Main Street, it seemed the whole town was out enjoying the respite from the winter weather. A few people recognized him and smiled and nodded. But largely, he went unnoticed. He stepped onto the lift bridge, walked about ten feet, and stopped to look out at the ice chunks breaking up in the canal. After a few minutes, a woman's voice spoke to him from the edge of the bridge.

"Thinking of jumping, Congressman?"

Alex turned and saw Kitty grinning.

"I just changed my mind," he said.

He walked over and gave her a hug. "What are you doing down here? I thought you were a city girl now?"

"I may live in the city, but I'm a Stonebridge girl at heart. Just enjoying the nice weather like everyone else. When did you get into town?"

"Got in yesterday for a meeting. Today's all mine, though. Would you like to take a walk with me?"

Kitty smiled and nodded.

They strolled up one side of Main Street and down the other, stopping only to get ice cream cones at a dairy store before continuing on. They ended up at the gazebo near the canal and sat on the picnic bench, licking their cones.

"So what were you so deep in thought about on the bridge earlier?" Kitty asked.

"I had just come from St. Andrew's. First time I stepped inside there since my mother's funeral. It felt good. Like old times. I got some things straightened out with God. Things I've been thinking about since you said them to me in January. About wanting revenge more than I want you. You were right about that, Kitty. And I almost blew it big time. When I prayed this morning at church, I forgave the priest, and decided to put that all behind me."

"Do you really mean that?" Kitty had a tender, but no-nonsense look on her face.

"Yes. I really do. I'm not carrying the bitterness anymore. It's just not worth it."

Kitty looked at Alex cautiously. "Well, I'm glad to hear that." She looked down briefly before continuing. "You should know that I'm working for Father Francis now, as his secretary."

Alex looked at her wide-eyed. "At St. Vincent's?"

"Yes. He had some staff adjustments, and he specifically requested me to come on as his secretary."

"But I thought you liked your job at the diocesan office?"

"I did, but this was better money and, I think, a better opportunity. You know, Father Francis is being considered as a replacement for Bishop O'Keane?"

"I heard that. Do you know when the announcement will be

made about that appointment?"

"It's in the pope's hands now. Could happen any day."

"So, I guess there's a chance you'll only be working for Father Francis a short time."

"Unless he wants me to come back to the diocesan office and work for him once he's bishop."

"You'd do that?"

"Certainly. Why wouldn't I?"

Alex thought for a moment of all the reasons why she shouldn't, but put them out of his mind. "Kitty, I meant what I said about forgiving the priest. I have. That doesn't mean I trust the man. Still, it's not for me to tell you who to work for. I would just caution you to be careful, that's all."

"I appreciate your concerns, Alex, but I'm a big girl. I think I can handle myself around Father Francis. Anyway, he's been nothing but a gentleman with me since I've started."

"I'm glad to hear that. But promise me you'll be careful."

"I'll be careful; I promise. I'm proud of you, Alex."

"For what?"

"I expected you to get upset when I told you I was working for Father Francis. You handled it very well."

"Well, I meant what I said. I've wasted too much time and energy agonizing about that man. I want to move on with my life."

"When do you head back to DC?"

"I fly back tomorrow morning. I've got some things I need to do in the office before the week begins."

"But you said today is free, right?"

"Yes . . ."

"I know a girl who'd be willing to go on a date with you tonight if you asked her nicely."

§

At 10:45 on Sunday morning, Alex arrived at the Rochester airport. After checking in his bag, he headed toward the gate, stopping at a newsstand to pick up the morning paper. He froze when he saw the headline: *POPE PAUL VI APPOINTS COL-LEGE CHANCELLOR NEXT BISHOP OF ROCHESTER.* He read the story and discovered that Father Francis consented to his appointment as bishop of the Rochester diocese and set the date for his episcopal ordination for Sunday, April 11, at Sacred Heart Cathedral.

Alex folded the paper and tucked it under his arm. Reaching into his briefcase, he removed his Daytimer and searched for Marge Reicher's phone number. He looked at his watch and calculated that it would be eight in the morning in San Francisco. A little early, but he wanted to catch her before she went on her rounds to Golden Gate Park. He found a payphone and dialed.

§

"Thanks for the news, Margie," Reed said.

"Is that the man you said was your father?" Marge asked.

"One and the same. I thought I'd see if I can scrape up some money to get there, so I can watch the special event. My mother said this was his dream, becoming a bishop."

"What will you do for clothes? I don't think they'll let you in wearing that."

"Guess I'll worry about that when I get there."

"No you won't, Big Guy. Tommy here is about your size. I'm sure we can find something of his you can wear. Isn't that right, Tommy?" Tommy nodded. "I'll talk to Herbie and see if we can scrape up enough for your round-trip bus fare and food. We got a few weeks. I'm sure we can do something to help you."

"That's awfully nice of you, Margie, Tommy. But I don't want you going to any trouble, now. And I won't be needing fare for a round-trip."

"Not planning on coming back, then?"

"Thinking it's time I got a fresh start, Margie. Maybe I can make something of my life back there."

"Do you think that friend of yours'll put you up once you get there?"

"Not sure. He's a big-shot congressman now. Probably can't be seen with the likes of me."

"He might have more heart than you give him credit for."

"Maybe so, Margie. But I'd rather not tell him I'm coming."

"Want to surprise him, huh?"

"Yeah, something like that."

Chapter 30

At noon on April 7, Herbie and Marge Reicher drove Reed to the Transbay Terminal on Missions Street to pick up the Greyhound bus that would take him on the first leg of his nearly three-day trip to Rochester. Herbie and Marge had picked up Reed early that morning and brought him to their home for a shower, a haircut, and a shave. After fitting him into a pair of dark slacks, a white shirt, and lightweight jacket of Tommy's, they fed him a hearty breakfast.

Standing inside the terminal in his loose-fitting clothes and with his clean-shaven face, Reed appeared more gaunt than ever. Yet, he looked more energized than Marge had ever seen him before. It convinced her she was doing the right thing, sending him off. She handed him a brown-bag lunch, which she had packed, and stuffed sixty-two dollars cash into his coat pocket. Reed pulled it out and tried handing it back to her.

"Margie, you and Herbie have done enough . . ."

"Now you put that right back in your pocket, Big Boy. You're gonna need that. Herbie and me don't want it back."

Reed bent down and hugged her, then kissed her on her forehead. He turned toward Herbie and shook his hand, thanking him for his kindness.

"You let us know when you get settled, now," Marge said, her eyes tearing up.

Reed put on his trademark smirk as he bent over to pick up his duffle bag. "Margie, I'll be doing so good you'll be reading about me in the papers."

Marge grinned and waved her hand at him like she was swatting a fly. Reed turned and walked off to board his bus.

§

"Are you sure you won't reconsider going to the ordination Mass tomorrow?" Kitty asked. "I'd love having you next to me."

"We've talked about this, Kitty," Alex said. "There's a reason Father Francis didn't send me an invitation. And a person in my position can't just go as someone else's guest. Anyway, I'd feel like a hypocrite going to the ceremony. I'll just sit here in the office and watch it on television."

"Do you wish you had stayed in Washington this weekend?"

"And spend part of my Easter recess away from you? Not on your life."

"You don't resent me for going to the ordination, do you?"

Alex took both of Kitty's hands and looked into her eyes. "I could never resent you. You need to be there. You're his secretary. And he's given you no reason to stay away."

"Can you and I go out to lunch after the Mass?"

"I'll look forward to it."

Chapter 31

Sacred Heart Cathedral stood ominously against the overcast Sunday afternoon sky. Its bells, housed in gothic twin sandstone towers, tolled a discordant sound as the faithful and the curious streamed into the hallowed house of worship. Reed Wentworth, blending in with a cluster of new arrivals, climbed the six steps to the front landing, and looked up to see a raised sculpture in the pediment above the doorway. It looked to him like a child kneeling and pleading for the love of its father.

Passing through the opened wooden doors of the cathedral, Reed stepped into the foyer and waited. The queue had backed up. The person behind him, apparently busy talking, hadn't noticed that the line had stopped. He bumped into Reed, pushing him into the back of the man in front of him. Reed felt the hard steel of the gun cylinder press into his chest through the inside breast pocket of his jacket, and he knew the man in front of him must have felt it too. The man, who was wearing a clerical collar, turned around and gave Reed a look of concern.

"Excuse me, Father," Reed mumbled.

The priest turned back, and the line started inching forward. That's when Reed noticed the priest was wearing a full-length black cassock and carrying something in his left hand. An older priest, similarly dressed, had been standing in an empty pocket of the foyer, outside the queue, and spotted the priest standing in front of Reed.

"Father Kaseman . . . what a surprise seeing you here," the older priest said as he walked over and extended his hand.

"Good afternoon, Father Vincenzo." Father Kaseman shook the priest's hand and continued walking in line while he spoke. "I wouldn't have missed this for the world."

"Will you be walking in the opening procession with us?" Father Vincenzo asked.

"No, I'm afraid not." He lifted the case and small tripod he was carrying by his side. "I'll be taking pictures from up in the choir loft."

"Well, that's an important job. I'm sure it's in good hands with you."

"Thank you, Father. Would you happen to know where Father Francis will be positioned in the line? I want to be sure to get a good overhead snapshot of him coming in."

"I believe he is the last person before Archbishop Rollins. But that should all be listed on the program being handed out at the next door." The line began moving at a brisker pace, so Father Vincenzo patted Father Kaseman on the shoulder. "Nice seeing you, Father. Say hello to your grandfather for me."

Father Kaseman nodded.

Reed made a mental note of Father Francis's placement in the procession.

When Father Kaseman reached the stairway leading up to the choir loft, he turned and glanced at Reed, then started walking up the stairs. Until then, Reed hadn't noticed the priest's limp.

Entering the nave of the cathedral, Reed grabbed a program and began looking for an empty seat on his right near the end of a pew. He spotted a seat midway down the aisle and headed for it. When he was almost there, he saw an older man crossing over from the left side of the aisle, racing to take the seat. They both reached the pew at the same time. Reed gave the man an evil look that was exacerbated by his sunken gray eyes and hollow cheeks, and the man turned away. Reed sat down and slipped his hand into his breast pocket.

§

Father Kaseman reached the top of the stairs and opened the door to the balcony. The organist was sitting in front of the pipe organ, which faced the back of the church, and she was adjusting her sheet music. She turned when she saw the priest walking in.

"Good afternoon, Father. I believe those who are walking in the opening procession are gathering in the school next door."

"I'm actually going to be taking pictures during the ordination." He looked around the choir loft and pointed to the left front corner. "You don't mind if I set my equipment up over there, do you?"

"Not at all, Father. As long as I can see out my rearview mirror, I'm good." She pointed to a mirror mounted on the organ, which enabled her to see what was happening near the altar. "I'm surprised they didn't place any television cameras up here. Would've been a great perspective, looking down on the congregation and the procession."

"I guess they're more interested in capturing the activities near the altar," Father Kaseman said, pointing. "I see they've got two cameras set up down there."

The woman looked through her mirror and nodded. She then glanced at her watch and spun around off the bench. "I think I'll go freshen up while I've still got a few minutes."

Father Kaseman smiled and dipped his head. When he heard the door close, he began unpacking his equipment.

§

At 1:40, Kitty was driving down Lake Avenue, about five minutes from the cathedral, when she heard a loud popping sound and suddenly felt the rear of her car swimming from side to side and thumping. She slowed the car gradually and brought it to the shoulder of the road. Stepping out wearing high heels, a dark skirt, white blouse, and red blazer, she walked around to the rear and saw that her passenger tire was completely flat. She looked at her watch and sighed, knowing her chances of being on time for the two o'clock ordination Mass were now slim to none.

§

At 1:50, Alex turned on the television in his office and sat back in his chair. The picture on the screen showed people still trickling in through the rear door. Alex set his glass of iced tea down on the table next to him and leaned forward, squinting to find Kitty in the crowd. The picture then changed to a long shot of the balcony and the back of the organist, who had just begun playing. Alex also saw a man with a camera in the right corner of the balcony. Periodically, he saw a flash from the camera when the man snapped a picture.

The picture on the television changed back to a wide shot, panning the crowd. Alex squinted again, looking for Kitty. His eye caught something to the left of the center aisle. A familiar face. The camera zoomed in slowly before it started panning again. For a split second, Alex had a better look at the man, but still couldn't place the face. Whoever it was, he had a sickly appearance. Alex resumed scanning for Kitty.

§

Reed looked at his watch: 2:00. He shifted in his seat and turned to see the beginning of the procession lining up at the door to the nave. The organist started playing the processional hymn *All Glory, Laud, and Honor*, which signaled everyone to rise. A sea of white robes began flowing down the main aisle at a leisurely pace. Reed looked at his program and noted that the first group of men, coming down the aisle in twos, consisted of students from the local seminary who were preparing for the priesthood. The first two students carried long upright wooden poles with a banner attached to each. The pair immediately following them held censers suspended on chains. They rocked the censors back and forth, emitting a thin cloud of sweet smoke. The remaining students had their heads bowed and hands folded in prayer.

Following the seminarians were the priests from parishes throughout the diocese. They, too, had their heads bowed and hands folded in prayer.

Reed looked down at his program. Only two more groups remained: the altar boys and the priests from the diocesan office.

Then the main attraction—the man he had come to kill.

He slipped his hand back into his breast pocket and felt the gun. It was the one he'd learned to shoot with as a boy. He had taken it with him when he ran away from Wentworth Estate. So much in his life had changed since then, but his Colt .38 remained faithful and true.

It was there for him in East Village when some drunk tried to take his wallet. He blew a hole through the sot's foot and warned him the next time it would go through his head.

It was there for him in San Francisco when he walked in and found his mother's boyfriend beating her senseless. He shot that man in the thigh. He would've put another bullet between the man's eyes, but his mother stopped him.

He felt surprisingly cool now. His hand quivered as usual, but at this range it wouldn't be a problem. He had rehearsed the movements in his head at least a hundred times during his bus trip. When Father Francis was just about to Reed's seat, Reed would step into the aisle and turn, pulling the gun from his breast pocket. He would then plunge it into the priest's mid-section and pull the trigger. He felt certain the priest would die. What happened to himself after that was inconsequential.

§

Alex took a sip of iced tea and watched the stream of robed figures moving down the aisle. The camera showed a single altar boy carrying a golden upright pole with a crucifix at the top. As the camera zoomed out, Alex could see two pairs of altar boys following the lead boy. Behind them was a group of four older priests, smiling with hands folded in front of them. Then Alex saw a lone man wearing a pink skullcap. It was the priest he used to loathe, but now, strangely, pitied.

The camera moved in for a medium close-up of Father Francis, his face expressing the same false piety Alex remembered seeing at his mother's funeral. With his hands folded reverently in front of him, the bishop-delegate turned from side to side, smiling saint-like at the people who came to witness the solemn event. Alex thought how sad it was that these spectators believed the man to be worthy of his sacred calling. And how sad it was that the priest was blind to his own hypocrisy.

Alex took another sip of iced tea as the camera zoomed out to a full shot of the procession. Father Francis was midway down the aisle. Behind him were some men wearing the white miters of bishops, followed by a man in similar attire, but apparently of higher rank. Alex's eyes were drawn to some movement on the left side of the screen. A man was slipping out from his pew into the aisle. *Probably some emotional zealot wanting to be seen*, he thought. The camera zoomed in on the man. It was the sickly person Alex noticed earlier. Only now he recognized who it was. The glass of tea slipped from his hand and shattered on the floor when he realized what was happening.

§

Time seemed to slow down for Reed, and his senses became more acute. He saw the priest turn in his direction when he stepped out from the pew. He saw the puzzled look on the priest's face when he slipped the gun from his breast pocket. He saw the priest grimace and heard him grunt when he plunged the barrel into his taut stomach. He felt the heat of the priest's breath, blasting from his flared nostrils. He smelled the scent of the priest's cologne and starched linen. He saw the priest's steely gray eyes show a glint of recognition. And he heard his own rasping voice when he blurted,

"Bless me Father, for I-Am-Your-Sin."

He started to press his finger against the trigger but was distracted by a flash from the balcony. He felt a jolt and a sudden burning sensation just below his chest. He looked down and saw a red spot blooming on the front of his white shirt. He looked back up at the priest, whose face was contorted, blood oozing from the corner of his mouth. And then the priest fell forward, pushing Reed to the floor.

§

Alex looked at the television in horror. He could hear the shrieks of the crowd as pandemonium broke out. He struggled in vain to find Kitty in the chaos that followed, but he felt certain there would be no more gun shots now that Reed had finished his deed. He was puzzled why people kept pointing to the balcony. Then the commentator mentioned it appeared someone had fired a gun from that direction. The camera zoomed in for a close-up of the balcony, and there were several men huddled in a circle, looking at the floor of the balcony. The organist was hysterical, looking in the direction of the huddled men, and a few women were attempting to console her. At this point, the commentator cut-in with an announcement:

> *It has just been confirmed by a physician, who had come to witness the ordination, that Father Michael Francis, Bishop-delegate of the Rochester diocese, is dead. He was killed by a gunshot wound that appears to have struck his heart. There is speculation the shot was fired from the balcony. The unidentified man who had apparently been trying to protect Father Francis was also hit by the same bullet. He is still alive. Police and ambulance crews are arriving on the scene. It is unclear whether anyone else has been hurt in the melee.*

Alex's phone rang, and he jumped. He then hurried over to pick up the receiver.

"Hi, you'll never guess what happened to me on the way to church . . ."

"Kitty, where are you?"

"What's the matter? You sound upset."

"Please tell me you're not at church."

"No, I'm at a service station, waiting for my car to get towed. I got a flat tire. What's wrong, Alex?"

"There's been a shooting at Sacred Heart Cathedral. Father Francis was killed." He heard Kitty gasp on the other end, and then she was silent. "Tell me where you are, Kitty. I'm coming to get you."

§

When Alex pulled into the Mobile station on Lake Avenue, he saw an ambulance and police car speeding past, going in a direction away from the cathedral. Kitty saw Alex getting out of his car. She rushed over, wrapped her arms around him, and began sobbing. He held her closely and kissed her head, until her chest stopped heaving. Then he pulled out a clean handkerchief from his pocket and dabbed her eyes.

"I feel like I need to go to the cathedral," Alex said.

"I'm going with you."

"Are you sure you're up to it?"

"I want to be with you, Alex . . . Do they know who shot Father Francis?" Kitty started to choke up, again.

"I'm not really sure . . ."

§

By the time Alex and Kitty arrived at the cathedral, much of the parking lot was empty. Three television vans were parked beside the front curb, along with six squad cars. A dark gray station wagon with tinted windows was parked on the sidewalk, backed up to the bottom of the stairs leading to the front entry. Its tailgate was open.

A police officer stopped Alex and Kitty at the front door. Alex identified himself, and the officer allowed them to enter. When they stepped into the nave, they saw a man and a priest coming up the aisle.

"It's Father Vincenzo," Kitty whispered.

Two men in lab jackets followed, pushing a gurney with the covered body of Father Francis. Father Vincenzo saw Kitty and stopped. She started crying and wrapped her arms around the priest.

"There, there," the priest said, patting Kitty's head. "I know he thought very highly of you, Miss McAlister."

"It all seems so senseless," Kitty said between sobs.

"It does indeed. Very senseless."

"Father, do you know where they took the other man who was shot?" Alex asked.

The priest deferred to the man standing next to him, who introduced himself as the Chief Medical Examiner. He told Alex an ambulance took the other victim to Highland Hospital about ten minutes ago.

"He's in pretty rough shape, Congressman," he added.

"Do the police know who did the shooting?" Alex asked. Kitty had moved next to him and had her arm around his waist.

Father Vincenzo looked toward the balcony. "A priest who worked for Father Francis for years. His name is Father Kaseman. He was the director of administrations at St. Vincent College until Father Francis fired him a few months ago. It obviously left him disgruntled. But who would have expected this . . ." The priest looked at the covered body on the gurney and choked up.

"We should be going, Father," the medical examiner said. Father Vincenzo nodded, and turned to lead the small recessional out to the awaiting morgue wagon.

Alex saw a few uniformed policemen and what appeared to be two plainclothes detectives standing midway down the aisle, at the spot where Reed and Father Francis had been shot. They were looking up at the balcony and discussing something among themselves. Alex and Kitty walked over, and Alex introduced himself.

"Were you able to identify the weapon the shooter used?" Alex asked one of the detectives.

"Had a suppressed Parker Hale M82 next to him when we rushed the balcony. Fine sniper rifle. Packs enough punch to go clear through two men. As we saw demonstrated today. Like to know how he got hold of it."

"I wonder how he got it up there without being noticed." Alex said.

"Told one of the officers he hid it under his cassock, strapped to his leg. Pretty ingenious, if you ask me. The guy who tried to save the priest had a Colt .38. He must've spotted the sniper when the priest was coming down the aisle. He could've been a hero if he'd gotten the first shot off. But, of course . . ."

Alex felt Kitty nudge him, and he saw she was growing uncomfortable with the conversation. "Well, I'm certainly glad I don't have your job, gentlemen," Alex said. "Thank you for your help."

"I'd rather investigate double homicides all day, every day than have to deal with Congress like you do," the detective said. "No offense, Congressman."

"None taken."

Alex took Kitty's hand, and they made their way out of the cathedral. When they reached the landing outside the front entrance, Alex looked down and saw the morgue technicians closing the tailgate on the gray station wagon at the bottom of the stairs. It's then that the full impact of the priest's death hit him. The last two lines from the foreboding poem delivered to him by the crazed woman in East Village two years earlier haunted his thoughts now.

On hate for a father doth feed
Whose guilt will be laid to your charge

"I need to visit Reed in the hospital," he said to Kitty.

"Of course. I think you should."

"I'd like to go alone. I need to ask him some questions he might not answer if you're with me."

Kitty touched his arm. "He's your friend, Alex. Do what you need to do."

§

A few reporters were congregating in the waiting area when Alex walked into the emergency room later that evening. Once they saw him, the reporters swarmed around the young congressman, asking if he was here to visit the shooting victim.

"I'm here to visit an old friend," Alex responded, and kept walking. When he introduced himself to the head nurse on duty and asked about Reed, she said he had been out of surgery for a few hours and was still groggy. His condition was listed as critical. He asked to go in, and she insisted that visiting privileges were restricted to family members only.

"I am the closest thing to family he has, nurse. You can either let me in, or you can call the Chairman of the Highland

Board of Directors for me. I have his home number right here."
Alex pulled out his Daytimer and started flipping pages.

"That won't be necessary, Congressman," the nurse said, giving him an irritated look. She pushed a button, and a buzzer sounded as the door unlocked. "ICU is on your right."

Once inside the Intensive Care Unit, Alex pushed open the door to Reed's room and found his friend alone, eyes closed, with a white blanket pulled up to his chin. Reed had a tube coming out his right arm and oxygen tubes in his nostrils. His breathing was labored. Alex walked over and stood next to the bed, on Reed's left, and gently brushed his friend's forehead with his hand. Reed's eyes fluttered, then opened, and turned toward Alex.

"Hey, kid," he mumbled. "Is he dead?"

"Yeah, he's dead, Reed."

"Who got him?"

"Some priest who used to work for him. Looks like Father Francis had more enemies than just us."

"Got me good, too . . ." Reed made a rattling sound when he gasped for air.

"Yeah, he did. But you're going to hang in there, right?"

"For what?"

Alex couldn't think of a response. What did Reed have to look forward to? A life as a heroin addict living on the streets. With no one to love. And no one to love him.

"Maybe now that the priest is gone, you can make a fresh start." It was all Alex could come up with.

Reed winced in pain. "My old man's . . . gonna love . . . hearing about this."

"You mean your grandfather?"

Reed nodded.

"They think you're a hero, Reed. They think you were trying to protect the priest. Your grandfather will be proud of that."

Reed stared at Alex for a moment before showing a faint smile. A short time later, he began shivering.

"I'm cold, Alex . . ."

Alex found a folded blanket on a nearby table and covered his friend with it. "Is that better?"

Reed gave a slight nod. His breathing required more effort now.

A nurse walked in and checked Reed's vitals and shook her head slowly. She had a grave look on her face. Alex followed her to the door.

"How is he?" he whispered.

"We've done everything we can for him, sir. It doesn't look good. All we can do now is make him as comfortable as possible. I'm sorry." She quietly left the room.

Alex found a chair, slid it over next to Reed's bed, and sat down. "This is all my fault," he said. "I should never have involved you in my vendetta against Father Francis. I've ruined your life."

Reed slowly lifted his left hand, and Alex clutched it.

"Glad I found my father . . . Now I know . . . Not your fault." Reed's breathing was shallow and quick.

"You forgive me, then?"

"Nothing to forgive . . ."

Alex let Reed's words sink in as he looked at his friend's pallid, sunken face, a face that showed the strain of two lifetimes, both badly lived.

"When you get better, Reed, I want you to come and stay with me. I can help you get back on your feet, help you get into the same art school your mother went to, if that's what you want. You and me, just like old times . . ."

Reed didn't respond but looked at the ceiling with a glassy, fixed stare. His lips had a pasty gray color, and his jaw remained partially open as he struggled to breathe through his mouth.

Alex felt Reed trying to squeeze his hand.

"So dark, Alex . . . I'm dying . . . I'm scared . . . Don't let me die alone . . ."

Alex brushed his free hand across Reed's forehead. "I'm

here, Reed. I'm not going anywhere . . ."

Peace washed over Reed's face. Forty minutes later, when he took his last breath, he was still holding the hand of the only friend he had ever known.

§

A light drizzle fell from the unrelenting gray sky, while Alex walked toward the entrance to the Monroe County Jail. After signing in, the congressman waited in a small, drab room for his escort, Sheriff Lombard. The sheriff escorted him to the six-by-eight holding cell where Father Kaseman had been placed in solitary confinement under a suicide watch. Posting an armed guard outside the cell, the sheriff opened the barred door and let Alex inside. Father Kaseman, dressed in an orange jumpsuit, sat upright on the edge of his bed, with his hands cuffed and resting on his knees, which were spread as far as the short chain on his feet shackles would allow. His eyes followed Alex, as he walked over to a stool and sat down.

"Father Kaseman, we've never met, but I believe we've shared a common disdain for one of the men you killed yesterday—Father Michael Francis. I'm here this morning primarily out of curiosity, but also to offer you some help, if possible."

"Congressman Spencer, please let me say how terribly sorry I am about your friend. It was never my intention . . ." Father Kaseman hung his head and slumped his shoulders and began crying. Alex waited for the priest to compose himself.

"My friend was in the wrong place at the wrong time, Father. Since you've already admitted to the police that you pulled the trigger, may I ask why you did it?"

The priest lifted his fettered hands and smudged a tear that was dripping down his cheek. "Father Francis was not the priest people thought he was. I worked for him for thirteen years, and I saw a lot and heard a lot . . . He was a womanizer, Congressman."

"How do you know?"

"When I first started working for him in the diocesan office, certain women from St. Andrew's would visit him regularly. It didn't matter what he was doing; he would drop everything if one of them stopped by. I became suspicious.

"We had an intercom system that we used to communicate between our two offices. The talk switch on mine would stick on occasion, and he insisted I get it fixed. I decided, instead, to swap our intercom units. When one of these women would visit, I would send them to his office and notify him they were coming down. On two occasions when he responded, his talk button remained activated, and I heard everything that went on. Everything."

"Why didn't you report him to the bishop?"

"He was a very important person in the diocese. I was a nobody. I'm convinced the only reason I got the job with him is because my grandfather is such a large donor. Before I started working for Father Francis, my grandfather always treated me like I was . . . inadequate as a man. After I was hired for the job, he seemed to respect me for the first time in my adult life. And, I'm ashamed to say, I didn't want to jeopardize that.

"Near the end of my time as Father Francis's secretary, something happened that assured I would never say anything negative about the priest, no matter what he did." Father Kaseman began to shift uneasily on the side of the bed. He hesitated to continue.

"You don't have to tell me, Father. I'm not your attorney."

Father Kaseman shook his head. "No, I need to talk about it. I've kept it inside for too long." He paused for a moment before continuing. "One evening, almost seven years ago, I was in my office, tutoring a seminary student who had stopped by for some assistance. I had done well as a seminary student, and enjoyed tutoring young men preparing for the priesthood. It gave me a little extra spending money and provided me an opportunity to do something beyond my mundane administrative tasks.

"Father Francis had left the office early that day to catch a flight for one of the business trips Bishop O'Keane often sent him on. My tutoring session turned into a . . . passionate exchange . . . with my student inside of Father Francis's office. To my horror, he walked in on us. His flight had been canceled.

"His face never expressed shock. I just remember seeing a very calculating look in his eyes when he turned and walked out the door without saying a word. From that day on, he held that incident over my head like a guillotine, which he threatened to drop if I showed the least bit of resistance to his schemes."

"How were you able to finally leave his service?"

"I have you to thank for that, Congressman."

"Me?" Alex asked, puzzled.

"When you discovered the irregularities in St. Vincent's allotment of financial aid, you made Father Francis more worried than I'd ever seen him. It was he who pressured me to falsify the data on many of those applications for federal aid. That's how we were able to secure so many good athletes for the college who may not have qualified for the financial aid needed to attend. He needed me to be the fall guy. Told me he'd give me a good recommendation to the diocese. If I resisted, well, he would just reveal our little secret and ruin me."

"Why now, Father. Why kill him now?"

"I may be the worst of sinners, Congressman, but I love God, and I love the Church. I couldn't bear to see a man as despicable as Father Francis make a mockery of all that is holy."

"And so you'd rather be known as a murderer than a hypocrite," Alex added.

"I'd like to be known as a man who finally had the backbone to do what was right."

"I'm afraid you'll have trouble convincing a jury of that, Father." Alex stood up, and smoothed the back of his slacks. "I know a very good defense attorney, if you need one. I went to law school with her. I'm sure she would relish a case like yours."

"Thank you for that."

"I'll put her in touch with you." Alex called to the guard, saying he was ready to leave. Before walking out the cell door, Alex turned to the priest and asked, "Where did you learn to shoot like that?"

"My grandfather taught me when I was a boy. Said it was a skill that might come in handy someday."

Chapter 32

A soft breeze blew through the gazebo in Simms Park where Alex and Kitty sat on the picnic bench, looking out at a log meandering in the torpid current of the canal. Alex scooped up a handful of pebbles and began tossing them at the drifting log.

"I feel so emotionally drained," Kitty said, breaking the silence. "Tomorrow will be a week since Father Francis and Reed were murdered, and I am as far from finding closure for this as I was last week."

Alex released the pebbles from his left hand onto the bench. He brushed his hand on his pant leg and placed it on Kitty's knee. He continued picking pebbles from the pile with his right hand and flinging them into the murky water. "It's going to take a while before either of us feel normal again, Kitty. But time has a way of bringing healing."

"I know you're right. I just wish I could make sense of it all. I mean how could Father Kaseman shoot and kill a man he worked with for all those years?"

"Maybe we'll know more if it goes to trial, but you're going to drive yourself crazy trying to figure it out now."

Kitty reached over and grabbed a few stones from the pile on the bench and pitched one into the canal. "A long time ago you told me you thought Reed was Father Francis's son. Did he ever find out for certain?"

"Yes, he did."

Kitty threw another stone and listened as it plunked into the water. "Was that why he was at church last week?"

"I think it was important to him to see his father, even if they didn't know each other."

"How ironic that he was almost able to save Father Francis."

"Reed's life was filled with irony."

Kitty turned her head toward Alex. "You could say the same about our lives, too."

"How so?"

"Well, for one thing, when your mother died and you moved away, I thought our chances of ever being together as a couple were gone. And now, here we are."

"There were certainly lots of twists and turns along the way, weren't there?"

Kitty wrapped her arm around his waist and nuzzled against his shoulder. "But those are all behind us now, right?"

"They are." He wrapped his arm around her and drew her close. "It's like a writer once said, 'We've been bent and broken, but into a better shape.'" Alex tipped his head and kissed her on the forehead.

"Since it's nearby," Kitty said, "let's walk to St. Andrew's and light a candle and say a prayer for Father Francis."

"And for Reed."

§

Alex pulled open the door to the sanctuary, and he and Kitty walked in, dipped their fingers in the holy water font, and made the sign of the cross. They approached the altar and smelled the distinctive scent of Easter lilies. Several of the white flowers sat around the base of the altar, and some were spaced along the first step to the right of the altar, near the heat vent.

They walked over to the votive candle stand, slipped some coins in the offering box, and lit a candle for Father Francis and a candle for Reed. Then they knelt on the padded kneeler and recited the Lord's Prayer in unison. At the end of the prayer, they heard footsteps coming from behind them, and turned to see

Mr. Knapp, the janitor, carrying an armful of potted Easter lilies toward the altar steps. Alex and Kitty rose from the kneeler and found a seat in the front pew for a few moments of reflection and quiet prayer.

Mr. Knapp set the flowers on the remaining steps to the right of the altar and limped back toward the heat vent to grab his broom. At one point, Alex glanced over and saw Mr. Knapp staring at him. Once the janitor saw Alex looking, he pointed to the heat vent.

"Sometimes . . . I heard . . . voices," he said.

Alex clutched the edge of his pew and leaned forward. "Pardon me?"

"Sometimes . . . I heard voices from here." He pointed to the vent, again.

"Voices? From the vent you say?" Alex quickly turned to look at Kitty, and noticed that the janitor had her full attention.

Mr. Knapp nodded, his face flushed with embarrassment. Alex's mind began to race, but he didn't want to scare the man by sounding too eager. He inched his way down the pew to get closer.

"Do you remember me, Mr. Knapp? I'm Alex Spencer. I used to go to church here when I was a boy."

"I remember. I felt real bad when your mama died. She was pretty upset when she left here that day."

"What day, Mr. Knapp?"

"The day of the accident."

"You saw her leave?"

"No, sir."

"Then how do you know she was upset?"

"I heard her talking to the priest."

"You heard her talking to Father Francis?"

The janitor nodded.

"How did you hear her talking to him?"

The janitor pointed to the heat vent.

"Mr. Knapp, are you telling me you heard my mother talking to Father Francis through that heat vent?"

"Yes, sir."

Alex looked at Kitty; her face was pale. "And you could understand what they said to each other?"

"Yes, sir. I know I should've moved away from it but . . ."

"But what, Mr. Knapp?"

The janitor was gripping the upright broom stick with both hands and shifting his weight from one leg to the other. "Truth is . . . well . . . I sorta liked your mama, and I didn't like the way the priest was talking to her."

"Do you remember what they talked about?"

"Yes, sir. Your mama told the priest she was . . . well . . . pregnant. Said he was the father."

"My mother told Father Francis that she was pregnant with his child?"

"Yes, sir."

"How did Father Francis respond?"

"Well, he was mighty upset. Said he was getting a new job with the bishop, and he was not gonna let something like this ruin things. He told her to . . . to make it go away."

"Make it go away? You mean the baby? He told her to make the baby go away?"

"That's the same thing your mama asked him. She said, 'You want me to make this baby go away? What's that supposed to mean?' The priest said, 'You know exactly what it means, and I can give you the name of someone who can do it for you.' Your mama got mighty angry with the priest then. She said, 'You disgust me. I'd sooner join you in hell than lift a finger against this child.' I sure did like your mama's spunk. The priest called her a fool, and then I heard the door slam."

"Mr. Knapp, did you tell anyone about this before now?"

The janitor looked down and shook his head.

"Why not?"

"I . . . I've got no skills. Got no schooling. Can't walk right. Who'd hire me if I lost my job? And I'd have lost my job for sure if I said anything. I know it ain't right, and I've been ashamed of myself all these years."

Alex could tell the man was being sincere. The agony on his face was almost painful to see.

"I was pretty sure you heard voices through the vent, too," Mr. Knapp continued.

Alex's eyes widened. "And what made you think that?"

"I was cleaning in the vestry one afternoon when you and an old man were in the sanctuary. I knew one of the young mothers from the church, Mrs. Foster I think, was meeting with the priest at the time. I saw you trying to get closer to the vent, and I figured you were listening for voices. When I saw you jump up and run out of the sanctuary, I went to the church office, pretending like I was getting something. That's about the time Mrs. Foster left the building. After she left, I peeked out through the blinds and saw you sitting on your bike, watching Mrs. Foster and shaking your head."

Alex nodded. "That's exactly right . . . So, clearly, you heard Father Francis with other women besides my mother."

"Yes, sir. But I'm just a nobody, and I knew there was nothing I could do to stop the priest. And, like I said, I'd have lost my job trying."

"And you're talking about it now because . . ."

"Because the priest is dead, and he can't hurt me now. And I needed to get this off my chest."

Alex put his hand on the janitor's shoulder. "I'm glad you did, Mr. Knapp. Very glad that you did."

The janitor leaned his broom against the wall and hobbled out of the sanctuary, saying he was going to get more Easter lilies. Alex turned toward Kitty and saw her looking at the heat vent, her eyes locked in a remorseful stare. He walked quietly back to the pew and sat down next to her, his hands clutching the edge of the seat. They sat in silence, but for the trill of a songbird, casting a soothing spell through the stained glass window.

Kitty reached over and grabbed Alex's hand. He turned to

see tears streaming down her cheeks.

"Oh, Alex. You must hate me for not believing you all these years. I am so sorry . . . so very, very sorry."

Alex wrapped his arms around her and held her tightly. She rested her head on his chest and wept.

"It's all right, Kitty, it's all right . . . It's all behind us now. I love you."

He ran his fingers slowly through her auburn hair to console her. He thought of his mother, and he thought of Reed. He thought of the exacting toll inflicted for his retribution. And he finally surrendered to his own urge to cry.

Made in the USA
Charleston, SC
25 January 2013